### *"Why special forces?" barked Lieutenant Colonel Jack Scatalone.*

Air Force Major Vanessa Blake shrugged. "I've got the skills. I've got the drive. I've got the desire. Why not?" she threw back at him.

He betrayed no reaction to her challenge. He asked stonily, "So it's still your goal to be the first woman to enter the Special Forces?"

The question made her feel naked. It was her most closely held dream, and she'd privately trained for it for years. But she wasn't the least bit comfortable sharing her life's ambition with this gruff stranger. She answered defensively, "I don't give a flip whether I'm the first woman or the last. I just want a shot at it."

He put the typed paper back in the file and closed it deliberately. He leaned back in his chair and looked at her long and hard. Finally he said, "Then today's your lucky day, Major."

Dear Reader,

Silhouette Bombshell is dedicated to bringing you the best in savvy heroines, fast action, high stakes and chilling suspense. We're raising the bar on action adventure to create an exhilarating reading experience that you'll remember long after the final pages!

Take some personal time with *Personal Enemy* by Sylvie Kurtz. An executive bodyguard plans the perfect revenge against the man who helped to destroy her family—but when they're both attacked, she's forced to work *for* him before she can work against him!

Don't miss *Contact* by Evelyn Vaughn, the latest adventure in the ATHENA FORCE continuity series. Faith Corbett uses her extrasenory skills to help the police solve crimes, but she's always contacted them anonymously. Until a serial killer begins hunting psychics, and Faith must reveal herself to one disbelieving detective.…

Meet the remarkable women of author Cindy Dees's *The Medusa Project.* These Special Forces officers-in-training are set up to fail, but for team leader Vanessa Blake, quitting is not an option—especially when both international security and their tough-as-nails trainer's life is at stake!

And provocative twists abound in *The Spy Wore Red* by Wendy Rosnau. Agent Nadja Stefn is hand-picked for a mission to terminate an assassin—but getting her man means working with a partner from whom she must hide a dangerous personal agenda.…

Please send your comments to me c/o Silhouette Books, 233 Broadway, Suite 1001, New York, NY 10279.

Best wishes,

*Natashya Wilson*

Natashya Wilson
Associate Senior Editor, Silhouette Bombshell

Please address questions and book requests to:
Silhouette Reader Service
U.S.: 3010 Walden Ave., P.O. Box 1325, Buffalo, NY 14269
Canadian: P.O. Box 609, Fort Erie, Ont. L2A 5X3

# CINDY DEES

# the MEDUSA PROJECT

Published by Silhouette Books

**America's Publisher of Contemporary Romance**

SILHOUETTE BOOKS

ISBN 0-373-51345-3

THE MEDUSA PROJECT

Copyright © 2005 by Cynthia Dees

Visit Silhouette Books at www.eHarlequin.com

**Printed in U.S.A.**

## CINDY DEES

started flying airplanes, sitting in her dad's lap, when she was three. She was the only kid in the neighborhood who got a pilot's license before she got a driver's license. After college, she fulfilled a lifelong dream and became a U.S. Air Force pilot. She flew everything from supersonic jets to C-5s, the world's largest cargo airplanes. During her career, she got shot at, met her husband, flew in the Gulf War and amassed a lifetime supply of war stories. After she left flying to have a family, she was lucky enough to fulfill another lifelong dream—writing a book. Little did she imagine that it would win the Golden Heart contest and sell to Silhouette! She's thrilled to be able to share her dream with you. She'd love to hear what you think of her books, at www.cindydees.com or P.O. Box 210, Azle, TX 76098.

# Chapter 1

*August 6, 8:00 a.m.*
*Free-fire zone Alpha*

Air Force Major Vanessa Blake ducked and spun, plastering her back against the muddy wall of her foxhole, narrowly avoiding a barrage of incoming fire. Enemy infantry had their position surrounded on three sides, and the only reason it wasn't all four sides was the river at their backs. Correction. The water moccasin-, alligator-infested river at their backs.

"Ammo check!" she called.

"Low!"

"Low!"

"Out!"

"Low!"

"Five minutes' worth!"

"Somebody get over to Echo position and pass that ammo around. We're not gonna last two more minutes at this rate!"

she ordered tersely. Crud. They were in a heap of trouble. She had only sixteen guys left standing out of fifty, and the enemy had close to forty. She had to do something radical, here. Something unexpected. *Think, Vanessa!* The woods around them had plenty of cover for enemy shooters, and that's why they were getting slaughtered like trapped rats in this foxhole complex. She had to turn the tables. Make the woods work against the advancing forces. She glanced up at the trees overhead. Big, mature oaks, mostly. Sturdy. Strong enough to climb…

"Guys," she called out low, "I've got an idea. Huddle." The enemy was close enough to hear her plan if she shouted it to the far end of the bunker.

"We're going to crawl out of here and climb the trees around this position. Then we'll let the enemy advance to the foxholes and pick them off from above. Set your weapons for single shots. We don't have enough ammo left to spray their lines with automatic fire. Use sticks and leaves to camouflage yourselves. Get up high in the branches, and when I give the signal, start firing down through the leaves. Think snipers, here. No wild shots. Wait till your targets are close enough to guarantee a hit. Take your time. Aim carefully. Keep your wits about you. Got it?"

The glum faces around her lit up with hope. They were all likely to die messy deaths before this day was out, but by God, they'd go out fighting if she had anything to say about it.

"We're gonna have to move fast. We'll split up and crawl out each end of the bunker. Stay behind cover as much as you can, but keep moving. We've only got a couple minutes to get into position. Let's do it," she said forcefully. She turned and led half the men in a crouching run to one end of the linked foxholes.

She slithered on her belly out of the red clay muck of the foxhole, her bulky rifle cradled awkwardly across her elbows. Belly crawling with a fast twisting motion of her torso, like the alligators that inhabited the area, she passed up a couple trees with nice, low branches for climbing. Better leave those to the guys with less physical strength than her. One by one, she dropped off her troops in an arc around the enemy's right flank. And then she was alone. Staying low, she tossed a length of nylon rope around the girth of a giant oak tree. Using the rope as a climbing harness, she shimmied up the tree as slick as any lumberjack.

She worked her way a good thirty feet up the tree and turned to survey the situation. Perfect. Clear line of sight down the brown-shirted line of enemy soldiers. She chambered a round in her rifle and took aim carefully. And fired.

A satisfying red circle blossomed in the middle of the chest of one of the enemy soldiers. One down. Shots began to rain down from all directions, and in a matter of seconds, half the enemy line was out.

"Fall back!" the enemy commander screamed. Chaos ensued as his forces attempted to obey in the midst of the death raining from above.

"Everybody down!" Vanessa shouted. "Charge!"

She shimmied out of the tree and joined up with her troops. They took off in hot pursuit, picking off stragglers as the skirmish turned into a lopsided rout.

*August 6, 8:15 a.m.*
*Free-fire zone Alpha*

"Jesus H. Christ. What a mess," Lieutenant Colonel Jack Scatalone announced in disgust from the fat edge of the battlefield as he watched the tide of the mock battle turn abruptly. He put down the field glasses and held out his hand. "Give me one of those toy guns."

"Are you sure, sir? Your uniform…"

"It can be cleaned," he snapped. "Or replaced. How do you fire this damn thing?" He inspected the oval canister attached to the top of the half-scale rifle that somebody had thrust into his hands.

"It's full, sir," his host stammered. "Two hundred half-inch paint pellets. It's really an honor to have you show us a couple moves." The eager kid quickly showed him how to pressurize and fire the paintball rifle.

He took off his wheel cap and stripped off his dark blue Class A jacket, with its multiple Special Forces badges and Christmas tree of ribbons. He passed them to a pair of waiting hands along with his crisply starched, light blue shirt and tie. He squatted, scooped up handfuls of red mud and streaked his face with the stuff. A little in his hair, and great stripes of it across his white T-shirt, and then he was off and running, low and fast. He circled wide of the current action, closing in silently from the left rear.

Rather than fire his weapon and give away his position with the popping sound of the air rifle, he stepped up behind his targets, pressed the rifle barrel into their ribs and murmured low in their ears, "Bang. You're dead, buddy."

He took out most of the right end of the line before Major Blake realized her troops were disappearing like magic. He heard her call for her remaining men to pull in tight in a close fighting formation.

*Thank you, Major.* Now her men were all nicely clumped for him to wipe out all at once. He moved in for the easy kill.

The eight remaining men had taken cover behind a huge, fallen log. He was going to have to circle around it and come in from the other side. But the poor bastards would be ducks in a shooting gallery. This wasn't even going to be a challenge. He eased forward, at one with the woods around him. One foot in front of another in complete silence, he glided forward. He hadn't been in the Special Forces for fourteen years for nothing.

Down a hill streaked with runoff gullies to that little stand of brush at the bottom. It would provide perfect camouflage for the shot. Dead leaves lay in an ankle-deep carpet in this part of the woods, and he eased each foot down separately to minimize the rustling noise of his passing. He crouched and braced the barrel of the toy rifle against a sapling. Peering through the leaves, he caught sight of the cluster of scared-looking soldiers. Bingo. He took aim and began to squeeze the trigger.

And jolted violently as an apparition in brown rose out of the flat ground beside him. Something hit him hard in the chest, stinging sharply. He looked down in disbelief at the circular splatter of red paint on his chest. Then looked up at the broad, white grin showing out of a face completely covered in mud and crushed leaves.

"Gotcha," the woman declared triumphantly.

Son of a bitch. She must have laid down in one of those runoff gullies and covered herself in leaves. And she'd done it so carefully he hadn't noticed the disturbance to the ground cover. He scowled narrowly. Okay, so Vanessa Blake was good in a game of paintball. Big deal. But that didn't mean she'd be worth a damn under live-fire conditions.

"Major Blake, I presume?" he said coldly.

She climbed to her feet and brushed leaves off herself. Not that it did a bit of good. She was caked from head to foot in red mud. "Who wants to know?" she replied coolly.

"I do," he bit out. "Lieutenant Colonel Jack Scatalone." He held out a hand to her. Normally he'd expect a salute from a lower-ranking officer, but they weren't in uniform, and she'd just killed him. Her grip was firm, confident, as she returned the handshake in a businesslike fashion.

"What brings you out here today?" She glanced down at his ruined navy blue uniform slacks. "You're not exactly dressed for this kind of fun."

"I was sent to fetch you." The words tasted sour in his mouth. He did *not* appreciate being the errand boy for anyone, even if his new boss was a four-star general.

One graceful eyebrow arched under the mud. "By whom?"

"If you're done playing toy soldier, come with me. I'll tell you more on the way."

"Do I have time for a shower?" she asked as she tromped out of the woods beside him.

It gave him a perverse sense of satisfaction to think about dragging her through the pristine halls of the Pentagon looking like a pig in swill. "No," he snapped. In fact, he probably had the time, but he'd cooled his jets long enough while she played toy soldier this morning. His foul mood didn't improve one bit when he and the major emerged from the woods. A rousing cheer went up, and a hundred weekend warriors grinned like idiots at the big, fat splotch of red on his chest. Bested by a *woman*. Dammit.

The good news was that he was going to get all kinds of opportunities to get his pound of flesh back from her. The major just didn't know it yet. But she would soon.

*August 6, 10 a.m.*
*northern North Carolina*

Vanessa studied the man driving the civilian car in hostile silence beside her. Dark hair, dark eyes, dark tan. Lean features. Hard. His profile could've been chiseled from rock. So could his personality. He hadn't said two words since they'd left the paintball range an hour ago. So much for telling her more about this mystery summons en route to wherever they were going. She'd met his kind before. Macho jerks who couldn't stand the idea of women infiltrating their precious military. She shrugged mentally. His kind were a dying breed. Women were here to stay and he could just get used to it.

She was surprised when he turned into what looked like a private driveway. A brick mansion came into view, but he kept on driving, around to the back side of the spread. What the heck? And then she spotted a hefty helicopter on the back lawn. Black, ugly and powerful-looking. A Black Hawk. Standard issue special ops aircraft.

Ah. Uncle Sam had used this house's private helicopter pad. For convenience or for secrecy? Fort Bragg wasn't much farther from the paintball range than this spread, and it had an entire airfield. Dang. Someone had gone to a lot of trouble to "fetch her" in the middle of her vacation. Her once-every-five-years, the-Air-Force-made-her-take-it vacation. Of course, she doubted her boss had high-stress mock combat in mind when he shoved leave orders at her and told her to relax. She grinned. This *was* relaxing. Or, had been until the colonel showed up. She waited silently while Scatalone tossed the car keys to a gray-haired man standing by the helipad. The guy looked retired military. Scatalone motioned her into the copter.

She strapped herself into a no-frills, nylon-webbing seat across from Scatalone. The bird lifted off without delay, and her stomach rumbled ominously. She swallowed hard and prayed that the secret nemesis of her career—persistent air-sickness—wouldn't reveal itself. Although the grumpy colonel's black patent leather shoes were caked in mud and looked liked hell, she didn't want to barf all over them.

How she managed to hang on to her breakfast through the interminable chopper ride she had no idea. It was probably just as well that she was filthy. Nobody could see the sickly green color her skin had to be.

She'd just about decided to let rip with the contents of her stomach when the distinctive skyline of Washington, D.C., came into view outside her window. Whoa. Who wanted to talk to her so urgently *here?* And about *what?* She was a know-nothing computer programmer working on a new database for a supply squadron in North Carolina. Not that she chose that career. Uncle Sam stuck her in a dead-end job to shut her up. To get her off everyone's case about the idea of letting her apply to the Special Forces. Not that her efforts had done a lick of good. Her dream wasn't to be.

They rushed north along the Potomac River and swooped in aggressively for a landing on top of a big red H painted in a white circle on the gray roof of the Pentagon. Almost back to terra firma. *Don't barf. Do* not *barf.*

The colonel was true to his word and gave her no opportunity whatsoever to clean herself up, refusing even her request for a rest room stop inside the Pentagon's plush heliport arrival lounge. Sheesh. She might accuse the guy of engaging in psychological warfare were he an enemy interrogator.

Clearly he was hoping to intimidate her. Throw her off balance. But he didn't know her well enough to realize she got a kick out of strolling down the high-gloss corridors of the Pentagon looking like the creature from the Black Lagoon. The looks all the scurrying flunkies threw at her in the halls were priceless. She was grandly amused by the time the lieutenant colonel turned into a rich, walnut-paneled corridor. Holy cow. The offices of the Joint Chiefs of Staff. Well, then. *That* was definitely intimidating. But damned if she'd let Jack Scatalone know it.

They stepped into a sitting area furnished like some old-world gentlemen's club with leather couches and thick rugs. Despite its soothing décor, the atmosphere in the office was electric. Like this place was the center of something important. Like life and death decisions were made here. Her adrenaline surged. God, she loved being where the action was.

Okay, so now she felt a little weird in her camo fatigues and full-body mud wrap. When they'd landed, Jack had shrugged back into his shirt, tie and Class A jacket, and he'd brushed most of the dried mud off his pants and shoes. In stark contrast to her, he looked reasonably presentable. To cover her discomfort, she occupied herself with picking bits of oak leaves off her clothes and tossing them into a trash can.

A thin, severe, gray-haired secretary stepped out of an interior office and looked down her nose with distaste at Vanessa. "General Wittenauer will see you now."

Wittenauer? The JSOC commander? The Joint Special Operations Command itself? Headquarters and operational command center for all interservice special operations units and missions. Except it was based out of North Carolina, not the Pentagon. Her pulse leaped in sudden anticipation. She'd applied to Special Forces school every year for the first ten years of her career, knowing full well that women were not accepted to that elite training. But a girl could always hope. Maybe that's why she'd been summoned to JSOC's Washington branch office....

Nah. Wishful thinking. She'd caused enough waves in those early years that she'd been shuttled off to a series of dead-end desk jobs ever since. The air force steadfastly refused to make use of more than one-tenth of her skills as a computer programmer. She managed last year to wangle an assignment to Pope AFB in North Carolina, right across the airfield from Fort Bragg, home of the army Special Forces. But that was as close as she'd ever gotten to the real thing. Her career had stalled out, and unless a miracle happened, she was never going to see lieutenant colonel in this man's air force.

It was a bitter pill to swallow. She'd joined the service with such high hopes of serving her country in a glorious fashion, heck, of at least making a difference. But all she'd managed to do was trap herself into the role of little cog in a big machine.

Cautiously, she followed Scatalone into the general's office.

Hal Wittenauer looked up from his desk. He nodded briefly at her escort and then turned his attention to her. His brittle gaze stabbed her like one of the carbon steel knives made famous by his black ops teams. Nobody'd told her to report in formally, so she mimicked Scatalone and just stood ramrod straight beneath the general's cold scrutiny.

The general finally broke the silence and addressed her in a growl. "Am I interrupting you?"

"Not at all, sir," she answered smoothly. "I was engaging in a little recreational activity on my leave."

"Rolling around in mud?" he asked skeptically.

"Playing paintball," she admitted.

Wittenauer looked over at Scatalone. "Your uniform seems uncharacteristically disheveled. Any problem finding the major?"

She saw the muscles in Scatalone's jaw ripple. "No problem, sir."

*Bull.* She blurted, "I killed him."

The general's rapier-sharp gaze snapped to her. If he was amused in the slightest, he hid it well. In fact, his jaw started to ripple, too. He stared at her for an inordinately long time. She held his gaze steadily. She'd waited for ten years to meet the man seated at this desk, and she wasn't going to go all girlie shy and abashed now.

Finally the general announced, "Brief her in, Jack. Let's give her a try."

A try at *what?*

"And for God's sake, get her cleaned up," the general snapped.

Scatalone led her out of Wittenauer's office and across the sitting area. "In here," he barked at her as if she were some raw recruit. Without comment she stepped into another office, much smaller than the general's but just as plush. These boys in D.C. sure liked their creature comforts.

"In there." Scatalone pointed at a door between two tall bookshelves filled with the memorabilia of a distinguished special ops career. A moment's envy filled her. But then she opened the door. Wow. A private bathroom? Nice. She locked the door loudly just to get Scatalone's goat and stripped out of her stiff, mud-caked clothes. She caught a glimpse of herself in the mirror. Lord, she looked like an alien invader with bright blue eyes.

She took a quick shower and rinsed out her clothes while

she was at it. Wet was better than muddy. She wrung out her fatigue pants and olive-drab T-shirt as best she could and shimmied back into the cold, cloying garments. Ick. No help for it. But at least she didn't smell like a North Carolina swamp anymore. She opened the medicine cabinet and borrowed a comb she found there to detangle her chin-length chestnut hair. Without a blow-dryer to straighten it, her hair was going to end up a mass of ringlets around her face. No help for that, either. Jack Scatalone would just have to deal with her looking like Shirley Temple.

She stepped out into his office. Scatalone looked up from his desk, did a double take and glared. What was his problem?

"Come with me," he growled.

She followed him down into the bowels of the Pentagon to a small PX. She had no idea there was anything like this compact department store inside the Pentagon. Like most past exchanges, it carried everything from sporting goods to clothes, from uniforms to children's toys. Although it was good to note that the Pentagon PX was noticeably shy on toys.

"Get yourself a uniform and whatever toiletries you need," Scatalone ordered.

"For how long?"

"Couple weeks. I doubt you'll last any longer than that."

"Is this a permanent reassignment?" she asked, surprised.

"I doubt it," he bit out.

What burr was up his butt? Or was he just a jerk naturally?

Uniform slacks, shirt, shoes, major's epaulets and an engraved-while-you-wait name tag went in her basket. She tossed in toothpaste, a toothbrush, a hairbrush, and deodorant, as well. But she'd be damned if she was going to buy tampons in front of the guy.

"That's it?" he asked in surprise.

Ha. She'd managed to throw him off balance. Sure, she wore makeup and perfume, and primped like any other woman, but for some reason, she felt compelled to match this guy's macho. "Whoops. Forgot one thing."

She bit her lip to keep from grinning as she hauled him over to the lingerie section of the store and picked up a fire engine-red ensemble of lace panties and push-up bra. Dirty old generals must choose the store's inventory, she thought.

"That's everything," she announced cheerfully.

His eyes were dark slits of irritation as he led her to the checkout counter. Excellent. But he turned the tables and surprised her when he pulled out a government credit card and charged it all before she could pull out her own wallet. Her purchases were bagged, and he led her back up to his office. Two minutes in his bathroom—whoa, his own bathroom? Plush assignment—and she was presentable again. She stepped out. And bit back a grin as his eyes dropped immediately to her chest. Thinking about that naughty red bra, was he?

"What gives?" she demanded. "Why did you and General Wittenauer drag me all the way up here to Washington? Have you got a computer problem you need fixed?"

"Computer…hell, no." Scatalone grabbed a thick file off his desk and headed for the door. "Come with me."

If he gave her the runaround for too much longer without some sort of explanation, she was going to walk out on him, lieutenant colonel or not. This time, he led her down to one of the deepest sublevels of the Pentagon—The Toilet, as it was fondly called in honor of the sewage that came in when the pipes burst. She'd worked down here before in the Central Computer Processing Center. They called on her occasionally to write programs for them. She was surprised when Scatalone led her past the computer complex, though, and down a darker, narrower hall. It was dry and musty, with exposed pipes overhead and paint reminiscent of the 1940s.

"In here." He ducked through an unmarked door.

He flipped on the lights and she looked around. It was a fairly large space, but every inch of it was crammed with tall filing cabinets. It felt like a tight rat maze. A single table stood in a small space in the center of the room.

"Okay, Colonel. Spill it or I'm outta here."

Amusement glinted in his eyes as he sat down at the table and gestured her into the chair across from him. He made a big deal out of looking at his watch, then he said flatly, "Four hours, nineteen minutes before you lost your patience. Not good enough, Major."

For *what?* What in the *hell* was he talking about? Of course, after that stinging rebuke, it wasn't like she'd ask him in this lifetime.

He opened the file and picked up a sheet of paper. "You went to MIT. Degree with honors in Computer Science. Studied Arabic, Spanish and Chinese. Why those three?"

"Hot spots in the world," she answered shortly. "Good languages to know."

He gave her an intent, assessing look. Finally he glanced down to the paper and continued. "Made the 1992 Olympic team in swimming, but a shoulder injury kept you from competing."

"Yes." That looked for all the world like her personnel file in front of him. Except it should be in San Antonio at the air force personnel center.

"Applied to spec ops school ten times," he read.

She folded her arms across her chest and pressed her lips together.

"Why'd you quit applying?" he shot at her.

"I was ordered to," she shot back.

One dark eyebrow went up. "By whom?"

"General Wittenauer's predecessor. He told me I was harassing his office, and if I didn't stop, he'd put a letter of reprimand in my record."

"And that stopped you?" Scatalone said scornfully.

Her eyes narrowed. "Sometimes you have to cut your losses and try again another day. Pursuit of my goal at that time had become counterproductive."

He shuffled through the rest of her file and didn't seem interested in anything else he saw. Not that a series of dead-end desk jobs should blow his skirts up. Without warning, he pinned her with a piercing stare. "Why Special Forces?" he barked.

His abrupt question startled her. Enough to pop an image into her mind. Of an old color photograph, its tones faded to green and yellow. Marred down the middle by a vertical white line where it had been folded long ago. Two grinning, shirtless young men hammed for the camera, their arms thrown over each other's shoulders. Young and wild. On top of the world. They died a week after the picture was taken. And one of them was her father, U.S. Navy SEAL Vince Blake.

She shrugged. "I've got the skills. I've got the drive. I've got the desire. Why not Special Forces?" she threw back at him.

He betrayed no reaction to her challenge. He asked stonily, "So it's still your goal to be the first woman to enter the Special Forces?"

The question made her feel naked. It was her most closely held dream, and she'd privately trained for it for years. It was why she put up with being pushed into a forgotten job. Why she worked out for hours every day. Why she pursued hobbies like skeet shooting and full-combat paintball. But she wasn't the least bit comfortable sharing her life's ambition with this gruff stranger. She answered defensively, "I don't give a flip whether I'm the first woman or the last. I just want a shot at it."

He put the typed paper back in the file and closed it deliberately. He leaned back in his chair and looked at her long and hard. Finally he spoke heavily, "Then today's your lucky day, Major."

# Chapter 2

Vanessa's heart nearly leaped out of her chest. *Please God, let this not be some sort of elaborate practical joke*. She sat very still, waiting for the colonel to continue.

He leaned forward and stared at her, his gaze deadly serious. "You've been chosen to pull together a team of six women who will be run through Special Forces training and evaluated to see if women are capable of performing the Special Forces mission."

Holy Mary, Mother of God. He wasn't kidding. Damned if her knees hadn't just started shaking.

He swept his hand around the room. "These are the personnel files of every female currently serving in the United States armed forces. We had them flown up from San Antonio for you. From them you will need to pick five women to join you on this project."

She eyed the rows of cabinets. There must have been a hundred metal, four-drawer stacks in the room. "How long do I have to pick the team?"

"Two weeks."

She stared at him slack-jawed. "You've got to be kidding. It'll take me a year to get through these files. What are the selection criteria?"

He shrugged. "There aren't any."

"What are we going to be doing? What's the mission? I need to know if I'm getting the right people."

"The Special Forces mission covers a broad array of possible scenarios. Surely you know that, Major."

Duh. She'd read everything she could get her hands on about the Special Forces over the years. She knew as well as any outsider what the spec ops guys did. They went into impossible situations against impossible odds and achieved impossible goals. "So you want me to pick five women out of thousands upon thousands, and you're going to measure the future of all women in special ops based on whoever I come up with. And I have two lousy weeks to find the right five?"

"If you can't do it, we'll find somebody else for the job," he said silkily.

"That's not the point. You're setting this thing up to fail from the very start if you don't give me enough time to find the very best women available."

He lounged in his chair and crossed his arms over his chest. "*I'm* not setting you up to fail, darlin'."

His implication was clear. Someone else sure as hell was. She could imagine the wrangling that had to have gone on in the chauvinist-laden halls upstairs over this one. "Who shoved it down Wittenauer's throat?" Because without a doubt someone had, given how pissed off he was to see her. Best to know up front who her enemies were going to be.

Scatalone shrugged. "That's above my pay grade to know."

Interesting. He didn't deny the fact that someone *had* twisted Wittenauer's arm.

"When you're done for the day, come back up to my office. I'll get you to the quarters I've arranged for you while you're here." He pushed to his feet. "I'll leave you to it, then. Two weeks, Major." And with that, he left.

Great. He was probably going to stick her in some flop-house nightmare—just to make her feel *really* welcome.

She turned to face the maze of metal cabinets. And took a deep breath. *She'd done it.* She was going to get her shot at the brass ring. An urge to whoop aloud nearly overcame her. Only the thought that Scatalone was probably standing outside waiting for her to lose her cool kept her jubilation in her throat. She did indulge in a heartfelt fist pump, though. And then she stepped up to the nearest filing cabinet, pulled out a file randomly and opened it. An army admin type. Enlisted. No problem. Single mom. No way.

She pulled out a dozen more files, and the women inside were equally dismally suited for special ops. This was never going to work. It was like looking for five needles in a mile-tall haystack. Surely the armed forces personnel centers wouldn't release their only copies of all these files to the Pentagon. There had to be some sort of backups. And she'd bet her next paycheck they were electronic.

She picked up the ancient black rotary phone hanging on the wall beside the door and dialed the Pentagon operator. It took only about four phone calls to track down the guy she needed to talk to in San Antonio. "Hi, Sergeant McAllister. This is Major Blake. I'm sitting in the basement of the Pentagon right now with a whole bunch of personnel files on female soldiers."

The sergeant exclaimed, "So you're who they went to! What in the world are you guys doing with all those files? We've been dying to know what's going on and who had the clout to get them relocated like that."

"I don't really know myself. But I've been asked to sort these puppies and select a few women for a test program, and there's no way I can do it in hard copy."

"No kidding," the sergeant commiserated.

"Do you happen to have an electronic version of this stuff?"

"I'll do you one better than that," the guy replied. "I can send them formatted for promotion boards."

"What does that mean?"

"All their training and skills are rated on numeric scales and can be compared easily against one another in a computer sort."

Fantastic. "That's perfect! How soon do you suppose you could e-mail the files to me?"

"Right now. But it'll take a couple hours to send. The files are huge. And you'll need a ton of storage space on your computer."

"No problem. Here's where to send them." She rattled off an e-mail address she'd set up on one of the Pentagon's mainframes the last time she was here. The guy agreed to get right on it and she hung up. Now for a decent computer to work on. She headed for the central processing center they'd passed on the way to this dungeon. The guard at the main door stonewalled her, but when several of the computer techs inside recognized her and called out greetings from across the room, the guard let her in.

A staff sergeant who was one of the best hackers she'd ever known came over to her. "Good to see you, Jerry," she greeted him. "I can't believe you're not in jail yet."

The young man grinned. "They have to catch me first."

She shook her head. "Hey, I need a favor. General Wittenauer's given me a project to do, and it's going to involve running a massive file sort. Any chance I could use a terminal here to write the program?"

"No prob."

"And I could use a little time on one of the supercomputers to run it," she added.

He shot her an interested look. "How much time?"

"A minute ought to do it."

He nodded slowly. "I might be able to work you in tomorrow night, late. Let's go take a look at the schedule."

In short order, she was booked for two minutes of run time

on the Pentagon's newest and fastest supercomputer, and she had a temporary badge granting her entrance to the computing center. Now to figure out what qualities she wanted the program to search for and in what order she wanted her candidates ranked. She worked throughout the afternoon, racking her brain for every skill she could think of that might be useful in a female Special Forces soldier.

Highly intelligent. Foreign-language speaker. Technical skills. Physical fitness. Upper body strength. Stamina. Mental toughness. Team player. A bit of an attitude. Some of the attributes would be hard to measure in the cold, numeric world of a computer, but once she got an initial readout of possible candidates, she'd narrow it down herself from there.

It was nearly six a.m. before she made her way back upstairs to Scatalone's office.

"Where in the hell have you been?" he growled. "You weren't in the file room."

"I had a couple things to take care of," she answered noncommittally.

He gave her a scornful look like she'd been slacking off all afternoon. "Your hotel is down the street. It's about a five-minute taxi ride except at rush hour, when it can take longer to drive it than walk it."

Wow. A hotel room? At best, she'd been hoping he'd stash her in the visiting officer's quarters at Andrews AFB, which was the air force base nearest to the Pentagon. The commute from Andrews into Virginia was a bear in the morning, and she'd been dreading it.

"I'll drive you to the hotel if you like," Scatalone offered gruffly.

She blinked. Had he just shown real, live human consideration? There was a person under that gorilla exterior? Get out. "Uh, sure. Thanks," she replied, surprised.

He dropped her off in front of The Ritz Carlton, Pentagon City. It was a shockingly swanky hotel that served mainly vis-

itors to the nearby Pentagon. Yup, all those defense contract
dollars hard at work. Scatalone told her brusquely that Uncle
Sam was picking up the tab, and room service was authorized. Checking in was a breeze. It seemed the colonel had
taken care of everything already. She stopped by the hotel's
gift shop and stocked up on makeup, moisturizers, hair con-
ditioner, the tampons she'd need in a couple days, a half
ounce of outrageously expensive perfume and a box of her
favorite Swiss chocolate. Now she was ready to face the
colonel tomorrow.

After working most of the night in her room on the logic
of her computer sorting program, Vanessa slept until nearly
noon. She had nothing to do until she ran the actual sort tonight, so she got up in leisurely fashion, primped to her heart's
content and wrestled her curly hair into a semblance of order
with the help of the hotel's complimentary blow-dryer. It
was just after lunch when she strolled into Scatalone's office.

He looked up from his desk, his expression thunderous.
"Where in the Sam Hill have you been? I had to cover for you
with the general this morning."

She jolted in alarm. "Did he need to speak to me?"

"No. But he wanted to know what you were doing."

She let out the breath she'd been holding. "I worked all
night and didn't go to sleep until about six this morning. I
wasn't aware I had to report in to you or the general at a set
time every day." She added with a tinge of sarcasm, "Is that
what you want? A daily written report? In triplicate, perhaps?"

His gaze stayed narrow, but the tense set of his shoulders
relaxed. "Just get the job done on time."

She bit back the smirk that threatened. Two weeks. Ha!
She'd have it done in two days. "I'll do my best, sir," she answered earnestly.

"Don't 'sir' me. Makes me feel like a damn staff weenie.
My men call me Scat."

She nodded, taken aback. It was an honor to be allowed

to use an SF guy's field handle. But Scat? Who picked a handle that was a glorified word for animal poop? She shrugged. Each to his own.

One of his eyebrows was creeping up. He stared at her expectantly.

"What?" she asked sharply. She was really getting tired of his cryptic silences and stony demeanor.

"Don't you have work to do?" he asked.

Actually, she didn't. Not until the computer run tonight. But she wasn't about to tell him that. She left his office and hit the Pentagon's gym, where she worked up a good sweat and blew off some stress. After a leisurely shower, she made her way to the computer center.

She ran a last check of her program on some test files to be sure it was bug free. Then she poked around in the Pentagon's electronic personnel files to see what she could learn about Jack Scatalone. She poked. And poked some more. Finally she called over Jerry the Wonder Hacker to ask what was going on.

He leaned over her shoulder and stared at her computer screen. "What's up?"

"According to every military roster and file I've accessed, Jack Scatalone doesn't exist. But he's working upstairs as we speak. What's the deal?"

"Scoot over."

She moved aside as Jerry typed at the speed of light. It took him only about three minutes to sit back with a satisfied, "Aha."

"Well?" she demanded.

"He's Delta Force. When guys join the Delta detachment, everything about them is classified, and their very existence is wiped out of the system. Only a handful of people can access their files. I could try to break in, but I helped design some of that security, and it's a bitch."

Whoa. Delta Force was the best of the best. An elite team within the elite Special Forces, trained specifically in counter-terrorism and hostage rescue. She frowned at Jerry and answered absently, "No, don't break in on my account. If he's Delta, what's he doing pushing a pencil at a desk here in the Puzzle Palace?"

Jerry shrugged. "Probably pulling a tour as a staff type. Happens to the best of them, you know."

Oh, how she knew. She'd pulled nothing but staff tours of duty in her twelve-year career.

"Hey, Major. It's getting close to time to queue up your program," Jerry announced. "Got it ready to go?"

"Yup, let's do it."

And ten minutes later she had her list. Plus, Jerry was kind enough to print hard copies of the personnel files of the top fifty candidates for her to look over. That way she wouldn't have to hunt around for the next week in the jumbled filing cabinets downstairs to find the darned things. With a warm thanks to the computer tech for his help, she scooped up the foot-tall pile of paper and headed for the hotel.

*August 8, 3:00 p.m.*
*the Emirate of El Bhoukar*

Sweat poured down First Lieutenant Daniel Defoe's face and into his eyes. It stung like hell. But he dared not lift his hand to mop it off. An enemy sniper would see the movement and nail him for sure. One-hundred-twenty degrees Fahrenheit and climbing out here in this damn desert. They were out of water. Low on ammo. Had barely enough cover to evade the snipers. Were ambushed and surrounded. The mission was blown completely to hell. In their line of work, once they lost the element of secrecy and surprise, their team was usually screwed. Which meant they were cluster-fucked right about now.

Their usual team leader, Lieutenant Colonel Jack Scatalone, was stuck in the Pentagon driving a desk on some classified assignment, and their number two, Captain Scott

Worthington, was down. Some sort of snake bit him around midmorning. Poor bastard was delirious with pain and poison. No use at all to the team. Jensen had hit him already with the broad-spectrum snake antivenin from the med kit and was pouring epinephrine and morphine into him to keep him alive, but it wasn't going to matter if they didn't get out of this death trap soon.

Snipers and machine-gun emplacements belonging to a nasty outfit calling themselves the Army of Holy War lined both rims of the valley above them. A couple of rocket-propelled grenades had whistled down their way, too. And to think, intel had said this valley was clear. They should have been able to move down it toward their target, no problem, the oil field at the far end of the valley. What a crock. Hell, they'd strolled right into the middle of a damn army. Of course, it hadn't helped that Captain Worthington yelped when the snake nailed him. Gave away their location big time. But he couldn't blame Scottie for hollering. The snake had been a monster. Some sort of adder.

He ducked as a spray of incoming rounds peppered the rocks by his head. "How we doing for firepower?" he grunted at Master Sergeant Harrison Walsh beside him.

"Not enough to take on this force. Our MP-5s can hit these guys, but we have to see them first. The bastards are holed up in all sorts of little caves and crannies. Short-range automatic fire doesn't have the punch to blast through solid rock. We've got about four dozen grenades, a bunch of C-4, a hundred yards of det cord and about three thousand rounds of ammo."

Not enough to trade fire indefinitely with these assholes. "Is there any support at all we can call in, Walsh?"

"Nada. We're not officially here. Neither the U.S. nor the Bhoukari government will acknowledge us."

"Alternate extraction points?"

"All in Oman. We've got to get back across the border for a pickup."

Crap. The border was a hundred miles to the east. It had

taken them over a week to hike into this area. No way would the captain make it that far. They had no diplomatic clearance to head for Yemen to the west, either, and the Gulf of Aden was close to two hundred miles south of their position.

Surrendering wasn't an option. Not only did Delta Three never give up, but these terrorists would have a field day torturing the fabled counterterrorism gurus of the U.S. military. Even if the team survived whatever the terrorists did to them, they still wouldn't exist on anybody's official list of missing persons. Uncle Sam couldn't and wouldn't charge in to the rescue. He eyed the high mountain ridges around them. "Can we get a radio call out?"

Walsh shrugged. "If we time it right, we can hit a satellite uplink."

Defoe crawled on his belly and elbows toward the radioman's hiding spot behind a cluster of red sandstone boulders. This valley looked like freaking Mars. Hell of a place to die. He crouched beside their communications guy. "I may need you to make a radio call later. Can you set it up?"

"Who to?" Ginelli asked in surprise.

"To whomever will listen. Make it in the clear. In plain English. On whatever frequency the most people will hear. A universal emergency channel."

Ginelli gaped at him like he'd lost his mind.

He returned the look. Ginelli was a good man. Solid. Defoe explained, "This mission's a train wreck. Our cover's blown and we're severely outnumbered. The boss is dead meat if we don't get him help soon. And until we do that, he's going to hamper our ability to stay alive in a major way."

Ginelli stared narrowly at him. "You're not planning to hand him over, are you?"

"Not to these maniacs. But he's got to have medical care. From a hospital."

"Higher-ups are gonna have a conniption if we break silence."

"Those higher-ups are sitting at their desks with their feet propped up, drinking a cup of coffee right now. It's the captain's neck on the line. And he'd do the same for any one of us."

Ginelli nodded grimly. "Your call. You're the one who'll catch hell for it."

Defoe looked up at the enemy positions all around them. "Those bastards could come down off the ridges any minute and overrun us. We'd take a lot of them out, but these Army of Holy War types are fanatics looking to die. They'd keep coming until they got us. Overwhelm us with sheer numbers. Spot says he's counted over a hundred of 'em."

Ginelli grinned. "Kinda nice to know six of us are so badass it takes twenty to knock one of us out."

Defoe returned the grin briefly. "Damn straight. Be ready to make the call. You'll have only a few seconds to get it off when the time comes, and the captain's life will depend on it. Don't use any names, ranks or military references. Come up with a story about being a lone civilian pilot who's come under attack, been shot down and you don't know why. Do a lot of yelling and Mayday calling. Request close air support or extraction."

"You got it, L.T. I'll be standing by for one hysterical radio call."

*August 8, 10:00 a.m.*
*JSOC headquarters*

Vanessa marched up to General Wittenauer's secretary resolutely. Darned if the woman wasn't almost more intimidating than her boss. "I understand Colonel Scatalone is in a briefing with the general. When they're done, I'd like a moment of their time, if I could."

A pair of gray eyebrows raised in condescending disapproval. "They will probably be too busy to see you today."

What was up with that? A crisis of some kind? Her pulse

jumped in consternation at the thought of what constituted a crisis inside these particular walls. "I'll wait."

The secretary sniffed and pointed at one of the leather sofas. "Sit over there, if you must."

Vanessa sat down and picked up a copy of *Aviation Week* from the coffee table. Two *Popular Mechanics,* yesterday's *Washington Post* and one *Sports Illustrated* later, General Wittenauer's office door finally opened. Scatalone stuck his head out into the waiting area. He looked like hell. "You wanted to see us?" he said shortly.

She picked up the stack of files from the coffee table and headed for the door. His uniform shirt was partially unbuttoned and his tie was missing. As she approached him, she noticed whisker stubble on his jaw. He looked like an expectant father who'd been pacing a waiting room for hours and hours. Had he been here all night?

Wittenauer didn't look any better. His sleeves were rolled up, and he was showing every one of his fifty-plus years this morning. He looked none too pleased to see her, either. She stepped farther into the office. An air of heavy events hung about the room. Something bad was going down.

"I'm sorry to bother you, sir. But I thought you might be interested in these." She set the stack of files down in the middle of his desk, facing him.

"What are they?" he asked.

"My team."

# Chapter 3

By sunset, the captain was in a coma. *Poor bastard wasn't going to make it much longer*. They were out of drugs and out of options. The lieutenant took advantage of a lull in the action— Muslim prayer time—to rig a litter out of a tarp for the captain. It was an ironclad creed in the Special Forces that they never left one of their own behind, dead or alive. The other guys huddled around the captain's prostrate form and looked at their new leader expectantly.

He laid out the options. "According to our exceedingly accurate and brilliant intel briefing yesterday, the Bhoukari government still controls the oil field. My plan is to head for its perimeter. We'll drop off the captain, fake a radio call from him pretending to be a civilian pilot who's been shot down, shoot off a couple grenades to make it look like there's been a crash and then activate the emergency locator transmitter in the captain's watch. Good Lord willing and the creek don't rise, someone will come out and find him. Give him some medical care. Then, the rest of us head back the way we came, make contact with the terrorists and continue the mission. Thoughts or comments on this idea?"

"The Bhoukaris will arrest the captain," Walsh, the team's sniper, said.

Jensen replied, "If he lives, and that's a big if, he won't be conscious for days. Maybe weeks. With the depth of the coma he's in right now, he's likely to have short-term memory loss anyway. He won't remember why or how he got to Bhoukar or with whom. Hell, he'll be lucky to remember his own name for a while."

No, the captain wouldn't blow their cover. Defoe spoke up once more. "Bhoukar won't kill a U.S. citizen if other countries know they've got him. That's why I need you to make that radio call, Ginelli. Let this whole part of the world know he's out here. It's not a pretty scenario, but he'll be better off a prisoner of Bhoukar than dead." The men traded grim looks as he continued, "Of course, that's if we can get him out of this valley alive."

Silent, determined looks passed all around.

Walsh spoke up. "I'll take point."

Defoe nodded. "Spot, you go with Walsh. Jensen will stay with the captain. I'll take the east flank, and Ginelli, you take the west flank. Me and Ginelli will scout the ridges and when the coast is clear, we'll help Jensen move the captain."

It was going to be a hell of a trick to evade their way out of there unseen with the captain in tow. But they had to try. Better to go down fighting than just to sit on their asses waiting for death to come to them all.

*August 9*
*secure briefing room, JSOC headquarters*

Vanessa paused for a moment outside the door. The women corresponding to that stack of files were seated on the other side of it. Four days to bring her to D.C., pick the team, and bring them all here. Scat and Wittenauer still didn't look entirely sure what had hit them. She grinned. Served them right.

She took a deep breath. And now it was time to convince five women to participate in this grand experiment. A couple of them would be easy sells. But the rest were unknowns.

She stepped into the heavily soundproofed and electronically protected room-within-a-room. The five women seated around the conference table went silent. Vanessa pushed the heavy door shut, and the green light went on over the door. She took the last remaining seat at the end of the table. "In case you hadn't guessed based on where we're sitting, this briefing is classified."

A chuckle around the table.

"In fact, it's so classified, I think somebody really would shoot us if we talked about it outside this room."

Another chuckle, but with an edge this time. Good. They'd caught the underlying seriousness behind her light remarks. But then, she'd expected this group to be quick on the uptake.

"My name's Vanessa Blake. Thanks for coming here today on such short notice. I apologize for any disruption I've caused in your lives."

A dark-haired, caramel-skinned captain spoke up. "Just why are we here, anyway?"

She identified the speaker. Aleesha Gautier. Jamaican by birth, emergency room doctor, trained surgeon, fluent in French, Spanish and Portuguese, currently doing research in chemical weapon countermeasures, collegiate swimmer and avid scuba diver.

Vanessa leaned forward. The moment of truth. Could she convince these women to be part of the Medusa Project?

"A few days ago, I was dragged to the Pentagon out of the blue in much the same fashion as you all were. General Wittenauer, commander of the Joint Special Operations Center, asked me to put together a team—myself and five other women—to participate in an experiment called the Medusa

Project. He put me in a room with the personnel files of every woman currently serving in the armed forces and told me to find the five best. And here you are."

The group rustled in surprise.

"I don't mean to throw a monkey wrench into the works here," a tanned gorgeous blonde said, "but I'm not in the armed forces anymore. I got out two years ago."

Vanessa nodded. Misty Cordell. Former air force test pilot, top stick in every squadron she ever flew with, stunt pilot and acrobatic pilot as a hobby, fluent in Russian and German. Champion surfer and triathlete for fun. "Correct me if I'm wrong, but aren't you furloughed from your airline job right now?"

"That's right," Misty replied, surprised.

"When I did searches for the best female pilot in the armed forces, your name came up every time. You have a regular commission, which means the military can reactivate you immediately if you choose to participate in the project."

"And what might that project be?" Misty asked lightly.

"To form the first team of women in the Special Forces."

They all stared at her. The marine officer, Karen Turner, grinned in open jubilation. According to her records, she'd been pressing to get into Special Forces work for years but had run into the same no-girls-allowed wall that Vanessa had.

But the officer to Vanessa's right, Isabella Torres, looked doubtful. Crud. Isabella was, bar none, the top photographic image analyst in air force intelligence *and* a cryptography expert, not to mention she was fluent in Spanish, French, Italian, Farsi, Hebrew and Arabic.

Vanessa turned to Isabella. "You don't look overwhelmed at the idea."

"Honestly, I never thought about it because it's off-limits to women."

Vanessa smiled. "It's not off-limits anymore. The testosterone fortress has finally been breached."

Katrina Kim spoke up. "What would the training entail?"

Vanessa turned to the petite, elegant half-Korean woman. Another person who'd fought for years—in her case to become an army Special Forces sniper—but been excluded from her goal because of her gender. "I have no idea what our training will be like. I expect it will suck worse than just about anything any of us have ever experienced. My guess is that JSOC will give us the roughest, toughest, nastiest bastards on the face of the planet to train us, and while they're at it, they'll do their level best to break every last one of us."

Karen Turner leaned forward, her grin even wider. "Sounds like fun. Where do I sign up?"

Vanessa grinned back. She'd had no doubt the power lifter and Far East studies expert would leap at this opportunity. But then, Vanessa spoke seriously. "I'm not going to blow smoke at any of you. Assuming we can survive the training, and that's a big assumption, being in special ops will be dangerous work. On top of that, we'll live under intense scrutiny, be subject to second-guessing every step of the way, get caught in the middle of political wrangling way above our pay grades, be the topic of controversy and negative public attention, and face discrimination and harassment by our male counterparts. I have no doubt this will be the most difficult thing any of us do in our entire lives."

She looked around the table at the sober faces. "None of you has ever turned away from a challenge, ever given up on a goal because it was hard or because someone told you it was impossible. You're all smart, talented, ambitious, stubborn women. You're all physically and mentally tough enough to do this. As a group, we have the skills to take on just about anything that comes our way. Based on what I've learned about you ladies in my research, I'd trust each and every one of you with my life. And that's why you're sitting at this table today."

She let that sink in for a minute. "Take some time to think about it. Talk to one another and to me. You can't go halfway with this project. If you agree to do it, you have to be willing to go all the way. If you can't commit to that, say no, and we'll find someone else.

"One reminder. Everything about this project, including its name, is classified. Don't talk about why you're here outside this room. I've got this soundproof cracker box booked for the entire day, so if any of you want to come down here to talk freely, it's yours. I'll be available all day.

"We'll meet again tomorrow morning at ten o'clock and you can give me your decisions then."

*August 8, 8:00 p.m.*
*the Pentagon*

A voice on Wittenauer's intercom announced, "Sir, a priority call for you from Al Khobar Ops on secure line one."

The general leaned across his desk and lifted the appropriate receiver to speak to his Saudi control center. "Go ahead," he said tersely, his voice rough from lack of sleep. One of the joys of his job. Sleepless vigils for missing men.

"Captain Takai, here, General. Delta Team Three missed its check-in six hours ago, and just missed its backup check-in as well. We received a report from the USS *Lincoln* carrier group about fifteen minutes ago that they picked up a Mayday call from a male American civilian claiming to have been shot down in the vicinity of where Delta Three last reported in."

Wittenauer swore under his breath. He could see where this was going. And he didn't like it one bit.

"This guy was screaming for close air support and emergency extraction. It may be a ruse by the Army of Holy War terrorists to draw in a U.S. search and rescue team, but the *Lincoln* said the guy sounded legit. American and real tense. They heard gunfire in the background on his radio. He reported that he was badly wounded and pinned down. Right next to the Al-Khibri oil field."

"God *damn* it," Wittenauer bit out. "Is it our guys?"

"Possibly, sir."

"What's the satellite imagery showing?" the general growled.

"Next pass is in fourteen minutes. Last pass—" a pause "—fifty-two minutes ago showed a whole lot of activity not far from Al-Khibri. Image analysts say it looks like the Army of Holy War is engaged in combat there. We're operating on the assumption that Delta Three was involved in that encounter."

"And your assumption about their current status?" the general asked.

"If they broke silence to make a radio call for help, they're most likely dead by now, sir."

*August 10*
*Hart Senate office building, Washington, D.C.*

Senate aide Sean Bradford spoke to another aide as a closed session of the Senate Arms Committee came to an end. "Senator McClure's going to have another stroke when he finds out the committee approved the funding for the Medusa Project behind his back."

"No kidding. But that's what you get for being in the hospital in this town. They kick you when you're down."

Bradford shook his head. "Wouldn't want to be the women in that project when the old man finds out about this. He'll rip the rug out from under them so fast it'll make their heads spin. Every poll we've ever done in his district is strongly against women in combat. If the old geezer wants to be reelected in November, there's no way the Medusa Project can succeed on his watch as chairman of the Senate Arms Committee. His congressional district is as conservative as they come. McClure's got to kill the Medusa Project."

"Do you think they'll even make it through their initial training?" the other aide asked.

"No way. Women can't hold up under that kind of pressure. And they're not strong enough physically."

The second aide looked skeptical. "I dunno. I think they could pull it off."

Bradford scoffed. "Twenty bucks says they don't last a month."

"You're on." The second aide gathered his notes and stuffed them into a red folder marked "Classified." "After we get this stuff under lock and key, are you up for a bite of lunch?"

"Nah." Bradford sighed. "Gotta go brief the senator. Let's just hope the news doesn't kill him."

*September 2*
*North Carolina*

Vanessa flopped down in her porch swing and chugged the bottle of water she'd left sitting beside it before her run. She was taking her own advice. She'd told her team to put their affairs in order and spend the next four weeks getting into the best physical shape of their lives.

It had been difficult explaining to her colleagues at Pope why she was suddenly wrapping up all her projects, putting her paychecks on automatic deposit and her bills on autopay, and giving away her cat without spilling the beans about what she was about to do. But Wittenauer had been clear. Nobody—*nobody*—was to know what they'd been offered. Thankfully, all the women had accepted the offer.

Her daily runs, six miles along the perimeter of the tightly guarded compound known as "Wally World" in a remote corner of the army side of the base next to Mott Lake—supposedly where Delta Force trained in urban warfare and hostage rescue tactics—took on new excitement. Finally. She had a shot at seeing what lay on the other side of that fence. Were it not for the grueling weight training and cardio workouts she pushed herself through in addition to her runs, she doubted she'd be sleeping at all with the amount of adrenaline zinging through her system. But as it was, she collapsed into bed every night, too exhausted to think.

It was hot tonight. Sticky. The cicadas were loud, drowning out everything else. Perspiring freely, she mopped her face and neck with a towel. Ten more days before their training started. She felt ready for it now. But then, ignorance was bliss.

The sound of a car engine pulling into her short driveway made her yank the towel down. A black Jeep with a roll bar and no roof turned its lights off. The engine stopped. A man in jeans and a dark polo shirt jumped out of the front seat. She couldn't see his face as he ducked under the crape myrtle at the corner of her porch. But his physique was to die for in the close-fitting shirt. Hard. Muscular. Ripped even for around here, home of the 82nd Airborne, the army rangers and, of course, the fabled Delta Force.

And then he stepped into the yellow glow of the porch light. She lurched in surprise.

Jack Scatalone.

"What are you doing here?" she blurted.

"Making a…social call," he said, as short on words as always.

She was abruptly vividly aware of her spandex shorts and sleeveless muscle shirt clinging wetly to her body. "Well, then, by all means, come up on the porch and be social," she replied dryly.

He stepped onto the veranda and parked one hip on the wide balustrade. He crossed his arms, and his biceps bulged in a display of power she could only envy. "Busy?" he asked.

"Nope. Just finished a run."

"How far?"

"Six miles," she replied.

"How fast?"

She glanced down at her watch and pushed the button that called up the stopwatch feature. "Thirty-eight minutes, five seconds."

"Bring it down to thirty-six minutes," he commented.

Shave off two minutes? In less than two weeks? Yikes. She started calculating how many seconds she'd have to drop each day to make that target.

But Scatalone's voice interrupted her mental math. "I want to show you something."

She blinked up at him. What in the world could he possibly have to show her here and now? "Okay. What is it?"

"Come with me."

"Right now?"

"Yeah."

"These clothes okay?" she asked.

"Fine. Why? Don't want to look like a jock?"

She scowled. "This, from the guy who hauled me in front of a four-star general wearing an inch of mud?"

Without warning, he grinned. His smile was sudden and devastating. And disappeared as fast as it came. Wow. He was *gorgeous* when he did that.

"Let's go. I'll drive," he announced.

She followed him to his Jeep and climbed in the passenger side. The vehicle was perfectly clean. No junk on the floor or stuff in the door pockets that might give her a clue to the mystery that was Jack Scatalone.

"So," she asked casually, "are you unattached or do you have the most understanding wife in the world?"

"No wife."

She couldn't resist poking. "A friendly, charming guy like you? Why ever not?"

His jaw rippled briefly, but he didn't so much as scowl at the barb. Spoilsport. And then he actually gave her a serious answer, of all things. "It's too damn hard to live life when I'm on the inside of the fence looking out and a family is on the outside of the fence looking in. I've seen too many guys wreck their careers and themselves trying to bust through the fence. It never works."

She had a pretty good idea she knew what fence he was

talking about, but she asked anyway, "And what fence, exactly, are we talking about here?"

"The one separating us from everyone else. Once you cross through it, you can kiss the real world goodbye."

"What do you mean?"

"If you make it through your training, you'll never go back to normal again. You won't fit in."

A vague memory of her father flashed through her head. Sitting in an armchair, drinking himself into a stupor, longing for the good old days. Three times his tour of duty with the SEALs ended, and three times he went back for more. Until finally he died. He never made it back to the real world. She'd been five the last time she saw him, too young to take it personally when he couldn't find a way to fit in with his family. But her mother was nearly destroyed by it. Had it not been for her stepfather, she'd hate to think about what would've happened....

Jeez, her brain was spinning off in morbid directions tonight. She replied lightly, "Who knows what's normal and what's not, anyway? I always thought it was a matter of opinion."

He grinned without humor. "When you're done with this project, you'll know. Although some folks would argue the real world is on our side of the fence and the rest of you live in fantasyland."

Yippee. Some profound philosophical epiphany about the nature of society awaited her at the end of the rainbow. She just wanted to make it through training in one piece. She'd worry about deep thoughts after that.

They drove the rest of the way in silence. She didn't usually frequent this part of town. Thick with tattoo parlors, adult video stores and bars. He pulled in at a beer joint she'd never heard of. Looked like a complete dive. "You have something to show me at a *bar?*" she asked.

"Yeah. Not chicken, are you?" he challenged.

She rolled her eyes. A completely transparent ploy. As if she actually needed to be dared to go inside with him. She was curious to see what he thought was so important that he'd show up at her house on a Friday night and take her to a sleazy bar.

The first thing that struck her as they ducked into the dark, low-ceilinged, smoky interior was the decided lack of women. The place was populated almost exclusively by rugged males, many of whom were built a lot like Scatalone. There was a noticeable dip in the volume of the voices as she stepped into the room. Okay, then. He'd brought her to some guy's-night-out joint. No girls allowed. She felt like an unwelcome intruder. But then she shrugged off the feeling. Been there, done that.

A big, blond guy stepped up to the bar on her right and spoke over her head to Scatalone as if she weren't there. "Hey, Scat. Long time no see. Been busy?"

Vanessa caught the undertone in the guy's voice. He was asking if Scatalone had been out on a mission of some kind.

She glanced over in time to catch Scatalone roll his eyes. "I wish. Been in D.C. At the Pentagon."

The guy grinned. "Ever notice how that place is shaped like the world's biggest asshole? My sympathies, man." A bartender thunked the guy's beer down in front of him, and he picked it up and drifted off.

"Who was that?" she shouted over the din.

"Guy I used to work with," Scatalone shouted back.

She looked at the retreating blonde's back. Special Forces guy? Didn't wear it on his sleeve like most of them. Usually she could pick out the I'm-a-badass swagger from twenty paces. She glanced around the room again. A lot of these men had a quiet confidence about them. They were the kind you wouldn't want to mess with in a dark alley.

A second man drifted up to Jack's other side. Vanessa barely made out the guy's words under the general din. "Any news on your guys?"

Jack's jaw set into a good approximation of steel. "Nope," he bit out.

"Too bad, man. You need help, you give me a call."

Was that gratitude that flashed in Jack's eyes? An actual emotion? Wow. And what was the deal with his guys, anyway? Surely the guy hadn't been referring to the Medusa Project. Maybe Jack's Delta team? Was it in trouble?

"Who are all these guys?" she asked aloud as the second man strolled away.

"Don't know them all," Scatalone replied dryly, dodging the question.

Uh-huh. That's what she thought. These were his Delta Force buddies. Hungrily, she looked around the room. And could not believe she was going to have the chance to become one of them. She felt for a moment like she was living in a dream.

And in that moment, the purpose of tonight's outing became clear to her. He was trying to show her she didn't fit in. She wasn't one of the guys and never would be. She leaned close to him and practically put her lips on his ear so he could hear her without her having to shout. "You know, Jack, I don't want to be one of these guys. I like being a girl. I just want to do the same job."

He lurched, but she couldn't tell if it was her breath on his ear or her words that did it. A pair of beers finally arrived, and he snatched them up. She followed as he made his way to a tall table at one side of the room. They perched on a pair of high stools and she took a drink of the dark, stout beer. Scatalone downed half of his in one gulp. Mad? Rattled? Worried about his team? She couldn't tell, but, man, would she like to know which it was.

Another powerful man sauntered up to them. "Yo, Scat. Me and my buddies were trying to figure out if that's a man or a woman you brought in with you."

A nanosecond of hurt pierced her defenses before she

closed off the feeling. She couldn't help it if she had no makeup, her hair was slicked back with sweat from her run, and she was sporting a muscle shirt. Besides, she was proud of her sculpted arms and shoulders. She'd worked damn hard to get them, and she was going to need them real soon.

Scatalone leaned back and looked pointedly at her. Punting the moron her way, was he? Only one way to deal with jerks like this. Vanessa eyed the guy levelly. "Didn't your mama teach you how to tell the difference?" she asked coolly. "Men have a dick and no brains, and women have brains and no dick."

Guffaws sounded from several nearby tables. She could swear that was a smirk she saw flit across Scatalone's face. The moron retreated, scowling.

"Gotta work on your techniques for winning friends and influencing people, Blake," Scatalone commented, sipping at his beer.

She was really tempted to tell him to kiss her butt. But she refrained and smiled politely instead. "Any pointers you'd like to share with me?"

He merely smiled and raised his glass to her. An acknowledgment that she hadn't risen to his bait, perhaps? Lord, he was hard to read.

The mass of men ebbed and flowed around their table, ignoring her for the most part. A lot of the folks in here knew her companion, though. They uniformly seemed to like and respect him. Which spoke volumes about his competence at what he did. This looked like the kind of crowd where respect had to be earned. The hard way. And maybe that was the point of tonight's field trip, too.

A disturbance broke out near the bar. Some sort of metallic pinging. The noise spread, rippling across the room as everyone reached for their pockets. Even Scatalone dug in his pocket and pulled out something. Metal glinted dully in his hand, and then whatever he was holding dropped to the floor.

In a few seconds the sound stopped, leaving silence in its wake. And a hundred guys staring at her.

She looked over at Scatalone. "Mind telling me what this is all about?" she asked evenly.

"Drinking coins. Whoever drops theirs first owes the place a round if everyone else has a coin. But, if someone doesn't produce one, then they owe the room a round."

She nodded slowly and stood up. Everyone in the bar knew damn good and well she wouldn't have one of those coins. They'd blatantly set her up. "Well, then," she called out in a carrying voice, "the next round's on me!"

She made her way over to the bar to put the tab on her credit card. She didn't usually carry a couple hundred bucks in her fanny pack when she went out for a run. Scatalone *knew* they'd do this to her. Jerk. He'd zinged her good. But it didn't mean she wouldn't go down without a fight.

She leaned across the bar and yelled to the bartender, "Do you have any cases of canned beer in the back?"

"Yeah," the guy shouted. "Why?"

She headed for the end of the bar. "Come with me."

The guy followed her into the relative quiet of a grease- and filth-coated storeroom that would give a health inspector heart palpitations. She looked around, searching for the refrigerator. "Do you store any cases of canned beer cold?"

"Yeah," the guy said cautiously.

She turned her most charming smile on the bartender. "Would you mind helping me with a little prank? These guys all think they're so tough, and that they can take advantage of a poor innocent woman like me. They're out there chortling because my friend suckered me into buying a round for the whole place."

A smile began to unfold on the bartender's face. "What did you have in mind?"

"I figure if we take the cases of beer, unopened, and give them a good shake, nobody'd be suspicious."

The guy nodded, grinning openly now. "I figure you're right."

"It's gonna make a mess. Put the bill for the cleanup on my credit card."

Chuckling, the guy waved a hand. "No problem. It'll be my pleasure to see a gal get the best of this bunch. Place could use a good mop-down anyway."

She snorted. The place could use an industrial decontamination. The two of them grabbed cardboard cases of beer out of the refrigerator and shook them hard. Vanessa really put her back into it, motivated by the smug look on Scatalone's face when he explained the coins to her. When all the cases were so shaken the cans were starting to warp, she and the bartender hauled them out front.

She carried a couple cases to the edge of the bar, near the exit. Fortunately, everyone was so busy passing beers around that nobody seemed to notice the state of the cans. She climbed up onto the bar and lifted her unopened beer in a shouted toast. "To Jack Scatalone, the man who put the jack in jackass!"

Everyone shouted with laughter, and she ducked for cover behind the bar as they opened their cans. Beer sprayed *everywhere*. It looked like an automatic car wash, so much foam went flying. A second shout went up, this time of surprise as everyone was drenched with airborne beer. As the foam settled, she stood up, grinning, and made her way to the exit. Fast. She paused in the doorway only long enough to call out, "See ya 'round, boys."

And on that note, she bugged out. No sense hanging around for a payback from that crew. She didn't even want to think about what they'd be capable of cooking up. She climbed into the Jeep to wait for Scatalone. He emerged, soaked in beer, a couple minutes later. She smiled broadly at him as he climbed into the driver's seat.

"You've done my reputation irreparable harm, you know," he said mildly.

"Yup," she said cheerfully.

Jack drove in silence while she debated asking him a question she'd been uncomfortable asking him before now. "So. Why this job? Why do you do it?"

His fingers tightened on the steering wheel and his knuckles went white for just a moment, but then his hands relaxed. "When I got into it, I was young and stupid and gung ho. I liked the idea of saving the world on a regular basis. Didn't want to sit out my whole career hoping and praying some war broke out somewhere so I could go kill a Commie for Mommy."

"And now? When you're not so young and stupid?"

He glanced over at her. And she reeled at the black abyss yawning dangerously in his hard gaze. "This job's a one-way ticket. Once you step inside the fence, there's no going back. Ever."

His words resonated in her brain, bouncing back and forth like echoes of an organ in a stone cathedral. Her mind teetered precariously in the moment, poised on the edge of understanding something huge. Of unlocking a secret her father had known. Maybe the one that had cost him his life. Or at least his family.

But it slipped through her fingers, just beyond her grasp. She stared at her escort's profile, frustrated. He'd been trying to tell her something, but she didn't have quite enough knowledge or experience to catch his meaning. She sighed. If it was that important, her instructors would undoubtedly impart that lesson to her again later.

He drove her the rest of the way home in silence. And, to his credit, he didn't even mention the beer stunt.

As she climbed out of the Jeep, she broke the heavy silence. "Thanks for the field trip. It was extremely educational."

One corner of his mouth turned up wryly, but he didn't take the bait. "See ya in a couple weeks," he replied.

A couple weeks? Now what did that mean? Was he going to be involved in the Medusa Project in some way? Oh, dear God, make it not so.

*September 4, 3:00 a.m.*
*the White House*

A Secret Service agent shook his shoulder gently. "Mr. President. You have a phone call."

President Henry Stanforth sat up in bed and rubbed his eyes. "What time is it?" he asked blearily.

"Three a.m., sir."

He groaned under his breath. It was a courtesy between world leaders that they generally tried to reach one another during their respective waking hours. Crisis of some kind, then.

"The emir of El Bhoukar is on the line."

Bhoukar? A crisis there could be one of only two things. Oil or terrorists. Stanforth shrugged into a bathrobe and stepped out into the brightly lit hallway. A briefer from the situation room fell in beside him as he padded down the hall toward the elevator in his bedroom slippers.

"Sir, an American has been arrested in Bhoukar. Apparently they've had him for a couple weeks, but he just regained consciousness. They only now ascertained that he's American. The Bhoukaris believe he's a fellow named Scott Worthington."

"And he's important because?" Stanforth asked shortly.

"Because if that's who he really is, he's a Delta Force operative who was in Bhoukar illegally."

"Delta Force? What are they doing in Bhoukar?"

"Checking out a lead on possible terrorist interest in a new oil field that's under development in the northern part of the country."

Terrific. Terrorists *and* oil. Then the information clicked in Stanforth's brain. Several weeks ago. A line in a daily briefing about Delta Team Three going into Bhoukar from Oman to have a look around. He'd okayed it along with a dozen other minor covert operations by various agencies. "Delta Team Three?" he asked.

The briefer gave him a surprised look. "Yes, sir. That's correct."

Stanforth nodded. "Well, at least we know I'm not losing my memory." As he walked past the night secretary's desk and into the Oval Office he said, "Mr. Thompson, patch the call through to my desk."

He padded across the United States seal on the carpet and sat down in his leather desk chair. "This guy speak English?" he asked as he reached for the receiver.

"Three years at Oxford, sir," the briefer replied.

Hallelujah. Messing around with translations tripled the amount of call time, and he always suspected he lost too much of the nuance in what the other person was saying.

"Name?" Stanforth asked as he picked up the receiver.

"Emir Yusef Al-Whabi. Call him Your Highness," the briefer supplied rapidly.

"Good evening, Your Highness," Stanforth said smoothly. "I'm sorry to keep you waiting. What can I do for you?"

The Bhoukari emir replied, agitated, "Your people assured me that the American Special Forces would not get caught. The only reason I allowed them into my country was because I had this assurance. But now this American boy, Scott Worthington, is lying in one of my hospitals, and I have to give some sort of explanation to my people and to the Arab world."

"He's in a hospital, you say?" Stanforth asked, stalling for time to think through this problem.

"Yes. He's gravely ill. Mostly comatose. Struck down by an adder, I'm told."

"As in a snake?"

"Yes, President Stanforth. They are extremely dangerous vipers."

Surely the Delta Force guys had no identification of any kind on them. So how did the Bhoukaris know who this guy was? "And you're sure it's this Worthington fellow?" Stanforth asked. "He had identification on him?"

"No identification. Which is strange, you'd agree?"

Stanforth grunted. Not going to touch that one with a ten-foot pole. "Then how did you identify him?"

"My most excellent intelligence service matched him to a picture of a cadet in a West Point yearbook. This is the cadet's name."

"Ahh," Stanforth said wisely, as if that explained everything. "So for all we know, he might just look like this Worthington. We don't actually know if this man is who he says he is. Why, he might not even be American for all we know." *Come on, Al-Whabi. Catch the hint I'm trying to throw your way.*

"Hmm. I see your point," the Bhoukari leader said. "Although he did respond when doctors said the name to him. Murmured it aloud when they asked him if it was his name. I do not know how long this will satisfy the media in my country. Al-Jazeera reporters and their ilk have become very aggressive in the last couple years."

"Haven't they, though?" Stanforth commiserated. "Too much corrupting Western influence, apparently," he said lightly.

The emir replied dryly, "Indeed. Of all the Western vices we had to import, why did one of the first have to be obnoxious journalists?"

Stanforth laughed pleasantly and hung up the phone. And as soon as the receiver was in its cradle, he looked up at the situation room briefer grimly. "I want to know how in the hell a Delta Force officer got caught by the Bhoukari government. What was he doing, and what can he reveal to the Bhoukaris when he wakes up? Tell the Secretary of Defense I want a full brief. Tomorrow."

"Yes, sir. Good night, sir."

# Chapter 4

*September 19, 8:00 a.m.*
*Washington, D.C.*

Vanessa walked into the nondescript office building at Andrews Air Force Base. An airman gave her directions to the room number printed on her classified orders. She still felt wobbly from the flight up from Pope Air Force Base. They'd sent a turboprop King Air, called a C-12 in the air force, to pick her up. Her stomach had *not* appreciated being vibrated half to death inside a flying lawnmower.

The other five women were already waiting in the room. Everyone looked up sharply as she entered. Apparently they were as wired as she was. And fitter than the last time she'd seen them all. Good. They'd need it. That thirty-six-minute run time had been a bitch to hit, but by God, she'd done it.

Aleesha Gautier, the doctor, commented, "Looking a little green about the gills there, Major."

She grimaced. "Airplanes and I don't get along too well."
A door opened behind her and she spun to face the intruder.
Jack Scatalone. *Oh, Lord.*

"Good morning, ladies," he said briskly. "I'll be your primary trainer and evaluator over the next few weeks. Grab your bags and come with me."

Oh. My. God. Trainer *and* evaluator? Could it get any worse than that? The bottom of her stomach dropped out, free-falling to somewhere in the vicinity of her ankles. She picked up her olive-drab duffel bag resolutely. It wasn't inordinately heavy, but its wide nylon strap dug into her shoulder.

The equipment list that had come with her orders was minimal. Several sets of camo fatigues, jump boots in addition to her regular combat boots, and some basic field supplies—canteen, compass, pocketknife and first-aid kit. She'd thrown in a few more basic survival items like water purification pills, camo paint, a fishing kit inside a film canister and a handheld mirror.

The women stowed their bags in the back of a dark blue van and then piled in the rows of bench seats. Jack drove. He retraced the route Vanessa had just taken across base toward the airfield. Somebody please tell her she didn't have to get right back on another airplane.

Jack flashed his ID and drove onto the tarmac to the rear ramp of a four-propeller C-130 cargo plane. Just peachy. From a lawnmower to a giant eggbeater. Her stomach gave a warning rumble, and she wasn't even on the damn plane yet. The other women threw her sympathetic looks as they got out and climbed up the shiny metal ramp into the plane's no-frills interior. They edged past a row of wooden crates chained to the floor. About midplane, there was an empty pallet position. A row of aluminum and nylon webbing seats had been installed along the right-side wall. A loadmaster took their duffels, stacked them and threw a cargo net over them. He cranked down a pair of crossing cargo straps to hold them in place and gave the group a disinterested safety briefing involving how to buckle a seat belt and not jumping out of the plane without permission before leaving them to settle in.

Karen Turner, the tall marine, stepped up close to Scatalone and not so subtly crowded him toward the rear end of the seats. Katrina and Isabella rolled in on either side of him, sitting down and immediately launching into an animated conversation across him, forcing him to lean back to stay out of the way of the discussion of the latest Paris fashions. Through a wave of nausea, Vanessa noticed Misty slipping off toward the cockpit, while Aleesha put a firm hand on her elbow and guided her to the other end of the row of seats. Misty was back in a minute with four white tablets that she pressed into Vanessa's hand.

"Take those," Misty murmured as she slipped into her seat and strapped in.

"What are they?" Vanessa choked out as she swallowed the bitter tablets dry. One stuck in her throat, and she gulped hard, forcing it down. The aftertaste was like battery acid.

Misty replied under the noise of the engines starting, "Double dose of Dramamine. Kills motion sickness. Got it from the crew's med kit."

Dang. The women had pulled off that maneuver like a well-oiled machine. It boded well for the team that they were already willing to set aside individual egos. The plane rolled forward. A quick lurch as the brakes were tested, and then the plane eased forward again. Oh, God. Her tongue felt thick, and her gut gurgled and roiled. But within a minute or two, her eyelids felt heavy and her limbs went weak. Gotta love good drugs.

*September 19, 7:00 p.m.*
*near the Al-Khibri oil field*

Defoe slid back down behind the ridgeline. "Walsh," he murmured low. "Didn't you pull some duty guarding oil rigs when we invaded Iraq?"

"Yeah. Why?"

"Would you be able to tell a big oil well from a little one?" Defoe asked.

"I guess so. Why?" Walsh replied.

"I thought Bhoukar didn't have major oil fields. Just little strikes here and there. Enough to keep their economy afloat, but that's about it."

He'd caught the interest of the other guys. Ginelli piped up, "That's right. There haven't been any big finds in the Middle East for decades. All the jumbo strikes were made by about 1970."

Defoe nodded. That's what he thought. "Walsh, take a look at the new rig they're putting up down there. Is it just me, or is that a big damn wellhead they're building?"

Defoe followed the sniper and slithered back up to the top of the ridge. Night was coming and they had to be careful. The Army of Holy War had thugs watching the oil field, and they came out thick after dark. They'd been as riled up as killer bees ever since Delta Three had slipped out of their grasp. It'd been a hell of a close call to get the captain down to the fence past all those Army of Holy War types, set off his ELT—emergency locator transmitter—and get out of there before the Bhoukari government soldiers came pouring out of their barracks to investigate. The good news was the surge of Bhoukari troops had pushed most of the Army of Holy War back into the hills. Gave his team time to slip away into the night undetected.

It was a stretch to say the mission was back on track, but at least they were back under cover doing the recon they'd been sent to do, and so far, they were undetected. Hopefully the captain had lived. Defoe prayed nightly that Captain Worthington wouldn't give away their mission under interrogation. It had been a huge risk to turn the captain over to the Bhoukaris for that very reason. But he knew Scott better than his own brother. The guy would never, ever, betray his team. Defoe would bet his life on it. *Had* bet his life on it.

"Yeah," Walsh murmured. "That's a big mother."

Defoe's attention jerked back to the oil rig in front of him.

"See how close it is to the well beside it, too?" Walsh asked. "That means there's a honking deposit of oil down there. No need for two wells so close unless there's a butt-load of crude in one spot."

That's what he'd thought. Okay, so Bhoukar had made a major oil find. Why were Army of Holy War terrorists sniffing around it? Hoping to destroy it, maybe? Out of character for them though. They were still a small, emerging terrorist group and couldn't afford to piss off their Arab backers. They attacked Western targets. Non-Muslim targets. Mostly outside the Middle East. Surely they wouldn't destroy a big oil find in a poor Muslim country that desperately needed the revenue to feed its faithful. Sure, the Bhoukari government didn't exactly have a warm relationship with terrorists, but they weren't openly at war with each other either.

Walsh froze. Murmured under his breath, "Movement at two o'clock. Army of Holy War patrol coming in on foot."

*September 19, 1:00 p.m.*
*the belly of a C-130*

One minute she was out cold, and the next Vanessa startled awake as the plane bumped onto the ground in a landing flare. She blinked, disoriented. What time was it? She checked her watch. They'd been flying a little more than four hours. Where were they? From the windowless belly of the cargo plane, there was no way to know.

They didn't taxi for long. And then, a different loadmaster walked past them and manipulated the buttons beside the back exit, lowering the combination metal ramp and door to the ground. Her stomach felt fine. Dang, those pills were good even if they did knock her on her butt. Anything not to puke her guts out in front of Jack Scatalone.

Speaking of the devil, he ordered briskly, "Let's go, ladies."

Curious, Vanessa picked up her bag and followed him outside. She inhaled a long pull of dry, thin air indicative of high altitude. And then she got a look at the range of snowcapped peaks to the west. Pike's Peak. They were in Colorado Springs. Of course. The air force academy was here, with its extensive and *private* training facilities. Smart choice. The whole base was fenced and patrolled. Not to mention the school year had started and the cadets would be ensconced in the main campus, attending classes.

"Let's go, Blake," Jack barked.

She started and realized the others were already mostly loaded into another navy blue van with small yellow print on its door to indicate it was property of the United States Air Force. Jack drove again. A security cop waved them through the main gates at the academy and Jack wound away from the cadet area toward the dry mountains north of the seventeen soaring aluminum spires of the cadet chapel.

He pulled to a stop in a wide, flat area that could house an entire tent city. What little grass there was lay flattened and brown in the dust. A single square tent, maybe ten feet by ten feet, stood by itself in the middle of the expanse. Beside the tent sat a roughly four-foot-square wooden crate and a toolbox.

Vanessa caught a hint of dismay from her colleagues. She grinned broadly. "Hell's bells, Colonel. The air force didn't have to go to all this trouble to create such an elaborate training facility just for us. I'm overwhelmed."

A chuckle passed through the van. Jack glanced at the rearview mirror, and, disconcertingly, met her grin with one of his own. Except his had a distinct edge. He stopped the van and climbed out.

"Welcome to Jack's Valley, ladies. Although I'd enjoy taking credit for it being named after me, it was called that before I got here." He gestured at the lone, standing tent. "That is *my* hooch." He pointed at the wooden box. "And *that* is yours. If you want a roof over your heads tonight, get that thing up in the next couple hours. I'll be back in a while."

And with that, he climbed in the van and drove away. Vanessa stared at the retreating trail of dust. Everyone turned to look at her. She shrugged and said dryly, "The man definitely needs work on his social skills. Let's see what we've got in the box."

Karen grabbed a crowbar out of the toolbox and pried the lid off the crate. All the women crowded around to look inside. Folds of musty-smelling, dark green canvas filled it. Another tent. Except it took all six of them to lift the darned thing out. A tangle of ropes followed the wad of canvas out of the box, while rows of wooden stakes lined the bottom of the crate. And there was no sign of instructions.

"Anybody ever put up one of these things?" Vanessa asked.

Karen replied, "I've seen it done. Not too hard. Just heavy work. We need to smooth out a flat stretch of ground, spread the tent out, drive in stakes, then hoist the interior poles and stake the exterior ropes."

Sounded easy enough. But as they sweated through horsing a quarter ton of canvas into the shape of a tent, she revised her estimate. Thankfully, everyone kept her cool and offered helpful suggestions as needed.

Finally she stood back from lashing the last rope in place. "Do you suppose Scatalone expects to come back here and find us sitting on the box bitching at each other?"

The women laughed knowingly. They'd all been solitary females in oceans of prejudiced men long enough to appreciate the comment.

Misty asked, "Anybody got something to eat? Or drink? I'm parched."

Vanessa smiled grimly. "I believe that would be lesson one from our erstwhile instructor. We're supposed to think about that before we get out in the field. Any ideas on procuring some water and chow?"

Karen grinned. "Let's raid his tent. I bet he's got some snacks stashed in there."

They headed as one for the smaller tent, but paused when they got to the front flap. Apparently breaking and entering to rob a superior officer's quarters fell under the job description of the team leader.

Vanessa pushed aside the heavy canvas and stepped inside the dim space. It was painfully neat. A camp cot with a sleeping bag and pillow lying on it. A folding table, closed and leaned up against the back wall at the moment along with a pair of folding chairs. Three wooden crates turned on their sides and stacked to make an impromptu set of shelves. A lantern, a couple MREs—Meals Ready to Eat—in their brown plastic pouches, a canteen and a utility vest sat on the shelves. She picked up the MREs, stuffed them in her shirt and headed for the footlocker in the corner. She opened the lid.

And jumped as something snapped, almost like a mousetrap. Lesson number two. If it looked too easy, it probably was. *The bastard had trapped his footlocker.* He'd figured they'd come in here looking for food. Now what was she supposed to do? When he saw his trap sprung, he'd know for sure they'd poked around in here. Did she go ahead and grab whatever food she could find, or did she back out now and take nothing at all?

She stared into the trunk full of ammunition, trip wire, knives and electronic gadgets, only about half of which she could identify. And at the bottom, four more MREs. She stared at the lure of the food. The setup was too perfect. Six MREs for the six of them. In general, the mission of the Special Forces was to work undetected. If they were going to rob their instructor, they'd better do it only when they could get away with it.

She left the four MREs buried in the bottom of the footlocker and put the other two MREs back on the shelves, in as close to the same spot as she could remember. She called out to the women outside, "Let me know if you see anyone coming."

They acknowledged her as she returned to the trunk. The trap had gone off when she lifted the lid, so it had to be attached to that in some way. She ran her fingers gently around the rim of the lid. Aha. A thin filament, so fine she barely felt it, in the back near a hinge. She grasped the thread and traced its course carefully down into the contents of the trunk. It led her to a mercury switch, a tiny, banana-shaped glass tube with a bubble of mercury floating inside it. She found the noise-maker attached to the switch. It was an easy matter to reset the snap-pop gadget, but it was another matter entirely to reattach the delicate filament and rebalance the mercury switch in place. Her fingers felt big and clumsy. Note to self: the team's surgeon got to be the trap expert. How in the world had Jack ever set this thing up with his big, blunt fingers?

She closed the trunk lid carefully and stepped back. Just when had she noticed his hands, anyway? The thought disturbed her. She slipped out of the tent carefully, using her baseball cap to brush away the dusty footprints from her boots.

"Find anything?" Misty asked.

"Yeah. Traps. There's food in there, all right, but he booby-trapped the trunk most of it's stored in."

The women absorbed that in silence. Jack had just defined the rules of engagement for them. No holds barred. The six of them squarely against him. Vanessa palpably felt the women coalescing into a team. And then another thought struck her.

"What are the odds he left us out here completely by ourselves to settle in? What do you want to bet he's been watching us all along? *Don't look,*" she added under her breath sharply as everyone's gazes immediately swung toward the hills around them. "Anyone got any ideas?" she murmured low.

"Wanna try to find him?" Aleesha suggested.

She'd been hoping someone would say that. Vanessa replied, "If nothing else, let's set up a perimeter surveillance to keep the bastard from sneaking up on us and surprising us. I bet he'd just love to make us scream like hysterical teenagers."

Misty tilted her head quizzically. "Why don't you like this guy?"

That was a no-brainer. "Because he wants to see us fail."

They decided to fan out around the two tents in a loose wagon-wheel formation. But first they went into their own large, bare tent to get ready. Vanessa pulled out her camo face paint kit from her paintball days and passed it around. Darkness fell fast as the sun dipped behind the wall of mountains to the west, and as the night deepened, the six of them liberally sprinkled themselves with twigs, leaves, grass and dust they brought inside for that purpose. One by one, they eased out the back of their tent, keeping low to the ground.

About two hundred feet out, Vanessa lay flat beneath a clump of desert sage. She'd give her right arm for a pair of night-vision goggles right about now. Not to mention a slice of pizza. She hadn't eaten since 4:00 a.m. when she'd gulped down a bagel and a cup of coffee in her kitchen in North Carolina. Amazing how, in one day, that place could seem so far away.

Her eyes adapted to the deepening blackness of the night. She lay completely still, searching in a slow, sweeping pattern for movement of any kind. If Jack Scatalone was, in fact, Delta Force, the odds of her untrained team spotting him were nil. But it was a good morale booster to give it a try anyway. It also announced to him that they were going to take this training by the horns and give it their best shot. All in all, she was pleased with how their first day had gone.

As if a switch had been thrown, the creatures of the night abruptly set up a loud chorus. So much for hearing the jerk coming. She laid there for a long time. Eventually, she eased her wristwatch into view. Almost 1:00 a.m. Maybe she should call this game quits and send her team to bed. Lord knew, they'd need the sleep over the days to come. Except something in her gut said it was important to make this statement to their evaluator. She remembered his rebuke that very first day in the Pentagon concerning her patience. She'd sit this one out a little longer. But lesson number three had been learned. Next time, she'd set up a sleep-watch rotation so her team could get some rest.

Three hours later, her eyelids felt like concrete and she struggled to string coherent thoughts together. The night's chorus of insects and frogs was finally petering out. She knew every twig of every tree in front of her and had all but counted the blades of grass within her line of sight. Nothing was moving out there.

Then the back of her neck tingled. It wasn't anything she heard or saw. More like intuition. She rolled over fast, onto her back. Just in time for something impossibly heavy to land on top of her, crushing her from head to foot. Her breath whooshed out of her as a big hand slapped over her mouth. She was pinned in place, flattened like a bug under the weight of Jack Scatalone.

He stared down at her, his gaze boring into hers. Was that anger in his intense expression? Amusement? Insanity?

He murmured, "Do you always do things the hard way?"

"That's the way I like it," she retorted under her breath.

Definitely a scowl on his face now. Speaking of hard, the word could describe his entire body. There was no melting together of male and female flesh, no molding and fitting, no easy slide of body on body. Tension zinged through every inch of him, alert and wary, as he pinned her down. Ah. *He thought she was going to fight him.* And so she relaxed beneath him. She let every muscle go soft, let her thighs fall open to cradle his hips closer against hers. Her belly and breasts softened against the hard planes of his body, welcoming him nearer.

He lurched up and away from her as if she'd electrocuted him, popped to his feet and took a quick step back. "Game's over, ladies," he called out irascibly.

The other five women rose out of the dirt and scrub nearby. Vanessa was proud of them. They'd hidden themselves remarkably well and shown excellent patience through the night. She felt bad that they'd had no supper or sleep, and that might come back to bite them in the butt, but next time, she'd do better when planning for them.

The women gathered around.

Jack growled, "Since you saved me the trouble of waking you up and you're already dressed, let's get going. We've got a lot to do today. Form up for a run."

Vanessa sized up the group. She'd normally put the shortest women in front to set the pace. But Katrina, the smallest of the bunch, was a frigging marathon runner. Isabella was the most unknown physically. She'd set the pace today.

Vanessa said briskly, "Isabella and Aleesha to the front. Katrina and Misty, you bring up the rear." That way, the marathon runner and the triathlete in the back could help anyone who got into trouble. Because she had faith Jack was about to run them into the ever-loving ground.

And he did. The altitude was a bitch. None of them had had any time to adjust to it, and Vanessa's lungs shouted in protest by the third mile. By the fifth mile, her whole body screamed for oxygen. Jack ran along easily beside them, giving them a lecture about the best way to establish a defensive perimeter and a sleep-watch rotation. She struggled to comprehend his lesson and keep moving her feet forward at the same time.

She needn't have worried about Isabella. The intel analyst set a steady pace and had a determined glint in her eye. Anything she might lack in physical prowess she more than made up for in grit.

Vanessa was profoundly relieved when Jack finally called a halt beside a water buffalo—a wheeled iron platform with a bladder of water mounted on top. This one looked to hold a couple hundred gallons. Everybody'd made it. Nobody'd complained or dropped out of the run. They all had to be hurting as bad as she was, but they'd gamely pressed on. She made eye contact with each one of them and nodded briefly in silent praise. She didn't have breath to do more.

Jack gestured to the water tank. "This is ours. You'll need to pull it back to camp."

Ouch. Hadn't seen that sucker punch coming. They'd just finished a grueling six-mile run, and now they had to repeat it, towing a good thousand pounds of water and a couple hundred pounds of steel water tank? She eyed the buffalo. It had a long tongue for hitching it to the back of a truck. The thing was going to be awkward as hell to grab on to and wrestle back to camp.

She announced, "First thing we're gonna do is empty a little of its weight into our systems. Everyone drink your fill."

Aleesha spoke up. "Take several small drinks instead of one big one. That way you won't puke. Wouldn't want to mess up the pristine beauty of the colonel's dirt, after all."

While Vanessa waited for her third turn at the water spigot, she considered how best to move the unwieldy wagon. It made sense to rig up some sort of dogsled-type hitch where they'd use their legs to pull the weight and their arms would be free to swing naturally as they moved. Man, what she'd give for a length of rope right about now. Yet another lesson. Go ahead and carry a bit of extra equipment, even on a simple run. You never knew what contingencies might crop up. She looked around for something to serve as a harness and spied a coil of rope around one of the back support posts of the buffalo. And she'd bet the wagon had a spare tire stowed on it somewhere.

Thankfully, several team members had pocketknives. They hacked up the rope and the spare tire, fashioning rubber padded straps to sling across their hips. These were connected to the wagon tongue with lengths of rope. It was an easy matter now to lean into the crude harnesses and move the water buffalo.

Vanessa remembered something about pairing up oxen with others of similar strength. She took the lead with Karen this time. Then came the two runners, with Aleesha and Isabella bringing up the rear.

The trip back took considerably longer. Jack demanded that they run, but it was really more of a slow jog. Thankfully, he called a stop to rest partway back and let them drink more water. The buffalo might not have been appreciably lighter after their drinks, but psychologically, it felt like it.

It was full morning before they finally lumbered into their little camp. Lord, she was tired. And she feared the day was just beginning. Somebody'd dropped off more gear in their absence. A pile of boxes and canvas bags stood in front of the big tent.

"Unpack your stuff," Jack ordered before he disappeared into his tent.

The women rolled up the sides of their big tent to let in the dusty breeze. Vanessa picked up the first box on the pile and carried it inside. It took them an hour to set up the cots and footlockers and sort the gear evenly among their trunks. They gulped down dry, C-ration oatmeal bars, and then they all collapsed on their cots. They'd been down about ten minutes when Jack's voice boomed at them, "Up and at it!"

Vanessa knew pain, but Jack Scatalone showed her heretofore unimagined heights of misery in the next twelve hours. He put them through endless push-ups, sit-ups, pull-ups, leg lifts, squat thrusts, interval sprints and anything else he thought of that might cause pain. The really annoying part was he did every last bit of it right along with them. And he talked casually all the while, instructing them on pushing beyond their limits, on the importance of performing physical feats the enemy thought were impossible. Talk about the razor's edge of survival. Being stronger, faster and fitter than the other guy often tipped the scales. Vanessa fell into a semi-trance of agony where little but Jack's words penetrated her brain.

Of all people, Misty, the flippant, California beach-girl blonde, was the team's mental salvation through that first endless day that too slowly faded into night. As a triathlete, she had a better sense of how far the human body could be pushed than the other women. Countless times, when Vanessa or one of the others was sure they'd hit the wall, Misty would be there, quietly encouraging them. Telling them she'd done worse and survived. Telling them to pace themselves and focus on their breathing. All Vanessa could add was to gasp that she was proud to be suffering alongside them.

And somehow, they all made it. Vanessa was too damn exhausted to bother looking at her watch as she fell into bed sometime after midnight. Her last conscious thought was that Jack Scatalone could go to hell.

In his tent, Jack sprawled in a camp chair, his feet propped up on his cot. Christ, those women had worked him out good. He'd figured they'd be in good shape for women, but he hadn't counted on just how much pain they could take. He knew damn good and well he'd pushed them far beyond their limits, but they'd hunkered down and sucked up the pain with a stoicism he'd rarely seen in his male trainees.

He picked up his cell phone and dialed the Pentagon. "Scat here."

The duty controller answered quickly, "General Wittenauer's waiting for your call. He wants to know how it went. Said to patch you through to his house no matter what time you called. Stand by, sir."

Jack waited while the call was put through to his boss's home. And then the familiar growl came on the line. "How'd it go?"

"They toughed it out, sir."

"Damn. I was sure they wouldn't make twenty-four hours. You didn't go easy on them, did you? I'm counting on you to give them the real deal's worth. Push them harder."

Jack frowned. He couldn't push much harder himself. "Never fear, sir. They've been here one day. They're already running on twenty-four hours without sleep. Give me a week and we'll see how they're doing."

"Senator McClure's due out of the hospital in a week. This whole Medusa fiasco better be finished by then or there'll be hell to pay."

"I can't guarantee they'll quit by then, sir. These dames are pretty tough."

"I only gave this thing the go-ahead to get it off the table once and for all. You know what you have to do, son. Now go do it."

Jack clenched his jaw. Twenty-four hours ago he'd have agreed readily that it was a good plan to give the girls what they wanted and shut them up once and for all. But sometime today a tiny doubt had begun to niggle at the back of his mind. He wasn't entirely sure he could force these women to quit, no matter what he threw at them.

"Any news on my team, sir?"

"Delta Three's still in place. They're reporting in on schedule. Due for another call in a couple hours, in fact. Nothing new on Worthington though. The Bhoukaris still have him. And they're still refusing to give any updates on his condition beyond the fact that he's alive."

Jack closed his eyes. He'd trained Scott Worthington from a raw recruit into a damn fine team leader. At least the kid wasn't vulture bait. But what in the hell was happening to him? And what was he saying to his captors? Jack could only hope Scott wasn't being tortured. He knew without a shadow of a doubt that Scott would hold out until death, but, Christ, what a lousy way to go.

And now he was supposed to train six women to perform the grueling, and sometimes Herculean, feats of a Special Forces team? Who in the hell were these women trying to kid? They couldn't hack it in a real crisis. And it was his job to show them that.

## Chapter 5

She couldn't do it. She couldn't take one more step. Seven days on practically no food or sleep, endless runs and drills and exercises, and it was all blurring together in a hellish hallucination in her mind. It was raining tonight, and she was shivering so hard she couldn't talk. She didn't even want to guess how hypothermic she was. And the bastard just kept on hammering at them.

Vanessa glared blearily at the back of Jack's head as he set the pace in front of them, this time running them up and down hills that would give a dirt bike pause. At least there was the satisfaction of seeing dark circles under his eyes, and a certain haggardness about his face. Without that evidence she'd think the man was a machine.

Day blurred into night blurred into day, and only Aleesha's

scratched hash marks on the side of her footlocker told Vanessa they'd survived a week.

She noticed Jack changing direction ahead of her. She staggered in relief as they made the turn for camp. Three miles back to the tent and maybe a half hour of rest. It sounded like manna from Heaven. And then Kat stumbled into her and would have fallen if Vanessa hadn't caught her. She wedged her shoulder under Kat's and called out hoarsely, "A little help back here."

As one, the group slowed, and Isabella wedged her shoulder under Kat's other armpit as the Korean woman collapsed.

"Let's get a move on," Jack barked, running backward in front of them. "Pick up the pace back there."

Vanessa staggered along at an awkward jog, dragging Kat's limp body for a couple hundred yards. It was all she could manage tonight. Gasping, she signaled Karen to take her place. The five remaining women tag-teamed dragging Kat along until the slender woman recovered enough to move under her own power again. Lord knew, Vanessa'd been dragged along the same way a couple times herself. They all had.

They never talked about it. But somewhere along the way, the six of them had come to a tacit understanding that they'd stick out this hell together. They'd all succeed or they'd all fail. Nobody would be left behind, and nobody would quit. Even if it meant dragging one another up hills like they'd just dragged Kat and tugging one another up by the belt when exhausted arms wouldn't do one more push-up. They shared their food and water, and they shared their strength and determination. And somehow, they'd managed to survive so far. But Vanessa had real fears about how much longer they could go on like this. Even indomitable Misty was way beyond her limits.

But the most important lesson she'd learned over the course of this nightmare: don't think beyond pushing through the next moment of pain. Take the moments one at a time, and somehow they would string themselves together into a minute. An hour. A day.

Aleesha croaked from behind her, "I'm done."

Vanessa dropped back to take her place under Aleesha's shoulder. Only one more big hill to climb. Their camp, and bed, was on the other side. She looked over at Karen, who'd taken up station under the doctor's other arm. "Let's show… the bastard…what we're…made of," Vanessa panted in rasping rhythm to her stumbling steps.

The marine's gaze met hers in silent communication. One more hill. They could do it. Vanessa dug deeper than she thought humanly possible, and dragged her uncooperative body and Aleesha's up that hill. One step at a time. Until finally, blessedly, the ground leveled out. The road began a gentle descent toward camp. The last hundred yards felt as if she were floating outside her body. A warm blanket of mist seemed to enshroud her, and, weightless, she glided through it. A large, dark form took shape in front of them. Vaguely she followed the other women toward it.

And then someone lifted the weight off her shoulder. Guided her inside a cave. Sat her down on the edge of a flat, soft surface. Swung her feet up and laid her out flat.

A deep, male voice intoned from somewhere in her delirium, "Sleep now."

Her lips curved in a peaceful smile. She'd died, and God had finally given her permission to rest. Ah well, she'd given it her best shot.

She dreamed of her father, as always a shadowy figure to be worshiped from afar. She dreamed of him letting her sit on his back while he did push-ups, of him showing her how to hide the best at hide-and-seek, of him helping her put on camo paint to scare the boys on the block. In his own way, he'd loved her. And when he died, she'd vowed never to forget him or his silent but unwavering love. Through all the ensuing years—as her mother attacked his choices, attacked his inability to let go of his work, attacked everything he'd stood for—Vanessa had secretly held fast to her memories of him. She clung to the lone photograph of him, the only memento she'd managed to hide from her mother's grief- and rage-filled expunging of her father from their lives. For if she didn't hold his memory dear, who else would?

Vanessa woke up slowly from her dreams, disoriented. Where was she? She ached from head to foot. Bright light seeped in between the cracks in dark canvas walls. Dear God, she'd overslept! She lurched upright, and then moaned in pain as needles pierced every inch of her body. The other five beds were occupied with her comatose comrades. She lay back down, carefully this time, and slipped into unconsciousness once more.

*September 26*
*a hospital in Bhoukar*

He was in Hell. His entire body was on fire, licked by flames slowly roasting the flesh off his bones as the poisons raced through his system. He smelled his own skin, redolent of raw meat and almonds. Didn't gangrene smell like almonds? He'd rather be cooked than rot away to nothing. He wanted to tear at his body, to scream with the agony. But thrashing around would only make it worse. How did he know that? Had he tried fighting the pain already?

Nobody'd ever mentioned that it was never dark in Hell. The fires burned all the time, sending white-hot pain past his eyelids constantly. Even his eyeballs hurt. He'd been damn miserable a few times in his life, but nothing had ever come close to this. He was going to go mad if the pain didn't stop soon.

One more minute. If he could make it one more minute without screaming, that would be a victory. Too long. Ten seconds. He could do it. One… Two… Three…

*September 27*
*Jack's Valley*

A sound by his head intruded upon his exhaustion. Jack roused groggily from his sleep state and looked around. Canvas walls. A tent. Oh, yeah. Jack's Valley and six of the toughest ladies he'd ever come across. What *was* that sound? He turned his head, wincing at the pain that shot across his shoulders. His cell phone. This had better be good. He was whipped after what he'd just put himself and his trainees through.

"Yeah?" he growled into the phone.

"Good day, Colonel," General Wittenauer snapped back.

Shit. Jack swung his feet over the side of the cot and sat up. "Sorry, sir. I was asleep."

"At this hour?" the general exclaimed.

Jack looked at his watch. Almost noon. He'd put the team to bed at four a.m. Thank God for eight hours of uninterrupted sleep. He needed about eight more to feel human again though. "We had a late night. What can I do for you, sir?"

"Tell me they quit."

Jack laughed without humor. "Hardly. The more I push them, the more stubborn they get. They've got as much guts as any man I've ever trained."

"Goddammit! You said you'd end this in a week. Senator McClure's office is calling me every fifteen minutes, and I can only dodge them for so long. Now how much more time is it going to take for you to break them?"

Jack scowled. What he was about to say was going to send the old man into orbit. Tough shit. "I want to give them a shot, sir."

As expected, the volcano blew spectacularly. "You *what?*" Wittenauer roared.

"I mean it. They've impressed the hell out of me. I think they might have what it takes to do the job."

"Get over it, Scat. No way is the American public going to buy women as commandos."

"The public has bought into women in combat. Why not women in the Special Forces? I've been giving some thought to mission profiles where women might be exceptionally effective, maybe even more so than men."

"Stop right there, Jack. It ain't gonna happen. Not on my watch, and not on Walter McClure's watch. You end this thing. End it now."

His temper under very tight rein, Jack ground out, "Is that a direct order, sir? Because I'm telling you, I'm not taking the fall for sabotaging this project. I think they can do it."

"No, goddammit, that's not an order. I can't go on the record with something like that, and you know it. But make it happen. You understand me?"

Jack set the phone down gently, even though his impulse was to heave it across the tent. Congress had funded the Medusa Project for up to six months of initial training. And Hal Wittenauer could just suck it up and deal with pissy senators until the money ran out.

Jack glared at the tent wall. After what he'd just put those women through, no way was he going to stand up in front of them and tell them the project was over. They'd goddamn well earned a shot at their dream.

Vanessa woke again. But this time she felt rested. Refreshed. If you could call being so sore she could hardly sit up refreshed. She gaped at her watch. Four o'clock? In the afternoon? Jack had let them sleep for twelve hours? An alien creature with compassionate tendencies must have possessed him overnight.

She lay on her cot, savoring the late-afternoon breeze crossing her skin. Never in her entire life had doing absolutely nothing felt so delicious. She sensed a movement at the entrance to the tent and raised her head. Jack. She started to jerk upright, but he waved her back down. What the...

He came and sat down on her footlocker as she swung her aching body slowly into a seated position.

"Anyone on the team know how to pick locks?" he asked quietly.

She looked him in the eye. The usual derision and hostility he showed them was absent. Instead, his gaze was clear and golden brown. Calm. Pleasant, even. Yup. Aliens got him. "I do," she answered cautiously.

He flipped her a small, oblong leather zipper pouch. "I hotwired the water heaters in the shower building up the hill a couple hours ago. If you can get the door open, you all can take showers today."

What was the catch? "How long do we have to do it?" she asked suspiciously.

"As long as you need. You've got the day off."

She frowned. "What happened? Is everything all right?"

He raised a sardonic eyebrow at her. "You mean why am I not being my usual bastard self?"

She met his gaze squarely. "Exactly." A pause. "Sir."

"You survived Hell Week. It's my assessment that you ladies have sufficiently learned the lesson that you can push yourselves a hell of a lot further than you thought you could a week ago. You've set the bar on your physical limits up where it needs to be for Special Forces work."

Warmth flooded her. They'd climbed over the first hump. But the way he was frowning, she suspected more mountains lay in front of them. "So what's the problem?"

He looked up quickly, his troubled gaze snapping to hers. "What do you mean?"

She said quietly, "One of the tools women soldiers bring to the table is well-developed trust in their intuition. Mine says there's a problem with our training that you're not telling me about."

He looked startled. Which meant she was right. But he didn't comment right away, which meant he was still working on a way to deal with it himself. Finally he said, "There's high-level pressure coming down to end this."

Oh, God. Not after all they'd been through. Alarm clenched her heart like a vise. She put a hand on his upper arm. "Don't do it to us. For God's sake, give us a chance."

He jumped at her touch but didn't pull away from it. He muttered something under his breath about Wittenauer shoving something up his ass. And then he looked up at her. His dark gaze was determined. Defiant even. "You gotta have a little faith, Blake. I'm not going to pull the rug out from under my snake ladies. If this project fails, it'll be your choice to quit, not mine."

The mythic Greek Medusa, with snakes for hair, had been a tough broad who went after what she wanted until she got it, too.

"I'm not quitting," Vanessa declared. "Ever."

"Neither are we." She jumped as normally quiet and reserved Katrina chimed in from the next cot over. Vanessa looked up. All the women were awake. And nodding.

Jack took a long look around the room. He exhaled heavily and stood up. A certain tension around his neck and shoulders relaxed as if he'd come to a decision of some sort. "If you ladies don't want to stink like a sewer, you'd better get cracking on that shower door. Rest up, because tomorrow your real training begins." He strode out of the tent.

"Real training?" Karen exclaimed. "What has the last week been? Finishing school?"

Everyone laughed, but the sound turned into a chorus of groans as they rolled out of bed.

Vanessa asked, "Any of you guys ever pick a lock, or am I our only hope for cleanliness?"

They all shook their heads in the negative.

"Grab your shower stuff. I'll show you all how to break and enter while we're at it."

They huddled around the door to the cinder-block bathhouse a few minutes later. In addition to a regular double action cylinder lock, it had a padlock on the door for good measure. Why the air force was so tense about keeping people out of a simple shower building was beyond her. Now that she thought about it, that padlock looked awful shiny to have been out in the elements for any length of time. The *bastard*. He'd had this installed especially for them. Just when she thought he might be human after all, he went and pulled a stunt like this.

She demonstrated using the various picks and rakes that were the tools of the lock-picking trade to her comrades. She'd taught herself how to do it out of a mail-order instruction manual a few years back, when she'd still harbored hopes of being let into Special Forces school with the boys. They each took a try at it, and as she'd expected, Aleesha the surgeon was a natural. Karen, on the other hand, was having yet another unsuccessful go at the padlock when Jack strolled out of his tent and walked up the hill to where they knelt on their knees.

"Worshiping at the altar of the shower gods before you go in?" he asked dryly.

Vanessa scowled up at him. "Taking the opportunity to teach my teammates how to pick a lock. Now if you don't mind, Karen's about to pop the second lock, and we're going to be occupied for a while. Girls only."

For all the world, that looked like a glint of approval in his dark eyes. Thankfully, the tricky padlock popped open with a loud click just then. God bless Karen's timing. Vanessa stood up and came face-to-face with Jack. She glared up at him and sparks leaped back and forth between them like opposite poles of a Vandergraff generator. Their gazes clashed for a moment before he whirled and strode away.

It was a good thing Jack wasn't around to hear their showers as all six of them moaned in orgasmic pleasure. The feel of hot water pounding Vanessa's muscles and washing away the sweat and filth of the last week was beyond amazing. She felt like a new woman when she eventually emerged.

When they got back to the tent, Aleesha pulled out a jar of green goop and began to rub it on her legs. The foul odor of rotting grass filled the tent.

"Good grief, what is that slop?" Vanessa asked in dismay.

Aleesha put on a thick Jamaican accent. "Don't be talking down my mama's secret voodoo cookin'. No mon, de bad spirits come git you."

Vanessa grinned. "Voodoo, eh?"

Aleesha answered in her normal voice, "Yeah. It's an old folk remedy. A muscle relaxant, actually. Stinks to high heaven, but works great. Want some?"

Vanessa reached for the jar. Heck, with the amount of pain she was in, she'd try just about anything. Before long, all of them smelled like rotted grass clippings. But darned if her aches and pains hadn't diminished noticeably. She just prayed there wasn't something typically Jamaican like marijuana mixed into the recipe.

"Does anyone know something cool the rest of us could learn while we're sitting around?" Vanessa asked. "Heaven forbid we rest and relax. I'm sure if we did, we'd get dinged on our evaluation."

Karen piped up. "How about tying knots? I'm fifth generation navy, and it's a family tradition to know all kinds of wild nautical knots. Might come in handy if we ever decided to *lynch* anyone." She threw a significant look at the side of Jack's tent.

They all grinned.

Sounded interesting, and furthermore, not the least bit physically demanding. Soon, Vanessa was elbow deep in tangles of rope. She threw out casually, "So. Anybody leave boyfriends back home?"

The tent filled with talk and laughter, and Vanessa let out a sigh of relief. The kind of hell they'd just been through could change a person. Scar them. Break them. But they'd truly survived the last week. Not only physically, but mentally, too.

*October 12*
*Al-Khibri, Bhoukar*

Defoe was starting to worry about his guys. They'd been out here for weeks now, and the pressure and boredom had to get to them sometime. But what choice did they have? The area was crawling with Army of Holy War thugs, and there was no way Uncle Sam could send in another team to relieve them. The situation definitely called for eyes-on recon.

In one of their rare incoming transmissions, they'd gotten word that Captain Worthington had been picked up by the Bhoukaris and was alive at last report. That was a great morale booster, one that had lasted for a couple days. And then there was the cave Jensen found. A couple ridges to the east, their medic had stumbled across a seasonal goat herd's stopover. It yielded several crates of canned food, which saved them from having to trap and eat lizards and snakes. But even better, it had a spring. Way back against the wall of the cave, a sluggish trickle of water ran down the sandstone wall into a depression, where it collected and evaporated off.

They rigged a water skin inside an empty food crate and stuck it under the spring. In a day's time, the skin caught enough water to fill all their canteens and water bladders—three-foot-long rubber balloons about six inches in diameter that could be strapped across a guy's back. They carried enough water for a day or so if a person wasn't too active. Usually, there was enough water left over from the spring for a couple guys to wet a rag and wipe off the worst of the filth, too.

Defoe set up a rotation where, every other day, a pair of the guys humped out to the cave, caught eight hours of real sleep in its relative cool, got a pseudo bath, and then hauled back water and rations for the team. The dank cave wasn't exactly a Holiday Inn, but it was keeping them sane. He was counting the time until it was his turn to go back—three days, four hours, ten minutes. Not that he was obsessing or anything.

"L.T. Come see this," Spot called out in a low voice from his vantage point atop the ridge.

Defoe slithered up beside the spotter, who passed him a foot-long telescope. He made out a bunch of men outside the Army of Holy War's main cave entrance, hugging and making lots of hand gestures. "Looks like some new arrivals. Big celebration," he murmured.

"Reinforcements?" Spot asked doubtfully.

"If we're lucky, they're only replacements. Let's keep an eye out for troops leaving the area now that new ones have come in."

Spot nodded and resumed the watch.

*October 15*
*Jack's Valley*

"It's all about patience, ladies."

Vanessa watched closely as Jack showed them how to wire an explosive charge.

"Better to do it right than do it fast. Unless, of course, you're about to die anyway."

Of course, they wouldn't be allowed to blow live ordnance here. It wasn't a designated explosives containment area, and it had been too dry a summer on the front range of the Rocky Mountains to risk starting a wildfire.

To say the next phase of their training was turning out to be a breeze was inaccurate, but in comparison to that first week, it was a veritable picnic. They started out before sunrise with a morning run that ranged from four to as many as ten miles. Then breakfast while getting a lesson in something like trip wire placement or tracking. Another workout, usually calisthenics and something heavy like rock climbing or rappelling. Then lunch over another lesson. Usually they did something major in the afternoon like parachute training or running a leadership reaction course. Today they were slated to run the air force academy's obstacle course. After supper the past few nights, they'd been going out after dark and hiking around the mountains. Jack was teaching them to navigate and move stealthily at night, and it was a hell of a lot harder than it looked. Especially walking silently when you couldn't see the twigs and leaves you were about to step on.

"Earth to Blake, come in, please," Jack growled. "This is the only walk-through of the obstacle course you're going to get."

"Uh, sorry," she mumbled. The man packed so much information into so little time, she felt as if she were drinking out of a blessed fire hose. Sometimes her brain went into overload and turned to mush. Like today. Exhaustion, probably. Although nowadays, her perception of what constituted fatigue was greatly tempered by her memory of Hell Week's ungodly sleep deprivation.

Nothing looked inordinately difficult about the obstacle course as Jack demonstrated how to go under, over, or through each station. It was mostly walls to climb, logs to balance on and run down, tires to dance through and, of course, a slime-filled pond to swing across on a rope.

Jack lined them up at the starting line. "If you all make it through the first time in under seven minutes, you can have a shower tonight."

Okay, that made it tough. It was at least a half-mile long, in addition to some real time eaters like the low crawl under a length of heavy cargo netting. He staggered their starts by thirty seconds. Vanessa went last. She was huffing like a racehorse when she got to the finish line, but she made it with fifteen seconds to spare. Everyone else had made the time limit, too. Hallelujah. *Hot shower, here I come!*

"Get a drink, and let's do that again. With feeling this time, ladies."

Vanessa breathed deeply, trying to restore oxygen to fatigued muscles as fast as possible.

"And this time, let's make it interesting. You'll run it as a group, but three of you will do it blindfolded."

Blindfolded? He had to be kidding. They all had to have been gaping at him, because he growled, "One of these days, you're going to be out on an op and someone on your team's gonna get hurt. You aren't gonna leave them behind, are you?"

"Of course not," Vanessa retorted scornfully. "Since when has this group ever left one of its own behind?"

He grinned, sharklike. Uh-oh. Bad things always followed that loaded smile. "Twelve minutes. All six of you, through the course. Blake, Torres, Cordell. Put these on." He passed them wide strips of heavy canvas. Vanessa tied the strip around her head. She felt Jack step up close behind her, his presence very male and very overpowering. He gave a yank on her blindfold to check its security.

"Whenever you're ready, ladies," he announced.

"Put your hand on my shoulder." That was Karen. From directly in front of her. "I'll describe what's coming as we go. Follow my instructions. I'll take care of you."

"Got it," Vanessa answered gamely. Lord, she felt vulnerable. Off balance.

"Go!" Jack barked.

Karen's shoulder lurched away from her hand. Crap. She bolted forward and stumbled against the marine, who'd slowed to let her catch up. It took a few steps, but they settled into a rhythm of running together.

"Up a hill. Curve to the right. Downhill to a wall with cargo netting on it. You go first. I'll be right behind you."

Vanessa grabbed the thick matrix of rope, feeling her way up it as fast as she could. She tried not to think about how far above the ground she was right now. She had to trust her comrade to take care of her. It hit her that trust was the point of this whole exercise. They staggered and stumbled their way through the course. And then they got to the rope hanging over the pond.

Aleesha took charge. "I'll go first and stand on the far side. Karen and Kat will run alongside you on the near side and point each of you at the rope. I'll yell jump. Just let fly and grab for the rope. It'll all but hit you in the face. Let go when I tell you to."

It was only a pond. If she missed, she'd just get wet and Jack would no doubt give her hell. There were worse things in life. But, damn, the idea of jumping out into space blind, with only a fraction of a second to find, feel and catch a rope was daunting.

"You first, Vanessa," Karen murmured in her ear. "Show the others how it's done."

Yeah, right. She took a running start, and Kat adjusted Vanessa's body slightly to the left as she charged forward hell-bent for leather. Aleesha shouted, "Jump!" and she took off into space, her arms and legs flailing like a long jumper. A rough slap in the face, and she grabbed for the rope. It slipped for a moment, but then her gloved hands caught and held it. She swung out into space.

"Drop!" Aleesha shouted.

Vanessa let go and slammed onto the ground. She rolled to the side and climbed awkwardly to her feet as Isabella made the jump, and then Misty. All three of them made it. Vanessa's first inclination was to just stand there and be amazed, but they had one last wall to scramble over, and then a sprint to the finish line. When they were done Vanessa ripped off her blindfold and looked at the stopwatch Jack held up silently.

Eleven minutes and forty-seven seconds. *Kick-ass.* The women let out a cheer.

"Okay, next drill. Turner, Gautier and Kim, lash one arm down to your sides."

Vanessa blinked. With all the climbing, crawling and swinging required, how in the world were they going to do it with half the team minus an arm?

"Twelve minutes," Jack stated calmly.

The course was a pain in the rear when handicapped thus. Then it was time for the rope swing over the pond again. There was nothing they could do to help their teammates but cheer them on. Kat and Aleesha went first. Both women were slight of build. They grabbed the rope high overhead with their good arm, and managed to slide only partway down the rope before they dropped to the other side. But Karen wasn't so lucky. She was big and muscular. Normally she had plenty of upper body strength for any job at hand. But supporting her body weight one-armed wasn't in her.

She gave it a good try, but as the rope swung lazily out over the water, she slid down the rope and dropped into the black slime. Vanessa grabbed a long stick the thickness of her wrist and threw the end out to Karen. She dragged the marine out of the pond, and the team took off running for the finish line.

They all bent over, breathing hard as Jack announced, "Twelve oh five. No showers for you tonight. And one of you's a whole lot uglier than usual."

Vanessa snapped upright, offended.

So did everyone. Karen stared, frozen, through a mask of black mud at him. He stepped right up to her, taunting, "What? Nobody ever have the *cajones* to call you ugly before? The men in your life too chickenshit to risk you breaking them in two? There's a name for manly chicks like you."

Vanessa stepped forward. "Don't say it, Scatalone," she snarled.

He rounded on her. "Oh, look. The team leader has to take up for the big nasty one. How quaint."

What in the *hell* was he doing? He'd never attacked one of them in this fashion before. And then Vanessa heard a sound behind her. A hoarse, rasping noise. What *was* that?

Son of a gun. Karen Turner, the toughest marine this side of the Halls of Montezuma, was crying. Jack had nailed her Achilles' heel and attacked it with a vengeance.

Vanessa rounded on the taller woman. She ordered sharply, "Look at me, Karen."

The marine looked at her, white tracks showing in the black muck on her cheeks. Misery swirled in the green depths of her eyes.

Vanessa said forcefully to all of them, "We're the Medusas. And we *all* kicked butt on that obstacle course today. But Karen has earned the right to have the first call sign of all of us."

Karen stared at Vanessa, her distress overtaken by surprise.

Vanessa announced, "Your handle's going to be Python."

The wind whooshed out of Karen's fragile emotional sails once more, and Vanessa grabbed the marine's wet, slimy shirt to hold the distraught woman's attention until she could finish what she had to say. She stepped forward and got right in Karen's face for good measure. She growled up at her, nose to nose, "I'm naming you Python not because they're the most muscular snakes in the world, but because they're the most beautiful. Got that?"

Karen stared at her doubtfully. But then something in her gaze shifted. Focused. Crystallized. Finally she answered slowly, "Yeah. I got it."

Vanessa let go of the taller woman's shirt. Still forcefully, she said, "Don't you ever forget it. You're beautiful, inside and out, no matter what some asshole like Jack Scatalone says."

The two women's gazes met for another long moment of shared understanding.

And then the asshole in question cleared his throat. "If you're done with your touchy-feely naming ceremony, we've got places to go and things to do."

# Chapter 6

Vanessa waited until well after all sounds from Jack's tent had ceased. His cot was only about eight feet away, separated from her by a couple layers of canvas. She crawled out of her sleeping bag wearing her shorts and a muscle shirt. She slipped on her combat boots and eased outside, next to his tent. No light showed from within. Taking her time—*surprise, Jack, I've learned to have plenty of patience*—she slipped off her boots and lifted the tent flap. She glided silently inside. Last time she'd seen them, Jack's lock picks had been on the stack of crate shelves.

His form was motionless on his cot. No reason he should be sleeping light tonight. There was no threat out here. Testing the wood floor that was standard in command tents before each step for creaks, she made her way painstakingly across the tent. There. On the middle shelf. The leather pouch. She ran her fingers all around it, checking for threads. She wouldn't put it past the bastard to have every last thing in his tent booby-trapped. All clear. She lifted the leather pouch slowly and slid it into her shorts' back pocket.

Now for the egress. The part where she tended to rush. She glanced over at Jack's sleeping form. Her adrenaline surged. As if he'd woken up. But she was looking right at him, and he hadn't moved a muscle. She checked his eyes. Definitely shut. Nonetheless, she froze. And stood there a long time. A good ten minutes. Still, the tension in the room didn't go away. She had a sinking feeling that with her next step, he was going to whip off that bed and drop her like a rock. She'd been on the receiving end of his lightning-fast and lethal fighting skills already. It wasn't fun.

How much longer to stand here? She gave it another ten minutes. Tried to slow her breathing and relax her body. To think invisible. To *be* invisible. It was minuscule, but eventually she sensed a lessening of the tension in the air. As if she'd passed some undefined test of wills and now it was safe to proceed. It was probably just her overactive imagination getting the best of her. She eased forward by inches, trying to flow like water toward the door. And then she was outside. She released a long, slow breath of relief.

Still moving silently, she crept back into the women's tent. She put her hand over Karen's mouth, the standard wake-up of Special Forces to let a team member know there was danger near. Karen's eyes snapped open.

"Wanna shower?" Vanessa whispered, holding up the lock picks.

Karen grinned and nodded. The marine rolled out of bed and put her hand over Isabella's mouth. The women woke up one another in turn and gathered their shower supplies silently. They headed for the front door, but Vanessa stopped them and gestured toward the back of the tent. She got a few questioning looks, but they followed her gamely. For some reason, she had a gut feeling that if they strolled right past Jack's tent on this little extracurricular outing, he'd bust them into last week.

She eased up the back wall of the tent. Paused. Had a long look around. All quiet. Perhaps the most surprising thing about their training so far was how slowly spec ops forces did everything. She'd always envisioned quick hits with bullets flying and wildly racing escapes. The exact opposite was true. They took as much time as required to infiltrate without discovery, they caused the least possible fuss in accomplishing their goal, and then they eased out of an area as unobtrusively as possible. No showboating for these folks.

When everyone was done with their showers and dressed again, Vanessa formed them up. They'd stay together this time, moving in a line formation and taking care to make only one set of tracks. Last one in line would countertrack and erase any signs of their passing. They swung wide of the tents and approached their tent from the side opposite where Jack's stood. They entered under a side flap this time. Vanessa stood guard outside and was the last in. She breathed a heartfelt sigh of relief as she lowered the tent flap silently. They'd made it.

"Good evening, ladies," a male voice boomed.

She jumped violently. The bastard was standing right beside her in the dark. Her heart pounded like a jackhammer and adrenaline screamed through her blood. *Busted.*

"All of you, get into bed. And stay there this time. You." He jabbed a finger at Vanessa. "Come with me."

He moved off into the night. Fast. She hustled to keep up with his long stride as he took her a good quarter mile away from his tent. Normally, she'd call it good management to criticize a subordinate in private. But since when had Jack shown sensitivity to his underlings? Suspicion and a faint niggle of fear danced around the edges of her mind.

Finally he stopped. Turned aggressively to face her in the

moonlight. She was vividly aware of her braless state, more clearly revealed by the thin muscle shirt than she'd like. It made her feel vulnerable. Exposed. But if he noticed, he didn't react. He towered over her, his jaw tight. His silence was more menacing than if he'd yelled his head off. He held out his hand. She put his lock picks into his palm.

When he finally spoke, his voice was low. Cold. But the whiplash in it still stung. "What part of the dangers of flaunting my authority don't *you* get?"

"What part of giving my team a morale boost after a rough day don't you get?" she shot back.

"You may be Special Forces and operate outside the law when you're on a mission, but you're still in the military, hot shot. You're still required to obey superior officers and maintain good order and discipline. As team leader, it's your responsibility to keep your troops in line, not lead them into trouble."

She glared at him, unconvinced. It *had* been the right thing to do, and she knew it in her gut. She supposed he was required to bust her chops for getting caught, too. Each in their own way, they were trapped in their respective roles in this little play.

Rather than debate the point further, she asked, "So how did you catch us?" Might as well learn something out of this night's debacle.

"I heard you moving in my tent."

She stared in surprise. "How? I didn't make any noise." She was sure of that.

He broke a branch off a tree and shredded it into little pieces before he looked up at her. "Maybe I should say I felt your presence," he finally answered.

She nodded. Yup, she knew exactly what he meant. "Just like I felt it when you woke up."

"Ah. That's why you froze for so long. I wondered if you were chickening out and considering putting the picks back."

She snorted. "Hardly."

He jumped on that one. "Retreating to try again another day is a viable option. Don't ever take it off the table as something to consider when the mission's going to hell fast."

"So how do I reduce my presence in a room so you can't feel it?" she pressed.

He frowned. "It's a zen thing. You absorb all your energy into yourself and don't project anything of yourself. You're extroverted and charismatic, so it's going to be hard for you to learn. Someone quiet like Katrina is going to come by it naturally. She's your mouse. Use her for infiltrating populated areas, just like you've pegged Aleesha to do your breaking and entering."

Vanessa nodded. If she could ever amass a fraction of the knowledge this guy had in his head, she'd count herself lucky.

"Tell me something, Blake. Why are you putting yourself through all this misery?"

His barked question jolted her. Rather than give a knee-jerk answer, she paused to consider her response. Oh, yes, she'd definitely learned patience these past few weeks. "Are you asking why I want to be in the Special Forces or why I chase after pain?"

He just stared at her expectantly. Apparently, he knew the technique—restate a question to buy yourself more time to think about your answer.

"I've always wanted to do it," she stated cautiously. She sensed a trap somewhere in this line of questioning. She just didn't see it yet.

"I'll tell you why I think you're doing it," he retorted.

She looked at him expectantly. This should be good. Here came the standard you're-frustrated-you-weren't-born-a-boy-and-secretly-wish-you-had-balls routine.

"You're trying to form some kind of bond with your real father. He was a SEAL. Died when you were a little kid. And you figure if you can do the same job, become the person he was, maybe you'll connect with your old man. Get to know him through his work. Fill that void in your life."

She blinked, stunned. A) How in the hell did he know her

father had been a SEAL, and B) had he just hit the nail on the head?

"What of it?" she managed to mumble.

He stepped forward until his face was no more than a foot from hers, and his eyes burned with the passion of a zealot. Each damning vowel he cast struck her like a dagger blow. "It's a shitty reason to put yourself through all this suffering. Someday you're going to be lying in a jungle, hungry and thirsty and hot and exhausted. You'll be eaten alive by bugs, your position will be in danger of being compromised, your team will be off its game. And you're going to think, 'What the hell am I doing out here? My old man can take this job and shove it.'"

He leaned in even closer, his intensity all but choking her. "And you're going to get yourself and your whole damn team killed. Because that's when you'll make a mistake. Your give-a-shit factor will drop to zero and our national security's going to take a hit or some innocent's going to die because you just don't care anymore."

She stared, shocked, into his blazing eyes. *Was he right?*

"Get out, Vanessa. Quit now before you lead five fine officers to their deaths while you work out your personal demons. It's not fair to them and it's not fair to our country."

Dear God. She suddenly felt sick to her stomach. A single thought pierced her numb brain. *What if he was right?*

"Get out of my sight," he snarled. "You make me sick. Playing at being a hero and putting all of us through this hell for nothing. Go to bed, toy soldier."

She turned and staggered blindly away from him. Into the vast, black wilderness of her soul.

*October 23*
*Jack's Valley*

Listlessly, Vanessa celebrated along with the other women when Jack announced that this would be a light afternoon. A down day wasn't in his vocabulary, but once every week or so, he let up on them for a few hours.

She laid on her cot and pulled the tattered picture of her father out of her footlocker. She vaguely remembered his face from her own childhood memories. Mostly, she just remembered this image. God, he'd been young. Twenty-eight when he died. Five years younger than her now. Had he been like Jack? Passionate about his work and utterly ruthless about doing it? Would he have ripped someone's guts out and flung them in his face to see if the trainee had what it took to survive Special Forces? Had somebody done that to him? Maybe that was why he'd cut himself off from his family and kept volunteering to go back for tour after tour in the SEALs.

According to her mother, he'd had to get special permission to go back for the last tour because he'd been in the field so long. That had been the straw that broke her mother's back. Vanessa remembered the argument between her parents the night he left for that last tour. Her mother made it clear that if he came home again, he should expect to find divorce papers and an empty house waiting for him.

At the time, Vanessa had secretly raged against the threat, secretly ached for her father's pain. But in retrospect, she could understand her mother's agony as well. If she were married to a bastard like Jack Scatalone, and he stomped all over her heart, she'd be plenty pissed, too.

And it wasn't as if her father was running away from her and her mother. Rather, he was running toward something else. Something out here in these sleepless nights and weeks of grueling training. What was it that would drive a man to emotionally abandon a family who loved him and worried about him? She had no idea. So far, she hadn't discovered anything out here worth losing all that.

Vanessa looked up, startled, as Aleesha sat on Vanessa's cot without warning. She tucked the photograph under her pillow unobtrusively and asked, "What can I do for you, Doc?"

"I'm making a house call, here."

Vanessa blinked. "I'm not sick. I feel fine."

"No, you don't, girlfriend," Aleesha said wisely. "You've been sick in the heart ever since Jack caught us sneaking those showers last week. What's up?"

She should have known the others would pick up on her personal crisis. Be it of faith or confidence, she didn't know which. But she was a mess for damn sure. The doubts Jack had planted in her head were only getting worse as the days passed. Maybe she *should* talk to someone about it. Lord knew she wasn't having any success wrestling down the beast on her own.

"Jack found out my father was a Navy SEAL," she said heavily.

Aleesha looked stumped. "Congratulations?" she said questioningly.

Vanessa laughed. For the first time in over a week. God, that felt good. "He died on a mission when I was five."

"Wow. That sucks," Aleesha commented. "And why has Jack knowing this sad fact put your knickers in such a twist?"

She felt yet another smile cross her face. It gave her the courage to make her confession. "It was my head he put into a twist. He questioned my motives for wanting to be in the Special Forces."

Aleesha waited. "And?"

"And that's it. He told me that someday I'm going to be in the middle of a mission gone bad, and I'm going to give up. I'm going to realize that connecting with my old man isn't worth all the misery, and I'm going to walk away from it all just like that."

"That's what's got you all messed up? You're afraid you're going to quit?"

When Aleesha put it like that, it did sound a bit ridiculous.

The doctor continued, "After the crap he put us through that first week? Good grief, Vanessa, you're the reason we're all standing here today. We didn't want to disappoint you. You were the team's rock throughout that whole ordeal. You were the one who told us over and over that it was worth it. That we were doing something important. That we'd know for the rest of our lives whether we'd given it our all. You showed us how to dig just a little deeper every time we thought we'd hit the bottom of the well. You don't know the meaning of the word quit. How can you possibly think you'd quit just because the going gets tough? Heavens, you don't even really get going good until things *do* get tough."

Vanessa stared hard at Aleesha. Lord, she wanted to believe her. A slow warmth grew deep down in her gut. And with it came a realization. She loved these women like sisters. Friends. Comrades in arms. *Family.*

And maybe that was it. Maybe that was why her father walked away from one family. Because he'd found another one. One that would drag him up the next hill if he couldn't make it on his own. That would suffer beside him no matter how bad it got. That would *die* for him.

Jack might be right. Maybe she was chasing after a ghost out there in the killing fields. But hell. Who didn't have an agenda coming into a job like this? No normal, sane person would volunteer for such dangerous, difficult work. The important thing was that she'd never abandon these women. Ever.

She looked up at Aleesha. "Thanks. I needed that."

The doctor shrugged. "Have voodoo, will travel."

Vanessa nodded slowly. "You know what? I think you need a handle other than Doc. You gotta figure every medic on every team out there gets called Doc. You deserve something better. Special."

The tent went silent. She had everyone's attention all of a sudden.

"What did you have in mind?" Aleesha asked, a grin spreading across her face.

"Well, in keeping with our Medusa theme of dangerous snakes, I was thinking of Mamba."

Aleesha grinned, clearly pleased. The others cheered. Karen came over and slapped her on the shoulder. "Welcome to the Medusa club, Mamba."

Aleesha grinned. "I think our fearless leader could use a name, too. Anyone got any ideas?"

Misty spoke up from the other end of the tent. "Huddle up, gang. I've got an idea."

Vanessa waited on her cot while the others held a whispered conference. In a few moments, they all turned around, grinning. Misty walked over, holding a black-bladed commando knife. "Kneel and be named, Vanessa Blake."

She grinned and slid off her cot onto her knees as ordered. Misty touched the blade to both her shoulders and pronounced solemnly, "I hereby dub thee, Viper. Arise and go forth, O venomous one, and kick some serious ass."

Viper. That had a good ring to it. Strong. Dangerous. Definitely not a quitter. The debilitating doubts of the past week weren't defeated, but they were tucked away for now. She had to give Jack credit. He'd messed up her head good. And then the lesson of what he'd done hit her. He'd found her mental Achilles' heel and exploited it, just like he'd found Karen's weakness when he called her ugly and mannish. He'd forced them both to face their demons. To make peace with them now so they wouldn't become issues in the middle of an op. God, he was a calculating, vicious, brilliant bastard.

She'd be on alert from here on out. If he pulled a mind game like this on any of the others, she'd know how to get them through it quicker and less painfully than her own experience. Suddenly the mantle of team leadership didn't feel quite so heavy on her shoulders.

There was a rustle at the door. Jack stopped abruptly, taking in the scene of Vanessa kneeling with Misty's knife at her neck. "My apologies. Did I interrupt an execution here?" he asked.

"Volunteering to help?" Vanessa retorted as she jumped to her feet.

His hard gaze met hers. "No. I work alone in that arena, thanks."

She looked away. She wasn't quite up to squaring off with him just yet. Maybe in another day or two she'd be back to her old tricks, thwarting him at every possible turn.

"Full combat gear. Outside in five minutes," he barked.

Vanessa scrambled to suit up in fatigues, combat boots, utility belt, ammo vest, helmet and autoweapon. The MP-5s they carried were all unloaded, of course. But they still trained at hauling around the weapons and getting comfortable with the autoweapon slung over a shoulder or across their backs at all times.

He ran them at a stiff pace to the assault course. They passed it all the time in their daily runs, but they'd never been on the course itself. Vanessa stared as a second surprise awaited them—the only other human beings they'd seen since they'd arrived. She followed Jack up to the formation of twenty or so young men in fatigues and got a glimpse of their uniform insignia. Cadets. From the academy.

"Ladies, I invited these fine young men here to help with your training. They'll act as aggressors on the assault course." He turned to the cadets. "These are the ladies you're helping me to train. Your orders are to give them as good as you've got out there. Don't hold back because they're females or officers. Got it?"

The cadets nodded, but Vanessa caught a hint of surprise in their reactions. Poor kids no doubt thought they were incoming academy staff. Probably were scared spitless at the possible recriminations if they kicked some lady officer's butt.

Jack gave the six women a quick walk-through of the course as the sun raced for the line of mountains in the west. Lots of climbing and crawling, over-and-under-type stuff. No problem. Back at the starting line, he handed them each a pugil stick. The padded staffs used for hand-to-hand combat resembled nothing so much as a giant, five-foot-long Q-tip. She took her place at the starting line. Jack called go, and she took off running.

The first obstacle was a low crawl under a maze of ropes. Kid stuff. Then a high crawl on her hands and knees through a concrete drainage pipe. A sprint up a hill, and just over the top, the first cadet jumped out at her. She clocked him with all her strength and knocked him flat on his ass, barely breaking her stride.

The rest of the course went pretty much the same way. The women collected at the finish line to catch their breath, while the cadets staggered in from their various locations. Poor kids looked dazed. Didn't know what had hit them. She caught the twitching of Jack's lips as he gathered the cadets close.

"Okay, now that you've met these ladies, let me say it again. Give it your best shot out there. We're going to run the course again, and this time, clobber the bitches."

Vanessa couldn't help but grin. Now, the course might just get interesting. She noticed the cadets' faces mirrored about equal parts anticipation and apprehension. She took pity on them. "We don't work here, and you're never going to see any of us again. Go ahead. Give us your best shot. We can take it."

That perked them up.

One of Jack's eyebrows lifted lazily. "Back to your old piss-and-vinegar self, I see. Welcome back, Major. What took you so long?"

She threw him a baleful look that delivered a clear "Screw you" message.

He grinned in her face and gestured to the starting line. "You're up, Blake. I want thirty seconds faster than last time."

"You know," she remarked as she eyed the first obstacle, "I'm going to start sandbagging these courses the first time through so I've got plenty of slack in my time to get faster."

"Not when I start using live ammo, you won't," he retorted. "Go!"

The cadets were definitely more aggressive this time around. Smarter, too. A couple of them got in good licks on her, but her speed and quick reflexes kept her clear of any knockdowns or seriously bruising blows. It wasn't the cadets' fault. They were up against six partially trained commandos with something to prove. And the young men were hamstrung by their gentlemanly urges and ingrained respect for superior officers. Vanessa tucked the reaction away for future reference.

Jack said briefly, "You ladies stay put. Gentlemen, come with me." He grabbed a bulky bag and slung it over his shoulder, then disappeared over a hill with the cadets in tow. The other Medusas looked at her, and she shrugged. Who knew what evilness he was cooking up now? They'd find out soon enough.

In a few minutes, Jack stepped back into the clearing by the start line. "Look at me, ladies," Jack ordered casually.

Vanessa looked over at him. And lurched as a blindingly bright spotlight lit up in her face. Jeez, that was intense. She flinched from the beam with her eyes screwed tightly shut, but the damage was done. Spots danced on her eyelids. Jack's voice floated out from behind the ray of brilliant light. "Now, you're ready to go."

The light went off as suddenly as it had gone on. Blackness closed in all around her. Her night vision was completely blown. She couldn't see her hand in front of her face.

"Ready, Blake? You're up first."

He had to be kidding. She couldn't see the path, let alone

the trees around it. "I'd never move at night with vision like this," she protested.

"Sometimes you gotta do what you gotta do," he replied shortly. "On your mark, get set, go!"

She took off running totally in the blind. She cast back in her mind for the shape and look of the course. As she stumbled into a rope at about knee height, she dropped to the ground and started belly crawling. *C'mon, rods and cones. Adapt already.* She squeezed her eyes shut through the whole low crawl. Her vision was a tiny bit better as she got up to head for the drainage pipe. Now she could see black and darker black. She stumbled up the hill and crested the top. And a shape leaped out of the darkness at her.

Whap! Something hard and thin whacked her painfully across the back. Ouch! That was no pugil stick! Felt like a damned broomstick. But by the time the third kid had smacked her, she revised her guess to frigging baseball bats.

She pushed onward doggedly. The trees were starting to take faint shape around her, and the pale ribbon of the path became visible underfoot. Another cadet jumped out at her. She swung at him, deflecting his pole up and away from her face. Whack! A second cadet from the other direction. She dropped to the ground, sweeping her feet in a wide, vicious arc at knee height. The kid went down with a grunt. And then she noticed something. The cadet was wearing a rectangular apparatus strapped over his eyes. Night-vision goggles! She and her team were out here, as blind as newborn kittens, and their aggressors had not only real staffs, but NVGs. For the thousandth time, the old refrain entered her head. *The bastard!*

Fine. He didn't want to play by any rules? Then neither would she. She chopped the downed cadet in the left temple with the side of her hand. She was careful not to hit him hard enough to do any lasting damage, but he went limp under the blow. She dragged him off the path into a patch of low weeds.

Probably poison ivy. She apologized mentally to the young man. And ripped the NVGs off the kid's head and pulled them over her own eyes. Much better. The forest jumped out at her in green relief. She raced through the trees, paralleling the trail to the next curve. She slowed and approached cautiously. Yup. Two more cadets waiting in ambush.

She sneaked up behind the first one and ripped off his NVGs. He squawked, drawing the attention of his buddy. She used the distraction to slip around behind the second kid and nab his NVGs as well. And then she was off and running again before they had time to react. She disarmed four more cadets of their vision advantage.

"Everything okay over there?" Isabella's voice came from behind her. She'd made up the two-minute stagger in their start times while Vanessa was slowed down taking out aggressors.

"I could use a little help," Vanessa called out low.

Isabella ran up and Vanessa bent down long enough to pick up a pair of NVGs and toss them at her comrade. "Put these on. Don't hurt anyone, but help me drop the last cadets up ahead."

Isabella complied and crowed quietly, "What have we here? No wonder I sailed through the course without opposition. Thanks, Viper. By the way, the walking wounded are all making their way in this direction."

Vanessa nodded. "I'll be back to pick them up in a few minutes."

Isabella grinned. "Got it."

Vanessa pointed down the trail. "These are the last four aggressors. Everyone on the course was toting NVGs and these sticks." Vanessa kicked one of the long poles the cadets had dropped.

"The bastard," Isabella hissed.

Vanessa grinned. "I'm going to trot up over the hill and finish the course. You stay here and wait for whoever's behind you to catch up. When she gets here, pass off control of any cadets you collect here to her and finish the run. Tell the last woman to stay here with the prisoners until I come back to get them."

Isabella grinned. "Have fun," she murmured gaily.

Oh, she planned to. She took off the NVGs. Thankfully, her eyes were adapted enough by now to see reasonably well. She hopped onto the path and set off at a steady run. The last rise loomed and fell away, and the finish line opened up before her. A lone aggressor stood between her and the white strip of chalk. This aggressor had no NVGs, but did hold a long, wooden staff. Because of the full-face cage on the helmet he wore, she was almost on him before she recognized him. Jack. *Crap.*

# Chapter 7

"You mean to tell me we still can't confirm if this guy's dead or alive?" Just what he wanted to hear the minute he got back from his first real vacation in a year. Another intelligence snafu that was going to cost him face with the emir of Bhoukar.

Down the table the CIA briefer squirmed. "Uh, that's correct, Mr. President. Bhoukar has proved to be an extremely difficult country to penetrate with human intelligence resources. The dark-skinned population combined with the insular clan and tribal structure of informal society—"

Stanforth cut off the guy's politico-babble with a sharp slice of his hand through the air. "Save it for congressional funding hearings." He turned to the other man at the table, a briefer with the JSOC. "What do we *speculate* is going on with Worthington? And save me the disclaimers. Just tell me what you think."

The briefer cleared his throat. "We think the Bhoukaris wouldn't hold on to an unidentified American's body if he'd died. So, we *speculate* that Captain Worthington is alive. We also believe that the Bhoukaris have made no firm ID on him. They think they know who he is, but they're not sure. And they're not willing to make a public political stink about it until they're certain. If Captain Worthington is alive, conscious, and has full memory, he still hasn't talked. We think this is the case because once they have confirmation that American spec ops are operating on Bhoukari soil, we *speculate* the news will magically leak out of Bhoukari government circles and show up all over the international media, particularly hostile presses."

"What are we doing to set up damage control?" Stanforth asked.

"Sir?" the JSOC briefer replied nervously.

Stanforth replied patiently, "You're military. I'm not going to bust your chops for not thinking of this one." He cast his razor-sharp gaze down the table at the CIA man. "But you, on the other hand, had better get cracking on some sort of prepositioning campaign, politically and in the American press, to cover my ass if and when this thing hits the fan. My butt's flapping in the wind right now, and I don't like the feeling one bit. There's an election in two weeks, for God's sake. If this story breaks wrong, my party could take a serious hit in the midterm elections. And we barely control Congress as it is. With the House swinging more against us every day, I can't afford to lose the Senate."

"Right away, sir."

He flipped the briefing paper aside. "Next topic."

*October 22, 9:00 p.m.*
*Jack's Valley*

Vanessa took a deep breath and squared off against Jack. He was taller, stronger and faster than she was. And he wouldn't hesitate to hit a woman with a big stick. In short, he was her worst nightmare in an opponent. She accepted that he was going to tag her successfully and that it would hurt. With that long staff, the best bet seemed to be to get close, inside his full-swing radius where he could do less damage. What if she intentionally took a few strategic hits from him in the name of closing in? And once she went hand-to-hand, if he were anyone but a spec ops trained soldier, she'd be in great shape.

It was a good theory. But in practice, it didn't work worth beans. He saw through her strategy in about two charges. He kept jumping back, into the primary range of his long weapon. In Robin Hood's terms, he gave her a sound drubbing.

Change of theory. Time to distract him. Get inside his head. She grunted, "So why are *you* out here? Getting a cheap thrill from beating up a bunch of women?"

"I derive—" a sharp blow to her left ribs "—no pleasure from hitting you." He switched hands and came at her from his left.

She shifted grips to meet the new attack. "Why'd Wittenauer stick you with this job? Did you screw up or something?"

"My only screw-up—" a mighty blow to her head that she barely got her pugil stick in front of "—was letting my team go on a mission without me, while I—" a quick blow to her right ankle that stung like hell "— stayed home baby-sitting a bunch of female wanna-bes."

She dodged another ankle blow. Her leather combat boots absorbed some of the force of his hits, but not nearly enough.

"And now, one of my guys is missing—" a fast blow to her shoulder "—and I'm stuck here, teaching you How to be a Toy Soldier 101, instead of looking for my man." He came at her with a flurry of heavy blows, only about half of which she was able to block.

He finally snarled, "Get out of here."

"Glad I could be your punching bag to help you work out your frustrations," she gasped before she staggered away from him, her head ringing. The stars cleared from her eyes just in time for her to welcome Isabella across the line after her own encounter with Jack. The woman was bleeding from a new cut across the bridge of her nose. Vanessa told her, "Stay here and cheer for the others. I'm going back into the woods to collect the rest of the cadets."

Isabella winced as she spoke. "Be careful. Jack's in a vicious mood tonight."

"You noticed?" Vanessa asked, fingering the throbbing lump on her right temple.

Pushing aside the pain, she waited until Jack was facing up the hill, waiting for his next victim, and she took off running quietly. She ducked behind a stand of trees and then cut cross-country into the heart of the assault course. As she'd surmised, the cadets who weren't already captured had gathered in a clump to discuss what they were going to do next. They were arguing over whether to mount their own attack on the crazy women or just walk down to the finish area. She saved them the choice by sneaking up on the nearest one of their number. Man, she hadn't realized how good she was getting at this stealth stuff until she strolled up behind the kid and put a knife to his throat. The cadets froze.

"Here's what you're going to do, gentlemen," she said clearly. "You're going to get into a line and follow that trail until you join the rest of your buddies. If you don't, I may get nervous and have an accident with my extremely sharp knife and your friend's throat."

As one, their faces transformed into masks of horror. Good grief. They believed her threat! She'd half expected them to laugh at her. Apparently, she was mastering the whole dangerous and menacing thing, too. The cadets obediently marched down the trail toward the end of the course. Katrina was there with four hostages.

"Hey, Kat. I'll take charge of your cadets now. You finish the course, and I'll walk in our friends here when you're done. Oh, and Jack's waiting at the bottom of the hill with a staff to kick your butt."

Katrina rolled her eyes. "Thanks for the heads-up."

Vanessa turned to the cadets. "Here's the deal, guys. If you want to see a good show, I'll let you all go up to the top of that hill with me and watch the colonel square off with her. It's not in her personnel records, so he doesn't know she's a fourth-degree black belt in karate. Could be fun. But you have to promise not to try any stunts in the meantime and to walk in with me afterward as cooperative hostages."

The cadets knew a good deal when they heard it and nodded their agreement.

She led them up the hill and motioned them onto their stomachs. She was just in time to see Kat come to a stop in front of Jack, who towered over her by at least a foot and a good hundred pounds in bulk. Sheesh, Kat looked like a child next to him. Maybe she ought to head down the hill now and give the diminutive woman a hand.

But then Jack attacked and Kat slid out of the way as fast as lightning. One second she was there, and the next she was behind him. She popped him on the back with her pugil stick and he spun, with a startled look on his face, and settled into a serious fighting stance. Uh-oh. But Vanessa shouldn't have worried. Kat was fast enough to block Jack's staff with her pugil stick, and she did so over and over as he mounted attacks from every conceivable angle and direction. Problem was, whenever she found an opening, Kat lacked the power to deliver a debilitating blow to Jack with her soft, oversize Q-tip. Vanessa lost count of how many times Kat tapped Jack with the stick, only to have him spin away unharmed. The sparring went on for a good ten minutes.

Finally Jack stepped back, disengaging. He spun his stick once, snapped it into a vertical position in front of him and dropped his chin in a quick, formal bow. Kat leaned her pugil stick against her hip and returned the formal bow, her closed right fist cupped in the palm of her left hand at chin level. Then Jack growled something too quiet for Vanessa to hear and Kat bolted like a frightened rabbit for the finish line.

Time for the grand finale. "Okay, guys, let's go." She stepped behind the cadet nearest her and put her blade across his neck. The kid tensed up like he was about to panic and do something stupid. "Relax," she murmured in his ear. "I won't hurt you. This is just to get the colonel's goat."

Thankfully, the kid didn't pass out on her. But she thought Jack might when he caught sight of her marching the entire cadre of aggressors into camp, minus their NVGs and staffs. The colonel said not a word, but looked about ready to rupture a vein in his neck. Point made. Vanessa released the kid in front of her and gave him a gentle push toward his buddies.

"Thanks for all the fun and games, guys," Vanessa said cheerfully. "I hope you had as good a time as we did."

Jack sent the young men back toward the academy campus with a word of thanks. Then he turned to the women. Vanessa already had her team formed up and waiting for the run back to their camp. She had no doubt this run was going to be a monster. And it was. He led them right past their tents and kept on going. He didn't turn back until every last one of them was gasping for air like fish out of water.

The last couple miles back to camp hurt like all get out. But it was worth it. To have gotten under Jack Scatalone's skin was a major accomplishment in her book. He finally stopped them in front of the tents.

"Pack," he ordered them tersely. "You're out of here tomorrow."

They fell out of formation and headed for their tent, huffing. But Vanessa followed him toward his. He turned, one eyebrow arched in question. "What?" he snapped.

"Where are we going?" she asked.

"I'm not sending you home if that's what you're worried about," he bit out.

It actually was, but she certainly wasn't going to admit that to him. She shrugged and turned away, but stopped when he spoke behind her.

"You've gotten cocky enough that it's time to take you to the big leagues. Knock the starch out of you. Tomorrow we head for Bragg. To the spec ops training compound to see how you hold up to some advanced training."

*Yes!* The home of the Special Forces, location of close-quarters battle facilities, live-fire ranges, urban assault training areas, legendary aggressor forces—the works! They were, indeed, headed for the big leagues. And they'd earned it. She checked her excitement and looked up at him seriously for a moment. "For what it's worth, I hope your missing man's okay."

He scowled at her, but the expression didn't reach his eyes. "Me, too," he said gruffly.

She returned to the women's tent, jubilant. "Guess what?" she crowed.

"Don't keep us waiting," Karen said eagerly. "I know that look in your eye."

"We head for Bragg tomorrow. Advanced SF training. We made it to the next step."

A heartfelt cheer went up. Misty Cordell rummaged in her trunk. "I've been saving something for a special occasion." She pulled out a large, gold foil box. "It's a pound of chocolate truffles. I planned on consoling myself with them if I washed out. But this is a much more worthy occasion."

A moan of anticipation and appreciation went up from all of them. Vanessa waited until they were all seated on their cots, sucking on the heavenly chocolate to say, "I believe we have another inductee into the Medusa club, tonight. Kat, you may be little and inconspicuous most of the time, but when you rear up and fight, the world had better look out. In honor of your amazing performance against His Highness in one-on-one combat, I hereby dub you Cobra."

Everyone cheered and Kat blushed, as shy as always.

Jack rolled over in the next tent. Through the layers of flimsy canvas, he always heard every word they said. They knew it, of course, but didn't generally care. His Highness, huh? Guess he was doing his job right as a trainer if that's how they saw him.

Cobra. A good name for Kat Kim. She'd surprised the hell out of him when she'd stepped up to him fearlessly tonight and declared, "Try me," with all the confidence in the world. Plucky little thing. They all were plucky. They'd known full well he'd knock them into yesterday with that staff, and not one of them had shrunk from the beating he gave them.

And he had to give Vanessa credit. She didn't miss a trick. Good tactic to turn the mental tables on him like that. Not to mention her stunt with the cadets. He grinned into the darkness. Probably scarred the poor boys for life. If she'd have been a man, he'd have pegged her in a minute to be a team leader. His brain screeched to a halt. The thought replayed itself. She had all the charisma, smarts and chutzpah he looked for in a Special Forces team leader. Two months ago, he never would have guessed a woman could successfully demonstrate any combat leadership skills, let alone all the skills the demanding job of being an SF team leader required.

He was going to catch endless shit, both from Wittenauer and his colleagues, for bringing his snake ladies to Bragg. But damned if he wasn't looking forward to showing off his students to the SF community. When had the irritating, stubborn, cussed lot of them wormed their way into his good graces, anyway?

*October 24*
*Al-Khibri, Bhoukar*

Defoe wiggled backward carefully, easing his body by inches underneath a beige ghillie net. He'd already piled a layer of small rocks and dirt on it and now had to get under it without disturbing the debris. Bit of a trick. But he made it. He settled into the spot he'd picked. He lay on the top of the eastern ridge flanking Al-Khibri. Over his left shoulder he had a clear view of the Army of Holy War cave complex behind him, one ridge to the east. Straight ahead lay the big, brightly lit wellheads of the oil field itself. One of the wells was pumping now, its giant hammerhead rotating ponderously, round and round, extracting black crude from deep under the earth.

His team was strung out in a line along the ridge, spanning a couple hundred yards. Ever since the big, celebratory arrival of more Army of Holy War troops—if a motley assortment of robed, ragged, randomly armed nomads could be called troops—the atmosphere outside the oil field had been electric. Something was fixing to go down. Soon. And whatever it was, they were sitting right on top of it.

The night grew cold, and he fought off a case of the shivers. What a hellish climate. It got up to ninety degrees in the daytime, even at this time of year, but ice formed in his canteen at night. How any creature survived out here was beyond him. Two a.m. came and went. His and Walsh's shift ended at three-thirty, and then Ginelli's and Spot's silent, vibrating wrist alarms would wake them and they'd take up the watch. Small rodents and the occasional huge insect crawled past in the sand and rock scree in front of him. And a few men moved around the oil rig now and then. But all else was quiet.

And then, without warning, Walsh's whispered voice came over his earpiece. "I've got movement from the caves. Two guys on foot. Moving perpendicular to our position. Two hundred yards northeast of me, moving due west. Scouting."

"Roger," Defoe breathed back into his own throat mike. He turned his head by slow degrees until he was looking back over his shoulder. No movement in his sector. Only two guys? They usually went out in groups of six to eight. Ah well, he'd call the alert anyway. "Everyone up. Look sharp. Patrol incoming from the north."

Any traffic on their headsets should wake the rest of the team. With their necks riding on being sharp, Deltas had a tendency to sleep real damn lightly. A mere whisper of sound was enough to wake them.

Spot murmured almost immediately, "I've got movement. Patrol. Moving east, fifty yards south of my position. Six Tangos."

South? But Walsh had just reported the patrol to be to the north. Shit. Two patrols? Not good.

And then a muted noise drifted to his ears. It sounded for all the world like a mechanized, tracked vehicle. He'd swear it was a light-armored personnel carrier if he wasn't out here in the middle of freakin' nowhere.

"Two groups cresting the east ridge directly opposite my position," Ginelli murmured tersely. "Twenty men total."

"I got eight guys coming straight at me. Moving fast. Heavily armed." That was Jensen.

Well, at least everyone was awake. Was that the ground rumbling underneath him? His already hypersensitive senses went into overdrive. He could swear he smelled the terrorists getting closer. That was definitely the stale redolence of goat shit on the air.

Men were pouring out of one of the main cave entrances now. And goddammit, they didn't look like they were headed to a party. Had Delta Three's questionable luck finally run out? Were they about to be overrun?

A large movement caught his attention at his eight-o'clock position. The entire wall of the cliff looked like it was collapsing! Were they witnessing some sort of evacuation?

And then a tank—a goddamn *tank*—emerged from the rubble and dust. Like Phoenix rising from the ashes. Men were streaming out of the other caves like bees defending the hive, moving directly toward them now. The team didn't have a fraction of the ammo they'd need to take this force out. "Hold your fire till the last possible second," he ordered in a bare whisper.

"How the fuck did they make us?" Spot whispered, although there was really no need for quiet beneath the din of the tank and the two armored personnel carriers grinding loudly toward their position. "I'm lookin' and I can't see a one of you guys. And I frigging know where you are."

Defoe frowned. Was his initial assumption wrong? Was the Army of Holy War coming for them at all? But if the Delta team wasn't the target of this full-scale assault then what... shit. *The oil field.* The bastards were going to take over the oil field!

"Hold your fire," he whispered frantically. "Lay low. They're headed for Al-Khibri." And then he was out of time. Too risky to say anything more. The first foot patrol was heading up the slope toward his position. He drew in his energy, went utterly still. Calm. Detached. Cold. Just like Colonel Scatalone had taught him. He let the terrorists flow past him like water. None of it touched him.

Until one of the bastards nearly stepped on top of him. Another did momentarily snag the bottom of his boot in the edge of Defoe's ghillie net. That near miss had almost blown his Zen state straight to hell.

And then the Holy War bastards *laid down* on the ridge in a ragged line, not twenty feet in front of him and the rest of his team. Peering at the oil field through binoculars. It was creepy as hell. He laid there, smack-dab in the middle of at least a hundred terrorists, and they never had a clue that five Americans were parked literally within feet of them.

He was a cool customer, but his nerves were screaming by the time the Army of Holy War terrorists finally started to slither down the rock face in front of him. One of the personnel carriers would have run him over if he hadn't parked almost beneath a waist-high rock. As it was, the vehicle's tracks swung perilously close to his head when it detoured around the boulder. Close enough to smell tread grease and get stung by the gravel it threw up in his face.

And then the foot soldiers moved. They crept past him for nearly a half hour. He scanned the ridge in both directions, looking at the long line of men. The terrorists had just walked right through their position. It was nothing short of a miracle that they weren't discovered. More of the bastards still milled around back by the caves behind them. It wasn't like he and the guys could stand up, take a good stretch and boogie out of there with all the activity around them. The team was completely, irrevocably pinned down.

He could only pray the terrorists successfully took over the oil field so they wouldn't be obliged to retreat back the way they'd come.

Moving millimeter by millimeter, he eased his telescope up to his eye. The assault on Al-Khibri wasn't pretty, nor was it fancy. The tank headed straight for the fence line. It was an ancient Russian model that he was impressed still ran. How in the bloody hell they'd ever gotten it inside that cave, he had no idea. He wouldn't put it past the lunatics to have assembled it part by part inside the compound. If so, it was an even greater miracle that the big old Bertha of a tank worked.

A row of hurricane fence and some barbed wire weren't going to stop the big, heavy tank. It rammed straight through the barrier. The more nimble personnel vehicles passed easily through the newly made gap behind Big Bertha. Grenade-tossing terrorists leaped out of the bellies of the armored vehicles. That first Holy War group took heavy casualties, but they drew out the Bhoukari troops, who mostly milled around in a confused and disorganized mob. The way they were arrayed around their attackers, he'd lay odds a bunch of the Bhoukaris took friendly cross-fire injuries in the mêlée around the three intruding vehicles.

And then the main terrorist force attacked on foot. It was swift and brutal. Whatever Bhoukari troops hadn't fallen in the first volley of gunfire were cut down like paper dolls in the second wave of the attack. The Army of Holy War terrorists started jumping around, waving their rifles in the air and firing into the sky. He noted that the Army of Holy War leaders managed, with some trouble, to corral a portion of the celebrating soldiers and have them sweep the buildings beside the oil rigs for survivors. Over the next few minutes, a few scattered gunshots from inside the army barracks drifted to him on the still night air.

And in about ten minutes, it was all over. He'd just witnessed the takeover of a major oil field by a dangerous and violent terrorist group. And now they controlled the output of the field and all the wealth that oil represented. Well, well, well. Weren't the boys back home going to be thrilled to hear about this....

# *Chapter 8*

October 24, 9:00 p.m.
*Fort Bragg, North Carolina*

It felt strange to be home. Although she wasn't allowed to go to her house, of course. They'd stay in a barracks in the middle of a thickly wooded area. *Inside the fence.* She'd finally made it to that hallowed training ground where the best of the best honed their skills.

Jack's words that night at the bar came back to her as their bus drove through the heavily guarded gate. *It's a one-way ticket. Once you go inside the fence you'll never go back.* Maybe she'd finally figure out what he'd been trying to tell her. Her father must have passed through a gate like this on a navy base somewhere, once upon a time. Had he been as pumped up at having made it as she was? Had he been naive and excited, or was he too macho at twenty-two years of age to wallow in such feelings? No answer came to her as Jack showed them to the aged, sturdy and unquestionably ugly Quonset hut they'd call home for the next few months. They unpacked and went to bed early.

She had trouble sleeping. In the dim moonlight filtering through the window, she pulled out her father's picture and stared at it. Surely he'd felt this same burning need to prove himself, to be the best. He must've been good at what he did, because he survived three operational tours before a bullet with his name on it finally caught up with him. She'd bet it surprised the hell out of him, too. A person had to believe they were invincible to even attempt this kind of work. Sure, she knew in her head that any of them could die at any time. She also knew this job was all about being better than the other guy, and in her heart, she was absolutely certain she and her team were the best. Now, it was up to them to prove it to Jack and everybody else who was watching them.

She jolted awake to the usual first sound of their morning—Jack hollering, "Fall out in five minutes! Light-battle gear, ladies."

Vanessa leaped out of bed almost by reflex. Five a.m. And another day in paradise began. She jumped into fatigues, boots, utility belt and vest, and grabbed her MP-5. It wasn't loaded yet. But soon, though. Very soon they'd stop being toy soldiers and take their place in the front lines.

Jack wore a black T-shirt, jungle-green camo pants and combat boots this morning. As always, he ran alongside them easily. He directed them onto a dirt road, more a wide path, really. "This is the inner ring. Five miles around. The outer ring's eight. But today, we'll take it easy."

The sea-level air felt thick and heavy after six weeks at six-thousand-feet altitude. Gave her a bit of a buzz, in fact. Or maybe it was just the exhilaration of the moment.

"You look full of it this morning, Major Blake. Why don't you do the honors?" Jack said with exaggerated courtesy.

She scowled at him out of general principle, but was glad

to be the pacesetter today. She couldn't help setting a brisk pace, but everyone seemed in high spirits and ran easily behind her. They'd been running for about ten minutes when the air got dusty around them. Like someone had passed this way recently, kicking up a lot of dirt.

A surge of excitement went through Vanessa, and she picked up the pace a bit. Another five minutes brought them within earshot of a group of male voices singing a filthy song about whores in various parts of the world.

"Shall we?" she murmured over her shoulder.

"Oh, yeah," Karen answered. The others added their agreement instantly. She glanced over at Jack, running casually beside her. He grinned and shrugged. Her call. She nudged up the pace another notch. Enough to bring them up on the tail of the group of two dozen male soldiers.

"Coming through," she called out.

The last couple rows of men jolted. "What the..." someone squawked.

The women dropped into single file and motored up alongside the formation.

"'Morning, gentlemen," Vanessa said lightly. "Fine day for a run." She pulled up even with the front rank. Patent shock filled their faces. She wondered briefly if they were more stunned to see women in their inner sanctum, or that the women were comfortably keeping up with them at a sub-seven-minute-mile pace. The guys' pacesetter picked up the speed to match hers.

"Wanna run with us?" she asked lightly. "Cool. We'd enjoy the serenade. I believe you guys left off at the 'Little Girl from Manila Bay.'"

"What the hell are you talking about? You think you can keep up with us?" he growled. "C'mon, men. Let's quit pussy-assing around and get a move on."

She shrugged. No sense grandstanding and pissing off these guys even more. Their testosterone-induced egos were already severely threatened.

The guy pushed the speed close to a six-minute-mile pace. Ah, but her team did that all the time. At altitude. She matched the pace and made darn sure it looked effortless. It was approaching the limit of what she did without sucking some hard wind, but what the men didn't know wouldn't hurt them.

Misty struck up a conversation with some poor shmuck beside her. Vanessa grinned at how *not* out of breath her teammate sounded. Misty had told her once it was an old triathlon trick she'd learned to psych out her opponents. "So how far you guys going this morning?" Misty asked.

The guy panted, "Five miles."

"Great!" Misty gushed in breezy California beach girl fashion. "That's what we're doing today, too. The boss is taking it easy on us so we can learn our way around before we get serious about training. We're doing the outer loop tomorrow morning. You guys want to meet us there? It'll be fun."

"We've got other shit to do," the pacesetter at Vanessa's elbow growled over his shoulder at Misty. "Important shit."

Vanessa grinned at him. "Is there any other kind?" she asked dryly.

"Let's go, ladies," Jack announced abruptly. "Social hour's over." He moved ahead of Vanessa, and she sped up to catch him. She was in a full-out run now, the long-strided, arm-pumping, deep-breathing variety. The other women breathed deep and hard behind her, but kept pace with her and Jack. The group of men didn't follow.

Thankfully, they rounded a bend in the road, and the soccer field-size open area where they'd started came into view. That all-out sprint only lasted a quarter mile or so, but she had the feeling they'd just made a giant statement to the spec ops community.

They crossed the finish line, and Jack hit his stopwatch. She didn't bother to look at hers. They'd been fast today. Wicked fast.

"Well, that was fun," Misty commented cheerfully, her

breathing not appreciably strained. *Damned triathlete.* Vanessa took another couple great lungfuls of air and retorted, "One small sprint for women, one giant leap for mankind."

Jack stepped up to her. "You didn't make any friends out there this morning."

She straightened to look him square in the eye. "It's not about making friends. It's about earning respect. Nobody around here's going to give us an ounce of it. We're going to have to wrestle it out of their grudging fists every step of the way. Just like we did with you."

"You think I respect you?" he demanded.

She raised a sardonic eyebrow at him. "We're here, aren't we?"

He turned sharply and strode away. "Fall out for calisthenics," he barked over his shoulder.

Vanessa's chin was parked on top of a pull-up bar when the group of men they'd passed came huffing into the parade ground. The guys openly gawked as she and her teammates pumped out sets of pull-ups. *Yup, boys, some girls do have upper body strength.* She also noticed a clump of black-shirted men gathering at the other side of the parade field. Here to watch the girl monkeys perform, no doubt.

Vanessa hopped up from the ground, fifty push-ups the wiser. She moved over to where Jack stood, clipboard in hand. "Sir?"

He looked up. "Speak."

"I'm sure you've already thought about this, but I have to ask. A whole bunch of people have seen us today. I thought General Wittenauer wanted to keep our project strictly classified."

He glanced over at the cadre of instructors, who were making no secret of scoping out the women. "You're worried about a security breach? Here?" he asked scornfully.

"Not a security breach. Someone with an agenda. With a strong opinion about women in the Special Forces. It wouldn't take much of a slip for word to get out. Have all these guys been briefed on our status?"

Jack gave her a hard look. "The instructors who'll be working with you know who you are. The rest of them would be too damn embarrassed to let anyone outside the fence know a woman is doing their job. I think your secret's safe, Blake."

She shrugged. "Your call. I'm not ashamed of what we're doing or how we're doing it. But the less the outside world knows about us, the better we'll be able to do our job when we go operational."

He nodded crisply, then snapped, "Get back in line. It's starting to look like you're telling me how to do my job."

"No, sir. Never, sir," she shot back as she dropped for another round of push-ups.

She thought she heard him mumble under his breath, "Mouthy broad." But she wasn't sure. She grinned at the wet grass under her nose.

*October 24*
*Congressional Country Club, Bethesda, Maryland*

General Wittenauer knocked a clod of matted grass clippings off his cleated shoe. "You have the honors this hole, Senator." He watched impassively as Walter McClure, a senior member of the Senate Arms Committee, teed up his golf ball and proceeded to hook it into the trees beyond the left rough.

"Bad luck, sir," Wittenauer murmured. He laid off his drive, swinging at only about eighty percent power, and hid a grimace when his ball sailed 260 yards and rolled gently to a stop in the middle of the fairway. If being a good golfer cost him the funding increase he desperately needed to meet all the manning requirements JSOC was mandated to fill over the next five years, he was going to wrap his favorite persimmon driver around a tree and quit playing the damn game.

"I heard you were good, Witt, but nobody warned me you were this slick," McClure commented slyly.

Were they talking about golf or not here? Wittenauer

wasn't sure. God, he hated playing politics. Give him a nice, bloody war any day over the backstabbing bullshit congressmen pulled. "I'm just a crusty old fart getting close to retirement," he finally replied.

McClure snorted. "After that end-around you pulled on me with getting Medusa funded while I was out of commission?"

"That wasn't me, sir. Believe me," Wittenauer answered fervently. He was as opposed to women in the Special Forces as anyone.

McClure pounced. "Who then?"

Wittenauer lined up his chip shot and swung through the ball, pitching it up on the green about six feet from the hole. He was left with an easy birdie putt. "Dunno, but it happened above my pay grade," he finally commented.

McClure misread the break of the green and wildly missed a long putt that would have given him a bogey. He glared past the hole at Wittenauer. "Are you telling me the White House drove this thing through?"

"I'm telling you no such thing," Wittenauer said sharply. "I'm simply telling you the Secretary of Defense handed me a pile of money and told me to make the project happen."

"This administration's not in favor of women in combat roles, such as Special Forces," McClure declared, "and neither are my constituents. I'm two weeks away from an election, and I cannot afford to go against the will of the people."

Wittenauer snorted to himself. Since when did power brokers like McClure give a damn for the will of the people? Aloud, he said, "I can understand your concern, sir. I hear your party hopes to retain control of the House in these midterm elections. It would be controversial, indeed, for this administration to put women on the front lines of the most violent situations in the world today."

"The hell with the House. Do you know what it would do to my ability to get reelected? This is the first time in twenty-four years a single issue has come along that might, no shit, cost me the next election. I'm not going down in flames for a bunch of women who want to play commando. What the hell was Stanforth thinking, pushing the Medusa Project through?"

Interesting. McClure was genuinely afraid he was going to lose his job over it. That explained a lot.

Wittenauer shrugged. "Maybe the idea is to let the women have a go at it, fail spectacularly, and put the matter to rest once and for all. You make fifty-one percent of the voting population feel like equals, and you still manage to close the door in their face."

"Way I hear it, those broads aren't going down easy," McClure commented slyly.

Wittenauer shrugged. "Yeah, but we just threw them into the tank with the big sharks. They'll be chewed up and spit out any day now, sir."

"You better be right, General. It could have a negative affect on my ability to get you guys funding if the public thinks you're using the money to send women off to die."

And there it was. The threat he'd been waiting for the whole golf match. Shut down Medusa or take it in the shorts when funding time rolled around. Wittenauer smiled brittlely at the senator. *The son of a bitch.* Almost made a man want to see those women succeed just to spite the old bastard.

*October 25*
*Fort Bragg*

"Cease-fire!" She could hardly hear Jack over the din of six rifles shooting on the target range simultaneously. "Weapons down! Check your shots!" Jack ordered into the abrupt silence.

Vanessa grabbed the binoculars that hung next to her firing position. A white outline of a man on black paper came into view. And then a loose cluster of holes, all inside the nine ring or better. Every one of her shots would have been classed a successful kill. Out of curiosity, she swung her binoculars to the next target over. Katrina's. Good grief. Every shot was in a tight little cluster, dead center on the target. She hadn't been on her college's champion rifle team for nothing, apparently.

"Show-off," she muttered at Kat, who grinned back at her.

Jack strode up behind the two of them. "It's all well and good to hit the target, Kim, but you've got to do it before the other guy has all day to shoot you first. Let's see you quick draw. Everyone else, off the firing line."

Vanessa dropped back along with the other four women. Katrina reloaded while Jack loomed beside her.

"Ready. Fire!" he ordered.

Vanessa saw what he was talking about. Katrina drew up the rifle deliberately, exhaled smoothly and then fired. It was poetry in motion, but it was way too slow for combat conditions.

"Accurate, but you're dead. Cobras are supposed to strike like lightning," he added sarcastically, referring to her nickname. "Faster."

He had her do it again and again. But every time, her ingrained training made her firing motion too slow.

Finally he got irritated. "What you need is someone firing back at you." He disappeared into the weapons bunker. And returned a minute later, carrying a jumble of straps, two large, black pistols and a pair of leather hip holsters.

Vanessa helped Katrina strap on a plastic chest piece wired to sense a laser shot. The pistol Jack handed Kat put out a red laser beam. Katrina tried drawing from the holster a couple times and adjusted it lower on her hip.

"Ready?" Vanessa asked her.

Katrina nodded, her delicate jaw set.

Vanessa murmured, "Don't let him intimidate you. Women have faster fine-motor reflexes than men. This fight's at least even, if not tilted your way."

Jack paced about twenty-five yards away and turned to

face the women. "Everyone stand back. So this fight's fair, Blake, you call the draw."

Vanessa nodded. The two combatants stood with their hands at their sides, relaxed. "Ready...fire!" she called.

Jack's red laser tagged Katrina's breastplate and made it beep before Katrina hardly had her pistol out of the holster. "Faster, Cobra," he taunted. He holstered his weapon. "Again, Blake."

He beat Katrina two more times in a row, but each time she got quicker. Another couple draws and she'd have him. And then there was a disturbance at the far end of the firing range, behind Katrina. A foursome of black-shirted instructors strolled into view.

Vanessa walked over to them and announced as required, "The range is hot, gentlemen."

They nodded in acknowledgment.

"One more time for all the marbles," Jack called out, swaggering into position.

Vanessa's eyes narrowed. He was grandstanding for his buddies. But she could fix that. She sidled over behind Katrina, directly in Jack's sight line. She signaled subtly with her hand for the other women to form a line between her and the male observers. They slid casually into position. Jack nodded his readiness at her.

"Okay, Kat, be fast," she murmured to her teammate. Vanessa pulled her T-shirt out of her pants and grabbed its bottom hem. "Here we go."

She nodded at Jack to signal she was about to make the call. "Ready..." At the speed of light, she flipped up her T-shirt, flashing the red lace push-up bra from that first day at the Pentagon. Jack gaped. "Fire!" she shouted.

Jack's breastplate beeped loudly. Vanessa yanked her shirt back down and stepped forward to congratulate Katrina. The other women grinned broadly as Jack stormed down the course toward her. Fortunately, the cadre of instructors pushed past her, waylaying Jack with good-natured slaps on the back and offers to bring the old man his cane. He scowled over their heads at Vanessa and mouthed, "Later," at her.

Ah, but it was worth it. She wouldn't forget that look of slack-jawed shock on his face for a long time.

Misty murmured laughingly in her ear, "You are so dead. But, God, that was priceless."

*October 27*
*a hospital in Bhoukar*

Scott blinked up at a bright fluorescent light overhead. Awake. *I'm awake.* Vague awareness of having been out of it for a long time assaulted him. He lifted a hand off the mattress. It was bony. Emaciated. Wow. He'd been unconscious for a good long time to have wasted away like that. He cast his mind back in time. Snippets of unbearable pain flashed through his fuzzy memory. Of being carried on a makeshift litter and seeing stars overhead. There was pain associated with that memory, too. A snake had hit him in the leg. Ah. The source of the pain.

He remembered humping across a red desert. Hot as hell. And crawling with terrorists. Further back, he recalled getting on a C-17 at Fort Bragg. That was a lifetime ago. An image popped into his head of a Labor Day barbecue at Colonel Scatalone's house with the rest of the team. The name Delta Three popped into his head. Mustn't repeat that one.

A flurry of activity made him start. He turned his head painfully, but whoever'd been there rushed out of the room, just beyond his field of vision. He heard an excited voice out in the hallway. Announcing in Arabic that the prisoner was awake. Whoa. Prisoner? Shit. A litany of training rolled through his head from somewhere deep in his brain. No names. No ranks, no admission of military affiliation. And for God's sake, no information. Not about the mission, not about the team, not about the very existence of Special Operations Detachment Delta.

A thin, dark man rushed into the room, slowing when he saw Scott's gaze upon him. "Greetings, my friend," the man said in Arabic.

Scott gave him a blank look.

"I said hello," the guy repeated in Arabic.

More of the blank look.

"Hello. Is there anything you need?" the man said in British-accented English.

Odds were with his light brown hair and blue eyes, these guys had him pegged as an American. Or a Westerner at a minimum. "Uh, I need to take a piss," Scott replied.

The man blinked. Not a topic most Muslims would bring up with another person. Unclean subject matter. "The doctors assure me that your...need...is taken care of."

So. The guy wasn't a doctor. An interrogator, then.

"What is your name?" the man barked abruptly.

Old trick. Try to surprise an answer out of the subject. Scott considered the question at his leisure, unfazed by the tactic. "Well now," he drawled, "that's a very good question. I can't seem to recall at the moment. Ain't that the damnedest thing?"

"We have reason to believe your name is Scott Worthington. Does that sound familiar to you?" The guy peered closely at him, no doubt looking for some flicker of recognition.

Scott gazed back, wide-eyed and unresponsive. "Nah, I don't think so. Sounds too hoity-toity to be me. I'm more the Billy Bob Ray type."

"What were you doing in Bhoukar?" the man shot at him.

"Bhoukar? *Bhoukar?* How the hell did I get there? I had no business there. At least not that I remember."

"What sort of business?"

Shit. What cover story had his team put in place for him? For surely they'd turned him over to the Bhoukaris under

some pretense. No Delta ended up in enemy hands by accident unless their mission went seriously to hell. His kind
died fighting. "What happened to me? Why am I in a hospital?" he asked, ignoring Beanpole's question.

"After your airplane supposedly crashed, you were bitten
by a puff adder. However, we found no evidence of any airplane near where you were picked up."

An airplane crash. He wouldn't have been wearing a flight
suit, so his team had to have passed him off as a civilian pilot
of some kind. A small plane, or the guy'd be talking about
him being a passenger. He thought fast. He needed a good lie
about why he'd be running through Bhoukar in a bug
smasher.

"Damn!" he exclaimed. "My bird's gone? Bloody sand
must have swallowed it up. Godforsaken deserts in this part
of the world...no offense intended, there, Ali."

"The name's Akbar," the man said haughtily. "And why
were you flying over restricted Bhoukari airspace?"

"Last I knew, I was en route from..." He hesitated, frowning like he was working hard to remember. He let his face light
up. "From Diego Garcia to Cairo!" he finished with a flourish.

"Why?" Akbar snapped.

He made a big production of fishing around in his memory. "Can't rightly say. I imagine I was doing a courier run
or some such thing. Express mail or something like that."

"Try to remember." Akbar took a step nearer the bed, the
guy's fingers uncomfortably close to the IV tubes running
into the back of Scott's hand. If the bastard had a hypoder-
mic concealed in that oversize nightgown of his, Scott would
have to be damn quick to get the needle out before the drugs
hit him. Could be dicey since he had no idea what shape his
reflexes were in at the moment.

He stared up into the man's black eyes. A lie always
worked best if it was outrageous. The truth-is-stranger-than-
fiction tactic. "I've got it!" he all but shouted.

Akbar went about two feet straight up in the air.

Scott bit back a grin. "I was hauling a dead guy. Some bastard fell asleep on the flight line at the air base on Diego and got run over by a maintenance van. Big dude. I was hauling the coffin out. Damned thing kept sliding around in the back of Marilyn—that's my plane—and kept fucking up, pardon me, screwing up my center of gravity. I fought that goddamned box for an hour. Finally put on the autopilot and climbed in the back to tie the sucker down." He frowned. "I don't remember any more than that. Did you find the dead guy at least?"

"No," Akbar answered. Poor bastard looked taken aback.

"Damned shame. His family's going to have a hissy fit if you guys don't find him and dig him up. Folks take losing the body of a loved one real poorly where I come from."

"Uh, I'll pass that on to my superiors."

Scott had to work hard to bite back a grin at that one. He could just see a platoon of pissed-off Bhoukari soldiers digging around in the desert sand in hundred degree heat, looking for a corpse that didn't exist. Ah well. Akbar would get tired of this game eventually. But at least the joke was on Beanpole for now. A freebie morale boost was never a bad thing. Especially since the look lurking in the back of Akbar's black eyes promised this game was going to get real ugly before it got better.

# Chapter 9

*October 30, 10:30 p.m.*
*Fort Bragg*

She couldn't stand waiting for the payback from Jack any longer. She was sleeping like crap and jumping at every shadow. Time to take the bull by the horns. Vanessa stepped onto the porch of the tiny bungalow in the row of cottages the instructors used when they had a class of recruits in training. One of the black shirts pointed her to it when she'd asked where to find Colonel Scatalone. Here went nothing. She knocked on the screen door.

"Come," he called.

She stepped inside cautiously. Dim light glowed from a single lamp on a desk. Jack stood in front of it, poring over a topographical map spread across its surface. He straightened abruptly as he saw who she was.

"Close the door."

She pushed the wooden door shut behind her, blocking out the night. And any chance of a rescue from a passerby. The sound of crickets went away.

"And you're here why?" he bit out.

"Preemptive strike. Thought it might be good to clear the air between us," she explained. Thank God her voice was steady, because abruptly, her pulse was not.

He gave her a long, hooded look. Was he pissed off, or merely plotting his revenge? "I assume you're referring to your stunt on the firing range?"

She nodded. Crisply and professionally, she hoped.

"Come here." His voice was low and sexy, his black gaze compelling.

No way could she fight the pull of the man. He was a damned magnet. She walked slowly, unwillingly even, toward him until she stood an arm's length away.

He turned and stabbed a finger at the map. "If you were here and got into trouble, where would you go?"

She blinked, stunned. He wanted to talk military strategy? She looked down, disoriented, at the map. The swirling topographical lines came to life before her. Mountainous country. Not high peaks like the Rockies, but a heavily broken landscape cut by gullies, cliffs and valleys. And the spot he pointed out was at the eastern edge of a lone plain in the middle of the wasteland.

"What kind of foliage is there?" she asked, captured by the problem.

"None. It's rocky desert."

Ugh. Made the scenario a whole lot tougher. No ground cover.

"Any caves in the area?" she asked.

"Plentiful. Occupied liberally by scorpions and terrorists."

Bummer. "I'd still scope out a cave. The climate's got to be a bitch if nothing will grow there. A team would need relief from it. I'd look for something high up the side of one of these ridges. Good vantage point to watch the comings and goings below me, because it looks like the only traversable paths or roads will have to follow the bottoms of the valleys."

He nodded slowly. "If you had a target to recon here—" another stab at the map with a long, blunt finger squarely at the middle of that wide plain "—where would you hole up?"

She leaned closer to the map. Her nose all but hit his arm. She noticed out of the corner of her eye that his biceps were bunched and tense. Was it her proximity or the question at hand that had him so wired?

"Barring any other factors, I'd head for this ridge, right here. Best spot to watch the target and still be able to check my six o'clock for hostile activity out of all those caves behind me."

"Very good, Vanessa."

So it had been a quiz. But if he knew the answer already, why had he bothered to ask her? "Where is this place?" she asked.

"Bhoukar."

She grimaced. "Nasty corner of the world." And then something hit her. "Is this where your man went missing?"

"Yeah."

"Did the rest of your team make it out all right?"

"They're still there."

She looked down at the map. "Parked on that ridge?"

He nodded. "If a big force of soldiers headed for your target from these caves here and passed right across the ridge where you'd camped out, what would you do?"

If hostiles came up from behind, the only place to run would be down onto that open plain. Probably suicide if there truly was no vegetation to use for cover. The back side of the ridge she'd chosen was a gentle slope. Probably eroded sand with no good caves in it. She glanced up at him. His eyelashes were long and dark, his eyes blazing beneath them. That must be what had happened to his team. Ouch.

She answered slowly, "I'd hunker down and hide as best I could while the hostiles passed by because there's not a blessed place to run that has cover."

He stared down at the map a moment more. And then his gaze shifted to her, piercing her like a bayonet. She was close enough to catch a whiff of his lethal aftershave. Lord, she loved the smell of it. And that scared the hell out of her. But, if she took a step back right now from it and from him, he'd know he'd gotten to her. And it was nothing short of suicide to give an opponent like him the power of such knowledge.

Without warning, his voice lashed out at her. "You used sex against me on the firing range."

She absorbed the cut of his words, and then replied evenly, "Of course I did. It's a weapon in my arsenal. Why wouldn't I use it?"

He stood up to his full height, and she found herself staring at his muscular chest. The black T-shirt clung to a great display of bulging muscles. Sometimes she forgot how big a man he was because he was as graceful and silent as a cat. She lifted her gaze slowly to his face. And when her gaze touched his, he moved so fast she barely saw what happened. One minute she was staring up at him, and the next, she slammed backward against the wall, his hard body pinning her immovably in place. Her hands wrenched up over head, locked there by his iron grip. One of his knees forced her legs apart and she straddled his thigh suggestively, her feet barely touching the ground.

They stared at each other for a moment that stretched out tighter and tighter, sex abruptly hanging thick in the air between them. Their gazes clashed, along with their wills. They frustrated and foiled each other at every turn, were adversaries in everything they did. And it was no different in this instance. She tested his strength, and he leaned into her more heavily. His chest smashed her breasts, and she gasped at the delicious sensation. She'd never needed to be dominated, but, God, it was exciting to be with a man who could do it. The fact that his fingers didn't hurt her wrists, and his muscular thigh only provoked zinging shafts of pleasure low in her belly was further provocation to her abrupt and overpowering reaction to him.

And then his mouth swooped down, capturing hers. It wasn't a violent kiss, but it was a demanding one. His whole body came into play, his arms sweeping around her, his flat, hard belly plastered to hers, his long legs planted against hers. How her arms ended up wrapped around his broad shoulders, her fingers tangled in the short hair at the back of his neck, her tongue inside his mouth, she had no idea. But she knew if she didn't devour him first, he'd surely devour her.

He lifted her off the floor, sliding her up the wall to fit against him more closely. His head slanted down and he all but inhaled her. Lust erupted like Mount Vesuvius between them, consuming them both like a raging river of lava, destroying everything in its path. His mouth was hot on her neck, his hands hotter as they slid up under her T-shirt against her bare flesh. His body singed her fingers as she returned the favor and practically tore his shirt off in her haste to feel his naked skin.

"Sweet Jesus, but you're a tiger. Where have you been all my life?" he gasped against her shoulder.

"Hunting for you," she gasped back, already reeling with the power of the explosion building inside her. He grabbed her rear end and dragged her tight against the hard length of him, and she detonated like an entire battery of rockets. Lights burst behind her eyelids and pleasure ripped through her. She stumbled forward, turning with him as they pivoted toward the bed. They fell onto it ungracefully and she laughed at the glorious tangle of their limbs. Desperation to have him inside her coursed through her. She surged up against him, and he met her advance with a counteroffensive of his own. She reached for his belt and lurched as his hands abruptly grabbed her wrists in a viselike grip that forcibly stilled her.

"What the fuck are we doing?" he panted. "We've got to stop this. Now."

She froze. And stared up at him uncomprehending. *C'mon, brain. Kick into gear, here.* But the thick cloud of lust in her head refused to clear.

He rolled away violently, flopping onto his back beside her. He flung a frustrated arm up over his face. "We can't do this. I'm your instructor, for Christ's sake. It's fraternization."

The word seared across her brain, burning off the fog of desire in an instant. Leaving only horror behind. Good God. He was *right*. She struggled up onto an elbow and stared down at him in shock. What in the bloody hell had just happened between them? They both knew better. Were both professionals. Highly disciplined. In control at all times. *Never* indulged in ill-advised peccadilloes. She knew that about him without even having to ask. In the two months she'd lived with the man, day and night, he'd never once come close to crossing the line. But Mother of God, they'd blown the line right off the map tonight.

She staggered to her feet. Took two stumbling steps back. "I'd better go," she mumbled.

He looked up at her, his eyes glazed with self-recrimination. "Christ, I'm sorry. My fault," he said bleakly.

She glared down at him. "Don't go playing martyred hero on me and take all the blame. It took two to tango. I'm every bit as responsible as you. And I'm sorry, too. I swear, I won't let it happen again. And I know you won't, either. This stays just between us. Consider it forgotten," she babbled in her mortification.

He nodded tersely. Swallowed hard.

And somehow, she managed to turn and force her feet to walk out of that room. Into the loud, dark, enveloping night outside. She paused on his porch to collect herself. To recover her breathing to something resembling normal. And a galvanizing realization hit her like a Mack truck. *She'd lied.* There was no way she could *ever* forget what had just happened between them.

*November 1*
*Al-Khibri, Bhoukar*

Defoe inched down the slope underneath his ghillie net. After a long night wildly celebrating their victory, the remaining members of the Army of Holy War had retreated into their caves to sleep off the party. But that left him and his team moving during the hottest part of the day.

They'd been moving for two hours and had managed to creep barely a hundred yards. He'd just drunk the last of his water, and at this rate, it could be a good twenty-four hours before he scored any more. Headache city, here he came. Of course, this whole damned mission was one giant headache. He never wanted to see another hunk of red sandstone for as long as he lived.

"Looks good, boss," Jensen reported. The medic, on point, had reached the top of the next ridge.

"Are we clear to move on foot to your position?" Defoe asked.

"Yup. Clear to proceed."

Praise the Lord. He stood up slowly, unwinding the kinks in his back, and climbed the ridge in a running crouch, his ghillie net still draped over his back. He dropped to the ground beside Jensen. One by one the others joined them. He stared at the Army of Holy War cave complex through his field glasses for a good long time. The only things moving between the team and the caves were waves of heat, rising off the valley floor, obscuring the view like sheets of wavering water.

He was tired of this game. He wanted a drink, he wanted shade, he wanted to report in to HQ, and then he wanted to get the fuck out of this place. "Let's follow this ridge south a mile or so and swing east around the Tangos. Then we cut a straight trail to Shangri La." A good nickname for their secret cave. Cool shade and water sounded like paradise on Earth.

"All of us?" Ginelli asked in surprise.

"Yeah. We've seen enough. I dunno 'bout you, but I've had about all the fun I care to out here. The politicians can figure out what to do about this mess."

The other guys nodded their fervent agreement. They eased down off the ridgeline and spread out in a covert march formation. Defoe took point. He checked himself when he began to rush. No time to screw up now. They were almost out of here. If they made good time, they could be home for Thanksgiving. *Slow down. Stay sharp*. He took a careful look around and announced quietly over his throat mike, "Let's move out."

*November 2*
*Fort Bragg*

Vanessa plastered her face against the dirt as another rocket-propelled grenade screamed overhead. Lord, the live-fire obstacle course was a good show. She'd never seen so much stuff blow up so close or so *loud* in her life. And she was the kid who always crowded up front at fireworks displays. The adrenaline of crawling under live fire was incredible. The trick was to stay low and not do anything unpredictable. Not with gunners raking fire across the course.

She could physically feel Jack's eyes on her. Ever since that blazing kiss, she'd been almost psychic about him. Being hyperaware of him like this was getting downright spooky. Like she was turning into some sort of obsessed stalker. She anticipated his thoughts, his words, even his decisions, almost before they happened.

Boom!

And if she didn't keep her mind on business, she was going to get herself or someone else killed. Berating herself for yet another slip in concentration, she yanked her thoughts back to the task at hand—slogging through this muddy, mine-infested, trip-wired, trapped, bitch of a course.

"Up the wall, gang," she shouted over the scream of what sounded like a jet engine. She grabbed a rope and levered herself up the fifteen-foot-high structure, walking her feet up the slippery surface. She straddled the top, waiting for everyone to make it before she slid down the far side and fell to the ground, rolling to absorb the impact.

They leapfrogged past one another, whoever was in the lead waiting until everyone else had cleared an obstacle before falling in at the end of the line. It slowed them some, but insured that everyone made it through the course. Finally Vanessa staggered to her feet, muddy and exhausted, and flung herself across the finish line.

Jack stood there, stopwatch in hand. His uniform was pristine, the look on his face disapproving. Breathing like a race-horse, she waited for the verdict. "The men do this course in a maximum of fourteen minutes. You just managed to cruise through it in seventeen and a half. Not even close, Blake."

Crap. She bent over, grabbing at her trousers, panting for air. She hurt from head to foot. Three and a half minutes to make up? She cast her exhausted mind back through the course. Where had she lost that much time? Where to find the extra seconds?

It boiled down to strength. They just weren't as buff as the men. They couldn't power up the walls or through the end-less low crawls, which relied solely on upper body strength for dragging the rest of the body through. She'd never pre-tended that the women could match the guys, but this glaring demonstration of deficiency in that area was depressing.

Misty walked over to her, breathing hard for once. "What if we tag-teamed the low crawling? Pushed off each other's shoulders with our legs as we go through it? We could boost each other up the walls, too. Leave Katrina for last, then we could pull her over because she's so light. We send Aleesha ahead in that middle section to mark the trip wires while you and Karen muscle that damn log through the tunnel."

Vanessa nodded. It could work. It would take split-second timing and perfect coordination, but they might be able to outsmart the course. But first she had to rest. The whole team had to rest. She walked over to Jack, forcing back a grimace of pain. Her shoulder felt like she'd wrenched it half out of the socket with that jump from the last wall.

He turned from where he was conferring with a half dozen other instructors. "What do you want, Blake?" he snapped.

"We'd like to try it again."

"Now?"

At least she'd managed to surprise him. The guys behind him momentarily looked startled, too, before they lapsed into their usual looks of disdain. "Actually, we could use a few minutes to catch our breath. But, yeah. Tonight."

He stared at her, his eyes hard. And then he nodded. Once. He spoke over his shoulder, "You heard the lady. Let's reset the course and reload, gentlemen."

The instructors dispersed. She turned to go and then paused. Felt Jack's gaze on her. She looked back over her shoulder. "Thanks."

"Fourteen minutes, Blake."

They formed up at the starting line again. Why in the world they were voluntarily doing this thing a second time, she wasn't quite sure. But it was too late to reconsider. "Everybody clear on how we're going to do this?" she asked.

Nods all around. "Then let's do it," she said briskly.

It went like clockwork. Better than clockwork. Like brain surgery. Everyone pulled her weight and each of them did exactly what she was supposed to do. No screwups anywhere. They busted their butts from start to finish, and she couldn't

have been prouder of them if they'd run the thing in ten minutes. As one, they threw themselves across the finish line an
eternity later.

Vanessa closed her eyes briefly as Jack looked down impassively at the stopwatch.

"Fourteen minutes, fifteen seconds."

Damn. No, wait a minute. They'd just come within fifteen
seconds of making the Special Forces men's times. That was
*incredible*. They'd shaved three minutes off their time by ex-
ercising perfect teamwork. She lifted her head and threw her
shoulders back. "I don't know about the rest of you," she declared, "but I'd say that was a good day's work."

Misty blinked up at her from where she'd flopped on the
ground. "How's that?"

"We just proved the superiority of brains over brawn.
When we tried to brute force our way through the course, we
were dismally slow. But when we put our minds to it, we just
about kept up with the guys. And we were tired from the first
time through. Next time we'll make it, easy."

Everyone's shoulders abruptly squared.

"I think it's time for another name," she announced.
"Misty, step forward."

The blonde, who normally played things as cool as a cu-
cumber, actually looked nervous. Vanessa grinned at her comrade. "For reminding us that sometimes brains and cunning
are more important than sheer brawn, and for reminding us
to come at problems from the unexpected angle, I hereby dub
you Sidewinder."

The other women clustered around to congratulate their
newest inductee.

The instructors began trickling over to check out the time.
They all knew the women had been close to making it. And
if she wasn't mistaken, there were a few furtive looks of respect being thrown their way. Even after Jack announced

that they'd missed the max time by fifteen seconds, Vanessa swore she caught a couple of impressed looks.

Jack formed them up for the run back to their barracks. And then he stunned Vanessa by commenting loudly enough for the other instructors to hear, "A good day's work, indeed. Spec ops is all about teamwork. And you ladies showed me tonight that you get it."

Stunned silence met his compliment. None of them knew how to react to praise from their relentless and usually merciless taskmaster.

"Let's move out," he snapped, back to his usual, irascible self. "We've got places to go and things to do."

*November 2*
*the White House*

"Sir, we have a situation."

President Stanforth leaned back in his leather chair and folded his hands across his stomach. He replied dryly, "One would surmise that's why we're all here in the Situation Room." The JSOC briefer squirmed and he took pity. "Let's hear it, son."

The army officer filled him in quickly on the observations Delta Three had made of a hundred heavily armed terrorists taking over the Al-Khibri oil field.

At the end of the briefing, Stanforth leaned back in his seat in disbelief. He glanced over at his Secretary of State. "You mean to tell me we offered to help the Bhoukaris throw these terrorists off the Al-Khibri oil field, and the emir turned us down? Why in the hell would he do that?"

The Secretary of State frowned. "United States interference in Middle Eastern events continues to be wildly unpopular among the Bhoukari, and the emir has his reputation to protect—"

Stanforth cut off the party-line recitation. "We're talking about tens of millions of dollars of revenue to these terrorists instead of to the Bhoukari government. For the emir, that translates to food in starving mouths. Medicine to sick kids, for God's sake. Why would he turn down an offer of assistance, especially when we guaranteed its secrecy?"

The Secretary of Education spoke wryly from down the table. "As secret as the last Special Forces mission to Bhoukar where the existence of one of our guys ended up splashed all over the international press?"

The Defense Secretary scowled and retorted, "They never proved his identity. It's all just rumor and speculation that Worthington's actually SF."

The Secretary of State responded sharply, "Rumor and speculation are more than enough to start wars in that part of the world."

Stanforth raised a hand, cutting off the argument. "Gentlemen. My question remains. Why would Bhoukar turn down an offer of covert assistance in booting out a group of terrorists who now control potentially the largest oil field in that country? Something doesn't add up here. We're missing a piece of the puzzle." He caught the movement out of the corner of his eye as the National Security Adviser squirmed in his seat. Good. He needed answers, and soon. The midterm elections were only days away, and like the Bhoukari emir, he couldn't afford a blowup in the Middle East right now.

*November 18*
*Fort Bragg*

Their first field op. At the moment, they were lying in a wide, grassy field, under heavy camouflage. And two enemy positions on either side of them were communicating back and forth. Their mission was to intercept the traffic and relay it to headquarters, or in this case, to Jack and a bunch of his black-shirted cronies.

Isabella wasn't one of the top cryptographers in the air

force for nothing. She made short work of finding the enemy frequency and deciphering the skip pattern they were using to jump from frequency to frequency to avoid detection. In a matter of minutes, she relayed verbatim reports of the transmissions back to Jack. He must have said something to the "enemy" positions, because abruptly Vanessa heard the chatter switch from English into complete gobbledygook. But Isabella merely grinned and continued to transmit steady streams of intel over her headset.

During a break in the transmissions Isabella murmured, her eyes twinkling, "They were speaking Farsi. Thought they were being real sneaky. Too bad my nanny was Persian."

The other women grinned back.

"Crap. They just changed the jump pattern." Isabella fiddled with the knobs on her radio and scribbled down the frequency on a piece of paper. She scanned until she caught another frequency and then a third. She smiled down at her paper and murmured to herself, "Aw, come on, guys. Challenge me a little." Louder, to the rest of the team she murmured, "Watch this." She dialed in a frequency on the radio.

All Vanessa heard for a moment was static. And then, without warning, a male voice transmitted something. Isabella had gone to the next frequency before the bad guys even got to it.

Isabella whispered, "Anyone recognize it? Sounds Asian."

Karen spoke up. "It's Japanese." She took over the translation.

After three more frequency pattern changes and four more languages—German, Romanian, Chinese and Tagalog—all successfully translated by the Medusas, Jack called out, "Okay, ladies. You've made your point. Let's call it."

Grinning, they stood up and waded through the tall grass to where the cluster of instructors stood waiting for them.

Jack said to his colleagues, "I'd say this round went to the ladies, gentlemen."

Vanessa looked at him sharply. That almost sounded like

pride in his voice. Since when had he become their unofficial advocate within the Special Forces community?

She clapped Isabella on the shoulder. "You rock, lady," she crowed. "I think that display of brains just earned you a handle. You lay in the grass all quiet, nobody notices you until you nail them, and when you strike you knock them dead. So, for our last, but certainly not least, inductee into the Medusa club, I dub you Adder."

Vanessa caught the look of acute pain that flickered across Jack's face. What was that all about? She could only pray she wasn't as open a book to him as he was to her. She caught his gaze and grinned. "Well, we're all named now. I guess that makes us officially a team."

"'Bout damn time that dawned on you," he snapped. "You've been a team since about twenty-four hours into your training. I couldn't pry you six apart if I used a crowbar."

Vanessa was arrested by his assessment. In fact, all of them stopped in their tracks at his declaration. She and her teammates stared at him for a minute, and then they all let out a cheer. The Medusas were official.

# Chapter 10

November 22
Fort Bragg

Vanessa winced as General Wittenauer snapped, "All right, Jack. This had better be good."

Why had Jack done it? Why had he called the Medusas' biggest opponent and invited him to come down to North Carolina and watch the women in action? Was Jack convinced they were good enough to make a believer out of Wittenauer, or was he attempting to hasten the end of the project so he could rejoin his team?

She couldn't blame Jack for chafing to get out in the trenches. If one of her teammates was missing in a hostile place like Bhoukar, she'd be frantic to do something to find them, too. Frankly, she was surprised he hadn't snapped under the strain. Of course, it couldn't be helping his stress level that attraction crackled and sizzled between them every time they got close to each other.

"All right, ladies. You heard the general," Jack snapped. "Let's make this good."

The six women lined up yet again at the starting line of the live-fire obstacle course. They were getting sick and tired of running the damn thing as a teamwork demonstration to every new class of recruits for every spec ops program in the land. Even today, there were two dozen ranger trainees lined up behind the general to see the show. The Medusas had long since shaved off the extra fifteen seconds they needed to make the fourteen-minute max run time on the course.

Vanessa muttered to her teammates, "All right. Let's show this male chauvinist pig why we belong here."

They nodded back at her grimly, jaws set in determination.

"On your marks. Set. Go!" Jack barked.

They ran the course almost by rote nowadays, pushing off, climbing over, boosting, and dragging one another through it like a well-oiled machine. Jack had laid off them for most of the day, and they were fresh tonight. They felt noticeably faster than usual as they flew through the familiar obstacles. They burst across the finish line as a group and came to a stop, breathing heavily. They'd all pushed wicked hard this time.

Every eye in the finish area riveted on Jack. He looked down at his stopwatch and announced loudly, "Twelve fifty-six."

*Yes.* Vanessa pumped her fist at her teammates. They'd finally broken the thirteen-minute mark. A few of the ranger trainees whistled under their breath.

Wittenauer scowled even more darkly and snapped, "And what'll happen when they're out in the field, getting shot at?"

Jack replied evenly, "Are you asking my opinion, sir?"

Vanessa caught the edge underlining his words. He was irritated, but concealing it very well. A person would have to know him like she did to pick it up.

"No, I'm not," the general retorted testily.

"Nonetheless, sir. I'd like to answer that question. When

the Medusas come under fire in the field, they'll do their job like any other spec ops team."

Wittenauer didn't deign to reply. He merely turned and stalked back toward his staff car, its blue, bumper-mounted four-star flags fluttering lightly.

Lord, Jack was tense. Vanessa sidled up to him. "What an asshole," she murmured.

Jack's surprised gaze jerked down to hers.

She grinned at him. "There, now you don't have to think it to yourself anymore. I said it aloud for you."

The corner of his mouth turned up wryly. "Thanks."

"Any time, boss," she replied.

"I'm not your boss," Jack snapped. "He is." He jerked his head toward the retreating general.

Now why was Jack so irritated again? Did it bug him that bad to be her instructor? Her gut said he resented the professional association standing between them, preventing them from indulging in another one of those outrageous kisses. She heartily concurred with that assessment. But there wasn't anything either one of them could do about it.

Jack said briskly, "Fall out, ladies. Head back to your barracks. And keep your noses clean the next couple days while the bas— While Wittenauer's here."

"Got it. Operation Bastard Placation in effect," Vanessa retorted jauntily.

Jack grinned reluctantly and headed off toward the staff car and its fuming occupant.

One of the obstacle-course instructors strolled over to them as they strapped on their canteens and picked up their rifles. Vanessa straightened and waited silently for the guy to speak. It wasn't often that one of the other black shirts intruded on Jack's team. "You know, he's not a bad guy."

"Who? Wittenauer?" Vanessa asked.

"Yeah. He's fought like a demon to get us more funding and more warm bodies to cover the expanded spec ops mission that got dumped on us a few years back."

"Well, bully for him," Vanessa replied tartly.

The instructor growled, "Scat laid his neck on the chopping block for you chicks by calling the general down here. The least you can do is be grateful."

She nodded, all sarcasm aside. "We are. We owe him big time."

"Just pray he didn't flush his career down the toilet. We'd hate to lose him from the unit. They don't come any better than Jack Scatalone."

She looked the instructor squarely in the eye. "I agree with you wholeheartedly. We'll do our best to cover his ass for him."

The guy nodded tersely and strode away from her.

The other women moved up beside her. Isabella asked, "What was that about?"

"The black shirts are worried that Jack nuked his career by asking Wittenauer to come see us."

Misty piped up, "He'll be okay. Those Delta guys have a way of landing on their feet."

*November 23,*
*eastern Bhoukar*

"Why in the hell are they pursuing us?" Defoe murmured to no one in particular over his throat mike. Ever since they'd bugged out of the Al-Khibri basin, someone, several someones, had been hot on their heels, tracking them through the desert.

"Dunno, boss."

"Any guesses as to who it is?" Defoe asked the team.

Ginelli answered wryly, "Three guesses and the first two don't count. Those are Army of Holy War scouts back there."

Defoe sighed. Ginelli was right. He had to be. Not another soul knew they were still out here. How the Army of Holy War had pegged their presence was anybody's guess. He only prayed the terrorists hadn't picked up their last transmission, where they reported the takeover of the Al-Khibri field and their intention to head out of the country toward the extraction point. But he knew, deep down in his gut, that was exactly what had happened. It was never a good thing when terrorist technology approached the same level of sophistication as the good guys'.

"Suppose we should circle back and nail the bastards?" he asked. He was too damn exhausted to make decisions like that on his own at this point. The whole team was beat, and they all were operating on group think. It was the only thing that had kept them—kept him—from making a couple of serious mistakes in the last few grueling days of movement through the desert. The team had countertracked the living hell out of itself, but the canny nomad bastards kept picking up their trail. He wished he knew what basic mistake they were making that allowed the terrorists to find them again and again each time Delta Three slipped away from them.

"Might not be a bad idea," Walsh replied to his suggestion to take out the terrorists.

"What do the rest of you think?" Defoe asked.

"We could sure as hell move faster if we got them off our tails," Jensen replied.

"Maybe we could get positive proof the Army of Holy War guys have infiltrated our communications technology," Spot added.

It sounded like they had a consensus in the team to circle back and kill the bastards. "Okay, then. Let's do it. We hunker down and rest through the heat of the day, and at dark, we set up an ambush."

*November 23*
*Fort Bragg*

Vanessa blinked awake, the night and the forest thick and black around her. Isabella's hand was over her mouth. Isabella indicated with quick hand signals that the recon team had returned. Vanessa nodded and eased out of her sleeping nest under a thicket of brambles to where the team was gathering.

The Medusas crouched together in the dense shadows, their black-and-green-striped faces fading eerily into the dark. If she didn't know they were right beside her, Vanessa would never have seen them. She spread out a laminated map on the ground and cupped a red flashlight, shining it on the map.

Karen pointed at a spot on the map about a quarter mile away. Eight fingers. Eight men. Another finger signal. Heavily armed patrol. Two guards posted. The rest sleeping in a circular formation. Vanessa nodded and flashed a hand signal back. Who were they? Friends or foes?

Kat flashed an emphatic signal for foe. Then she added in a whisper, "We overheard them say that when they catch us they're going to, and I quote, 'goose-step those pecker-envying bitches across the parade ground naked.'"

The women traded grim looks. Spec ops troops didn't make threats like that lightly. They could all do without such humiliation.

Karen breathed, "Our security's definitely compromised. One of our contacts today must have been a double agent."

Vanessa nodded. She'd had a funny feeling about a couple of the "freedom fighters" who'd supplied them the coordinates of their target earlier in the day. The mission was to find a chemical weapons lab, gather proof that it was, indeed, a chemical weapons facility, destroy it, and then get the proof away safely.

She had a bad feeling about this exercise. Wittenauer had without a doubt loaded the deck against them on this op. So far their pursuers had been ranger trainees who, although good, weren't flawless. But her gut said that at some point, things would change. She'd caught sight of a whole squad of black shirts drawing weapons and explosives from the armory yesterday afternoon. Exactly the kind of stuff she'd take out on a field op in heavily wooded terrain. Like the forest surrounding them now.

"I think everything our contacts told us has to be classed as suspect," Vanessa murmured. "The bastards are setting us up, all the way. I wouldn't be at all surprised if the lab's a fake."

Aleesha nodded. "My gut instinct says you're right."

Vanessa continued, "I say we eliminate the contacts so they can't report on us any further."

Nods all around.

She looked at Kat and Karen. "Were our contacts in the group you found?"

They nodded, and Kat murmured, "Both of them. We probably need to take out the whole team. I think they're all double agents."

Vanessa agreed. Better safe than sorry. She scanned the map. "If we go here and climb this ridge, we can set up an ambush for these jerks following us." Everyone nodded, but her internal alarm system twitched. "Problem is, it's too obvious a ploy. I think everyone will expect us to do that."

Karen murmured, "We know where they are now. We could just go slit their throats in their sleep, tonight."

Vanessa turned the idea over in her head. Their followers outnumbered them. But they would undoubtedly set up a sleep-watch rotation where only a couple guys were awake at any given time and the rest were down. It was an aggressive move Karen had suggested. Probably wouldn't be expected this early in the exercise. Vanessa murmured, "You realize, of course, that when we take out the amateurs, Wittenauer's going to bring in the big guns. We're going to have a Delta team on our tails the minute we take out the trainees."

Misty grinned. "Bring 'em on."

The other women shrugged equally unconcernedly. Well, she certainly couldn't fault her team's confidence.

"Okay, then. Everybody gear up. This is going to have to

be silent all the way. Here's how we'll do it." She mapped out their approach to the enemy position and designated who would take out whom. Nobody had any questions when she was done explaining it.

"Let's go kill us some bad guys," she murmured.

*November 23,*
*eastern Bhoukar*

Defoe sent Spot wide around the enemy position. He had the best eyes on the team, and he'd verify that the four terrorists were otherwise alone before they made their strike on the bastards. Walsh would take out the terrorist's radio, and Spot, Ginelli, Jensen and he would each take out one of the remaining Tangos. If this was, in fact, an isolated scouting patrol, speed would be more important than silence. The idea would be to kill these guys before they could get off a distress call to anyone.

Defoe stared down at the terrorists' crude camp. These guys might look like simple goatherds, but he in no way underestimated their skill. Anyone who could carve out a life for themselves in this harsh environment was a tough customer deserving of respect.

Spot murmured, "All clear beyond the ridge. Nothing but rocks out there."

Excellent. Defoe keyed his throat mike one last time. "Let's roll."

He slithered forward, inching his way across the ground silently. He was never going to complain about jungle ops again as long as he lived. At least there was some freaking cover in a jungle. This business of living on his elbows to avoid showing a silhouette against the open landscape was for the birds.

It took them a solid hour to move down the ridge and fan out into position all around the camp. Walsh indicated with a hand signal that he had eyes on the scout party's radio. Defoe waved him forward. They'd let Walsh get right on top of the radio before the rest of them struck. He watched Walsh's progress over the next half hour. If he took his eyes off the guy for more than a few seconds, he had a hard time picking him up again when he looked back. A brief moment of pride surged in Defoe's chest for his men. Although he supposed Jack Scatalone should get the credit for training them all.

Why in the hell these bastards hadn't set out a watch mystified him. Unless…shit. Unless one or more of the terrorists were faking being asleep and were just lying there silently, listening to the night sounds. It was a Delta technique to use ears, rather than eyes, on the watch. Defoe tuned in to the night chorus more closely.

So far, so good. The crickets and various insect buzzes and hums sounded right. Dammit. So much for speed. They'd need to move like glaciers not to disturb the noisy little critters of the night. He signaled the change in approach to Ginelli, who was on his immediate right. Ginelli relayed the signal to Jensen. Defoe gave the signal a few minutes to make its way to everyone on the team. He took a deep breath and released it slowly. *Patience, buddy.* Their success and survival tonight was all about patience.

*November 23*
*Fort Bragg*

Vanessa eased a few inches forward. The guy standing watch in front of her shifted slightly and then settled back into quiet. It had taken them almost four hours to move into position around this team. The guards were alert and wouldn't be easy to sneak up on. Then, there'd been a shift change. That had been a boon for the Medusas. While the guards were busy exchanging hand signals and shifting positions, her team had spurted forward the last dozen yards and moved into its final position.

Now she was waiting out the guard. Letting the guy in

front of her get bored. A little tired and dull. No sense taking the guy on at full speed. She'd been sitting here almost an hour. The guy's eyes weren't drooping in the least, but the tension around his shoulders had eased off in the last few minutes. He was relaxing a little. Vanessa eased a few more inches forward. She was approaching the guard from his left side and slightly behind him. It meant slipping between the guard and the guy sleeping next to him in the formation. Space to operate was a little tight, but if she was quiet enough, the close quarters shouldn't matter.

And then the guard in front of her moved. She froze in place, doing that Zen thing Jack had taught her—pulling in her energy to stop projecting her presence. What in the hell was the guy doing? He was standing up! He rose to his feet slowly in front of her. He was either too tired to stay awake on his belly or he had a severe leg cramp. More like a brain cramp.

As he continued to move toward vertical, she mirrored his motion, moving upward behind him as well. She happened to have a clump of bushes between her and the other members of the guy's patrol, so she had cover at her back. Her target leaned against a tree and bent over to massage his calf. He was about to learn a hard lesson about taking the pain and keeping his butt on the ground where it belonged.

She eased forward the last step and leaped on him silently. She covered his mouth with her left hand and put her razor-sharp field knife against his neck. The guy froze in shock.

"You're dead," she breathed in his ear. "I just slit your throat."

The jerk unlocked his knees without warning and dropped toward the ground. *Bastard!* Good thing she already had both arms around him. She managed to catch him and break what would have been a noisy fall. She eased two hundred pounds of pissed-off ranger to the ground. He glared up at her as she stepped over him. She gave him a sharp hand signal to stay put and stay quiet. He nodded fractionally, his eyes glittering slits of irritation. *Get over it, buddy. I only capitalized on your mistake.*

She eased back down to the forest floor and crept forward on her belly. Now for the guy sleeping beside the guard. Her next victim didn't appear to have been disturbed by the faint sound of the guard dropping. She gave it ten minutes anyway, just to be safe. Patience was the name of the game. When the guy finally shifted slightly, a natural movement of someone sleeping soundly, she eased forward.

He was equally shocked to wake up to her hand plastered over his mouth and her blade to his neck. He looked more chagrined than pissed off, though, and nodded meekly at her signal not to move or make any sound. She noticed slow movements from all around her. Her team looked like a half-dozen shadows flowing silently toward the center of the clearing. She signaled for a head count of bad guys taken out.

Six, plus her two made eight. The patrol had been eliminated. She held up two fingers then made a slashing motion across her throat to indicate her two kills, then signaled them all to sweep the area for any stragglers they might have missed. Silently, they eased back out into the blackness of the forest.

*November 23,*
*eastern Bhoukar*

It took nearly an hour to move that last fifty yards. Inch by painful inch, Defoe worked his way forward, his ghillie net secured to his back like a turtle shell. And finally they were inside the camp. He peered over a backpack at the guy using the other end of the rucksack as a pillow. Sleeping eyes either moved back and forth beneath the eyelids or twitched slightly in place. This guy's eyeballs were perfectly still. Yup, the bastard was awake.

Where were the guy's hands? Defoe raised himself up a few more millimeters to check. Hidden underneath a blanket. He couldn't make out the bulge of a rifle. Probably holding a knife, then.

He eased his own knife out of his teeth and into his right hand. The cloth grip fit perfectly in his palm. He'd have to go for a throat shot. Straight through the larynx to keep this guy from shouting out a warning. Defoe moved his eyes slowly, casting them around the camp. Everyone should be in place by now. They'd go on his signal. Tonight that signal would be him lunging forward and skewering his target.

And then his target moved. Got up on his knees. Defoe froze in place. He eased the knife blade an inch to the side, sliding it underneath a layer of sand. The target muttered something to himself and fumbled at some sort of tie at his waist. Christ. The guy was going to take a leak.

Defoe closed his eyes as the stream splashed not a foot from his face. He'd swear he felt a few droplets against his cheek. The acrid smell of urine filled his nostrils. Perfect. The smell of it would camouflage the scent of blood when he killed the guy. Might buy the rest of the team a few extra seconds to make their own kills.

And then the guy flopped back down onto his back, pulling the blanket over himself with a knife in his right hand. The target rolled onto his side, and it was the last thing he ever did. Defoe lunged up silently, landing on the side of the guy's head with his knee as he slammed his blade into the guy's throat. A single, surprised gurgle, and the guy went still. A good, clean kill.

There was a sudden movement not far from him, and Defoe yanked his knife clear, spinning to face the new threat. It was Jensen, signaling the all clear. Everyone had successfully made his kill. He looked around for Walsh, who crouched beside the dead radio.

His radio operator motioned him over. He stood up and moved quickly to Walsh's side. And looked down to see what had put that look of disgust on his man's face. *Son of a bitch.*

The terrorists had a state-of-the-art, U.S. Army issue field radio. Complete with encryption and frequency scrambling capabilities. How in the *hell* did they get hold of that?

*November 23*
*Fort Bragg*

Vanessa looked around the clearing at their eight hostages. They'd bound and gagged the guys just to be sure none of them decided to be spoilsports and send up an alarm. Given the glares a couple of the guys were throwing at them as they searched the men's gear, it had been a good call.

"I got something, Viper," Isabella called out low.

Vanessa walked over to see what the woman had found. A one-time use code pad. And a list of radio frequencies with times noted beside them. A couple of the times had asterisks scribbled beside them. She'd lay odds those were scheduled report in times for this team. Next one was at six a.m.

Vanessa grinned widely. Bingo. The odds had just been evened up in their game of cat and mouse with Wittenauer. "Let's grab their radio," she murmured to Isabella. The woman glided away into the dark to fetch the piece of equipment.

The Medusas drank their fill of the men's water and supplemented their sparse food rations with the rangers'. They also took extra ammo and the team's Claymore mines, which the Medusas hadn't been issued for this op. Extra go-boom potential never hurt.

"Okay, let's secure these guys and get out of here," Vanessa ordered quietly. The Medusas tied each of the rangers to a separate tree, well away from their comrades. Vanessa stood back to survey their work, and her skin crawled at the hell to pay gleaming in the team leader's eyes.

"Take their boots," she ordered her team in quick decision.

The rangers struggled, but it was an easy matter to wrestle off their footwear. The Medusas tied the laces together and slung the combat boots over their shoulders. Now, she felt better. She gave her team the order to form up and move out. Karen disappeared into the forest on point. Aleesha fell in behind her, followed by the others in single file. When Vanessa was the last one left standing in the clearing, she flashed a grin at the rangers. "It's been a pleasure doing business with you, gentlemen," she murmured. And then she, too, bugged out of there.

*Damn, that was fun!* On a real op, she'd be worried about the patrol getting loose, calculating how long it would take them to hike in their socks to somewhere they could call in reinforcements, estimating about how wide a net would be cast for them after they'd shown themselves like that. But this was just training and she could afford to enjoy the rush of embarrassing the hell out of a bunch of rangers.

Precisely at six a.m., Vanessa called a stop. Isabella cranked up the captured radio and encoded a morning report using the one-time pad. "Quiet night. Targets camped two clicks east-northeast of our position, coordinates to follow. Stop."

Almost immediately, a reply came back. Isabella copied down the fast Morse message. Vanessa was good at Morse code, but Isabella was a goddess with it. Vanessa waited impatiently while Isabella ran the letters through the one-time pad, chortling as the message unfolded.

"Well?" Vanessa demanded.

"It says, 'Keep driving the sheep toward the corral.'"

"Sheep, eh?" Vanessa commented. "Maybe we should show them we're wolves under all that soft, cute fleece." She looked at her radio operator. "Acknowledge the instruction and ask for any further directions."

She waited impatiently while the message and reply were encoded, transmitted and decoded.

Isabella looked up, less amused this time. "It says, 'Don't

let the bitches catch you. Wittenauer's breathing fire to see them taken down.'"

Vanessa's jaw tightened all of a sudden. "By all means, let's not get caught. Let's look at that map again. I'll be damned if I'm going to stroll into their 'corral' for the slaughter."

The location of the supposed chemical lab was suspect at best. It was tucked up against the base of a steep ridge, a cliff, really. A river ran parallel to the ridge, creating a narrow land corridor with limited approaches to—or exits from—the lab. Vanessa ran her finger down a red line drawn on the map. "They expect us to approach the lab by paralleling this road down this corridor of trees. What say we cross the river and run up along this ridgeline instead? We'll drop down the cliff face from the opposite direction, here. And for God's sake, we're not going in at four o'clock in the afternoon like the contact said. More like four a.m., I'd say."

Misty frowned. "Night climb down a cliff could be dicey."

Vanessa grinned at her. "That's why we're Medusas."

Misty grinned back. "Let's do it."

# Chapter 11

November 25, 2:00 a.m.
Fort Bragg

Vanessa stared over the edge of the hundred-foot vertical drop. She gave her climbing harness one last tug and then stepped off the precipice. A person did have to ask herself why she was out here at two o'clock in the morning in a cold rain, climbing down a viciously slippery cliff in total darkness, for the purposes of scoping out a pretend weapons lab in a pretend hostile country, guarded by pretend bad guys. All psychobabble about connecting with her father aside, only a violently overdeveloped competitive streak could account for this insanity. Hoo-hah.

Although she let out her rappelling line quickly, she descended more slowly than usual. She had deep respect for the combination of treacherous conditions and her team's fatigue. They'd hiked nearly twenty miles in the last twelve hours, after working all night last night to knock out the ranger team. Just like Jack had taught them that very first week of training in Colorado: Do something the other guys think is physically impossible, and you buy yourself time and the element of surprise. Since the folks running against them knew they were women, she was counting on them to underestimate her team's physical capabilities. By her calculations, the bad guys wouldn't expect them to show up at this spot for another day at least.

She jerked her attention back to the task at hand. This was no time to be daydreaming. She assessed the conditions for the climb back up the cliff as she went. There was plenty of loose shale to knock off with a misplaced foot. And her team was going to be tired long before they finished hauling themselves up this cliff. Good call to leave Karen and Misty behind to manage the ropes from above and help pull up anyone who ran out of strength. Isabella and Kat would provide cover and eyes outside the building, and she and Aleesha would run the gauntlet of traps and tricks she was certain awaited them around and inside the supposed weapons lab.

The ground came into sight below, a vague black wetness between her feet. One last release and grab of the rope sliding up her back, and her feet touched down. She signaled Kat and Isabella to fan out. They unslung their rifles and melted into the dreary night. She nodded at Aleesha, and they headed for the low, wooden building some fifty feet in front of them.

Each step was an exercise in controlling her nerves. Trip wires, faint depressions in the ground to indicate mines, infrared sensor beams all awaited them as they moved forward cautiously. Aleesha took the lead as they neared the building. She pointed out two probable land mines to Vanessa, who nodded and stepped over them. Not three steps later, Vanessa tugged sharply on her teammate's shirt, halting her in midstride. Aleesha looked over her shoulder questioningly, her foot suspended in midair. Vanessa pointed out a vertical metal spike, maybe two inches tall, that Aleesha's foot would have landed on had she stepped down. A third land mine. The doctor nodded and stepped over the device.

They stepped over six trip wires and ducked under a couple more. As they'd expected, the entire building was one giant trap. But after nearly thirty minutes of work to cover the fifty feet, they stood outside a dirty glass window, peering inside. No sign whatsoever of a chemical lab. There were, however, a couple chairs, some rope, manacles, brass knuckles and car batteries. *A prisoner facility.* This had all been an elaborate setup to begin their POW training.

Vanessa signaled Aleesha to take some pictures of the bare interior. Her teammate pulled out a silent shutter camera loaded with infrared film. She took several shots of the space, then bent to photograph underneath the building, no doubt to show that the pier-and-beam structure concealed no secret underground facility.

Aleesha froze, bent over. And gestured for Vanessa to have a look. She bent slowly. The entire underside of the floor was wired with explosives. Of course, this was a training scenario, and the blocks of C-4 were no more than rubber marked to simulate the plastic explosive. But it was still a daunting sight. A trap, indeed. A death trap. Vanessa signaled Aleesha to take a picture of their intended fate.

Pictures done, Vanessa reached into her backpack and pulled out the two Claymore mines they'd stolen from the rangers. She handed one to Aleesha and pointed to the far corner of the building. She took her own Claymore and gestured that she'd head for the opposite corner.

Aleesha touched her sleeve. She breathed, "These will blow up the building."

Vanessa shrugged. She was more than a little annoyed at Wittenauer, who had tried to yank their chains on this op, and at Jack, who hadn't given them any warning about the scenario they were walking into. It was standard procedure to notify trainees when they were about to go into their resistance-and-escape training. The very real Claymores would send both men a message about jacking around with the Medusas. She murmured, "A realistic response to realistic training."

Aleesha grinned and threw her a mock salute. Then she turned to set her mine. Vanessa eased step by painfully slow step toward the opposite end of the building. She paused twice, feeling the gentle pressure of a trip wire against her shin. Both times she eased her foot back before she snapped the thin wire. The rain came down heavily, running off the roof in a cold, soaking sheet of water that drenched her to the skin. But it was a boon in that it partially collapsed the freshly dug spots where mines had been buried. They were a piece of cake to spot in this kind of weather.

Taking no chances, she stopped shy of the end of the building and pulled out her folding periscope. She took a peek around the end of the building before she stepped out from behind its shadow. And was darn glad she had. A pair of ponchoed soldiers sat under a tarp stretched between two trees, not twenty feet from her. Well then, this corner of the building would have to do for the mine. Given the aged wood of the structure, it should go up in flames nicely, regardless of where the explosions lit off.

She crouched and eased the Claymore behind the foot-tall concrete piling. No sense killing the poor schmucks pulling guard duty. The piling would shield them from the direct force of the blast. Very gently, she pushed down the switch that activated it. And lifted her hand away gingerly. She backed away from the corner, fluffing flattened leaves, and using a stick to remove her footsteps. Dodging the traps was *fun* while moving backward. But that's why they got the big bucks. Yeah, right. A couple hundred bucks a month in hazardous duty pay added to their measly government paychecks. At least they got to blow up stuff.

Eventually, she felt Aleesha's presence approaching. She exchanged a quick thumbs-up with her teammate. The egress away from the back of the building was dicey in the downpour, made more so by the knowledge that even a "training charge" explosion might be enough to set off one of the real Claymores behind them.

But finally they reached the base of the cliff. Isabella and Kat eased up beside them. Kat indicated the two guards that Vanessa had seen by the building, but neither woman had seen any more. Two clicks on her throat radio, and four ropes came snaking down the face of the cliff. A hundred feet up in total silence, and they'd be clear.

*November 25, 5:00 a.m.*
*Bhoukar*

Defoe and his men buried the bodies in shallow graves. They didn't need a flock of circling vultures to point out their position to anyone else who might be out there. Walsh reclaimed Uncle Sam's radio from the terrorists and added it to their own gear. Oman, here they came. At top speed. Now that they'd taken care of their pursuers for good, they could beat feet out of this damned wasteland. They liberated the terrorists' water as well. It was stored in skin sacks that made it taste like warm goat piss, but it was water. And the skins, slung across their backs, were surprisingly easy to carry.

They made good time the rest of the night and into the next morning. Defoe called a stop at noon, when the sand and the air really began to heat up. They dug holes and stretched tarps across them for shade. They'd rest through the worst heat of the day. He took the first shift alone so the others guys could catch some z's before it got too hot.

A couple more days of movement like last night's would see them across the border. Damn, he was ready for something to go smoothly for once on this mission.

They humped hard all the next night, too, but they stopped earlier the following morning. They were getting low on water again. Defoe deployed the solar water collectors—big plastic tarps stretched over deep, freshly dug holes in the sand. They worked on the principle of capturing the humidity trapped in the hole as condensation that formed on the plastic sheet. He eyed the sky warily. He didn't like that pink-brown cast to the sky on the western horizon. Good Lord willing and the creek don't rise, that was just a weather front passing through, kicking up some sand, and not a full-blown sandstorm cooking.

*November 25*
*a hospital in Bhoukar*

Scott opened his eyes as a nurse sidled into his room. She looked over her shoulder furtively as she delivered a plate of boiled chicken and rice. He was sick of the bland food, but it was probably as good as the fare the hospital staff got. He sat up in bed as best he could with his hands manacled to the bed frame.

The nurse fed him his breakfast, and he murmured his thanks as usual. She smiled back at him, but the expression didn't penetrate the fear in her eyes. And then she did a strange thing. She pulled a pencil out of her robe and scribbled something on the paper napkin she'd brought in with his meal. He looked at the writing and frowned. It was in the Latin alphabet. N2O2SNA.

What the hell was that? He looked up at the woman and started to ask when the hallway door opened. Good ol' Akbar stepped into the room. She balled up the napkin and threw it on top of his plate. Silently, she took the plate away and exited.

N2O2SNA? He repeated the sequence to himself. A phone number? A zip code? He repeated it again. And then it hit him. It was a scientific notation. Christ. He lurched against his restraints. That was the chemical formula for sodium pentathol.

His brain went into high gear. Given in the proper dosage, the drug reduced inhibitions. Made a person willing to talk about things they might not otherwise admit. The nurse was warning him that Akbar was planning to use it on him!

He had to plant some image in his mind before he was hit with the drugs. Something to fixate on. Not Delta Three, but something close enough to it he'd mess up Akbar. He thought fast.

*Got it.* He envisioned the weekend trip he and his dad made when he was fourteen to a national paintball tournament. Perfect. If he slipped and said something of military significance, Akbar would think it was all part of the paintball game. Frantically, he recalled details of that weekend as Akbar's hand, holding a syringe full of amber liquid, reached for his IV.

*November 25, 6:00 a.m.*
*Fort Bragg*

As morning broke, gray and wet around them, Vanessa and the others lay on their bellies atop the cliff, peering down at their handiwork through binoculars. "We have to wait until those two soldiers move off before we blow the building. I don't want to kill anyone," she murmured. "Yet."

Misty murmured back, "If that were Wittenauer sitting there, that building would be a fireball right about now."

She grinned back at her teammate. "I can neither confirm nor deny that statement," she declared under her breath.

"Movement, Viper," Isabella announced. "Jeep coming down the road. Looks like replacement guards for our soggy pair."

"Everyone, look sharp," Vanessa bit out. "Cobra, get ready."

Kat nodded over the telescopic sight of her long-barreled sniper rifle and then settled into a nearly catatonic state behind her weapon. Talk about Zen. Vanessa envied the utter stillness she could settle into at a moment's notice. The army'd made a huge mistake keeping her out of the sniper corps. Their loss. The Medusas' gain.

The sniper reached up and rolled the condom off the end of her rifle barrel. Vanessa grinned. When Jack had passed out the foil packets marked with an army supply code and the words, 'Protector, Rifle Barrel, Rubber' they'd ribbed him pretty good over it. He'd actually blushed. But the suckers worked great for keeping sand or water out of a rifle. And you could actually fire a bullet right through the latex if you needed to.

"Jesus, that's Scatalone," Isabella whispered.

Vanessa's attention yanked back to the situation at hand. She trained her binoculars on the three men climbing out of the vehicle. She couldn't make out the men's faces, but she didn't have to. She recognized the set of his shoulders, the aggressive grace of his walk, the sheer presence of the man.

The night watch soldiers stepped out from under their tarp. A few more feet toward the jeep, boys. "On my call, Kat, shoot the Claymores."

"Roger. On your call," her sniper breathed.

Jack gestured toward the back of the jeep. All four men stepped toward the vehicle. Perfect. The tough jeep would provide an extra margin of protection from the blast.

There. The men put the jeep between themselves and the building.

"Now," she ordered sharply.

Vanessa saw Jack flinch as the first shot rang out. He was already diving for the ground when the Claymore blew. Good reflexes, there, Tonto. In a flash of blinding light, wood flew high up into the sky along with a whoosh of orange flames.

The metallic ping of the second shot as Kat took out the second Claymore was inaudible over the roar of the fire sucking air. So much for one training building. She saw Jack look around, scanning the trees quickly. And then his eyes traveled up the cliff face as he calculated the direction the shots had come from.

"Everyone freeze," Vanessa ordered. She counted the long seconds as Jack scanned the ridge they lay on. Finally his gaze slid away as one of the other soldiers said something to him.

"Back up, ladies." Vanessa slid backward on her belly, scouring red mud into her clothes. Ah well, all the better for camouflage. It reminded her of the first day she'd met Jack, a lifetime ago. A little less than four months.

She signaled them to their feet and led them away from the area. Fast. If she knew anything about Jack Scatalone, he'd be up on that ridge as soon as he could pull a team together. And with pissed-off Deltas, that would take only a matter of minutes. Isabella countertracked for the team. That girl had eyesight for details that wouldn't quit. And it was a huge benefit when it came to erasing every last sign of their passage.

They all but ran out of the area. Vanessa put a good four miles behind them before she even stopped to look at the map. They were on the far side of the air force base from the cluster of training buildings near their barracks where they were supposed to bring their photos of the "chemical lab." But then she had an idea. An inspiration, actually.

"Instead of heading back toward the training headquarters, what say we pay General Wittenauer a little visit in his room? Tonight. Late."

The whole team grinned widely. It lent an extra spring to their steps as they humped hard throughout the day. They'd been on the go almost nonstop for three days now, but Vanessa was hardly aware of it. Funny how a person's perception of fatigue could change. They swung wide around the edge of the training area, way beyond the likely perimeter of any search Jack might mount for them. It nearly doubled the distance they had to travel, but it was worth it. She couldn't wait to see the general's face when they woke him up tonight, Medusa-style.

Of course, maybe they should let the guy sleep. And just

steal his pants—all of them—and then leave. Or maybe they should take him hostage and goose-step *him* across the parade ground naked. As exhaustion began to pull at the edges of her consciousness, she kept herself alert by thinking up more dastardly stunts to pull on Wittenauer.

They made it to the clustered buildings of the main army post by nightfall, and all of them were able to get a couple hours' sleep. At midnight Vanessa woke the team. It was an easy matter to hot-wire a van and drive, as pretty as you please, into the VOQ—Visiting Officer's Quarters—parking lot. Karen, who'd procured the vehicle, turned off the engine and the lights. They slid down low in their seats and watched the parking lot for a half hour before Vanessa declared it clear. Fatigue had to be making her paranoid, because she'd swear Jack was nearby if she didn't know better. It was almost as if she could smell him on the air. Sheesh. She was losing her marbles.

"Okay, let's do it," she murmured.

Tall, buxom, blond Misty was elected to find out which room the general was in. She borrowed tiny Katrina's T-shirt and shrugged into the small garment. Then, wiggling underneath it, she unsnapped her bra and pulled it out the left sleeve. The effect was startling. "Damn, girlfriend," Vanessa murmured, "You could've made a fortune as a stripper with those things."

The tanned blonde tugged the shirt down farther over her prodigious chest and grinned back. "How's that line go? Yeah, but then I wouldn't get to blow up shit."

Vanessa retorted, "You're gonna blow the night clerk's mind in that getup."

Misty pulled her camo pants low on her hips, exposing a line of flat stomach. She slung her utility belt low on her hips, with manacles and a length of rope conveniently peeking out of its pouches. Next, she took her hair down out of its customary French braid and fingered it out into loose, sexy waves around her shoulders. Last, she bit her lips and pinched her cheeks, laughing ruefully, "Who'd have guessed I'd need mascara on a field op. I'll have to add it to my minimum equipment list."

Karen grumbled, "I'm not turning into a Bond girl, and that's final."

Everyone laughed quietly at that one.

Vanessa said lightly, "Okay, Misty, you've got five minutes to find out what room Wittenauer's in, or we're going to do it the old-fashioned way. By looking in the windows."

Misty gave a little shimmy that set strategic parts of her jiggling in the most fantastic way. "I'll only need two minutes. A minute fifty-five for the desk clerk to drool and five seconds to find out what I need to know."

Aleesha piped up. "I've got ten bucks that says you can't do it in two minutes."

Misty shook her head. "I am, of course, honor bound to accept that bet in the name of all the other nonsilicone breasts in the world."

Aleesha eyed her comrade's chest narrowly. "You're not saying those things are real, are you? Damn. They're practically miracles of genetic selection."

Chuckling, Vanessa intervened. "Get out of here, Misty. And the clock's running."

One minute, twenty-two seconds later, Misty was back. And about one minute ten of that had been spent walking to and from the check-in counter. She opened the door to the van and slid into the front seat in disgust. "Female clerk," she grumbled.

Vanessa grinned widely. "Too bad you didn't get to work out the girls. Did you at least get the room number?"

"Yeah. Suite A. First one on the left on the far side of the building. Ground floor."

It was almost too easy. They could pop the window lock and be in the general's room in a matter of seconds. Except something didn't sit right with Vanessa about this one. Sheesh. She really *was* starting to get paranoid. Nonetheless, she climbed out of the van. They stuck to the dark shadows, employing urban stealth techniques to make their way around the main VOQ building. They ducked low under windows, spun fast past doorways, and stuck to shrubbery and shadows for cover.

The rest of the team looked at her funny when she stopped under Wittenauer's window and pulled out her periscope. It was just a hotel room, for God's sake. Except she couldn't shake that bad feeling. She eased the scope's end up over the sill and had a slow look around the room. God, she needed a pair of night-vision goggles right about now. Those hadn't been issued to the team for this op. She made out the shape of a body sleeping in Wittenauer's bed. And she could see most of the room clearly, except for one corner shrouded in black shadows. She observed it for a long time. Long enough to feel impatience start to build up in her team. Tough. She was listening to her gut on this one. And something was wrong.

She pictured Wittenauer's build and had another look at the blanket-covered form on the bed. The general was in excellent physical condition, but he wasn't as thin or as tall as the person lying on his bed. The mattress was either in terrible shape and had swallowed a third of the general's midsection, or that wasn't Wittenauer lying there. She let her senses flow outward, trying to sense the trap. She didn't like that dark corner to the right of the window, either. Something or someone lurked over that way.

Two hostiles. One in the corner and one impersonating the general in his bed. She signaled the information to her team, who stared at her for a moment in disbelief, and then absorbed the new information and adapted. Stealth wasn't going to work in this scenario. Surprise would be their best weapon. They'd burst in all at once. Three of them jump whoever was hiding in the corner, two would land on whoever was lying in the bed, and one would use a gun to take out anyone hiding behind the bed.

She communicated her plan to the others with hand signals and a drawing in the dirt. They nodded their understanding.

Now for the window. If this were a real op, she'd just bust through it. But this was the VIP suite at Fort Bragg's VOQ. Aw, what the heck. They'd already blown up an entire building today. What was one more window? She eased a tarp out of her bag and wrapped its end around her forearm. The bulk of the tarp she folded into a pad over her right shoulder. All set.

She nodded a countdown to her team, who clustered behind her.

And then all hell broke loose. She dived through the window with a tremendous crack of splintering wood and shattering glass. She rolled and popped up onto her feet, and took a running leap for the bed. The person in the bed started to roll to the far side, but only made it halfway to the edge of the king-size mattress before she landed on him, spread-eagled over his entire body.

Vanessa vaguely registered sound and motion behind her as the others burst in and subdued the man seated in the chair in the corner. But what slowed time to a stop and riveted her attention completely was the burning black gaze of Jack Scatalone glaring up at her.

Sweet Jesus, she felt every hard inch of him pressed against her from head to foot. They had to stop meeting like this. Her insides went molten, and she had an overpowering urge to flow all over him and burn the night down around them both.

Silence settled over the room as quickly as it had been disturbed. And then Jack spoke dryly, his chest rumbling beneath hers. "I told you they'd come for you, General."

She scowled down at him. Becoming predictable, was she? She moved sinuously against him and felt his whole body go tense beneath him. Uh-huh. That got his attention.

She looked over her shoulder at the general, still restrained in his chair by three of her teammates. The guy's eyes glittered in the pink halogen light coming in the window from the parking lot.

"If I might offer you a word of advice, General," Vanessa said lightly. "Next time you want to ambush and humiliate us, send a real team to do the job."

Jack's chest vibrated beneath hers with silent laughter. Her gaze jerked back to his. And for the first time, they were comrades-in-arms against a common foe. Equals.

*November 25*
*eastern Bhoukar*

They weren't lucky. Defoe and his men had just enough time before the sandstorm blew in to build themselves a low, makeshift tent from their water collection tarps. They tied down the corners as best they could and lashed a piece of canvas across the entrance, but it hardly seemed to slow down the stinging needles of sand that pelted them. They took turns banging the underside of the roof, knocking sand off their shelter to keep them from being buried alive under the accumulating drifts of grit. The wind howled around them, screaming like a banshee. And as if that wasn't bad enough, the temperature dropped precipitously. They suffered and waited throughout the day. Dark crept up gradually until blackness completely cocooned them. It was cramped in their shelter and smelled of stale sweat and frayed nerves.

Defoe ventured out once to take a leak and barely found the tent again, even though he'd only taken a few steps away from the structure. He couldn't see a damned thing, not even his hand in front of his face. He crawled back inside on a blast of sand that drew a grumble from the other men.

All through that night and the next day, the sand blew relentlessly. On the morning of the second day, he thought he heard a change in the tenor of the wind. Maybe a softening of the harsh howling. Or maybe it was just a hallucination. He was starting to feel pretty detached from any reality he'd ever known. A weak shaft of light penetrated the shelter, her-alding dawn, such as it was.

Defoe wiggled out of his space blanket. Not as cold as yes-terday. But that wasn't saying much. A witch's tits were still history in this storm. Ginelli staggered back inside the shel-ter. "Hey! It's almost light enough to move out there. I fig-ure if we get on the compasses and stick to 'em, we could put a few more miles behind us."

Defoe couldn't blame the guy. He was eager to get out of here, too. At this rate, they'd be lucky to make it home in time for Christmas. Hell of a two-week recon in the desert *this* mis-sion had turned into. The proverbial three-hour tour. Except they didn't have the hot babes Gilligan had had to make his predicament bearable.

He looked around the tiny space. At least they'd caught up on their sleep while they waited out the storm. But the guys still looked haggard. At the end of their ropes. "All right. Let's pack up and blow this Popsicle stand."

They walked a couple hours in the swirling sand, pieces of cloth wrapped around their heads, covering all of their faces except a slit for their eyes. They entered a region of rocky ridges and climbed carefully over mounds of freshly deposited sand that obscured sharp rocks and crevices. It was treacherous terrain and their pace slowed to a crawl.

And then Spot piped up from behind him. "Uh, boss. I hate to break this to you, but we've got company."

Defoe froze, his heart sinking. "Report," he breathed, what little adrenaline he had left pushing into his veins.

"Trail of black specks behind us. Coming straight at us. Ten, maybe twelve guys. Moving fast. I've seen 'em twice now when the sand let up some."

"Any chance it's a mirage?" Defoe asked grimly.

Spot answered with disgust. "I wish."

"Everybody, reduce your profile," Defoe ordered. "Let's keep moving as deep into this rocky shit as we can." He looked up at the sky, which was taking on that damned pink-brown tint again. And prayed more sandstorm didn't close in on them.

It did. About an hour after dark, the wind gusted up around fifty miles per hour, and the blowing sand was so painful he couldn't open his eyes at all to see where he was going. Reluctantly, he called a halt. At least if they couldn't move, whoever was behind them couldn't move, either.

They waited out the night as the storm raged around them. The wind took on the sound of a madwoman laughing hysterically. Enough to make a guy a little crazy himself. His watch eventually said it was morning, but damned if it wasn't nearly as dark as it had been all night. He couldn't take this anymore, just sitting here doing nothing. None of them could. He didn't even have to ask if they wanted to pack up and move out, even though they couldn't see a goddamned thing. They tied themselves together with rope, lest one of them wander a foot or two away and be lost.

He shouldered his pack and stepped forward. One foot in front of the other, one step at a time closer to home. They stopped every ten minutes or so to take a compass bearing and correct to an easterly heading. Every time they stopped, they switched off the lead position. Might as well spread around the fun with sandblasting facials.

Defoe had been in front for about ten minutes in the third hour of their blind hike through the storm when a huge, dark shape suddenly loomed in front of him. He jolted to a stop and squinted up at it. It was really big. Something like ten feet tall. It let out a strange noise like a donkey braying and he lurched backward. And noticed another huge shape to his left. And one to his right. Jesus Christ, what was going on?

He scrubbed his hands across his eyes, knocking the sand off his lashes and blinking hard to make out what the hell had just surrounded them.

Camels. The only creature on earth who could and would move freely in a sandstorm. He exhaled in relief.

And then froze in shock. A dozen armed men slid off the camels' backs, pointing rifles at them. They were surrounded. And about to be captured. *Son of a bitch.* A perfect ending to a perfect mission.

*December 18*
*Fort Bragg*

After everything else they'd been through, their prisoner-of-war training was anticlimactic. The Medusas sailed through the supposed sleep deprivation, beatings, lousy food and endless interrogations. It certainly sucked, but it didn't come close to breaking any of them. And, better, it marked the end of their formal training.

They quickly knocked off advanced sky diving, advanced survival school, and an assortment of other miscellaneous courses. And then they were done. Just like that. They had at their disposal the full arsenal of basic Special Forces knowledge. Now it was up to them to go forth and apply it intelligently and with guts. All they had left to do was amass some all-important field experience.

A week before Christmas, Vanessa rode with Jack on a Learjet to the Pentagon for his classified final report on the Medusa Project to the Joint Chiefs of Staff and various congressional representatives.

This time, when she turned down the corridor leading to the offices of the Joint Chiefs, she was at her spit-shined best. A whole lot different from the first time she'd walked these halls. She was a whole lot different inside, too. She knew herself worlds better. Knew the world Jack Scatalone and men like him lived in. And knew—*knew*—that women belonged there. Not every woman, certainly. But then, not every man belonged there either. More than anything else, being in the Special Forces was a mind-set. And it belonged to women as well as to men.

She got to the big, circular briefing room about fifteen minutes early. A few staffers were there, but none of the main players had arrived yet. About five minutes prior to the briefing, Jack walked in, deep in quiet conversation with General Wittenauer. Actually, it looked more like an extremely restrained argument. Jack seemed beyond tense about whatever they were talking about. Wired to blow any second, in fact.

She sidled up to him. "Everything okay?" she murmured.

"Hell, no, everything's not okay!" he retorted.

She recoiled from the violence in his voice.

He continued under his breath, "My team's gone missing. There's been no word from them since Thanksgiving."

Thanksgiving? That was three weeks ago! No wonder the guy was about to blow a gasket. "Is there anything I can do to help? Anything the Medusas can do?" she asked in concern.

His gaze slid away. He sighed heavily. "Yeah. Forgive me for what I've put you through these past four months."

She shrugged. "Given the end product, none of us have anything to complain about. You're a hell of an instructor."

A troubled look flitted across his face, but before she could ask what put it there, a steady parade of generals arrived and Jack was sucked away to shake hands and make nice with the brass. The generals were followed shortly by the civilians— several congressmen and a bevy of congressional staffers. A gray-haired man in a dark gray suit shot her a malignant glare as he moved past her to his seat. The name card in front of him read Senator McClure. She recalled he'd barely won his Senate seat back for a sixth term in November. Clearly not a fan of the Medusa Project.

The doors shut a few minutes late, but finally Jack stepped up to the podium. Vanessa wiped her damp palms on her skirt.

She listened carefully as he gave a brief overview of the purpose of the Medusa Project, how the team had been selected, and the training the women had been put through. Even she was a little impressed to see all they'd done spelled out like that. And then Jack stepped around in front of the wood podium. "I'll go over the details later, gentlemen, but let me cut directly to the chase."

His gaze captured hers for just a moment and then jerked away. She'd never seen such a turbulent look in his eyes before.

He continued, his voice stony, "In short, the Medusa Project failed. Women do not belong in the Special Forces."

# *Chapter 12*

$V$anessa gaped in slack-jawed disbelief. He couldn't... He wouldn't... She leaped to her feet in outrage. *"What?"* she exclaimed.

Jack nailed her with the cold look of a superior officer to a subordinate and ordered in no uncertain terms, "Sit down, Major."

She sat. She'd obeyed that bark for too many months, was too conditioned to the sound to do anything else. Besides, her shock was such that her legs would no longer support her weight. Her brain went numb. She felt cold all over. Sentences refused to form. She barely heard the rest of the briefing. But the snippets she caught were pure, unadulterated bullshit. They'd done the job. They'd made the times. Pulled their weight. Worked together. Succeeded in field ops. They'd been smart, strong, stubborn and, dammit, successful!

Somewhere near the end of the damning litany of twisted half-truths, a slow burn lit low in her stomach. It gathered strength and power, and it roared like a Saturn Five rocket by the time Jack's briefing ended.

An eternity of living hell later, the meeting was adjourned. Vanessa bolted from the room. She had no interest in talking casually with anybody, nor did she particularly care to stick around for the jabs or condolences that would come her way. But she did loiter in the hallway outside, waiting. For Jack.

Several generals, followed by a cluster of staff officers, left the room. Jack was part of that cluster. She studied a plaque on the wall until the brass had passed, and then she stepped forward aggressively. He jerked as he caught sight of her. But he kept walking.

The other staffers slid away from her, distancing themselves from the political pariah she'd suddenly become.

"Why, Jack?" she demanded, her voice shaking with outrage.

"Not here," he bit out.

"Oh, no. You're not getting off the hook that easy. Right here. Right now," she said with deadly certainty, stepping in front of him and forcing him to stop in his tracks. He glared at her, and she glared right back, militant.

He grabbed her arm and ducked into a random office behind her. An air force tech sergeant looked up from his desk in surprise. The poor guy took one look at the two of them flinging visual lightning bolts at each other and vacated the room hastily.

"Is this about us?" she demanded. "Please tell me you didn't sabotage the future of women in the Special Forces because you're pissed off that I threw myself at you."

"You didn't throw yourself at me any more than I threw myself at you, and, no, this doesn't have a damn thing to do with that. How could you think that? Jesus, I busted my ass to be professional with you and your team and not to cross that line."

He was right. He had been a total pro about working with

women. Before *and* after that outrageously unforgettable kiss. Her accusation wasn't fair, and she knew it. "Why then?" she asked raggedly.

He stared at her, frustration hot in his eyes. He wasn't going to answer her. At least not voluntarily. But she *was* going to get answers. She had to face her team and tell them why they'd failed. And she damn well wasn't going to lie to cover Jack's ass on this one. He *would* answer the question.

He looked away from her, but she stepped to the side, injecting herself into his line of sight. "We ripped out our guts for you, Jack. We *bled* for you. We did everything you asked of us. And you *betrayed* us. We deserve to know why, dammit."

"I did *not* betray you," he ground out.

"What would you call it?" she threw at him.

He exploded. "I followed orders, goddammit!"

She gaped at him, appalled. *Orders?*

"The decision was made on the Medusa Project long before I ever pulled you off that paintball range. You ladies were never going to be allowed to go operational. Forces beyond even the power of the Pentagon were not going to budge on that one."

It was all well and good for him to say that, but the logic didn't hold together. He'd damn well trained them like they were going to make it all the way. "If you knew the project was doomed going in, why in the world did you make us suffer like you did?"

He exhaled heavily. "My orders were to break you. To make you quit. And, believe me, I did my best. But nobody— *nobody*—counted on how tough you all turned out to be."

"What was all that big talk of yours to Wittenauer at Fort Bragg, singing our praises? Was that an act between you two to throw us off the scent of the political inevitabilities? Was that a lie, too?"

Jack ran a frustrated hand through his hair. She'd swear

that was an instant of anguish that flashed through his black gaze as he looked over at her. "I tried. I swear. I really tried to make him see."

"To see what?"

"To see the six of you for what you really are, not colored by political maneuvering or blackmail over JSOC funding."

She stared at him for a long time, absorbing that one. He stared back, challenging her to believe him. Their gazes clashed, two equally matched Titan wills.

Finally he sighed. "I let you down. I did my best, but it wasn't enough. I'm sorry."

He was telling the truth. She could feel it, deep down in her gut. She'd been so blinded by her dream that she forgot— or maybe conveniently ignored—the political reality of the situation. Jack had warned her going in that people beyond the project were gunning for it. But, God, she'd gotten so close to grabbing the brass ring. The disappointment was all the more bitter for having glimpsed the world behind the fence.

"Tell me one thing," she said heavily. "Were we good enough? Could the Medusas have cut it in the field?"

"Hell, yes," he declared forcefully. Without hesitation. "Not only were you good enough, spec ops could use women like you. The Medusas could pull off certain missions that no male team could ever do. You could infiltrate the female side of seg-regated societies…move around in urban insertions with im-punity while the other side looks in vain for male operators…" He broke off. Then he looked her square in the eye and finished, "You'd have been a hell of an asset to the Special Forces com-munity."

Her throat abruptly went tight and she felt hot all over. The backs of her eyes started to burn and his face went blurry. She would *not* cry. Not now, and certainly not in front of him. She shoved past him and all but ran out of the room. She stum-bled down the pristine hallway in a haze of tears. Away from her broken dreams.

Jack watched her go. He didn't stop her. And it was just about the hardest thing he'd ever done. Every fiber in his being yelled at him to go after her. To comfort her. Commiserate with her. Tell her how goddamned much he admired her guts and determination, the way she'd laid her dreams on the line and hadn't held anything back. It was one of the things he liked the very most about her. And there were lots of things to like. He'd never met a woman as courageous or as big-hearted about life. He'd give his right arm to have a woman like her standing beside him. In the field *or* at home.

And he'd let her down. Seemed like he'd been doing a lot of that recently. He'd sent his team out on a dangerous op with a young team leader, while he stayed home and played pretend with a bunch of female wanna-bes. He'd failed to convince Wittenauer to give the Medusas a shot at the field. And then he didn't have the balls to stand up in front of that room full of generals and disobey his orders, to tell the truth about the Medusas.

It was all well and good that now the Special Forces would get the funding they desperately needed for more men, more training and new equipment. But he'd sacrificed the dreams of six fine officers to get it done. He ought to shrug and chalk it up to the casualties of war and politics.

But Vanessa's big, blue eyes kept staring at him in his mind. Betrayed. Wounded. Jesus, he needed to talk to her. Hold her. Make it better. But what the hell could he say? If someone had done to him what he'd just done to her, there wouldn't be anything anyone could say to him. He'd have murder on his mind and not much else. Dammit. They could've been great together. Hell, who'd have guessed his heart would end up a casualty of war, too?

He stalked out of the office and back into the hall. Where in the hell would he ever find another woman who understood him like she did? One who really grasped the world he lived in. Who could cross the fence and find him in the wilderness

when he got lost in his work. Who could give him a reason
to come out from behind the fence and go home to a real life.
A real family.

He swore violently under his breath. He'd seriously
wanted her for himself. And he'd killed his future with her
today as surely as he'd killed the Medusa Project. He stormed
into an office and slammed his briefing notes into the trash.

He'd let down Vanessa, and he'd let down the Medusas.
Hell, he'd let down himself. But by God, he wasn't going to
let down his Delta team any longer. That was one mess he
*did* know how to fix.

*December 27*
*Pope AFB, North Carolina*

Christmas came and went in a black depression for Vanessa. The Medusas had all been given two weeks' leave and
dispersed to spend the holidays with their respective friends
and families. To lick their wounds and pretend none of it had
ever happened. Vanessa sat in her little bungalow and stared
at the walls. She didn't have the stomach to face her mother
and stepfather and their middle-American life in their
middle-American home in a middle-American town, far removed from the death and violence of her world.

Although her mother rarely tiraded anymore, Vanessa
knew she still deeply resented her father's passion for his
work, his choice of country over family, his inability to dis-
engage from the world of black ops and be the man he was
before he went behind the fence. The fact that Vanessa had
joined the military at all grated on her mother, let alone the
idea that she'd pursue the same career field as her father. No
way could Vanessa tell her family what she'd just done, even
if the whole thing hadn't been classified.

And her pain was too raw right now to hide it from her
family.

Not only had her dream been ripped out of her very grasp, but a man she'd *trusted* had betrayed her. She didn't know which hurt worse. But she did know she was never, ever going to forgive him for it.

*January 3*
*Pope AFB, North Carolina*

Bursts of rage at the unfairness of it all still gripped her now and then. During one of those episodes, she put her fist through the mirror in her front hallway. She cut her knuckles, but cleaned and bandaged them herself when she recovered her senses. And then she finally cried. She finally let out all the disappointment, frustration and loss. And all it got her was puffy eyes and a runny nose. No answers lay at the bottom of a box of Kleenex.

Her problem ran deeper than just having her life's dream yanked out from under her. Being in the Special Forces was no longer what she did. It was who she was. Somewhere along the way, she'd become a special operator. And she wasn't going to be allowed to function in that way ever again. No wonder her father kept going back for tour after tour of duty with his team.

And no wonder Jack had been so surly at getting stuck training a bunch of women in a dead-end experiment when his team was out in harm's way without him. How could she ever face him again? She'd put her heart and soul into pursuing something she could never have. He must think she was one pitiful human being. Did he laugh about it to himself? Feel sorry for her? Or maybe he only felt contempt for her and her stupid dream.

The two of them could have been good—heck, great—together on a personal level. But that was gone, too. As intense as the vibes had been between them, every time she looked at him from now on, she'd see the one thing she couldn't have.

He so embodied the Special Forces, she could never separate the man from the job.

She had to return to the Pentagon to turn in officer evaluation reports on her five team members and to submit requests for reassignment to new jobs for each of them. She'd spent a lot of time on the phone during the holidays, doing her best to get each of them a plum assignment. They'd all earned something special after their tremendous effort. It wasn't much, but it was the best she could do. She'd never forget the grim, stunned silence with which they'd taken the news, the way they filed out of the room saying not a word to her or to one another.

She'd rather cut off her right arm than face Jack again, but if that's what it took to take care of her team one last time, then so be it.

She made her way on a cold, dreary day to the sprawling, gray Pentagon on the shores of the Potomac. An occasional stray snowflake blew in her face, stinging icily as she walked up the wide steps of the main entrance. After showing the appropriate identifications, she made her way to the JSOC's Washington office complex. And paused in front of the door to JSOC headquarters. She could do this. Just a few seconds to drop off the exit paperwork on the Medusas to Jack, and then she'd be out of there. And he'd be out of her life forever.

She opened the door and stepped inside the plush office. And was about knocked over by the tension permeating the space. It vibrated off the paneled walls and slammed into her with the force of a locomotive. She paused, arrested by the sensation. It went way beyond simple tension. More like silent panic. What was going on?

Brandishing her paperwork as if she needed the excuse to be there, she stepped up to the desk of General Wittenauer's secretary. The woman looked about ready to throw up. "Hello," Vanessa mumbled. "Is Colonel Scatalone in his office? I have some paperwork for him."

"No, Major Blake. He's *not* in his office," the woman said with a strange, and definite, emphasis.

Vanessa looked closely at the secretary, who stared back intently. What was the woman trying to tell her? Clearly, she was trying to convey some hidden meaning in her charged silence. Okay. So Jack wasn't in his office. Thank God.

"Maybe you should give that paperwork directly to the general," the woman said weightily, her voice thick with double entendre. This from the woman who guarded her boss's privacy as jealously as an angry she-lion guarded her kill? What in the Sam Hill was up with her?

"Good idea," Vanessa said hesitantly. "Is General Wittenauer in his office?"

The secretary sagged with relief. "Yes," she answered quickly. "I'll show you in right away. Come with me."

Thoroughly confused, Vanessa followed the woman into Wittenauer's office. And stopped in shock. When she stepped through the door, before the general realized she was there, she caught a glimpse of his unguarded expression. He looked like he'd aged twenty years since she'd last seen him. His face was haggard, etched with deep lines of worry.

"Excuse me, sir," she said quietly. "Your secretary said I should bring this paperwork directly to you." Vanessa held out the stack of forms.

Wittenauer pulled himself together, but she could see the effort it cost him. She continued, "I wrote up officer evaluation reports on each of the women on my team. But Colonel Scatalone will need to do one for me in the next couple of weeks."

"That could be a problem," Wittenauer bit out.

She was *so* missing something here. "What do you mean?" she asked. And as soon as the words left her mouth, certainty exploded across her brain that something was terribly wrong with Jack. Something that was all but killing Wittenauer.

"Nothing. We'll take care of your fitness report."

"Nothing, my ass," she snapped back at him, an intentional slap to yank the guy out of whatever psychological hole he was wallowing in.

Wittenauer's gaze jerked to hers.

"With all due respect, sir, don't bullshit me. Something's happened to Jack. What is it?"

Wittenauer scowled at her, but she didn't so much as blink in the face of his attempt at intimidation. It took a minute, but finally he relented. His shoulders drooped in exhaustion. "I can't tell you. It's classified."

Classified. That meant Jack was out on a mission. Where? And with whom? His team was missing, not available for a new op...wait a minute. His missing team. He wouldn't...

Oh, yes, he would.

"Jack's gone looking for his team, hasn't he?" Vanessa accused. "He's in Bhoukar. But something bad has happened to him. What is it?"

Wittenauer physically lurched in his chair like she'd shot him. "How the *hell* do you know all that?"

"I worked with the man around the clock for months, remember? He said a few things here and there, and I'm no dummy. It wasn't hard to piece together what was up with his team. Has Jack gone AWOL looking for them?"

"Not exactly," Wittenauer answered.

"Then what, exactly?"

The general leaned back in his chair and gave her a long, assessing look. She thought she heard him mumble under his breath "What the hell" as he leaned forward in sudden decision. "You're correct. Jack's team, Delta Three, went missing the day after Thanksgiving. We haven't seen or heard hide nor hair of them since then. Jack left on the twentieth of December on an off-the-record op to go find his guys. And now he's gone, too. He's missed all his check-ins since Christmas Eve. We've got nothing on him. No locator beacon, no satellite transmissions, no radio calls, nothing. He's dropped off the face of the earth."

Her gut ached like the general had just kicked her. Hard. She sat down heavily in the chair in front of Wittenauer's desk. "Maybe he's in deep cover and can't call in."

The general shook his head. "It was a straight recon mission. No contact with locals. And he had a silent, untraceable, high-frequency transmitter. No reason for him not to call."

Fear congealed Vanessa's blood in her veins as Wittenauer continued grimly, "It gets worse. We received an intel report last night of a single American prisoner being held in a military facility less than twenty miles from Jack's last known position."

Vanessa leaned forward and asked urgently, "Who's going in after him?"

Wittenauer laughed, a harsh, painful sound. "Going in? Nobody. He's in Bhoukar, for God's sake. The Bhoukari government practically broke off diplomatic relations with the U.S. over the last American Special Forces guy they captured, and they didn't even know he was a Delta operator. We can't acknowledge that Jack's one of ours, let alone go get him."

Vanessa stared at the general, and he stared back at her bleakly. They were both Special Forces-trained soldiers. And the inviolable Special Forces creed of never leaving behind one of their own ran bone deep in both of them.

Vanessa finally broke the charged silence. "Send the Medusas in to get him."

"What Medusas?" Wittenauer burst out. "You don't exist!"

She replied significantly, "Exactly."

Wittenauer stared at her, arrested by her meaning.

She continued in a rush before he could say no, "None of us has been reassigned yet. That's the paperwork sitting on your desk. The Medusa Project is funded for two more months. And you said it yourself. We don't exist. We don't show up on anybody's radar screen, foreign or domestic."

He stared at her doubtfully. "Go on."

"If we crash and burn out there, nobody will know. Throw out a cover story about a training accident to our families. I'm sure you know the drill."

He nodded impatiently, and she continued her line of reasoning. "If we get caught by the Bhoukaris, you claim it was the final training phase of the Medusa Project. You massage the Bhoukari government with some story about their excellent security and that's why we were assigned to get into and out of Bhoukar undetected. You bring us back home, declare the project a failure and shut us down."

She felt him actually contemplating the idea and pressed her advantage. "If nothing else, we'll put to rest once and for all the question of whether women can cut it in the field. And if we succeed—"

He cut her off with a burgeoning grin. "We'll cross that bridge when we come to it."

She subsided to let him chew on her proposal.

Eventually he looked up at her. "I won't order any of you to do this. Every one of your team members will have to volunteer for the mission. And you'll be under the same rules of engagement that Jack was. If you get caught, the United States cannot help you. Maybe your cover story will work and you'll get released. But maybe not. You'll be operating without a net."

Vanessa nodded briskly. "May I use your phone? I need a secure line to make five phone calls."

"Use Jack's office. And, Major…"

Vanessa stopped on her way out the door and looked over her shoulder.

"If even a hint of this gets out, I will disavow all knowledge of any mission to rescue Jack. The six of you will hang from the highest yardarm for disobeying orders in planning and executing this rogue mission."

"Understood. And, sir?"

He looked up, pausing in the act of stashing the transfer paperwork in one of his bottom desk drawers.

"Thank you."

He nodded shortly. And said gruffly, "Don't let me down. Bring him home."

She smiled grimly. The Medusas weren't about to let anybody down. Not General Wittenauer, and not Jack Scatalone.

Twenty-four hours later the entire team sat in General Wittenauer's office. Focused. Intent. Hungry. It wasn't as if there'd been any doubt that they'd all volunteer for the mission. Jack Scatalone might have been a born-again bastard during their training, but he was *their* bastard. And the Special Forces never abandoned one of their own.

Wittenauer himself gave them their intel briefing. Panels on the walls of his office slid back to reveal a large map of Bhoukar showing the track of Delta Three's mission up to the point of their disappearance. Overlaid on top of their path was Jack's insertion point and progress until he disappeared. The Medusas would be airdropped a few miles from the military facility where they believed he was being held. They'd approach by stealth, use whatever means the situation called for to get into the facility, grab Jack and back out. Assuming he was in good health, they'd hump out on foot to Oman. It would be a sixty-mile hike, but it was doable. If he was hurt, they'd carry him out. A daunting proposition, but doable, too.

Wittenauer gave them their insertion itinerary: McGuire AFB, New Jersey to Rhein-Main Air Base, Germany, where all the gear they'd need would be waiting for them, including indigenous clothing from Bhoukar. From there they'd head for Saudi Arabia, and then they'd take a helicopter out to the USS *Eisenhower* aircraft carrier group in the Red Sea off the Saudi west coast. The *Eisenhower* was about to cruise out into the Indian Ocean, and it would pass by the coast of Bhoukar forty-eight hours from now. A helicopter off the

*Eisenhower* would fly them directly to their insertion point low and fast at night, under Bhoukari radar. Wittenauer had already arranged for the *Eisenhower* to delay its departure for the Red Sea by eight hours, both to give the Medusas time to get on board and to time its passage by Bhoukar for late at night.

For the next two days, Vanessa lived on Dramamine and airsickness sacks. And learned the hard way that ships made her even sicker than airplanes. It was almost a relief to climb into a vibrating tin can of a helicopter. She was too sick to worry about the strange looks the aircrew gave them as they donned their distinctive Special Forces packs and prepared to jump out of the copter. Fortunately, the crew, on loan from a marine recon unit, had already been briefed not to say anything to anyone about the Medusas or where they were taken.

During the long ride to their drop point, she thought about her father. Had he been this pumped up on his first mission? Had the adrenaline been this big of a head rush? A person could get addicted to feeling this alive. Is that what had happened to him? Had the real world simply been too bland and boring to hold his attention? Maybe that was one of the things that had driven him back to the field over and over.

The helicopter swooped in low and fast, dumping them out into the sand and sandblasting the hell out of them as it jumped into the air and sped away. Silence enveloped them as they crawled to the top of the nearest dune to recon the area. All clear.

God, it felt good to have both feet back on the ground, even if the ground was covered in deep sand that sucked at her feet and made every step take the energy of two. They needed to cover the last ten miles to their target before daylight and set up surveillance on the Bhoukari army base where Jack was imprisoned.

Vanessa hiked up her pack and prepared to move out. As she set up the marching order, a stray thought came, unbidden, to her mind. They'd done it. They were in the field for real. On a no-kidding op. A grin split her face for just a second. And then she got to work.

"Okay, Medusas. Let's do it. We've got places to go and things to do."

# Chapter 13

*January 8*
*eastern Bhoukar*

Vanessa lay in a shallow depression, covered by a clever German-made ghillie net that was light beige on one side and brick red on the other. A holdover from the two Gulf Wars. Perfect for this rocky environment. She'd been watching the Bhoukari army base in front of her for hours. She couldn't see anything even remotely resembling a prisoner holding area in the cluster of buildings. It truth, it was more of an outpost than an actual military base. Beyond the fenced compound, a small, dusty town sprawled along a highway.

The military buildings were white plaster, low and squat, with the exception of one large, three-story building. A sign in front of it proclaimed it, in Arabic, to be a military hospital. If Jack was in this area, that's where he'd be. Every other building showed too much everyday foot traffic to be holding a politically charged prisoner with Jack's lethal skills.

They had two choices. They could go in by stealth and try to sneak up to the hospital, gain entrance covertly, move through the facility unseen, find Jack and sneak him out. A tough proposition on an enemy military base. Or, they could use subterfuge. A couple of them could dress up in the flowing robes and full facial veils of locals and walk in the front door, bluff their way close to Jack and then sneak him out. A male Special Forces team would be forced to go with the first option in most cases. But a female team had the choice. And the more Vanessa thought about it, the more she liked the second option. It was a great deal less risky, would go a whole lot faster, and in her opinion, had a higher chance of success.

She and Isabella, both fluent in Arabic, would go in. Isabella could pass for Middle Eastern at a glance. And, fortunately, before they'd left Germany, she'd been hastily fitted with a pair of brown contact lenses to disguise her blue eyes. There'd undoubtedly be armed guards outside Jack's door and maybe even a hallway cordoned off by his room. When they found his location, they'd improvise from there.

The team moved not long after dark. They took their time, working their way around the perimeter of the military base, staying behind boulders and outcroppings. Even though the routine of covert movement was familiar, the adrenaline of doing it out here was a whole new ball of wax. Every little roll of gravel, every whistle of the wind made her jump.

Finally they drew near the populated area outside the base's gates. During the day it would be noisy with cars and people. But right now, it was as silent as a tomb. Nothing moved, not even the wind. Worse, the moon shone close to full overhead. Less than ideal conditions for sneakiness. Oh well. They didn't get the option of choosing to work only when the moon and stars were properly aligned.

While the rest of the team stood off a couple hundred

yards and spotted for them, she and Isabella went in on their bellies. It took nearly an hour to creep to the back wall of a residential home facing out into the desert. Maybe she was being too conservative taking it so slow and going in under ghillie nets hooked to their backs. But this was their—her—first mission. And all of a sudden, she was feeling real damn insecure about leading a team to its possible death. She abruptly understood Jack's occasional comments about wishing she'd been able to work with a male team for a while to learn the ropes before she had to lead a team herself. Another "oh well" moment. Baptism by fire. At least she had her awesome team to support her. Together, they'd get through this.

She and Isabella lay side-by-side along the back wall of a two-story building. The temperature had dropped to near freezing, and Vanessa was miserably cold. Moving slowly under the net, she ate a protein bar and sipped at her canteen, but mostly she just gritted her teeth to keep them from chattering. Clearly her father hadn't done this job for the great climates.

Katrina's voice jolted Vanessa to full alert in the dim gray just before dawn. "Look sharp. Movement in the alley."

Vanessa eased her rifle into a firing position beside her cheek.

Kat reported, "One female. Carrying a bucket. Headed toward you."

Great. To think their cover could be blown by a chamber pot. Such an ignominious end before they'd even really begun their mission. She lay frozen in place, not daring to breathe as a black-garbed figure emerged. She watched as an arc of brown liquid flew out and landed with a sharp splat. And then the figure retreated. Vanessa exhaled slowly. Carefully. Inhaled. Pee-yew. Nothing like fourteenth-century sanitation to clear the sinuses and start the day.

"All clear," Kat murmured.

Vanessa looked at her watch. Six a.m. local. They had to

wait here a couple more hours until the day's traffic picked up. She could do this. It was all about patience. But the next three hours had to be among the slowest she'd ever experienced. Finally, when her watch read nine a.m., she'd had enough. She signaled to Isabella to get ready to go. The other woman nodded, a relieved look on her face.

Working fast, Vanessa sat up and pulled out a bundle of black cloth. She picked apart the knot holding it shut. A long, shapeless piece of rayon flowed on to her lap. The *abeya* German Intelligence had provided. She found the neck opening and pulled it over her head. Then, she picked up the second, smaller piece of gauze that had fallen out and wrapped it around her head. The long, loose end of the scarf she pulled across her face, tucking in the corner over her right ear and pinning it in place. Then she pulled out a flat makeup compact, an eyeliner pencil and a tube of black mascara. *If there is a God in Heaven, please let the rest of the Special Forces community never find out about us carrying makeup on our missions.* She lined her eyes heavily and applied a thick layer of mascara in the tradition of women in this region. Isabella nodded at her, her own *abeya* and veil in place and makeup complete. They were ready.

"We're moving out," Vanessa murmured into her mike.

Misty replied jauntily, "Roger. Go get 'em."

One last check to make sure no rifle butts or other incriminating shapes showed through the drapes in their robes, a last veil check, and Vanessa flashed a thumbs-up at her partner. They walked cautiously down the alley. The street noise grew close. Here went a little piece of military history. They stepped out into the street.

As they approached the military base, they watched the flow of traffic, mostly in cars but occasionally on foot, that went in and out of the front gate. The guards were relaxed. Bored, even.

The two of them walked side-by-side, mimicking the local

women, their heads down, their gaits slow and heavy. Not hard to do with an extra thirty pounds of gear stashed under her robe. An AK-47-toting guard waved them near. Peeking out of the corner of her eye, Vanessa saw he didn't have the rifle's strap over his shoulder or even looped around his arm. The proper technique for disarming him and turning the weapon on him flashed through her mind. Instead, she stared at his dusty boots and prayed her Arabic would pass for native.

"Please, in the name of God," she asked humbly. "We have come to see my husband." She gestured at Isabella. "Her brother. He was injured in a car accident and is in your hospital, where he is obtaining most excellent medical care. He broke his leg and his ribs—"

The guard nodded, disinterested. "Register in the guard shack."

They stepped into a tiny building and waited behind an elderly woman bent on the same task they were. The guard wrote the crone's name in a log for her and Vanessa watched the woman's wrinkled hand make an unsteady $X$ by it. Then it was Vanessa's turn. She reached for the pen and signed a false name in careful Arabic script. It had been a few years since she'd written the language, so it wasn't hard to pretend to be uncomfortable making the flowing lines on the page.

And then the guard waved them through. It was that easy. She walked, amazed, onto the base. She looked around from under downcast lashes, cataloging hiding spots, places to take cover in a firefight, possible egress routes from cover to cover toward the fence. She noticed they were quickly overtaking the tiny, bent form of the elderly woman who'd signed in before them. Isabella caught her eye and nodded fractionally toward the woman. Vanessa nodded back infinitesimally. The two of them slowed to walk beside the woman. They struck up a conversation with her and found out she'd been bringing her son food for the entire month he'd been here, recuperating from back surgery. Apparently the hospital food didn't meet her eldest's high standards in cuisine. So this fragile woman walked two miles each way, twice a day, to deliver meals to her son. Her spoiled rotten son, more like. Vanessa insisted on carrying the heavy tin bucket draped over the woman's arm.

When they stepped into the hospital, a nurse came up to the elderly lady right away. Apparently this woman was well-known to the hospital staff. The nurse thanked Vanessa and Isabella warmly for helping her, and they slipped right past the reception desk as they assured her it had been no trouble.

Inside. Now to find Jack. They wandered down the halls until they came to the end of the long, third-floor hallway. And saw the armed guard sitting outside a closed door. Tallyho. Target acquired. Good news: there was only one guard, and the room was not in direct view of the nurses' station. Bad news: the guard looked alert and had an AK-47 sitting across his lap at the ready. She and Isabella retreated to a waiting room at the other end of the hall to have a whispered conference.

Vanessa murmured, "We need to take out that guard."

Isabella grinned. "Either that or we need him to fall asleep on the job."

Vanessa stared at her. And replied slowly, "That's a great idea. Where do you suppose they keep the drugs in this place?"

Isabella replied, "I saw a sign for the pharmacy down on the second floor."

The pharmacy turned out to have big glass windows in its walls and a single, locked entrance. They'd have to get in—assuming they could get in at all—and get out fast before someone noticed them rummaging around.

"Cover me," Vanessa murmured.

She turned to face the glass wall and, grasping a handheld field telescope about four inches long, surreptitiously read the labels on the drugs stacked on the shelves inside the pharmacy. Thankfully, almost all the boxes and bottles were labeled in English. God bless the global American pharmaceutical monopoly.

Bingo. She recognized the name of a powerful narcotic used to knock out patients having emergency surgeries. It was a nasal spray that one good whiff of would knock a man out for an hour. They'd only need to knock the guard out for a couple minutes.

"Here comes a doctor," Isabella murmured.

Hallelujah. A bit of luck. The approaching white-coated physician stopped at the pharmacy door and punched in a number code on the pad beside the door. In plain sight of her. Vanessa memorized the number and then turned away so the guy wouldn't notice her interest. The guy left the pharmacy. Vanessa led the way down the hall lest they be noticed loitering and headed for the nearest nurses' station. She waited until all the nurses were either gone or involved in a conversation at the back of the area then murmured to Isabella, "Grab a couple charts while I keep a lookout."

Isabella moved across the hall, took a couple of metal clipboards from the rack at the nurses' station and slipped them under her robe quickly. They headed back toward the pharmacy. As they approached their target, Isabella passed Vanessa a metal clipboard, which she pretended to refer to. She stepped up to the keypad and punched in the code. A green light illuminated over the numbers.

It took all of ten seconds to grab a tiny spray bottle of the drug she needed. She was back out in the hall before the pharmacy door had fully closed. They moved down the hall. Okay, this was all going just too damn smoothly. Except now came the tricky part. Taking out the guard.

While Isabella kept a lookout, Vanessa quickly tore a square of cloth from a hidden drape of her robe. She wadded it up in her hand. Just the right size for a gag. She nodded at

Isabella. They moved slowly down the third-floor hall toward the guard, murmuring in apparent deep conversation over something. They hardly looked where they were going.

"You there. Stop," the guard ordered.

Vanessa looked at his boots while Isabella answered quietly, "Our apologies. Are we not allowed to be here?"

The guard lowered his voice to match hers, as if belatedly remembering he was in a hospital. "No. This area is off-limits. Go back."

Isabella replied, "We seem not to be able to find the room we seek. Perhaps you know where to find room 3205?"

Vanessa stepped closer as the guard pointed toward the far end of the hallway. She glided right up next to him and raised her gaze. The guy just had time for surprise to register in his eyes and open his mouth to speak when she reached out lightning fast with both hands. Her left hand went around his neck, and the right hand jammed the wadded cloth into his mouth. Isabella slammed the spray bottle at his nose and squirted the medication up his right nostril. He yelled, or tried to yell, but all that came out around the dry rag was a muffled sound.

And then he sagged toward the floor. Vanessa lurched forward and caught the guy under both arms. She couldn't hold his entire weight, but she did manage to guide his fall into the chair. "Block him from view," she whispered at Isabella. The two women used their voluminous robes to hide the guy while Vanessa yanked the gag out of his mouth and posed the guy with his chin on his chest and his hands folded in his lap.

"Give him another hit of that stuff," she whispered. "I don't want him waking up and sending out an alarm."

Isabella nodded and shot another dose of spray up the guy's nose.

One last check to make sure he looked peacefully asleep at his post, and then Vanessa nodded at her partner. They opened the door beside the unconscious guard.

Her attention riveted immediately upon the long, thin form stretched out on the bed, his wrists and ankles manacled to the metal bed frame. The stale smell of a urinal rose from that direction, and dark bruises and swelling were visible on the pale flesh, even from across the room. Her heart jumped into her throat at the thought of Jack suffering. She stepped forward quickly. And then stopped, staring down in shock.

The ill, broken man lying on the bed wasn't Jack.

But he sure as heck looked American, with light brown hair and pale, faintly freckled skin. Who was this guy? She glanced up at Isabella, whose expression reflected uncertainty as well. Vanessa leaned down and whispered in the man's ear in English, "Who are you?"

The guy's light gray-blue eyes flew open, intelligent even if they were swimming in pain. "A prisoner. Who the hell are you?" he retorted in whispered and clearly native American English.

"American Special Forces. Here to rescue you."

"Bull," he bit out. "There aren't any women in SF."

She grinned down at him. "There are now." She pulled her black robe open to show him a glimpse of a sawed-off MP-5 submachine gun and belt of grenades and ammo clips slung around her hips. His gaze snapped up to hers, questioning, mistrustful, as she went to work on his manacles. She popped the four simple locks in under a minute. "Can you walk?" she asked him under her breath.

"Looks like I have no choice," he retorted, sitting up weakly with her help. He rubbed his wrists gingerly.

Isabella pulled out the spare black *abeya* they'd brought along and passed it to Vanessa, who passed it to the American. "Here. Put this on."

He stared at it for a moment, then grabbed it and pulled it over his head. She draped a veil around the guy's light hair, then she pulled eyeliner and mascara out of her utility pouch. "Close your eyes and sit still," she ordered him.

He eyed the cosmetics askance. "What are you doing to me?"

"Disguising you as a woman so you can walk out of here with us. Now be quiet and close your eyes."

He scowled but complied. It was awkward putting makeup on someone else, but she did a passable job of it. The poor guy didn't look half bad as a woman, either. She pinned the end of the veil over his face and stepped back to check her work. She hiked the veil a little higher to hide the last hint of the beard that clearly hadn't been shaved in several weeks.

"We'll do all the talking," she ordered briskly. "If one of us goes down or it comes to a fight, help yourself to the spare firepower under our robes. Do you know anything about evasion and concealment?"

He threw her a withering glare. "I'm SF, too," he bit out.

Holy shit. She hadn't seen that one coming. "Well then," she commented dryly, "I guess you do. We've got an extraction team two hundred yards beyond the front gate of this military base at bearing one-five-zero. Mission radio frequency is one-three-eight-point-two. If you get separated from us, contact them."

"Who the hell *are* you?" he mumbled as they headed for the door.

"Later," she bit out as Isabella opened the hall door.

"Guard's still out like a light," her partner murmured over her shoulder.

She nodded and flashed the hand signal to move out. Isabella went first, followed by the American. Vanessa went last. Now their escape depended entirely on how long the guard stayed unconscious and undiscovered. How Isabella managed to set a slow, measured pace down the hall, Vanessa had no idea. Her heart felt like it would explode before they turned the corner into the main hall and picked up the pace. As it was, they had to behave themselves and walk out sedately. But in under two minutes, they were outside.

"Quit looking around," she grated at the prisoner as she saw his gaze flitting in every direction.

"I'm scoping out egress routes," he hissed at her.

She bit out, "Already took care of it. This is my op. You're the cargo. Now do as I say and look at the ground, like a good female."

The prisoner subsided and did as he was told. Thank God. They seriously didn't need to shoot their way out of the middle of a military base. Another five minutes at a steady pace brought them near the front gate. Just in time to hear some kind of commotion erupt behind them. Crap. That sounded like the hospital. It was maddening to have to keep plodding toward the front gate like this. She felt the soldier behind her getting jumpier by the second.

"Easy does it," she murmured. But she watched in dismay as the guard inside the shack ahead picked up a telephone and listened. She picked up the pace to a fast walk. Her robe billowed around her and she snatched it close lest it give away all the toys stashed beneath it. They were even with the shack now. The guard stepped into the doorway and looked toward the armed guard manning the gate itself. He opened his mouth.

Isabella peeled away from Vanessa's left side and called loudly in Arabic, "Mustafa! Is that you?" She walked right up in the guy's face, and he glanced at her impatiently. She continued, opening her arms as if to embrace him, "I knew it was you! It has been almost ten years since I saw you, but I would know the face of my fiancé's brother anywhere!"

Now she had his full attention. The American soldier slowed beside Vanessa, and she whispered urgently, *"Let's go."*

They passed the frowning guard and garrulous Isabella. Almost through the gate. And then they were outside. Vanessa risked looking back over her shoulder and saw the guard arguing politely with Isabella as he forcibly walked her out the gate by the elbow. The tall hurricane fence swung shut behind her. She argued through the links a few more seconds for good measure, and then she turned and headed toward them.

"Time to boogie," Vanessa murmured to the soldier. "She'll follow us and watch our six."

"Son of a bitch," the American breathed as they walked away from the gate. "We just *walked* out of there."

Vanessa grinned under her veil. "Welcome to women in the Special Forces."

She led him onto the sidewalk, which was moderately crowded with mostly women, all garbed identically in black *abeyas* and veils. A wail of sirens blasted behind them, startling her. Police cars. A lot of them. The soldier lurched, and she murmured, "Just keep walking. We look like every other woman out here. They can't unveil us all without causing a huge ruckus." Nonetheless, as they blended into the flow of black moving shapes, she let out a sigh of relief.

"Who are you?" he murmured.

"Let's get you out of here, and then we can play twenty questions," she murmured back.

To his credit, the guy nodded under his veil and cast his eyes down at the road. Another two minutes saw them ducking into their original alley. Vanessa reached under her robe and pressed her throat mike. "We're headed up the alley."

"Gotcha," Misty announced cheerfully. "Looks like good fishing."

"Ayup," Vanessa replied under her breath. "It's not Jack, but this guy says he's Special Forces. We'll get under the nets and make our way to your position. I want Cobra and Mamba deployed over toward the base to keep an eye out for pursuit. His escape was discovered just as we left the base."

"Roger," Misty replied. "Cobra and Mamba are moving out now."

Vanessa stopped, crouched behind the same house as before. She pulled her ghillie net out from under the back of her robe and spread it out over herself and the American. It was a tight fit, but it covered them both.

"Stay in your *abeya*," she instructed him. "If all hell breaks loose, hide in the city until we can hook back up with you." She passed him the spare radio they'd brought for Jack and the guy expertly untangled the wires and donned the throat mike. Yup, Special Forces all the way.

"The cargo's wired," she announced into her mike. "How do you copy?"

"Five by five," he murmured, transmitting clearly into her ear.

She gave him a thumbs-up and then murmured off mike, "The three of us are going to slime our way behind that first outcropping over there." She pointed to the nearest decent-size upthrust of red sandstone. "My team's got eyes on the base. If the search for you catches up with us before we get to those rocks, you keep moving under the net and head over there. My team will move you toward the extraction point while Adder and I cover your retreat."

"Got it," he replied crisply.

She and Isabella stripped off their cumbersome *abeyas* and stuffed them into the pouches that had held their ghillie nets. And then they lay down on their stomachs and began the slow crawl to freedom. It was awkward with two of them under the net, and she had to help the American with his *abeya* constantly. But after a few false tries, they found a rhythm whereby they weren't constantly sticking elbows in each other's eyes. The guy was good. He was weak from his ordeal, but he moved with wiry power and gritty determination. It took about thirty minutes to make the crawl.

They reached the rock. And then they were behind it. They leaned against it to catch their breath. Misty passed the soldier a canteen and a protein bar. He chowed the food and drank about half the water. He took the utility belt and

MP-5 Misty handed him and donned them with all the ease of a seasoned operator. "Thanks," he grunted. "Now I don't feel so damn naked." He looked around in patent disbelief at the four women crouched around him. "You're *all* women?"

"Yup," Vanessa answered, amused.

He shook his head. "Son of a bitch."

"Ready to move?" she asked.

"You bet," he answered briskly. "Thanks for pulling me out, whoever you are."

"Don't thank us yet. We've still got work to do before you're safe." She led the way through the rocks, using them for cover as she made her way on her hands and knees up the side of the near ridge. They belly crawled over the top, keeping as low a profile as possible. They took off running down the sandy backside of the ridge, putting a half mile behind them quickly.

"Cobra, Mamba, fall back. We're a thousand yards southwest of your position."

"Coming, Mother," Katrina quipped.

Vanessa and the American hunkered down again together under her ghillie net as the team waited for its last two members to join them. She swore under her breath as a pair of helicopters passed overhead, circling the area and then moving back toward town. God bless the ghillie nets.

"What's your name?" Vanessa murmured. "Or, you can give us a handle if you'd prefer."

He grinned. Cute guy. Probably a hunk when he wasn't twenty pounds underweight. "You saved my life. I figure you can have my name. It's Scott Worthington."

"Oh, my God," Vanessa breathed. "Delta Three. Jack's team. Do you know where the rest of your guys are? Were you separated from each other? What can you tell us about who nabbed you guys?"

The man beside her jolted. "What do you mean, 'you guys'? I was bit by a snake. I think my team dropped me off at the fence of an oil field guarded by the Bhoukari army to get me medical care. As best I can tell from the questions of my interrogators, my team faked me crashing a civilian airplane that had gone off course. I have no idea what happened to them after that."

"When did they drop you off?" Vanessa asked urgently.

"I don't know exactly. We inserted on the third of August. The snake bit me on the sixth of August as best I can remember."

"Damn," Vanessa mumbled.

"Why? What's happened to my team?" he demanded.

"They disappeared the day after Thanksgiving. And Jack Scatalone went looking for them a week before Christmas. He's missing now, too. We thought you were him when we came in for you. We had intel that a lone American SF prisoner was being held here."

"Right intel. Wrong guy. Sorry," Scott murmured. "What do you know about my team's last location?"

"They reported a takeover of the Al-Khibri oil field by the Army of Holy War—"

Scott whistled between his teeth.

"—and they were last known to be headed east, toward an extraction point in Oman. A sandstorm hit the region, and they were never heard from again."

"Do you have the last position report they called in?" he asked tersely.

"Yup, and we have the colonel's last known coordinates also. And, yes, they're fairly close together."

"How far away are they from here?" he asked.

Vanessa looked at him through narrowed eyes. He wanted to go with them to find Jack. It was tempting. An experienced Delta team leader. One who knew Jack at least as well as she did. Except the guy was in lousy physical condition. And who knew what his mental state was after his ordeal. As much as she'd enjoy the security blanket of having someone like him around, it wasn't the smart operational decision.

"The last positions of your team and the colonel aren't far from here. And you're not going with us. You've just spent months in a hospital bed, and you're weak, malnourished and beat up all to hell."

"I'm not beat up that bad. My guards more or less adhered to the Geneva Convention. They mostly tried to mess with my head. Worst thing they did was drug me a couple times. I'll be fine."

"You're right," she said firmly. "You'll be fine because you're getting out of here. Now."

"I want to stay," he insisted.

"I don't recall asking your opinion," she said, deadly cold. "Like I said before. This is my op. And you're going home."

He glared at her with a menace that Jack would have been proud of. And she glared back, cool and confident. Finally his gaze slid away. He sulked in silence for a couple moments. She could feel him turning over arguments to use on her to change her mind. But in the end all he said was, "Who are you?"

"We're the Medusas. An all-female Special Forces team that works for JSOC. We don't officially exist."

"Well, then I won't officially tell you that was one of the slickest bits of work I've seen in a long time. I can't believe the way you ladies waltzed right in and walked me out of there."

Vanessa grinned. It had been pretty sweet. In fact now that she thought about it, she felt like she could take on the whole world right about now. Ten to one her father felt this way after a successful op, too. Chalk up one more reason that daddy dearest stuck around for this stuff. She looked over at Worthington. "Do me a favor. The next time you see General Wittenauer, tell him what you just told me."

Misty spoke up from beside her. "Are you still trying to convince the old bastard to keep us on permanently?"

Vanessa replied lightly, "You know, my very first officer evaluation report said that I don't adjust well to failure." She grinned at her teammate and added, "I guess some things never change."

# Chapter 14

*January 11*
*extraction point Charlie, Bhoukar*

Vanessa watched the blacked-out helicopter rise overhead, whisking Scott Worthington off to safety. A blast of sand hit her face and she turned away sharply. She was glad they'd saved the guy, but the man she was desperate to find was still out here somewhere. What was that sick feeling way deep in her gut? Disappointment that Worthington hadn't been Jack? Fear for Jack? Missing the jerk? Did she actually harbor feelings for him? This wasn't just unsatisfied lust rumbling around in her gut. This was something else entirely. How that was possible after the hell he'd put her through for the past four months, she had no idea. But there it was.

Time for plan B. They'd go to the point of Jack's last position report and track his movement. She had no clue how the heck they were going to do that, but her gut said to get to the spot and improvise from there.

The "spot" turned out to be on top of a ridge looking out over a wide valley. Goats dotted the plain below. And where there were goats, there were people. A line of cave dwellings was visible tucked under the far rim of the valley. The satellite photos Wittenauer had shown them of this location hadn't revealed the caves. Her gut and her logic said those caves were the first place to start poking around for clues to Jack's whereabouts. They'd wait until nightfall and make their way across the valley to do a little recon. Meanwhile, she put the team on a sleep-watch rotation to keep an eye out for the humans who belonged to those goats.

Night came abruptly as the sun dropped behind the valley's western rim. She moved the team as soon as it was full dark. They walked south for about a mile until they were well out of sight of the grassy plain, its goats and probable people. Quickly and quietly, they crossed the valley floor, then climbed all the way to the top of the western ridge and proceeded back toward the north much more slowly. It was tricky work moving along the ridgeline while not showing themselves in silhouette.

In other circumstances, Vanessa would've loved to stop and look at the stars. She'd never seen such a thick display of twinkling lights against the black of the universe. But as it was, she mostly ignored the magnificent view in favor of staying alive.

They closed in on the caves a little after midnight. A lone dog barked to announce their presence, but a man's voice hushed it sleepily from inside a cave. The other women looked at her questioningly. They'd been able to walk right up to this compound and have a good look around totally unchallenged. Hard to believe the tough, desert tribesmen whom they'd been briefed lived in this part of the world were that lax.

Working on point, Vanessa eased farther north, directly above the middle of the compound. If they hunkered down here and listened through the day tomorrow, they'd know everything there was to know about this little settlement. She signaled her team down and watched with pride as they appeared to sink right into the rock. Jack had taught them well. She took one more step to get a better vantage point on the ledge below, and something snaked around her neck, yanking her backward.

It was powerful. Choked her hard. An arm. A male arm.

Her adrenaline roared, and she snapped forward at the waist to throw her attacker off balance. But the man leaned with her as if he'd expected the move. She twisted to the left, challenging the grip on her neck. Her skin burned as rough fabric scraped her throat, but it didn't break the grip. She dared not shout aloud, for fear of waking the whole village. But this guy was getting real annoying, and she was ready to breathe any time now.

She elbowed his ribs with all her might and elicited a muffled grunt out of him. Her knee swung up, but the nimble assailant dodged that one alertly. However, the move threw him off balance, and she swung her fist up at the side of his head. He ducked, but she dealt him a glancing blow.

*C'mon, Medusas, a little help, here.* Surely they saw the scuffle. Why weren't they taking this jerk out?

The guy made a fast grab and snagged her fist as it swung up again. She yanked hard against the grip and forced him to release her neck to grab her other hand. Dragging in a gasping breath, she spun to face him. And stopped. And stared.

Son of a gun. *Jack.* Scowling like Zeus, with thunder on his brow and lightning in his eyes. And the rest of the Medusas were just standing behind him, watching the show and grinning like Cheshire cats. Traitors.

"What the hell are you doing here?" he bit out in a bare whisper that still managed to sound menacing.

"Looking for you," she replied equally irritably.

"Well, you found me. Now get out of here," he growled.

"No can do. Our orders were to find you and bring you home."

"Your team was disbanded. Who gave you the orders?"

"Wittenauer," Vanessa bit out.

Jack gaped. "How'd you get him to send you out?"

She shrugged. "My outstanding powers of persuasion."

Jack glared at her through narrowed eyes. But jumped when a voice called out quietly from the ledge below in Arabic, asking him if everything was okay.

*"Naäam, anaa bikhayr shukran,"* Jack replied easily.

Fluent in Arabic, was he? Vanessa translated in her head, *Yes, I'm fine, thank you.* Not the way a prisoner would speak to a captor. Particularly with a Special Forces team armed to the teeth and standing in front of him, able to yank him out of here.

He looked down at her beige camo fatigues in disgust. "Is there any chance you ladies happened to bring along BMO gear?"

"BMO?" That was a new one on her.

"Black moving object," he retorted. "Traditional Muslim dress for women."

Ah. The visual image was crystal clear. "Yes, we did."

"Put it on," he ordered shortly.

Vanessa keyed her throat mike. "Everyone into their *abeyas* and veils." She pulled out her own voluminous black robe and donned it quickly over her gun, vest and various pouches. "Do you want full eye makeup, too?" she asked, one eyebrow arched at him.

"Not tonight. You've been traveling all day and folks will understand."

"What folks?" she murmured as he took her by the arm. They stepped onto the path, and a half-dozen armed men stepped out of the shadows to meet them.

"Those folks," Jack muttered. He spoke up loudly in Arabic. "Look what the wind blew in. My wife and all her friends. They came to visit me and got lost. Silly females wandered around in the dark instead of lighting a fire for us to see."

His *what?* She missed the rest of the exchange, still hung up on that wife thing. She nodded politely when introduced and stayed safely parked behind Jack's right shoulder, just in case these tribesmen were heavy traditionalists. In short order, the marital status of the rest of her team became the main topic of conversation. Jack casually asserted that none of the others were married, and there was a noticeable perk of interest among the men. Great. Just what she needed. To have her team bartered off for goats and camels. "Jack, what are you doing?" she muttered under her breath at him.

"Hush," he muttered back.

She gritted her teeth and played along. Not like she had any other choice. Why, oh why, had he blown their cover? He could've just tapped her on the shoulder and said hello. He didn't have to tackle her, dress her in robes, and drag her in here for all these people to see.

She noticed a couple of women peeking out of one of the larger cave entrances. When she made eye contact with them, they waved at her and her team to come join them. They smiled in friendly enough fashion as they held veils up over their faces. She took a step toward them. And stopped as Jack's hand snagged her arm.

He remarked in casual English, "You'll stay with me, *wife*. Your friends may go join the other unmarried women in their cave."

The Medusas threw her a questioning look, and she nodded slightly. They trooped off toward the cave, and within moments, a chatter of conversation erupted inside. Great. Her team got to have a slumber party, and she got to beard the lion in his den. Alone. Wasn't that just spiffy?

"Come with me," Jack directed her in Arabic.

She followed as he led her down the long ledge in front of the caves to a narrow entrance near the end, acutely aware of the tribesmen watching her suspiciously. It was painfully implausible that Jack's no-kidding wife would just show up like this in the middle of nowhere. But the locals seemed willing to play along with the polite fiction. For now.

Jack took a step forward and disappeared into an abrupt void. She followed him gamely into the cave opening and bumped into a wall about four feet inside. Ouch! She felt air currents on her right and moved cautiously that way, hands outstretched. The tunnel curved back to the left, and the thick black of true darkness wrapped around her. Her hands encountered warm, hard muscle. *Jack's back*. She pulled her hands away sharply, but not before she felt the rumble of a chuckle in his chest. Jerk.

"Go on in," he murmured from off to her left. And then a curtain of some kind moved aside in front of her and light spilled into the tunnel.

She stepped past him into a small chamber. A lantern cast a dim glow in the space, but after the tunnel, it looked as bright as day in here. She looked back over her shoulder. Jack stepped past what looked like a camel hide with the hair still on it, letting the flap of leather fall back into place over the opening. She gazed around the room. Carpets and tapestries hung from the walls, lending it a tentlike feeling. The domed ceiling was high and dry. A good thing in a cave. A pile of pillows and blankets by the far wall had to be his bed. A table and chair stood to her right, and a set of shelves was carved out of the rock to her left. Most of Jack's gear sat there. She saw his pack on the floor beside the bed. There was only the one chair. And Jack took it now.

She watched in dismay as he stretched his feet out in front of him and crossed his hands over his flat stomach casually. Whenever Jack acted this casual, it was a sure thing he wasn't feeling that way. "Talk," he ordered.

She'd forgotten what a stunning conversationalist he could be. "You went missing. Wittenauer was worried about you. I offered to bring the team to find you, Wittenauer accepted. End of story. Oh, except we already found Scott Worthington, extracted him, and sent him home."

That made Jack sit up straight. "Tell me about it."

She related the tale quickly, in dry, official language. Nonetheless, he sat back at the end of it, staring narrowly at her for a long time. "Well done," he finally said.

Pride exploded in her chest. That was as much praise as she'd ever heard Jack give anyone or anything. Usually a slow nod was the best she earned. But, dammit, she wasn't some raw recruit anymore. She was Jack's peer. Surely not his equal in experience or skill, but she had her own team and belonged out here in the field with him. She had to stop acting like an eager puppy in his presence.

He interrupted her train of thought. "And now you've come to bring the wayward soldier home," he said speculatively.

She didn't bother to answer. His brain was clearly engaged in some other train of thought as he made the comment. But when he didn't elaborate, she fired off a question of her own. "What exactly are you doing out here, living with these nomads?"

"Later," he bit out, signaling her sharply with his right hand to be quiet. He got up, intentionally scraping the chair as he pushed it under the desk. And said loudly in Arabic, "I have missed you, wife."

An eavesdropper outside? Maybe listening in to see who she really was? Jack turned off the lantern on the desk. God, it was black in here. He rustled loudly in her direction. What was he doing? She knew full well he could move as silent as a ghost if he wanted to. She jumped when his hands gripped her arms out of the darkness. He made a loud production of taking off her veil and robe, and he tossed the garments aside with a swish of billowing fabric.

His hands touched her shoulders again. Enough was enough. She grabbed his hands. "What in the world—" she started to say in English.

But then his mouth swooped down on hers, cutting off her words. Yowza. Lust ripped across her brain like chain lightning. That man could kiss a dead woman back to life. She surged up into the kiss as his arms swept around her, dragging her against him. God, she'd wanted to do this for a long time. Their tongues clashed in a primitive dance that left her panting for more as he pulled his mouth away from hers.

He froze, listening. She stilled against him, trying to hear what he did. But all she was aware of was the roaring in her ears and the throbbing beat of her heat in the nether regions between her thighs. Who the hell cared if the eavesdropper was convinced or not? She wanted more of that, listener or no listener.

"I think he's gone," Jack murmured, his breath hot on her hypersensitive ear.

"Who's gone?" she mumbled.

Jack murmured with all the casual control in the world, "One of the locals followed us. But I imagine the sound of us breathing heavy answered his most pressing question about you. They won't for a minute believe you're my wife, but at least they know now that you're my woman."

The words fired her blood, but the detached way he said them made her heart sink like a rock. She had to turn off her raging lust for him. Again. That toe-curling kiss had just been part of their cover. He didn't want her at all. It had been no more than a ruse to throw off their listener. But how in the hell was she supposed to leash the electricity zinging through her like a hot wire?

"And here I thought you were glad to see me." She sighed, trying to sound light and cheerful.

Humor flowed through his body. "I am. But not for the reason you think."

Damn. It really would have been nice if he'd returned at east a little of her lust. "Why, then?" she asked, resigned.

He spoke so close to her ear she felt his lips brush against he tender flesh. Her pulse leaped like a nervous schoolgirl's. He murmured, "I'm glad to see you because I missed you. 've been trying to find some excuse to kiss you again ever since the first time we did it."

Her brain vapor-locked. He'd missed her? Wanted to kiss her? Surely this was a hallucination. Her pulse doubled. Then doubled again. Not a chance she was reining in her crush on his guy now. Desire for him tore through her, leaving her weak with need. All the strength went out of her muscles and liquid heat roared through her.

He released her and stepped away from her into the dark. "Dammit, I'm an ass. I said too much. Forget it."

*Forget it.* Right. *Not a chance.* The mission, dammit, the mission.

# Chapter 15

Vanessa woke up slowly. She knew she was safe, but she couldn't for the life of her remember where she was. Bhoukar. *Jack.* She lurched up onto an elbow, glancing at the pillows beside her. Empty. She had no idea how she'd ever gotten to sleep last night, less than an arm's length from a man who fired her blood like no other. A lone candle burned in a stone niche on the far wall, and she made out a ceramic pitcher standing on the table beside a plate bearing grapes, olives and what looked like some sort of cheese. Goat's milk cheese, no doubt.

Moving slowly until she worked out the kinks of a couple hard days' work, she dressed in her fatigues, but pulled her *abeya* on over the camo pants and shirt. She took a long drink of the water from the pitcher, tore off a hunk of the surprisingly mild cheese and grabbed a handful of grapes. She reached the cave entrance but had to go back to retrieve and don her veil before she stepped out into the bright morning. The light out here was extraordinary. The sun shone so clear and strong it almost made the landscape at her feet look surreal in its bright relief. Jack stepped into her line of sight, no less dazzling to look at.

"Good morning," he said casually.

"Morning," she mumbled. Lord. She felt as if she were back in junior high, tongue-tied over the cutest boy in school.

"Quit looking at me like that," he ordered.

She frowned. "Like what?"

"Like I'm some sort of damned hero," he growled.

She laughed aloud at that one. "Jack, if you're not a hero, then they don't exist."

He rolled his eyes. "I'm only a soldier trying to do a job, and six of my trainees just threw a big damn monkey wrench in my plans."

She threw up her hands. "Hey, I'm not trying to horn in on your op. I'm only a soldier following my orders to find your happy ass and drag it back home where it belongs."

He snorted. "Someday you're gonna have to tell me how in the hell you convinced the Old Man to send you out here."

"I already told you. He was worried about you, and we don't officially exist. It was no skin off his nose to send us after you."

"He's solidly against women in Special Forces."

"Apparently not anymore. Sorry, big guy. You did your job too well in training us. You're stuck with us now."

Jack shrugged as if that prospect didn't bother him particularly. Aloud, he merely replied, "C'mon. Everyone's waiting for you."

She pulled her veil across her face and followed him to a section of ledge that widened into a gathering place of sorts. A couple fires burned, and women crouched around them cooking. As he led her toward the nearest one, she whispered to him, "Never fear. I won't ever tell that a bunch of women rescued you."

He scowled, and she grinned back at his irritated expression.

"You're killling me, babe," he retorted.

She recoiled. "Never. Good Lord willing, we'll both live to a ripe old age."

The corner of his mouth quirked up. "And sit around in our rocking chairs at the old folk's home trading war stories with each other?"

She looked him directly in the eyes. "Works for me."

He stopped, apparently arrested by her serious expression. "People die young in our line of work. I don't count on anything but the next moment."

He didn't have to tell her that. Jack was a good ten years older than her father had ever lived to be. And her mom had thought her father had pushed his luck! Sheesh. By comparison, Jack was living on seriously borrowed time. According to her mother, a girl'd have to be incredibly stupid to fall in love with a guy like him. Whoa. Where had the L-word come from? She wasn't falling in love with Jack. No way. She'd seen the kind of heartbreak loving that sort of man caused.

She blinked. And noticed she was standing all alone. Jack had moved to the other side of the common area while she zoned out. Picking her way over baskets and goats and firewood, she hustled to catch up with him. And spied the five black robes of her teammates. Yikes. Her team was done with their breakfast and nearly done cleaning their breakfast dishes with handfuls of sand.

She chided Jack, "Why didn't you wake me up earlier?"

His eyes glinted momentarily as he murmured back, "Since you had so much trouble getting to sleep last night, I figured you could use the extra rest."

Her jaw sagged. He knew she'd lain there for hours, thinking about him? Did that mean he'd lain there thinking about her, too? Before she could pull herself together to make a snappy retort, the Medusas greeted her. They looked relieved that she'd survived the night alone with Jack.

She asked her team, "How'd you guys sleep?"

Isabella grinned. "Great, once we got the local girls to quit asking us questions. They kept us up half the night grilling us about the outside world. Seems they don't have much contact with the rest of mankind around here." She added under her voice, "And they don't buy for a second that you're Jack's wife and that we're just your 'friends.'"

No surprise there. Vanessa took the steaming cup of black coffee Aleesha passed her and sipped at its knock-your-teeth-back contents. Jack took a cup of the brew as well. Vanessa set her hand-turned clay mug on the ground beside her. "Okay, Jack. Care to tell us why you're out here running around with the natives and not checking in with Papa Bear like you're supposed to?"

He snorted at her description of Wittenauer. "I dropped my backpack. My only radio that's not broken doesn't transmit out of this wasteland."

He had to have dropped it off a cliff for their tough field equipment to get that busted up. Or maybe he was lying. Maybe he simply chose not to report in after going against his orders and making contact with locals. Nah. Not Jack. He wouldn't be worried about changing the rules of engagement on the fly. Special operators did it all the time. She tuned back in as he spoke again.

"As for why I'm here, this is the Al'Mah tribe . Guess who they've been feuding with since Christ was a corporal?"

"I give," she answered.

"The Hakhir tribe. Which is notable for being the source of over ninety percent of the members of the Army of Holy War."

Vanessa's eyebrows shot straight up. "The ones who took over the oil field?"

"The very same. What's more, these Al'Mah guys are all kind of interested in taking a chunk out of their old enemy's hide. With my expert help, of course."

Vanessa frowned. "And why exactly are you taking it upon yourself to knock over the Army of Holy War? We've got no orders to do anything like that. In fact, the briefing Wittenauer gave us led me to believe the U.S. has been specifically told to stay away from the Al-Khibri oil field by the Bhoukari government."

"Ah, but Uncle Sam doesn't know one salient detail that I do."

"And what's that?"

He looked around at all of them. "I'd rather show you than tell you. I'd like your unbiased opinions on what you see, first. We'll go tonight."

After a quick radio call on their fully functional satellite radio relaying to Papa Bear that Mama Bear had found Baby Bear, the Medusas rested through the day, fielding constant questions from a bevy of Al'Mah women who made any excuse to talk to them. A couple times, Vanessa actually worried that the nosy women were going to lift her robes to see what she was wearing under them. The way she figured it, the Medusas moved the cause of women's liberation in the tribe ahead by about two centuries in an afternoon.

The sun began to drop in the west, and Jack gathered up the Medusas. "Go get your gear," he told them quietly.

Vanessa and the others retired to their respective caves and emerged in a few minutes. Her team nodded at her and she turned to Jack. "Lead on, Dr. Livingston."

He led them over the ridge above the caves and marched them straight west for a good hour. The sun was blinding despite the dark sunglasses she had on. Her cheeks got tired from squinting so hard as dying sunlight glared off mountains of sand. Once the sun set, Jack turned north and picked up the pace. The sand pulled at her feet and made for slippery, clumsy going, but she managed to keep up with the grueling pace he set. The sky went from mauve to gray to blue to black and the air grew chilly around them. An hour later, as they approached a tall, sandstone ridge, he slowed abruptly. Held up a fist. And signaled for silent running from here on out. She passed the signal back to her teammates. Vanessa and the others followed him single file up the steep incline. The rocks were sharp, and it took total concentration not to make a misstep. The moon wasn't out yet, and the desert was a sea of black.

Jack lay down to crawl the last few yards to the top of the ridge, and she stretched out on her belly beside him. Their shoulders brushed, and a jolt of sexual awareness rushed through her. She'd swear the same explosion of lust slammed into him, too, because he went as tense as a lion about to spring on its prey. But this was work. She fought off her desire and felt Jack do the same. She eased her field glass out of the long, narrow pouch at her waist and lifted her head to peer over the ridge.

A huge oil production facility rose out of the desert a half mile in front of her, lit up like a Christmas tree. She put the telescope to her eye and zoomed in on the tall oil derricks and cluster of buildings beside the hulking, steel giants. *Al-Khibri oil field.* She recognized it from the satellite pictures Wittenauer had shown them. Looking closer, she made out pairs of armed men patrolling around the oil rigs and along the high fence surrounding the facility. What was she supposed to be seeing out here? Methodically, she searched the place, looking for whatever it was Jack wanted her to see for herself.

It took about ten minutes but abruptly she lurched. And gestured for Jack to pass her his telescope. His had about another ten power of magnification than hers. She lifted the glass to her eye. Son of a—she was right! Those were bundles of explosives taped to the legs of the oil derricks. And there were more clustered around the wellheads. The entire place was rigged to blow.

She dropped to the ground to think about that, and Jack lowered himself beside her. They lay nose to nose and her heart slammed into her throat as his intense gaze bored into her. "Are all three wells booby-trapped like that?" she breathed.

He nodded grimly.

That oil field represented salvation for hundreds or even thousands of poor, hungry Bhoukari people. People like the Al'Mah tribe, who barely scratched out a living in the barren desert. And the Army of Holy War was preparing to wipe it out? It made no sense. They were Bhoukari Muslims, too. Why would they take food out of the mouths of their brothers? Not to mention alienating the radical Islamic community that would support them as they grew in scope as terrorists.

But then, maybe the plan wasn't to blow up the oil field. Maybe the idea was just to threaten to blow it up. Say, to blackmail a government into keeping its mouth shut. Into making that government hand over a chunk of the proceeds from the sale of Al-Khibri's oil. Into making that government keep secret the fact that a terrorist group controlled a major oil field within its borders. As the political ramifications unfolded in her head, Jack's harsh gaze met hers. Yup, he'd come to the same conclusion she had.

Isabella tapped her shoulder. She looked into her teammate's eyes and saw the same horrified awareness. Isabella flashed the signal for explosives and pointed down at the oil field. Vanessa nodded grimly. She looked over Isabella's back, and all the others were signaling explosives, too. They'd all seen the very same thing.

Jack tapped her foot. He'd wriggled backward a full body length and she hadn't noticed it. She did the same and her team followed suit. He led them back the way they'd come, swinging wide to the south before heading back east toward the Al'Mah camp. It was well after midnight when they walked into the cave complex. Jack signaled with a complicated whistle before they stepped down onto the common ledge. Apparently the Al'Mah were light sleepers and had even lighter triggers on their weapons. The rest of the team adjourned to the women's cave, and he and Vanessa retreated to his digs.

As soon as they were inside and sure they were alone, she turned to Jack. "You've got to report that to Wittenauer ASAP. Our satellite radio's working just fine."

He nodded his agreement. "Let's do it."

She went outside and ducked into the women's cave. She tiptoed around sleeping women on pallets on the ground in the light of the single candle burning on a rock ledge until she found her radio operator. She covered Isabella's mouth and whispered in her ear, "I need the Comsat radio."

Her teammate rummaged quietly in her gear and passed her the radio. Vanessa stepped outside. Jack joined her immediately and set a brisk pace northward. A couple hundred yards beyond the camp, he headed for the top of the ridge. They came out between several huge boulders that formed a natural hidey-hole. But the sky was wide open above, and that's all the satellite uplink needed.

Vanessa cranked up the radio, while Jack encoded a message holding a red penlight between his teeth to illuminate the code book and paper he scribbled on. She got a double beep in the headset indicating a good comm link and passed the clamshell earpieces to Jack. He put them on and spoke the series of random letters. He double-clicked the mike button to indicate the end of the transmission.

"HQ confirmed receipt of the message," Jack murmured as he took off the headsets.

Vanessa reached for the folding satellite antenna to start packing it, but Jack caught her hand in midair. His fingers were warm. Strong. Sexy as all get out resting against her wrist.

"Leave that set up," he told her. "I expect a reply within a couple hours. Set it to beep us with any incoming messages. This is a low-threat area."

Okay, then. So now they had a bunch of time to kill. A couple hours to be precise. Out here all by themselves. Under a romantic, starry sky. And she was supposed to keep her hands off him the entire time. This was going to suck. *Conversation.* She needed to talk about something innocuous to distract herself from the idea of jumping his bones. *Innocuous.* Think of something innocuous to talk about. *Crap.* Desperate, she finally said, "Well, this certainly turned out to be an easy first mission."

"Don't ever complain about an op going like clockwork," Jack replied easily, his low voice mellow in the velvet darkness.

"Yeah, but I was hoping to work out the Medusas a little bit. Show off our skills in a way that would convince the powers that be to reconsider."

Jack leaned back against a rock, stretched out his legs and relaxed. All tension flowed out of his limbs and he looked like a lounging god at one with his surroundings. She sat beside him, but couldn't match his state of relaxation. Instead, she hugged her knees to her chest to keep herself from fidgeting. Just being this close to him tied her up in knots.

The very fact that she had these feelings for Jack precluded her from doing anything about them. If all she'd been interested in was a casual fling for the sake of relieving some sexual tension, both of them might have been willing to scratch that itch. But as it was, she needed to stay totally away from him, lest he provoke even more uncontrollable and unprofessional feelings in her. *Sorry, Mom. If falling for a guy like this is stupid, then I'm dumber than a post.*

Her misery stretched out into a long silence between them.

Eventually, he said quietly, "I'm so damn sorry about what the brass did to you and your team."

She looked over at him in surprise. Real regret etched his features.

He continued, "It about killed me to give that briefing with you sitting there, looking at me. I still feel like a shit for not disobeying orders."

She absorbed that one for a moment. "Who made you do it?" she finally asked.

"Wittenauer gave me the order. But Senator McClure was the bastard pulling his strings. Threatened to yank JSOC's additional funding if Wittenauer didn't kill Medusa."

"Does one senator have the clout to do that?" she asked, surprised.

"He could make a good run at it. He's a powerful old coot. Been around since the Nixon administration."

She'd been naive to ignore the fact that someone powerful would inevitably get wind of the Medusa Project and want it shut down. Finally she replied, "I'm glad you didn't wreck your career on our account, since we were doomed anyway. I'd have had a hard time living with that on my conscience."

He shrugged. "I remembered what you said about cutting your losses when they told you to quit applying to SF school. I figured I'd better keep my career alive and obey orders so someone would be around to fight the good fight for the Medusas another day."

She unwound enough to lean back against a rock and grinned at him. "You're just saying that to butter me up."

His eyes blazed in the faint starlight. "If I wanted to do that, I'd kiss you again."

Her gaze snapped to his mouth. Thinking about kissing her, was he? Answering lust roared through her. She ought to tell him not to try it again or she'd have to hurt him. She ought to fight off the need raging through her. But she just couldn't do it. This guy was an addiction in her blood. Reluctantly, she accepted the fact that she'd definitely gone and done something really stupid by falling for him.

And there wasn't a damn thing she could do about it.

But what a way to go. She gazed at Jack's silhouette against the background of distant stars, and something powerful shifted inside her; it moved the axis of her universe to make room for him in her heart.

She was *so* hosed.

*January 14, 4:00 a.m.*
*the White House*

"Sir, there's a situation. Someone you need to talk to."

Stanforth rolled over with a groan. He'd been having a great dream that involved fishing and humiliating an old political rival, two of his favorite pastimes. "Who's on the phone this time?" he grumbled as he padded down the hall.

The Secret Service agent startled him to full consciousness with his reply. "It's not a phone call. You have a visitor."

"Who?"

"Come with me, sir," the agent said impassively, throwing a significant look at one of the night cleaning crews passing them in the hallway.

Ah. Not to be talked about in front of the staff. A big secret then. He could do without big secrets. It wasn't that he was a gossip or couldn't hold his tongue. But the secrets a president of the United States collected over a four-year term weighed heavy on a person's soul.

Stanforth blinked as the agent punched an elevator button that would take them well below ground. "Your visitor is waiting in the Situation Room, Mr. President."

The Situation Room? Crap. The big secret took on the proportions of a really big secret. Stanforth stepped out of the elevator and walked down the short hall to the Sit Room. He stepped inside and saw a lone, uniformed figure standing with his back turned at the far end of the room. The Secret Service agent closed the door behind him, leaving the two men alone in the conference room. His visitor turned around. Hal Wittenauer, commander of JSOC. No Joint Chiefs to chaperon their boy? No national security adviser in attendance, no CIA?

"Pretty early to be out and about, General," Stanforth remarked.

"I'm sorry to wake you, sir, but I think you'll understand when you hear me out."

That was a definite undertone of worry in Wittenauer's voice. The guy was taking a big risk to jump his chain of command like this. And they both knew it. "Well, I'm up now, so let's hear what you have to say." Stanforth took his usual seat and waved Wittenauer into the vice president's chair at his elbow.

The general sat down jerkily. Wired like a mine field, the guy was. "Sir, as you may recall, one of our Delta Force teams reported a couple months back on the takeover of a Bhoukari oil field by a terrorist group called the Army of Holy War."

Stanforth nodded. "Delta Three made the report, and the Bhoukari president told me to keep my big, red-white-and-blue nose out of it."

"Well, what would you say if I told you that a lone Delta operator has reported that every derrick and wellhead at that site is wired with enough explosives to blow the whole field sky high?"

Aha. The missing piece in the Bhoukari puzzle. So, the emir was being blackmailed, was he? That explained a lot. Stanforth leaned back in his chair, thinking hard. At best, a bunch of terrorists were getting a huge infusion of cash from selling the Al-Khibri oil or from government kickbacks for not blowing up the oil field. At worst, this situation could spiral into a terrorist incident demanding unilateral U.S. intervention that would cause a huge international brouhaha on nearly the same scale as the Iraqi invasion a few years back.

Belatedly he answered the general's question. "I'd say that information might explain why an antiterrorist government like Bhoukar has uncharacteristically bowed to a terrorist group like it has."

The general nodded. "And what would you say, sir, if I told you there's a fully operational U.S. Special Forces team in place only a couple miles from the Al-Khibri field that might be able to do something to change the situation?"

He stared sharply at Wittenauer. "I'd say you haven't been following orders, General."

The military man met his gaze squarely. "You'd be correct. My lone operator went into the area to see if he could find the Delta Three team that went missing the day after Thanksgiving."

"The whole team's missing? Why wasn't I briefed?" Stanforth demanded.

Wittenauer flinched. "I expect because there was such a stink when Worthington was taken prisoner. My superiors probably didn't want to further…inflame the situation until they knew more."

"You mean they didn't want to piss me off?" Stanforth snapped.

"That would be correct, sir," Wittenauer replied dryly.

Stanforth grinned. Gotta love that straight-up, military way of speaking. "Okay. So Delta Three's missing. And this lone wolf went in to find them. Has he had any luck?"

"No, sir. Actually, I sent in another team to go after him when he dropped off the map at Christmas."

"Jesus, man. Can't you keep track of any of your teams? I thought you guys were better than that!"

Wittenauer took the rebuke well. He sighed. "It's been a tough couple of months."

"Continue," Stanforth ordered.

"Okay. So Delta Three got lost, then my lone operator who went after them got lost as well. Then I sent in another team to find them all. They're the ones who found and liberated Scott Worthington, by the way. The Bhoukari story that they released him as a show of good faith to the United States is a load of crap. You'll get briefed on it later this morning, I imagine."

Stanforth's eyebrows shot up. "Oh, really? That's interesting. And here I was, thinking the emir had cleverly made me look like an aggressive, ugly American with his magnanimous gesture." He waved a hand at the general for him to go ahead with his story.

Wittenauer nodded. "My second team found Worthington, got him to an extraction point where he was airlifted out and then continued its mission. They found my lone operator next. His radio's broken, which is why he didn't report on the explosives all over Al-Khibri until earlier this evening."

"So now this team and your lone wolf have hooked up," Stanforth clarified. "Near the Al-Khibri field."

"That's correct."

"Do they have the assets to disarm the explosives at the field? All of them?" Stanforth asked.

"My operator says that with the full team there to help him, they do."

Stanforth thought about the ramifications of that for a minute. In a way, he was glad the Cabinet wasn't here to wrangle in committee over what to do with this information. Sometimes, he got a gut feeling on something or someone, and it was a pain in the ass to get the whole team on board with his intuition. He reached forward and picked up his telephone. "Get me the emir of Bhoukar," he directed the White House operator. "No translators, and I want a secure line on both ends."

It took about five minutes for the phone to ring back. Stanforth put the call on speakerphone so Wittenauer could hear and then picked up the receiver. "Good afternoon, Your Highness. If you would indulge me for a moment, I'd like to have an off-the-record conversation with you about a hypothetical situation."

The man at the other end of the line responded cautiously, "Of course. And would that be why you requested the private line and no translators?"

"Exactly," Stanforth replied.

"What is it you wish to discuss, Mr. President? Hypothetically, of course."

"What if a little birdie told me there might be a whole lot of explosives wired all over a certain oil field in your part of the world? This might explain a certain reluctance on certain people's parts to do anything to rock that particular boat. My question to you is, if there happened to be certain forces in that area who could eliminate these hypothetical explosives and the threat of destruction of said oil field, what would you have to say about it?"

There was a long pause on the line. Much longer than the one caused by satellite signals bouncing from the ground to satellites and back down to positions halfway around the world.

Finally the emir spoke. "Mr. President, I would say that such assistance, particularly if it was rendered in complete secrecy, would be greatly appreciated. I would not, of course, be in a position to acknowledge such assistance should it become widely publicized, however."

"Of course not," Stanforth replied smoothly. "Thank you so much for your thoughts on the subject, Your Highness."

"No, no. Thank *you*, Mr. President."

Stanforth hung up the phone. Wittenauer was looking at him like he'd lost his mind. "Well, there you have it. Tell your team to take out those explosives. Oh, and thank them for pulling out that young captain. I was getting roundly sick of all the infighting over at State about how to handle that one. Besides, I hate the idea of any American being held prisoner on foreign soil, especially a brave young man serving his country."

"There's a little problem with my team, sir."

It figured. Nothing could be easy that ended up in this room. "What's the problem, General?"

"They don't exist."

Stanforth came part way up out of his chair. "*What?* Do you mean I just promised assistance to the emir of Bhoukar that you can't deliver?"

"No, no. It's nothing like that," Wittenauer answered hastily.

He settled back down, thoroughly alarmed. "You'd better explain yourself fast before my cardiologist gets wind of what you just did to my blood pressure."

Wittenauer talked. Fast. "The team is on the ground with my operator. And they are fully operational. But the team is female."

"*Women?* Good God, man, are you trying to give me a stroke?"

"Let me finish, sir," the general interjected. "A test program was funded a few months back to train an all-female Special Forces team. It was called the Medusa Project."

Stanforth nodded. "I heard it was slated to fail by certain conservative, bipartisan elements in the Senate Arms Committee."

Wittenauer confirmed, "That's correct. An ugly political hot potato everyone wanted to kill as quickly as possible. The project was strictly classified."

"Go on," Stanforth said.

"Here's the thing. The project succeeded."

"You mean to say the women made it through training?"

"They not only made it, Mr. President, they blew the training out of the water. There are a number of mission profiles in which I believe they'll not only do as well as the men, but will outperform the men because of their unique ability to infiltrate places and cultures where men cannot go. The Worthington rescue is a good case in point. They dressed up like local women and literally walked in, put him in a woman's robe and veil, and walked him out."

Stanforth leaned forward, intrigued. "So why don't these women 'exist' if they're on the ground and fully operational in Bhoukar?"

"Senator McClure torpedoed the project. Pulled all kinds of strings to get it shut down. Except he failed to notice one pertinent detail. The funding for it doesn't run out until the end of February. I...neglected to reassign any of the Medusas immediately after the project was killed. When my lone operator went missing, the Medusas volunteered to go get him. This guy was their primary instructor in their training, and I'd venture to guess they're fond of him. Or at least loyal to him."

"Who sent American troops into Bhoukar without authorization from my office?"

"That would be me, sir," Wittenauer confessed stoically. "They don't exist on paper, so no official action was taken and no authorizations were required. Technically."

Stanforth asked sternly, "So you split hairs and went around me to get your guys back?"

"Yes, sir."

He glared at the general. And then retorted, "Damn, I wish I had more people in my administration who showed initiative like that now and again."

"I believe, sir, that most people would argue it's a bad thing to have the military of a democratic nation taking matters of foreign policy into their own hands and acting without the will of the people behind them."

Stanforth grinned. "Stop while you're ahead and don't talk me into court-martialing you."

Wittenauer shut up and looked relieved.

"So what do you need from me besides that phone call I just made?" Stanforth asked.

"I'd like you to consider recognizing the Medusas and authorizing their existence in an executive order. Something that stays very under the table. Very quiet. Between the office of the president and JSOC headquarters. This team will be most effective if their existence is buried completely."

"Not to mention you'd save yourself a world of political headaches," Stanforth added dryly.

"I'm just trying to do my job and defend this nation with the best tools I can bring to the task. We need these ladies, sir."

"Is it your position that the congressional legislation a few years back allowing women in combat covers these women as well?"

"Correct."

"And they'd be funded, run and monitored directly by JSOC headquarters?"

"That's right, sir."

Stanforth steepled his fingers and stared at his general. Finally he said, "Show me they can do the job. If they can take care of this oil field problem, I'll seriously consider your request."

# Chapter 16

*January 15, 5:30 a.m.*
*near Al-Khibri*

Vanessa jolted when a beep sounded beside her out of the night's deep silence.

Jack went alert and tense beside her as well. He pulled on the headset. She waited impatiently while he scribbled a long list of random letters and gave a double click to acknowledge receipt of the message.

He passed the paper to Vanessa to decode while he packed up the radio.

The first two words made her gape. *Presidential orders...*
"Uh, Jack?"

"Yeah?" he murmured.

"I think you might want to see this." He looked down into the code book at the words she was pointing to.

He swore under his breath. Together, the two of them

looked up the rest of the coded phrases. The president personally had ordered them to remove all the explosives from the Al-Khibri oil field and render it safe. It was neither required nor desired to engage the Army of Holy War in the process of accomplishing this mission. Holy cow. The president, himself?

"Looks like your team's going to get the workout you wished for," he commented.

She looked up at him in dismay. "Remind me not to wish for anything again. Ever."

He grinned and offered her a hand to pull her to her feet. He held her hand a little longer than was necessary and a thrill skittered down her spine. "Your team will do fine. I trained them, remember? Besides, I'll be there, too. You can help the Al'Mah folks create a diversion while I slip in and disarm the explosives."

Vanessa shook her head in disagreement. "The Al'Mah men will never work directly with a bunch of heathen, foreign women. The only reason they're tolerating us among them is because they respect you. Did you know they don't even let their women learn how to read? You're going to have to work with the men. Besides, there are a bunch of explosives to disarm. Even with all six of us working at, it'll take the Medusas a couple hours to do the job."

"Too dangerous," he objected.

"Jack," she said warningly.

"Don't you 'Jack' me. This has nothing to do with your being women. I would never send in a green team on an op that dangerous."

"In the first place, a green team is all you've got. And in the second place, you don't give the orders to the Medusas. I do. Or in this case, the president."

He glared as he shouldered the radio pack. "I'm not arguing with you about this."

"Good," she retorted, "because I'm not changing my mind."

They did argue about it. For hours. Finally, at midmorning, they laid out the mission to a council of Al'Mah leaders who were more than willing to help crush their ancestral enemy. As long as they didn't have to take orders from her. Jack suggested a dozen different methods of attacking the oil field to the native tribe, and it always came back to the same hang-up. The Al'Mah warriors would never follow a woman into combat. The tribesmen were all good with the Medusas going into the oil field under high-risk conditions and fetching out the explosives, but let a bunch of women tell them what to do? No way. The Al'Mah men made it crystal clear they'd never go for that. Not even if the women in question were commandos—which news the nomads took in stride surprisingly well.

Jack relented, but grudgingly. By inches over the course of the day.

Finally, with utter lack of fear or consternation, the Medusas got down to working out the final details of the mission. Vanessa couldn't have been any prouder of them. The plan ended up being quite simple. Jack and his tribesmen would make an assault on the north side of the oil field. Once the Army of Holy War soldiers were drawn to that fight, the Medusas would go in from the south and disarm the explosives on the oil wells. As soon as that was done, they'd radio the Bhoukari army to come get their oil field back.

At best, the Army of Holy War would be obliged to rewire the field, and that would take time. Plus, the Medusas would set up long-range sniper positions around the field and knock out any of the terrorists who tried to attach new explosives to the oil wells. Her team would move their positions every few shots and keep up the suppression fire until the Bhoukari government arrived to mount an assault on Al-Khibri and take it back. Easy as pie. Of course, if the mission were that easy, seven highly trained Special Forces operatives wouldn't be sitting out here in a desert planning it.

The seven of them set out shortly after dark. The first order of business was to map the locations of all the explosives on the oil field. They made the hike as before, heading due west, and then swinging north to approach the oil field from the south. But this time, they didn't stop at the ridge five hundred yards short of the field. They topped the ridge and crawled down it. On their bellies. In fine, talcumlike sand that got between their teeth and down the collars of their shirts and in their eyes.

Vanessa felt no shame in admitting to herself that she felt safer having Jack there with them. He had fourteen years of field experience under his belt. She could talk a big line all she liked, but if it came to a shooting match, he was in charge out here. It was testimony to his experience and professionalism that he hadn't disputed her earlier when she'd insisted the Medusas were her team, not his.

Her fingers touched Jack's boot. Whoops. Better pay attention. He'd stopped in front of her. She halted as well. A faint noise of wind sweeping the surface of the sand whisked lightly around her. They lay in a shallow depression. She couldn't see the oil field from here, just the glow of its lights in the sky overhead. The others joined them in the hollow.

Jack breathed to her, "We'll fan out around the place. Send out your team in pairs to map all the explosives they can see."

Vanessa nodded and murmured, "Python, Cobra, you go left. Observe from the west side." Karen and Kat nodded and moved off. "Sidewinder, Mamba, go east." Misty and Aleesha slid away into the dark. "Adder, move straight ahead another couple hundred yards and observe." Isabella nodded at her. She looked at Jack. "You want to swing around to the north side and observe from there, or shall I?"

"I'm leading the attack on that side with the Al'Mah. I'll recon it."

She nodded and transmitted quietly over her radio to her team, "When you've seen all you need to, come back to the hollow you just left. The backup meeting point will be due south of here, just behind the first ridge."

Jack nodded briefly at her and then disappeared silently into the night. Man, he was good. She spotted Isabella and crawled forward to catch her. They moved side by side under their ghillie nets, taking their time. They didn't have far to go, but it was wide-open desert and a dozen guards, albeit bored-looking ones, roamed the fence lines.

Vanessa reached forward with her arms for the hundredth time to make a slow forward pull, when something clicked under her right elbow. She froze. Oh shit. Her adrenaline skyrocketed. She whispered to Isabella, "Freeze."

Her partner complied instantly.

"Small problem. I think I just activated a land mine," she murmured. "We're lying in a freaking mine field. Keep an eye on the guards and tell me if any look this way."

"Roger," Isabella murmured.

Slowly, Vanessa used her left hand to scoop away sand from around her right elbow, being careful to keep exactly the same amount of pressure on the joint at all times. Her fingers encountered cool steel. She uncovered the device with the care of a paleontologist for a rare fossil. Fragmentation mine. She needed to get a finger on the trigger. Shift it back into its safety slot to disarm it. Never mind that she needed to do all that so as not to attract the attention of the guards only a few hundred yards away! She eased her left index finger under her arm. Careful. A little farther. There. The metal pin pressed against her fingertip. Very gently, she depressed it farther, sliding the trigger to the side, back in its safe position. Exceedingly carefully, she let up on the pin. It didn't move. She released it all the way. Clear. She exhaled very slowly. Lord, she needed to go to the bathroom. Her gut felt like water.

"I'm close enough to see the oil wells from here," Isabella murmured.

Vanessa nodded. She felt too shaky to move right now, anyway. She slid carefully to the side of the uncovered mine. Good bet there wasn't another one twelve inches away from the first one. She eased her field glass to her eye. It took a few minutes, but she got engrossed in the slow, methodical search for the duct-taped bundles on otherwise smooth, steel surfaces. On the three wells, she counted ten bundles of dynamite or C-4 per well. Two bundles of dynamite on the control building, and two bundles on a small cinder-block building next to the control building. Probably the water source for the facility. Thirty-four charges in all. There were probably a few more charges set where she couldn't see them. Plan on seven disarms per person when they went in. That was going to take some time. If she allotted ten minutes to get to each target and disarm it, Jack would have to hold the Army of Holy War's attention for more than an hour. That was too long. They'd have to move from bundle to bundle in more like five minutes, and even that was pushing Jack's capability. Two minutes apiece would be better. Dang. The Medusas were seriously going to have to put their money where their mouths were.

Vanessa let the photographic analyst beside her take her sweet time and use her phenomenal eye for detail all she wanted. Finally Isabella nodded and pointed behind them. She was ready to go. But how? They were lying in the middle of a mine field. "Get the spare radio antennas out," Vanessa breathed.

Isabella nodded and reached slowly into her pack. Vanessa took one of the thin rods, careful to hold her arm slightly off the sand in case another mine lay between them. Stretching out the antenna to its full length, she wiggled its point slowly down into the soil. The antenna encountered nothing. She withdrew it carefully and poked again.

Isabella caught on instantly. They both poked the space between them. Clear. Vanessa turned slowly, using the safe patch of sand to do a one-eighty on her belly. She took point. Foot by nerve-racking foot, she poked and prodded a path to safety. Twice she encountered solid objects and veered around them. Isabella stayed right on her heels, following in her exact path.

They were the last to return to the hollow. Vanessa sagged in relief as she slid into the rocky depression.

"Run into a little trouble out there?" Jack murmured.

"Mine field. We'll need to come in from the east or west to avoid it, unless anyone else hit mine fields, too."

"Nope. You were the only ones that lucky," he replied.

Whoopee. She felt like she'd just burned a year's supply of adrenaline in a couple hours. She took rear guard as they made their slow retreat. The sky was growing pink in the east before they finally stumbled into camp, exhausted by the night's strenuous workout in the sand. Thankful for the cave's darkness as its thick, leather panel shut behind them, Vanessa crawled in among the pillows and crashed.

It was nearly sunset again when something warm touched her shoulder. Jack's hand. She'd know that touch anywhere. She blinked up at his face, the mere sight of him bringing a smile to her lips. "Hey," she mumbled sleepily.

Blatant desire blazed in his eyes for a second, but then he blinked it away.

Dammit, she didn't have time for this right now. She needed to focus entirely on the mission and not on the way her heart beat double-time every time he even looked at her. Jack left the cave and she sponged off using a rag and the basin of water on the table, then changed clothes and ate a tasteless supper.

Jack returned with the rest of the team in tow and a diagram of the oil field under his arm. He'd mapped out all the explosive charges they'd spotted. There were thirty-eight in all. A little more than six apiece. She divvied out which explosives the team members would take out and did a quick review of how to disarm the types of triggers used on these devices. And they were ready to go. She nodded tersely at Jack.

Tonight was a repeat of last night. Except this time, thirty men accompanied them and they came in directly from the east. Jack would run the Al'Mah north along the last ridge before the field and then cut west, bringing his force in from the north. About half the Al'Mah led horses, little more than ponies, actually, but the stringy creatures looked every bit as tough as their riders. The Al'Mah warriors were also armed to the gills. It turned out they had stockpiles of weapons and ammunition that boggled the mind. No wonder they lived like paupers if they bought and maintained all this stuff.

Jack walked up to Vanessa. "Give me one hour to get these guys in position to the north while you move in. As soon as Tangoes are fully engaged with us, do your thing. Try to be out of there in thirty minutes. Call me when you're all clear."

She nodded. They'd been over the plan a dozen times already, and she'd been rehearsing it in her head for the last two hours of hiking. She knew it cold.

Jack leaned fractionally closer like he might kiss her, but then he jerked back. "One hour," he bit out. He turned and strode away.

*A hell of a send-off that would have been.* She whirled and headed for her team. The Medusas moved toward the southeast corner of the oil field. They'd move in from the east, then run right along the south fence to make their incursion into the field. They were not going to tangle with that mine field again if they could help it.

This was it. A no-kidding, full-blown, black op using her whole team. The real deal. Lives rode on tonight's work. Excitement roared in her gut. *Easy, girlfriend. Stay calm. Stay focused.*

It took them forty-five minutes to go down the east slope to a point roughly fifty yards from the fence. Right on schedule. The glow of the big overhead lights was palpable on Vanessa's skin under her ghillie net. God, she felt exposed. They eased forward until the fence loomed right in front of their noses. Now to move down the south perimeter. They'd made it within a couple yards of the spot they'd picked out to cut through the fence, behind a stack of barrels on the other side, when an explosion split the night. Voices all over the compound shouted wildly and men ran every which way. Jack's opening salvo certainly achieved the chaos he was hoping for.

Vanessa and Karen began snipping at the hurricane fence with wire cutters while Kat and Aleesha dug from underneath their nets, pushing sand back beside their bodies. The bottom of the fence was not deeply buried, and a gap formed under the hurricane wire. Vanessa peeled back a low, flat section of the fencing and slipped under. She lay on her belly, gun at her cheek and set on full automatic. Lots of movement across the compound. Nothing nearby. She waved the others through.

They left their ghillie nets behind and spread out quickly toward their assigned explosives. Their black clothes blended into the darkness as they darted from shadow to shadow. They all had to work alone because there were so many targets to neutralize. It also meant they had to carefully control their fields of fire if it came to a shoot-out so they wouldn't take out one another. Thankfully, they'd rehearsed scenarios like this enough times in North Carolina that they all knew where to go. Explosions and the rat-a-tat of weapons fire crackled on the night air on the far side of the field. No worries about anyone hearing them coming, at any rate.

Vanessa crouched behind a big crate and peered around it. A lone man stood in the doorway of the control building, craning to see the battle on the far side of the compound. She'd be in his line of sight when she headed for the explosives. She took aim and fired. Clean shot through the head. He dropped like a puppet whose strings had just been cut. Just like that. Her first kill. No time to stop and think about it though. It was time to move. She slid out of her hiding spot and sprinted for her assigned oil rig. She took up residence in the dark shadow of one of its giant steel legs. The first bundle of dynamite stared her in the face. She took a quick look at the timing mechanism and snipped the red wire. The electronic face of the clock on the detonator went blank. She ripped the bundle off the steel and shoved it in her empty rucksack. One down.

She was able to fly through the remaining three charges she was responsible for on the legs of the rig, but the one directly on the wellhead gave her pause. It was a big C-4 charge, big enough to mess up the whole well for good. This time two wires had to be cut simultaneously. She pulled out her second pair of wire cutters, aligned both carefully, then squeezed steadily with both hands. A single, audible snick. The detonator went blank. She chucked the bulky charge in her pack.

Now for the little pump house or whatever it was. Karen was responsible for the control building beside it. She ought to be headed that way soon. Vanessa kept a sharp eye out for her teammate but didn't spot her. She was either ahead of schedule or Karen was behind.

Vanessa eyed her target, a cinder-block building about ten feet square. It had a single door with three heavy padlocks. Wow. That was a lot for a utility building. A lone window, more a vent, really, sat at the very top of the building's east-facing wall. She made a crouching dash for the south side of the structure and flopped on the ground beside the first charge at the base of the cinder-block wall. She checked the charge carefully, tracing each wire to make sure there were no dummy wires or misdirects. And while she was at it, she heard an odd sound right by her ear. A faint scratching. Like an animal trapped in a cage and trying to get out.

*Snip.* The first charge was no more. The second charge was on the exposed north side of the building. It would be much

more difficult to disarm without being seen. She planned to
go west around the building to reach it. But a sudden intuition told her to go east. She'd gotten this far by following her
gut instincts, and she wasn't about to change her ways
now. She went east. Past that crazily oversecured door. And
something insane urged her to take a peek through that tiny
little window and see what merited all those locks. It was as
dangerous as hell. But she did it anyway.

She jumped up and grabbed two of the bars striping the
tiny vent and did a slow, careful chin-up. She peered inside.
*Holy shit.* She let go of the bars and dropped to the ground
in shock. A man had been staring back at her. Nose to nose,
doing a pull-up on the other side of the window at a range of
about six inches. Jesus. Her heart was pounding like a jackhammer. Why didn't he sound an alarm?

Crap. Now what? And then she heard a sound. A careful
tapping. Tap. Tap. Tap. A pause. Three slower taps. A pause.
Three quick taps. *Morse code. SOS.*

She tapped it back. The same sequence repeated again. She
laid down beside the door in a deep shadow. "Who are you?"
she whispered at the door seam.

"American prisoners," came the whispered response.

Holy Mary, Mother of God. Not part of the plan, here. Prisoners. Plural. What a mess. No time to talk to the Medusas.
They had their hands full getting the rest of the explosives
disarmed. She had a backpack full of explosives herself.
Might be able to blow the door with some of it or make a hole
in the wall. But she'd make scrambled eggs of the humans
inside the tiny structure. Those door locks would take forever
to pick. The door hinges looked solid. She'd create too loud
a blast if she tried to blow them. She couldn't afford for the
Army of Holy War to hear an explosion behind them and turn
around to come find her and the whole team. Jack and his men
were outside the fence and would never get inside in time to
save their lives.

"Any ideas on how I can get you guys out of there quietly?" she whispered.

"We've been digging at the mortar at the base of the south wall. We're almost all the way through to the outside, and it's pretty weak. If you worked on it from your side, we might be able to get through it fast."

"Done."

Vanessa risked a radio call. "Python, when you're done, come to the south side of the pump house."

She didn't expect a reply and she didn't get one. But Karen wouldn't let her down. She took her utility knife off her belt and tossed it through the high window vent to help the prisoners dig. Then she slithered around to the south wall. Using her Swiss Army knife, she gouged at the mortar between the blocks. True to the guy's word, her knife poked through almost immediately. In under a minute, the first block moved.

"Stand back," came a voice from inside.

She moved out of the way as the block abruptly lurched outward. Somebody was kicking it from within. As soon as she could get a handhold on it, she helped yank the block out. She bent to peer through the hole. A pale face peered back at her.

"Keep going," she murmured. She looked at her watch. Four minutes left in the thirty Jack had promised them. The explosions seemed to be reaching some sort of crescendo, in fact. Jack was going through ammo like candy over there. He couldn't keep it up forever. She urged the men, "Hurry. We're way low on time here."

"Roger," came the grunted reply from inside. The scratching noise she'd heard before was louder now. Frantic. Like several pairs of hands were digging for their lives. She passed in a couple sharp rocks and kept digging hard herself. She scraped her knuckles raw and broke her already short nails. Another block moved. They'd have to get out three more blocks for even the thinnest adult to squeeze through. Probably would take four more blocks. She looked at her watch. Two minutes left. Christ. Not enough time!

"Jack," she radioed urgently. "I need ten more minutes."

"Not a chance," he replied tersely. "Five at the outside."

"I'll take it," she answered.

A black form moved beside her. She lurched violently. Karen. "Help me dig," she grunted. "American prisoners." Karen took in the situation in a fraction of a second and passed her field knife in through the gap. She pulled out a small crowbar and started knocking out big chunks of mortar.

"Medusas, report," Vanessa murmured into her mike.

The other four women called in, and they were all on their last charge, or egressing stealthily. "Come to the cinder-block pump house," she directed them.

"Why?" Jack interjected.

"I've got American prisoners in here," she bit out. She dug for all she was worth. Another block moved. They were one minute into their five bonus minutes. Moments later another block moved. Then two more tumbled out in quick succession.

"Outside, now," she directed the prisoners. They started coming out. Five in all. Thin. Beat up all to hell. Wearing only Middle Eastern men's undergarments—loose, below-the-knee pantaloons held up by drawstrings. The first man jumped hard when Aleesha rounded the corner. Good reflexes. His hands had come up in a trained defensive position. The explosions were starting to peter out. Damn!

"One more minute," she begged Jack in a whispered scream.

The rest of the team materialized beside her in the next few seconds. Vanessa hand-signaled them to grab a man each and head for the fence. She was startled when the men moved into position beside her team members like they'd understood the signal. She signaled that she'd cover the retreat.

A furious burst of explosives rent the night. She fell back, running backward, MP-5 at the ready before her. A quick glance over her shoulder showed ten forms running low and fast for the hole in the fence. She backpedaled hard, keeping her gaze on the battle before her. So far all she saw were backs.

And then the explosions stopped. Crap. She was still about fifty feet from the fence and four bodies waited behind her to go through the gap in the fence. They were going to get caught. And Jack was out of ammo. They weren't going to make it.

And then she heard a bloodcurdling scream from the north side of the compound. Her head snapped up in surprise, and on the far side of the fence, beyond the mass of Holy War soldiers, she saw a line of Al'Mah warriors racing past the fence on horseback. She watched in awe as the tribesmen stood in their crude saddles, standing atop their galloping horses like circus performers.

Only one more body—Karen—to go through the gap.

Vanessa reached the fence. And began to crouch. But froze in shock as she saw the Al'Mah warriors with great deliberation untie their pants and drop their drawers. They *mooned* the Army of Holy War while balancing on their wildly racing horses. The terrorists yelled and shook their fists, trading shouted insults with the Al'Mah. Interesting that they didn't just shoot the riders. Old customs die hard. And an outrageous display of horsemanship like that probably wouldn't traditionally get shot at.

A tug at her ankle and she dropped flat, wriggling backward through the hole. As soon as she cleared the fence, hands were there, bending the wire back into place and shoveling sand into the depression.

"Get under your net," Misty hissed.

Still stunned by the display of bravado she'd just witnessed, she spread out her net. They began the slow crawl away from the oil field. Although she didn't have the awkward task of sharing her one-man net with another person, she did get the dubious pleasure of making the entire crawl backward. She kept her weapon trained on the oil field the entire two hours it took them to make their painstaking way over the ridge to cover.

She sagged with relief and exhaustion, her back against a boulder. "Cobra, we've got a small problem," she murmured to Kat, her sniper.

"What's that, Viper?"

"I didn't get the explosive charge on the north side of the well house. Any chance you could blow it up without damaging any of the oil wells? Wouldn't want to leave our job unfinished."

Kat nodded readily. "The charges weren't that big, and that one's set at a ninety-degree angle to the wells. It'll blow some debris around, but at worst, that would only cause minor damage to a wellhead."

"Do it, then," Vanessa ordered. She watched the sniper wrap the barrel of her rifle in a silencer blanket. It wouldn't completely cover the sound of the shot, but would muffle it enough to cause confusion about where it came from. Best-case scenario, Kat would hit her target, and long about when the sound of her shot reached Al-Khibri, the explosive charge would blow and cover up the first noise.

"I'm ready," Kat announced quietly.

"Want me to take the shot?" one of the prisoners asked. "I'm a trained sniper."

Kat replied coolly, "Watch this, Cowboy."

Vanessa pushed away from the rock. "You guys all know how to handle weapons?" she asked their guests.

"Yeah, we're soldiers," was the short, confident reply.

Could it be? Had they stumbled across the lost Delta Threes?

"Viper," Kat murmured, "We've got movement. About fifty armed Holy War men coming out of the compound in jeeps."

Crap. No time to talk to these guys just now. She made a

fast command decision. "Let's get our guests armed ASAP," she directed. If this turned into a firefight, she'd need every warm body she had shooting back at the terrorists.

The Medusas handed out spare side arms, knives, grenades, ammunition and the explosives they'd just brought out with them. The prisoners did, indeed, handle the gear with easy familiarity. "Everyone look sharp. Any chance you guys know how to do a fighting retreat?"

She sighed in relief when they nodded shortly. The ten of them stretched out on their bellies beside Kat, watching over the ridge. Thankfully, the jeeps headed north, no doubt pursuing the Al'Mah. Good Lord willing, the prisoners' escape hadn't been noticed yet in all the confusion after the Al'Mah firefight.

"Whenever you're ready, Cobra," Vanessa said into her mike.

A short pause. *Pop.* Sheesh. That sounded like a BB gun, not a .50-caliber, bull-barrel sniper rifle that could take out a fist-size target at a thousand yards.

*Kaboom!* An orange blast obliterated the cinder-block building as the C-4 lit off.

Isabella spoke up dryly, "While I can't make a positive bomb damage assessment until I see corroborating satellite imagery, I'd say that was a direct hit, boss."

"Hoo-hah," Vanessa murmured. "Let's get out of here. We've got to set up new sniper positions." She turned to the nearest prisoner. "Are you guys in good enough health to hike a bit?"

The soldier grinned wryly, his teeth a flash of white in the shadows. "If it means getting out of this goddamned hellhole once and for all, we'll hike all the way home."

She knew the feeling. She was getting real tired of this inhospitable corner of the world. He captured her attention again by saying, "Why don't you and your team go first. I'll cover your movement."

She grinned widely. "I'm the one carrying the fully automatic MP-5. You go first. I'll cover *your* movement."

# *Chapter 17*

*January 17, 5:00 a.m.*
*Al-Khibri*

After the Army of Holy War troops encountered sniper fire, they and their vehicles retreated hastily to the fenced oil field and hunkered down inside their concrete buildings. Her team and the liberated soldiers provided suppression fire all night, keeping the terrorists pinned down and unable to reset any of the explosive charges on the oil wells. Near sunrise, Jack radioed to inform her that more ammunition had arrived from the Al'Mah camp and his men would take over sniper duty for a couple hours.

Vanessa led her double team quickly to the east, winding deep into the network of ridges and gullies. It was a nightmare to navigate but it had plenty of cover in the form of boulders. They'd been walking about fifteen minutes when the guy who acted like the leader of the men dropped back beside her. "Am I correct that you need to find a place to hole up in this area?" he asked.

"Yeah. It's too late to walk all the way out to the Al'Mah village before daylight. We need to find cover, wait out the day and move again tomorrow night."

He stared hard at her in the gray half-light of coming dawn. "If you don't mind my asking, who exactly are you?"

"Afraid I can't answer that question," she replied.

He shook his head. "For all the world you're acting like a Special Forces team, but I know the government doesn't let women do that. You can't be real spec ops."

For a moment, she was frustrated that a contemporary of hers, a colleague in point of fact, didn't even acknowledge her team as "real" Special Forces. But then the beauty of that occurred to her. If her own coworkers refused to believe the Medusas existed—even after the Medusas had saved their necks—nobody else would believe they existed either. That element of invisibility was the reason the Medusas would succeed in the long run.

The guy was speaking again. "Me and the guys, uh, surveyed this area pretty thoroughly before the Army of Holy War picked us up. We know a great little hideout. A cave. With a spring. Not far from here."

"Sounds perfect. Lead on," Vanessa replied without hesitation.

She and the other women paused outside the cave while the guys slid up to the opening carefully. They squatted in the dirt and looked around, then the team leader waved them forward. "All our signals are still in place. Nobody's been inside since we were last here. There's even dust on our wires."

Nonetheless, she sent Kat and Misty in to clear it before anyone else went inside. While the pair checked out the dark corners, she turned to the lead soldier. "Show me the defenses you set up to guard this opening."

He pointed out a series of traps and trip wires that were as clever as anything she'd ever seen. Jack couldn't have done

better himself. These guys were *so* Special Forces. She said
quietly, "I see one possible approach from above, between
those two big boulders up there." She pointed to the offend-
ing rocks. "I'm gonna lay a trip wire in there, and then I think
we're covered."

The guy looked where she pointed and nodded. "There's
a nasty crevasse on the far side of those rocks that isn't passable, but a person can't be too careful out here."

Aleesha was dispatched to trap the narrow gap. She returned from the task just as Kat and Misty emerged from the
cave and reported it clear.

Vanessa murmured to Isabella, "We need to make a position report to Jack so he can hook up with us. Maybe he knows
these guys. For all I know, they're his Delta Three team."

"Why not just ask them?" Isabella murmured back.

"If they are the Deltas, they've just spent nearly a month
being tortured to reveal that information. They're pretty conditioned not to admit it right now. That's why I want Jack here
ASAP."

Isabella nodded and set up her radio. She made a quiet call,
murmuring into her microphone for a few moments. She
nodded at Vanessa.

"Everyone inside," Vanessa ordered quietly. "Python,
you're with me on first watch. Three-hour shifts." To the others, she said, "Get some shut-eye."

Her team members nodded.

The American soldier spoke up. "We can pull watch."

Vanessa smiled. Definitely operators. "I hate to break it to
you, but you guys look like death warmed over. Go inside and
get some food and rest."

The rest of the men filed inside, but the leader lingered
outside.

"What can I do for you?" Vanessa asked him.

"What kind of time frame are you looking at before
extraction? We've been out here a long time, and the past few

weeks haven't been fun. My guys need to get back to the real world. Soon."

A good team leader. Looking out for his men. Vanessa replied, "I'll see what I can do. I need you to sit tight for a few more days while we finish our job out here. But we'll get you home. I promise."

The guy grinned. "It's weird being on the receiving end of that line." And then he turned and went into the cave.

Oh yeah. They'd found Delta Three. Wait till Jack saw his team. She smiled to herself and made her way out into the rocks to pull first watch. Her three hours were nearly over and it was full daylight when her earpiece crackled briefly. "I'm coming in," a male voice murmured.

Jack. She spotted him making his way toward them from the east, moving fast out of the morning sun. His grace was beautiful to behold as he leaped from rock to rock, leaving no footprints to mark his passing. She stood up to wait for him.

He set down a heavy-looking box. Looked like ammo. Excellent. He asked without preamble, "So why'd you need me here so urgently?"

"I've got something to show you," she replied.

He ducked after her into the cave. People slept all over the floor. She reached for the nearest foot of one of the freed prisoners and gave it a shake. The guy sat up. And leaped to his feet as he saw who was with her.

"Defoe," he whispered urgently over his shoulder. "Wake up. Scat's here!"

Jack shoved past her to embrace the man in a short, hard hug. "You look like shit, Walsh," Jack growled affectionately. The other men woke up and all exchanged hugs and backslaps with Jack. "How the hell are you?" he asked them.

Defoe answered for all of them. "A whole lot better since these ladies pulled us out last night."

Jack's gaze met Vanessa's. He nodded once, shortly, in thanks and approval. She returned the nod crisply.

He looked back at the men. "Scottie Worthington's alive and well. These ladies found him and pulled him out of a Bhoukari hospital a couple days ago. Put him on a helicopter bound for the good ole U. S. of A."

The men eyed her anew. The one called Defoe said, "Guess we owe you even more than we knew."

She shrugged. "Just doing our job."

Jack grinned. "You reported in to Papa Bear with the news yet?" he asked her.

"Nope. I wanted an ID on our guests first. We figured they were Delta Three, but they weren't talking and we weren't asking. Do you want to make the call?" she offered.

Jack's grin got wider. "Yeah. Where's the radio? Adder, I need to phone home."

"E.T. at your service," Isabella mumbled as she rolled out from under her blanket.

*January 17, 10:00 a.m.*
*the White House*

Henry Stanforth said a last goodbye as a group of high-school students filed out of the Oval Office. They'd won writing competitions in their respective states and earned trips to Washington, D.C., to meet the president. His secretary stepped into the office as the noise of the teenagers trailed off down the hall. "General Wittenauer is on line four."

Stanforth nodded briskly. "I'll take it at my desk." He called after his retreating secretary, "Close the door behind you and don't tape this."

He sat at his desk and picked up the phone. "General Wittenauer, I'm surprised to hear from you so soon. Does this mean you have good news for me?"

"I do, sir. All the explosives at the oil field have been removed. The Bhoukaris probably have about an eight-hour window remaining to go in and do something before the Army of Holy War trucks in more explosives and men and rerigs the place."

"Excellent," Stanforth replied jovially.

"There's more," Wittenauer added. "The Medusas found my lost Delta team and pulled them out. Turns out the Army of Holy War captured them and was holding them at Al-Khibri. They're debilitated and banged up, but none of them are seriously injured."

Now that was good news. And it gave him an idea. "I'm glad to hear it, General. Just out of curiosity, is the Delta team operational?"

"I don't understand, sir."

"If they had to take care of one last piece of business before they were extracted, would they be up to it?"

Wittenauer was dubious. "They've been prisoners of a nasty outfit who's never heard of the Geneva Convention. I expect they got worked over pretty good. I wouldn't call them operational, no."

"Even if the job was to kill their captors?" Stanforth asked.

"Well, now," Wittenauer drawled. "That's different. Wild horses wouldn't keep them away from that op if they got the chance. Might be good therapy for them to kick some Army of Holy War butt."

"I'm going to make a phone call, General, and see if I can mend a fence between my country and Bhoukar. I may need to call you back in a few minutes and give those young men their shot at therapy."

"I'll be standing by, sir."

Stanforth disconnected the call and punched another button on his phone. "Get me the emir of Bhoukar. Yes, same as before. No translators and secure lines at both ends."

The British-accented voice came on the line in a matter of seconds this time. "President Stanforth, how are you today?"

"Very well, thank you. I thought you might be pleased to

know that the Al-Khibri field is completely free of explosives. I'm told it'll take the current occupants of the field another eight hours or so to change that."

"I am pleased, indeed, to hear this news. That is a very narrow window of opportunity, however."

Stanforth frowned. Sometimes he forgot that other countries didn't have the kind of quick-response, kick-ass, Special Forces capabilities at their disposal that he did. But it played into his hands in this case. "If I happened to have two full teams in a position to buy you a larger window of opportunity, Your Highness, what would you say to that?"

The guy answered instantly, emphatically, without even a moment's hesitation: "I'd say to kick the blighters' arses."

Stanforth chuckled. "Consider it done. Oh, and I won't be able to acknowledge having any part in taking down the Army of Holy War. I'm afraid you'll have to take all the credit. Call it an apology for the awkward position I inadvertently placed you in last fall."

The emir chuckled. He sounded completely mollified. "Fair enough. Apology accepted."

*January 17, 5:00 p.m.*
*near Al-Khibri*

Vanessa was back on watch when Jack crawled over to her in the late afternoon. "Come with me," he said shortly.

He jerked his head at Karen to go inside, too, then he stepped into the cave and handed off the radio to Isabella. Vanessa's pulse jumped. She knew that look. Something big had happened in Jack's latest radio call. He looked around at all of them. Then he announced quietly, "We've got new orders."

Vanessa thought she caught a faint groan under the men's breath. Poor suckers had been here for almost six months of grueling action. She couldn't blame them.

Jack ignored the sound and continued, "The twelve of us are ordered to engage and kill as many Army of Holy War terrorists as we can."

"Yes!" Defoe gritted out between clenched teeth.

She couldn't blame him for that reaction, either. There was nothing like a good dose of revenge after somebody'd messed with a person's team.

Jack continued, "The Bhoukari army can't get here until tomorrow. We're to prevent the terrorists from rigging the oil wells with new explosives until then. Free fire authorized."

Vanessa blinked. They could kill anyone and everyone they saw? Whoa. Deltas didn't get that order often. They were in the stealth business, not the all-out assault business. She said, "We'd better get eyes on the target then. Based on what I know of the Army of Holy War, they didn't sit around doing nothing today. Let the Medusas take the recon," she suggested. "The Deltas could use the extra four or five hours' sleep and another square meal."

Defoe drew breath to protest, but Jack cut him off. "Don't try to outmacho these ladies. In your current condition they'd leave you in the dust. Take the extra rest. It'll be a long night."

Defoe subsided.

A half hour later, Vanessa lay along the ridge due east of Al-Khibri. She lifted her field glass to have a look. Yup, as she'd expected. The terrorists had been busy since last night. There was a new trench surrounding the three wellheads. It was maybe six feet wide and no doubt shallow if it had been dug in a single day. She couldn't tell from this angle, but she'd lay odds it was full of oil that could be lit on fire at a moment's notice. A roll of concertina wire—barbed wire with razors along its edges instead of simple barbs—lay across last night's opening in the fence. And patrols were out in force. Getting through that fence again would be a bitch. There'd be no element of surprise at all. She estimated something like two hundred men crowded inside the compound now.

Reinforcements had arrived, no doubt from the Army of Holy War cave complex northeast of her position. The good news was she didn't see any sign of explosives taped to the oil derricks or wellheads. The Al'Mah snipers had done their job well today. Isabella took her place on the ridge, and Vanessa made her way back to the cave to relay what she'd seen to Jack.

"So, what's your recommendation?" he asked at the end of her recitation.

"I say we stand off with sniper fire only. Pick off as many of the terrorists as we can. Drive them inside or under cover and keep them away from the wells until the Bhoukaris get here. If they make a push to come outside and all twelve of us fire at once in a concerted barrage, we ought to be able to pick off a good thirty or forty of the terrorists before they get organized."

"And what if they mount an all-out assault and come after us?"

"We booby-trap escape routes for each team and run the terrorists through a killing field of explosives. We've got a ton of go-boom to play with after last night."

Jack nodded. "You want the teams to work separately then?"

"I want to surround the place and have incoming fire from every direction. Seems logical that we'd pull one team in one direction and the other team in another, if it gets hairy. We keep each team intact for escape and evasion because they know each other and work well together. And a team of six has enough firepower in a fighting retreat to hold off a good-size force of Tangos."

"Sound thinking. Where do you propose we deploy?"

She squatted in the dirt floor of the cave and drew a rough map. "The Medusas will spread out along the south side of the field. If the Army of Holy War wants to come get us, they'll have to go around their own mine field. We'll retreat south into the line of rocks here and set up our ambush for any pursuers."

She drew another arc on the north side of the field. "You array your guys here. If you run into trouble, you pull back to the east."

"Why not have us retreat to the north?"

She answered, "The terrorists will expect our teams to run in opposite directions, not at a ninety-degree angle to each other. It may buy one or both of us some time."

"And what if they bring in more reinforcements?" Jack asked.

"We know the Holy War caves east of the field have been emptied of men today, which means help has to come in by road. The only road into the field runs down from the northeast, here. You and your guys will have to cover it. Maybe block it or booby-trap it. Just don't blow up the Bhoukari army when it comes hauling ass down that same road."

He snorted. "Yeah, that would suck. We need them if we're ever gonna get out of here."

"How are we doing for weapons?" Vanessa asked. "The Medusas have six weapons that will shoot accurately at standoff range."

"I've got one, and we've got the one from Scott Worthington's gear that the Deltas stashed here."

"Eight total. We'll take four and you guys take four. We've got enough spare radios for everyone to be wired for sound. And we've got plenty of ammo thanks to the stuff you brought with you this morning."

Jack nodded crisply. "Let's leave at dark. The Al'Mah will be ready to go home by then, and it'll take a couple hours to set up the ambushes. The more time we spend shooting tonight, the more of these bastards we can take out."

Defoe muttered from his prone position on the floor, "That's why I love you, Scat. You're the bloodthirstiest bastard in the world, and you're on our side."

Jack growled, "The Army of Holy War hurt my guys, and now they're going to pay." He looked at Vanessa, his eyes as cold as death. "Let's make tonight an object lesson for terrorists everywhere in why it's not good to fuck with Delta teams."

*Teams.* Plural. He'd just included the Medusas in the inner circle of the elite. A warm, tingly feeling suffused her.

And she still hadn't shaken the feeling when she lay in position four hours later, waiting for Jack to call the attack. There were about forty guards milling around inside the oil field, and as soon as the shooting started, a whole lot more men would rush outside. She figured they'd get two good salvos of shots in before the ducks realized they were trapped in a shooting gallery and took cover.

She'd armed her fifth and sixth team members with pistols. They had enough range to hit the mine field, and maybe they'd get a lucky shot and detonate a mine, just to add to the overall panic and confusion in the compound. Jack's team had spent the last of the daylight rigging up a crude cannon, a lot like the potato cannons she'd built as a kid. They were hoping to lob some dynamite into the fray as well. Should be an exciting show. Well, loud, at any rate.

"Choose your targets," Jack murmured into her earpiece.

Time to rock and roll. Vanessa lowered her eye to the telescopic sight on her rifle. An armed figure came into focus.

"Fire," Jack said quietly.

She squeezed the trigger smoothly. Her man dropped. She swung her weapon an inch to the right. Another squeeze. Another man down. And now the targets were running all over the place like a mound of pissed-off fire ants. She searched for a stationary target and found one, crouched by the corner of the control building. She nailed him and swung her sight across the field. Another guy climbing a rig! She took aim at him, but he fell off the tower before she could pull off the shot.

"Here they come out of the buildings," Jack announced calmly. "Pick them off in the doorways."

She swung her aim to one of the large buildings. A man jumped out.

"Mine," Kat bit out over the mikes.

"Mine," came the call from Delta Three's sniper, Walsh, as the next guy jumped through the door.

An informal shooting rotation set itself up quickly as they took turns knocking out terrorists as they tried to rush outside. The Army of Holy War caught on after another dozen of their men went down.

"Cease-fire," Jack murmured. "Now we wait. They'll be on the phones, screaming for help right about now. Walsh, Cobra, you two stay sharp. They're gonna try to sneak a few spotters outside. The rest of you save your ammo. Deltas, shift position to cover the road."

Vanessa came up on the radio after him. "Move to your secondary firing positions, Medusas." She crawled backward behind the ridge and scrambled toward her next firing position.

Sure enough, about twenty minutes later, a concerted rush of men exited the barracks. And learned the error of their ways. They were mowed down to the last man. She counted about sixty bodies total on the ground. A sizable dent in the overall force. Another two hours passed with no movement whatsoever in the oil compound. Nobody was sticking his nose outside. Which probably meant backups were on the way.

And then Spot, the Delta team's spotter, came on the radio. "Traffic on the road. Coming at a high rate of speed. Contact in two minutes."

"Scramble," Jack ordered tersely. "Down to the roadblock."

Vanessa waited, tense, for a further report.

"Truck's stopping," Spot murmured a couple minutes later.

"I'm going in," Jack murmured. "I see something."

*What?* Vanessa's pulse leaped. What was he doing? What had he seen? Lord, she wanted to be over there, right now.

Spot murmured, "Scat's coming out from under cover. Hold your fire without positive target ID."

No kidding. She'd shoot every last Delta herself if one of them shot Jack. She blinked, startled by the violence of her protective urge. He was a big boy. He could take care of himself. Except she'd still kill anyone who harmed a single hair on his head. Whoa. She filed that one to think about later. When she wasn't smack-dab in the middle of a dicey op.

"Jesus," Spot whispered. "He's climbing in the back of the second truck."

Her heart rate jumped a full order of magnitude. What in the bloody hell was Jack doing? What could he possibly have seen that would merit taking such a risk?

*"Shit."*

That was Defoe. "What's happening?" Vanessa asked urgently.

"Trucks are moving. They got the roadblock cleared. About thirty guys piled out of the first truck and moved the rocks."

"What about the second truck?" she asked desperately. "How many men were in it?"

"No idea. None got out to help move the tree." He added tersely, "Don't blow up the trucks, Ginelli."

"Ya think?" the radioman retorted dryly.

Vanessa held her breath as the pair of trucks came into view a mile north of the oil field. They were moving fast. Too fast for a man to jump out of without breaking his neck.

"Don't jump, Jack," she whispered. "You're going about fifty miles per hour."

He didn't answer, nor did she expect him to. But, damn, she'd like to know what was in that truck with him.

"Christ, they're headed inside the compound and Scat's not clear!" Defoe shouted in a bare whisper.

"Keep your cool," Vanessa warned. "He knows what he's up to. What did he see in that truck? Any of the rest of you get eyes on the contents?"

Five negatives came across the radios.

"Get into firing positions aimed at the oil field. Jack may need cover. Medusas, move in closer. I want to be able to lay down a curtain of lead if he needs it."

She crawled as fast as she could down the side of the ridge and out into the sand. Her team swung east around the mine field, which put them in a less-than-perfect firing position, but did put the compound in range of all their weapons.

"Shit, shit, shit," Defoe began to chant.

"If you stubbed your toe, shut up," Vanessa snapped. "If you see something important, talk." The guy was too strung out to be on this op. He and his team had been to hell and back, and they weren't fit to be making decisions at this point. No time to talk it over with Defoe, though. She was taking control of him and his team.

"They found him," Defoe bit out.

A continuous string of "oh shits" detonated in the back of her head, too. But she had to keep her head in it. Keep thinking. Keep fighting. Keep working the situation.

"Give me a running report, Spot," she ordered.

"About twelve guys are pointing rifles at the back of the truck. Jack's getting out. Hands on the top of his head."

Fast, before they ripped his earpiece out, Vanessa barked, "We're coming to get you, Jack. Stay alive and stay sharp. We'll be there as soon as we can."

"Time hack," he grunted. "Two hours."

*Time hack?* She looked down at her watch as a matter of habit. Why did Jack want her to note the time just then? Very strange. She looked up from her wrist in time to see the radio ripped from his head.

"Change freqs," she ordered quickly. If one of the terrorists put on Jack's headset, she damn well didn't want the bastard hearing her teams' locations and next moves. She reached down to her radio's waist unit and dialed in the backup radio frequency they'd arranged before they left camp. "Everybody, check in."

Ten voices murmured their handles in her ear. "New backup frequency is 123.4," she announced. Easy to remember. Fast to dial in. She thought furiously. What had Jack meant by "two hours"? Don't do anything for two hours? He could hold out against interrogation for two hours? Her bet was on the latter. Besides, the Army of Holy War wouldn't expect an immediate and violent strike against them only minutes after they nabbed a hostile. Now was the time to move aggressively.

She keyed her radio. "Deltas, you come in from the northwest. Get close enough with that potato cannon to lob C-4 into the compound. And keep your sniper fire coming. We'll need the noise and the continuing diversion. The Medusas are going to come in from the east and pull Jack out."

"Too dangerous," Defoe argued. "You lay down suppression fire and we'll go in."

"Too dangerous because we're women?" Vanessa asked icily.

"Well, yeah."

"Stuff it, Defoe. We don't have time for that shit. Jack's life is on the line. You're laying down cover fire and *we* are going in. I'm team leader with Jack in custody."

"I don't have to recognize you—" Defoe started.

She cut him off. Sharply. "I outrank you, Captain. And I will shoot you myself if you disobey orders and cost Jack his life. I'm ordering you to do as I said."

Silence on the radio.

She spoke casually. Lightly. "Defoe, don't be an ass. Your judgment's so impaired by combat fatigue right now, you couldn't cross a street without fucking it up. My team's fresh. Jack trained us himself. We saved your butts, didn't we?"

Finally Defoe's voice came across the radio. Cool. Professional. Back in control. "You heard the major, men. Let's get that cannon down to the fence."

Vanessa sagged in relief. "Let's go, Medusas. We've got ourselves a hostage to rescue."

# Chapter 18

Vanessa sent Aleesha around to the west side of the compound to set a line of explosive charges along the western fence. While Aleesha was making her painstaking way to the fence, Vanessa ordered Walsh, the Delta sniper, to get into position to take out the facility's power generator. It was an eight-foot-long and six-foot-high metal behemoth behind the main control building. Hitting the huge target would not be a problem. But knocking it off-line might be. She needed him to take it out of service completely. Preferably in a single shot.

Meanwhile, the other Medusas worked their way carefully to the eastern fence. With maximum stealth they snipped the wires in the hurricane fence. Guards passed within ten feet of their positions on a regular basis. Fortunately, they were scanning the hills around the facility and not looking down at their own feet.

The team left about every fourth wire in place to hold the fence in position until it was time to go. Vanessa headed out for the west side of the compound. The breezy night had given her an idea. She had a little surprise in mind to make the opening gambit complete. She lay in a hollow about a hundred yards beyond the fence where Aleesha was still at work setting charges. Vanessa taped Scott Worthington's spare pistol to one of their sniper tripods and aimed it at the fence, about waist high. She took out a wind sock she'd rigged out of a piece of thin nylon she'd cut out of her rain poncho, and stuck its mounting pole, a spare radio antenna, deep in the sand. Then, she tied one end of a piece of trip wire to the end of the wind sock and looped the other end carefully around the pistol's trigger. Last, she dug a little hole in the ground and set an empty tin can in the bottom of the protected spot. She tied the wind sock down to the ground with a piece of string she'd looped around the middle of the candle. Once she lit the candle, it would burn down, burn through the string and release the wind sock to blow in the breeze. Every time a strong gust of wind came along, the wind sock would yank on the pistol trigger and the weapon would fire. It would create the illusion of someone out here taking random shots.

The trick would be timing the candle's burn rate. She'd timed an exact duplicate of this candle in training back at Fort Bragg, and it took fifty minutes to burn down exactly three inches. She put the thread three inches down the wax pillar and lit the wick. Her can and the hole in the sand provided plenty of shelter from the wind so the candle wouldn't blow out. Although she did notice that the flame flickered from time to time, flaring up and burning more brightly when a particularly strong gust of wind blew overhead. She adjusted her burn estimate. Forty-five minutes until the pistol fired.

"Thirty-five minutes," she murmured into her radio. "I need everyone in place by then." She followed the little hollow to the south, past the end of the mine field and checked her watch. Twenty minutes left to meet her own deadline. She low-crawled east around the back side of the mine field. Sixteen minutes to go.

Walsh radioed, "I've got a bead on the fuel line leading into the power generator. One shot should blow up the whole thing."

"Copy," she grunted. Low-crawling a half mile was hard work any way you cut it. "Report, Mamba."

"About fifty feet behind you," her trap expert replied.

Vanessa swung north as soon as she could and crawled toward the compound. The last twenty yards took the last twelve minutes she had left. Aleesha touched her foot about three minutes late, but well before the candle set off the pistol.

Vanessa breathed into her mike, "When the pistol I rigged fires, Mamba, blow the fence charges. Walsh, when the west fence blows, give it thirty seconds, then take out the generator. Also when the pistol fires, I need the Medusas to finish cutting the fence and open it up. As soon as the lights go off, we move in. Guard your night vision from the blasts."

And now came the wait. Adrenaline in high gear for the gunshot to set off the chain of events. It could come in a few seconds, it could be several minutes. She spent the time scanning the compound, looking for any sign of Jack. Nada. They'd taken him inside the one-story, concrete control building and nobody'd seen him come out. Despite the arrival of that truckload of reinforcements, the terrorists continued to hide in their barracks from the snipers who'd bedeviled them earlier. Probably waiting for daylight to venture out and reset the explosives.

Bang! *The pistol.*

Vanessa caught the movement out of the corner of her eye

as Aleesha mashed the remote-control detonator for her charges. Vanessa closed her eyes to preserve her night vision as a row of bright lights exploded beyond her eyelids, cracking like a string of firecrackers. Shouting erupted in the compound and a hundred armed men poured out of the barracks toward the western fence. Karen and Misty reached up and started snipping wires quickly and methodically. Vanessa couldn't hear her pistol decoy fire again, but she saw its muzzle flash a couple more times. Perfect. The terrorists were shooting at it like crazy.

And then the lights went out. All of them. The hum of the generator went silent and the entire facility plunged into total darkness. More shouting erupted, and gunfire sprayed wildly at the western fence. She could see dozens of men running around chaotically, backlit by their own muzzle-flashes as they poured lead at the supposed assault from the west.

"Let's go," Vanessa bit out as a section of fence abruptly rolled back.

The Medusas crawled through the fence and dispersed in a fighting line. They'd send their gunfire to the west, and the Deltas would send their field of fire to the south. Less chance of hitting one another that way. Vanessa darted forward, pausing for a moment behind the leg of the first oil rig. She shot a half-dozen terrorists using single shots. A stream of automatic weapon fire would tell the terrorists someone was behind them. But in the cacophony of shooting the terrorists themselves were creating, single shots were lost in the chaos.

She counted several dozen terrorists lying on the ground already. No time to do head counts right now. She had to get into that control building. She darted forward to the far leg of the rig. A couple more shots. A couple more dead terrorists. There was a long, open stretch of ground before her, and then a stack of oil barrels. A few flashlights were starting to swing back and forth, and several voices were shouting over the others in Arabic, trying to pull the mob into some semblance of order.

Kaboom!

A block of C-4 exploded in the northern corner of the com
pound. It rocked the ground and hurt her eardrums, i
was so loud. So much for order. The soldiers screamed an
hollered and ran around like chickens with their heads cut of
What a mess. She yanked out her woman's black veil, twiste
it into a thick rope and tied the makeshift turban around he
head. It gave her a similar silhouette to the terrorists.

She announced over her radio, "I've put on a turban. An
making a run for the last stack of oil barrels east of the doo
to the control building." She had no wish to be mistaken fo
a Tango in the dark and shot by her own people. A quick look
left and right, and she dashed for the barrels. Someone
shouted to her in Arabic, telling her to get inside the barracks.
She pitched her voice as low and rough as it would go and
shouted back an affirmative in Arabic. And then shot the guy
dead.

"I'm heading for the control building as soon as you lob
another block of C-4," she said into the mike.

"Double charge incoming," Defoe replied.

Boom! Boom! Another round of shouting, this time direct-
ing all the troops to the north fence to lay down suppression
fire against the infidels. "Return fire headed your way, Delta,"
she murmured. "I just saw an RPG going past." A rocket-
propelled grenade launcher could be a serious problem for
Defoe and his men.

"Take cover," Defoe ordered his men. "And launch a big-
ass brick of C-4 this time."

She had to give the guy credit. He was keeping his cool
under fire. And then she was off and running. The C-4 made a
tremendous blast, knocking her to the ground. She rolled and
popped back to her feet and kept on going. A guard swung into
the doorway of the control building, his rifle in a firing position.
She dived to the left, firing as she flew through the air. She landed
hard on her shoulder and grunted with the force of the impact.

Boom! Another incoming charge. That potato cannon was a godsend.

Kaboom! A huge, hot explosion seared the night air. The fuel tank next to the generator blew. She squinted at the control building. No silhouette in the door anymore. Either she'd hit the guy or he'd retreated inside. She ran up to the door and crouched beside it. The guy lay on the floor just inside, motionless.

"Viper, you're about to have company," Kat murmured. "Spin and fire on my mark, to your left." A pause. "Mark."

Vanessa spun and squeezed the trigger twice. A double tap to take out the Tango. The guy went down and didn't move. She jumped into the doorway, clearing left and right. A hallway going straight ahead, about ten feet long. Another hallway to the left, a door to the right, and a third hallway at a right angle to her straight ahead.

She stepped over the dead guard, kicked open the door to the room on the right and swept her weapon across the space. A break room of some kind. Empty. She stepped back out into the hall. And lurched as a hand grabbed her ankle and yanked her foot out from under her. It threw her off balance, but she managed to get the muzzle of the MP-5 down and shoot the possuming bastard in the face. His dead fingers fell away from her ankle.

*Where was Jack?* She concentrated on her gut for a moment. Straight ahead to the back hall. And then left. She didn't know how she knew, she just moved.

"Karen, drop!" Isabella bit out.

"Thanks," came Karen's voice a second later.

And then chatter began to fly as the women covered one another's positions. Sounded like they were in danger of getting pinned down, soon. She had to get Jack *now* and get the hell out of Dodge. Rather than slink around clearing the whole building, she took a giant risk and sprinted down the short hallway, careening around the corner into the longer hallway, firing as she went. Two men went down, and some-thing hot grazed her right shoulder. She didn't break stride as she raised her arm. Flexed it. Functional. Not much pain. Good to go. *The last door on the left.*

Jack was no dummy. He'd heard the gunfire out here. If he could move, he'd put himself low and in the corner behind the door. Out of her field of fire when she burst in to clear the room. She careened to a stop. As her foot connected with the door, just above the knob, she heard Jack shout, "Two!"

Two guards. She fired high as she exploded into the room. Chest level, to miss Jack if he was crouching like he ought to be. Somebody fired at her from the right, but the impact slammed squarely into her flak vest. It felt like someone with a damn heavy fist had just slugged her. She spun and double tapped the bastard. She spun back to the left. And froze. The second guard had an arm around Jack's throat and a pistol pressed against the side of Jack's head. *Shit.*

"Drop your weapon," the guard shouted at her in Arabic.

Yeah, right. Not a chance. She sighted carefully at the guy's wrist. The first bullet would knock the gun away from Jack's head. The second shot would take out the guard's eye. With cold precision she pulled the trigger twice, as quickly as her finger could twitch. Bam! Bam! The shots reverber-ated, deafening in the small space. Both men fell to the ground.

And then Jack shrugged off his guard's arm and stood up, scooping up his captor's pistol as he moved. Vanessa's gut turned to water. Lord, that had been a crazy thing to do. She could've killed Jack if she'd been just a millimeter or two off target. She'd killed the guard out of pure reflex without even a moment of rational thought. The guard threatened Jack; the guard died. Simple math.

"Let's go," Jack bit out, waiting in the door for her as she stared down at the guard's corpse.

"Right," she replied as she bolted into motion. They ran

down the long hall toward the exit. Jack took both rifles off
the two dead guards they passed in the halls. She crouched
beside him in the doorway of the control building and
scanned the field of battle. Not good. It looked like the terrorists were forming a line and preparing to sweep through
the compound from one side to the other in methodical fashion.

She ordered, "Adjust your fire, Delta. Disrupt their line."

"This thing aims like a blunderbuss," Defoe replied, frustrated. "But we'll do our best."

"Just don't hit the oil wells," she bit out.

Kaboom! Defoe came through like a champ, laying down
what had to be a five-pound brick of C-4 right in the middle
of the Army of Holy War formation. In the flurry of reaction,
Jack darted away from the building. She followed at top
speed. And dived for the stack of barrels she'd used on the way
in. A barrage of bullets pinged off the far side of the metal barrels.

"I'm getting low on ammo," Kat radioed.

"Me, too," Aleesha added.

"Me, too," Misty chimed in.

Crap. Vanessa was down to her last fifty rounds or so
as well. "Position report, Medusas," she ordered.

"All of us are at the wells," Misty answered. "We have you
in sight behind the barrels with Scat."

Defoe came up. "We're way low on ammo, too. Still flush
on explosives, but bullet-challenged."

"Keep the potatoes coming," Vanessa murmured back to
him. She leaned over to Jack and murmured in his ear,
"Everyone's low on ammo. Not enough to brute force our
way out of here. The Medusas are at the oil rigs."

"Let's join them and conserve our fire," he murmured
back.

She nodded. They waited for another explosion to rock the
ground, a double charge this time. And they ran for their

lives, side by side, to the hulking black shapes of the oil derricks ahead.

"Over here," someone called out in English. Vanessa followed Jack as he veered toward the sound. They dived to the ground beside the five women. Vanessa eyed the fence behind them. It was a good hundred feet away. Too far to cross without being picked off like ducks in a shooting gallery.

"Time from that hack I gave you?" Jack asked her.

Surprised, she looked at her watch. "One hour, fifty-seven minutes," she answered.

"We need to stall these guys for three more minutes. And then we'll have the diversion we need to escape."

"Here come the Tangos," Kat murmured.

Vanessa looked up sharply. Crap. Two lines of terrorists had started advancing across the compound, taking turns laying down suppression fire for each other. Three minutes? They had about thirty seconds at the rate those men were moving.

Vanessa's brain went into overdrive. She looked up overhead. Yeah. It would work. "We need a full out potato barrage, *now*," she ordered Defoe. Then, "Medusas, climb the oil rigs. We let them advance until they're right under us, and then we wipe them out from above. Single shots, fast and accurate. Make each bullet count. *Move.*"

Jack's gaze met hers. He remembered the maneuver from the paintball range so long ago. She grinned as they stood up and jumped for the first crossbar. She glimpsed Karen bent over at the waist. *What the*— And then Kat's petite form stood up on Karen's back and grabbed a bar. The taller marine jumped and caught the bar. Vanessa scanned the rigs. Five shapes besides her and Jack. Everyone was off the ground.

"Let's go," Jack muttered above her.

She lurched into motion, shimmying up the rig like a monkey. She stopped about forty feet up. The camouflage was minimal, but the heavy steel rig itself would provide a measure of cover. "Fire on my mark," she breathed into her radio. The front line of terrorists was maybe fifty feet away, the second line another thirty feet back. She waited. And waited. *Patience.* A few more feet.

The first line of terrorists was directly underneath the rig, and the second line of men about twenty-five feet away, when she breathed, "Mark," and pulled the trigger of her weapon.

They literally rained bullets down on the hapless terrorists. Half the Tangos were dead before they even figured out what was happening. Bullets zinged up into the rig, but by the time the terrorists got a bead on their location, another quarter of their men were down. The scale of the destruction was so big and so abrupt that the Army of Holy War's backbone broke. They cut and ran, scrambling back toward the two main buildings. Vanessa shot a couple of stragglers, and her team picked off some of the wounded who got up and tried to move away.

"Time?" Jack murmured.

"One hour, fifty-eight minutes and change."

"Tell the Medusas to start climbing down. Our escape will be forthcoming in under two minutes. And tell the Deltas to fall back as far and fast as they can for one minute. Then take cover."

What in the world had he done? She relayed the messages and started down herself. She lagged behind the others, providing cover in case anyone decided to come out and play while her team was vulnerable. Everyone else hit the ground, and she scrambled downward. She dropped the last ten feet and did a parachute-landing fall to absorb the impact. She rolled to a stop against Jack's side. And was startled when he threw an arm over her.

"Stay down," he ordered loudly enough for the whole team to hear.

Vanessa opened her mouth to ask what in the hell was

going on when a tremendous explosion split the night. This was unlike any of the previous bangs and booms from the "potatoes" Defoe and company had fired. This was huge. A hot blast wave slammed into her back, flattening her against the ground and knocking every last ounce of breath out of her lungs. She drew in a gasp of hot air, deafened by the blast. A loud roar was all she could hear.

But then an arm dragged her to her feet. Jack. She staggered upright, still gasping for oxygen. And gaped at the enormous fireball rolling up into the night sky. Half the control building and all the barracks were destroyed. A few men staggered out of the flaming ruins of the barracks, bloody and disoriented, in no shape to pose a threat. It would take a frigging truckload of explosives to cause a blast like that…a truckload. *That's what Jack had seen.* The second truck had been full of explosives. He was lucky the terrorists hadn't parked the rig right beside an oil well, but instead had pulled it around the back of the control building away from the wells. He'd jumped inside and wired the thing to blow in two hours' time. Long enough for him to egress the area. Or, as it turned out, long enough for the Deltas and Medusas to rescue him. A suicidal stunt if she'd ever seen one.

He tapped her on the shoulder, and she turned and stumbled after him. She helped him kick the feet of her teammates, signaling them to get up. It was too loud for any kind of verbal communication, but everyone got the idea when Jack pointed at the fence and made the hand signal for running. But just then, a wall of fire erupted in front of them. The trench full of oil had caught fire as burning debris from the blast landed in it. They were ringed by it on every side. The flames shot a good fifteen feet up in the air.

Jack took off running, straight at it. "Medusas, follow me!" he shouted over the roar of the fires. Vanessa took off running after him and watched as he took a running leap and disappeared into the inferno. Pure suicide. This was nuts! And then it was her turn to jump. Everything went yellow and hot around her, and then just as fast, she burst out the far side of the fire. She hit the ground, stumbled and took off running again. She reached the fence and turned in time to see her entire team explode through the fire, five black silhouettes flying through the air as graceful and powerful as wild horses running free. As one, they sprinted for the hole in the fence. She and Jack provided cover while the others took turns diving through it. No need for a stealthy withdrawal tonight. The whole damn region knew they were out here after that tremendous explosion. Vanessa crawled under the fence and came up running. She slogged through the sand at a dead run until her legs felt like spaghetti. And then she kept going on guts. But finally they crested the first ridge to the east. Safe. But still Jack didn't stop running.

They humped down the ridge to the floor of the next valley and met up with the Deltas there. Defoe slapped Jack on the back by way of greeting, and then all twelve of them turned to the east and took off running yet again. It was a matter of pride for her to keep up with the Deltas. Had it been anyone else running with them, she'd have begged for a breather a half-dozen times. But as it was, all twelve of them pulled into their cave together. At least the Deltas were huffing like racehorses, too.

"Reload," Vanessa gasped as soon as she could get the words out.

The Deltas hauled out one of the crates of ammo they'd stored in the cave, and everyone reloaded in efficient silence. Jack grabbed the last spare radio and wired up for sound. Then he murmured, "I'll go keep an eye on the oil field."

"I'll come with you," Vanessa murmured. "Everyone else, down for a rest." Adrenaline was still screaming through her veins. No way could she sleep. Besides, she had a bone to pick with Jack Scatalone.

# Chapter 19

*January 19, 7:00 a.m.*
*Al-Khibri*

Vanessa stretched out in the sand, peering at the results of their night's work on the oil field, while Jack did a circuit of the area looking for any roaming hostiles. The facility was a blackened hull, with only the wells standing intact among the ruins. Bodies lay everywhere, and a few people moved here and there among them, going through pockets and covering the faces of corpses. A couple more men dragged bodies toward the shallow trench that held burning oil last night and now served as a makeshift grave.

They'd done it. The Medusas had not only survived but succeeded on their first full op. Exhaustion tugged at her, as did elation. With this oil field and its income restored to Bhoukari control, thousands of hungry Bhoukaris would eat. The Army of Holy War's cash supply had taken a serious hit.

And then there was the Army of Holy War itself. They'd killed most of the two hundred terrorists encamped here. The frosting on the cake was rescuing Delta Three. All in all, a job well done. Satisfaction seeped through her.

Absolute certainty broke over her. She slipped the picture of her father out of her breast pocket and looked at it for a long time. *This* was why he did it. For the quiet satisfaction of knowing he was making the world a better place for his baby daughter. He'd never abandoned his family. He'd gone into this line of work because he cared so very much about them. She smiled. With her understanding came peace. It spread through her in a calming flow, enveloping her in warmth.

It was the very same reason she was out here. Because she cared about her family. And her teammates. Sure, she was motivated by larger ideals like duty, honor and country. But at the end of the day, it all came down to protecting the people she knew and loved.

She jolted as Jack flopped down beside her without warning. Too suddenly for her to stow the picture of her father before he saw it.

"Who's that?" he asked. "Your boyfriend?"

She looked up at him, startled. "No. My father. It was taken about a week before he died."

"Did he die on an op?"

She nodded.

"Do you know anything about how he died?"

"No. We were told he was on an important mission, and that his sacrifice ultimately helped the op succeed. But who knows? Uncle Sam could've said that just to make us feel better."

Jack shrugged. "His teammates know the truth. Why don't you ask them?"

Teammates. Good Lord. The idea had never occurred to her. And with the security clearances she had now, they could tell her the whole truth. All the horrible things she'd imagined over the years about the circumstances of his death suddenly flooded back into her head. She wasn't entirely sure she wanted to know the details. Maybe the government's polite fiction was the gentler thing to believe. She didn't like how off balance the idea of finding out the truth made her feel. She shrugged. "His team's probably forgotten what happened. It was a long time ago."

Jack went very still. And looked her square in the eye, his expression dead serious. "In this business, you never forget your teammates. And you *never* forget when you lose one of them. Trust me. I know."

What if he was right? What if she could find his old team and learn the truth? And then something else even more rattling hit her. She'd spent her whole life convinced that she was the only person in the world who'd loved her father. The only one who kept his memory alive. But she wasn't. Never had been. Somewhere, there was a group of dedicated men who'd served alongside her father. She thought about her feelings for her own team. Oh, yes. Her father's comrades remembered him. The sense of connection to her father grew even stronger. Once they got out of here, she was going to learn all about him. Impatience to get home, to make some phone calls, filled her.

Jack lifted his spyglass and had a look at the oil field. "We nuked it pretty good," he remarked. "The Bhoukari army should be able to waltz in and plant their flag in the sand."

"Any idea when they'll show up so we can get out of here?"

"Soon," he replied.

"About last night—" she started. And stopped. In the harsh light of day, it sounded pretty stupid to blurt out that she loved him and had been scared to death when he took such a huge risk by jumping into that truckload of explosives.

He glanced over at her. "Having first-timer's remorse over killing all those guys?"

She blinked in surprise. "Not at all. We did our job. They'd have killed us if we didn't kill them. If they didn't want to play by those rules, they shouldn't have joined a terrorist organization."

One corner of Jack's mouth turned up in a wry smile. "Thank God. I didn't pack enough hankies for six sobbing females."

She knew it for the compliment it was and returned the smile.

"Speaking of thanks," he said matter-of-factly, "thanks for saving my neck."

"You're welcome. But since you brought it up, care to explain to me why you pulled a damn fool stunt like jumping into that ammo truck by yourself?"

"I saw explosives markings on steel ammo boxes. Tossing a grenade in the back of the truck wouldn't have detonated it through the steel, and we had to knock out those explosives so the bastards wouldn't rerig the wells to blow."

"I'm not disputing that it was a good thing to destroy that truck. What I'm asking is why you had to do it in suicidal fashion. You could've let the truck drive over your booby trap and then blown the trap."

"Might not have blown those reinforced ammo boxes." His head jerked toward her. "And it wasn't suicidal."

She merely stared him down.

Finally he mumbled, "Okay, so maybe it was a high-risk move. But I got the job done."

"You are a valuable asset to Uncle Sam. He's put a lot of time and money into training you, and you don't have the right to endanger yourself unnecessarily like you did last night."

He rolled over on his side to stare narrowly at her. "I've been doing business that way for fourteen years, and I'm still here. Uncle Sam's got no reason to complain about my work."

She retorted, "Yeah, but I do."

His eyes became dark, unreadable slits and his face went still. Inscrutable.

What the hell. She was in the soup now. Might as well dive in all the way and make a complete fool of herself all at once. "I happen to give a damn about whether you live or die, Jack Scatalone. Yes, risk comes with this job. But I'm going to worry every time you go out in the field if I know you're taking *stupid* risks when the job could get done in a more sensible way."

He stared at her, stone-faced. And gave her absolutely no hint whatsoever what he thought of what she'd just said. Crap. She'd blown it big time. Her heart sank. Well, at least she knew now that they truly didn't have a future together. Hey. It had been a great fantasy while it lasted. She was tough. A professional who knew the score. Knew better than to get involved with anyone as long as she was doing such a dangerous job. But, God, it hurt. She started to roll over onto her belly to resume surveillance.

A hard hand shot out and grabbed her shoulder, stopping her from turning away from him. "Are you telling me you *care* about me?"

"No." She looked at him levelly. "I'm telling you I love you."

His fingers twitched, tightening painfully on her shoulder, but that was his only reaction. Finally he murmured softly, "Well, son of a bitch."

*Son of a bitch?* Was that all he had to say?

"Viper, Scat," a voice said abruptly in her earpiece, startling her.

"Go ahead," Vanessa murmured back.

Isabella reported, "We just got a radio call. Bhoukari army will be here shortly, and they've given diplomatic clearance to a U.S. helicopter to come pick us up. Contact time thirty minutes on our ride."

"Thanks. Do the guys know?" Vanessa asked.

Isabella chuckled. "Can't you hear them whooping it up in the background?"

Vanessa grinned. "We'll keep eyes on the field until the Bhoukaris arrive."

"Roger. Out."

Jack had turned and was peering at the oil field again. "Incoming," he murmured. "Must be our Bhoukari friends."

So. He didn't want to talk about her declaration, did he? Her heart felt like a lump of lead. Without any enthusiasm, she picked up her spyglass and watched four truckloads of Bhoukari soldiers pile out at the gates of Al-Khibri. The remaining terrorists immediately threw up their hands and lay on the ground. It took about thirty seconds for the Bhoukari army to secure the field. Vanessa grinned when a Bhoukari flag was unfurled with great fanfare and tied to one of the oil rigs. "Looks like our work here is done," she murmured to Jack.

"Yup. Let's blow this Popsicle stand," he replied. He slid backward off the ridge.

She followed him back to their camp in silence. If he wasn't going to acknowledge her declaration of love, she damn well wasn't going to bring it up again, either. *No tears.* She would not cry. Not in front of him and not in front of her team. Numb, she packed her gear quickly and carried it down the eastern slope to the valley floor. Frantic to stay busy, she helped the Deltas and Medusas clear and mark a landing site for the chopper.

And then a thwocking noise sounded to the south, coming at them low on the horizon. The black dot grew into a double-rotored Chinook. It blew sand into a blinding whirlwind that felt like stinging nettles on her exposed skin, but it was the most welcome pain she'd ever endured. Vanessa waited until everyone but Jack had boarded the chopper, then the two of them ran up to the door together. She flung her pack inside and jumped into the interior. A crewman slid the door shut, and the craft lifted away from the ground.

Vanessa's stomach gave an ominous rumble. "Uh, Jack, there's something you need to know about me and flying...."

*February 4, 2:00 p.m.*
*the Oval Office*

"Major Blake, it's a pleasure to meet you." Vanessa stuck out her hand and the president of the United States grasped it firmly. "Hell of a job you and your team did in Bhoukar," he said warmly.

"Thank you, sir." Her entire team stood behind her, along with all of Delta Three and General Wittenauer. And, of course, Jack. It was the first time she'd seen him in the two weeks they'd been home. She'd been kept busy since their return with debriefings, and he'd been settling into his new, permanent position as General Wittenauer's liaison officer to the Delta detachment at Fort Bragg. Whenever she slowed enough to think about Jack, it hurt. Bad. Like a field knife to the heart. She figured it might lessen to a dull throb in, oh, twenty years or so.

President Stanforth continued, "As you know, your participation in the events of several weeks ago in Bhoukar can never become a matter of public record. Nonetheless, I asked General Wittenauer to bring you and your team here today so I could personally award these to each of you." He picked up six dark blue boxes off his desk and handed one to each woman with a handshake and a murmured congratulations.

He gave Vanessa hers last. She opened the lid and looked inside. Nestled on a bed of black velvet was a Bronze Star. A medal for heroism in combat. One of the highest medals given by the U.S. military.

"I'm afraid you will not be able to display these medals on your uniforms, but they will be entered into a classified section in each of your personnel records. Perhaps someday the existence of the Medusas will be declassified and you can wear these with pride. But in the meantime, on behalf of a grateful nation, please accept my thanks for your outstanding service."

Since this whole crazy ride began, she'd never been closer to tears. Funny. She could stare death in the face and not flinch, but give her a sappy thank-you speech, and she was a puddle of mush. She noticed Karen surreptitiously wiping a tear off a cheek.

The president stepped around behind his desk and sat down. "And now we have a business matter to take care of."

"And what might that be, sir?" Vanessa inquired when he didn't continue.

"Your futures."

She nodded politely. A letter of recommendation from the commander-in-chief ought to be good for a sweet assignment for each of her team members.

The president pushed a piece of paper across his desk. "General Wittenauer, if you would sign and date this executive order, please?"

The general stepped forward. He scanned the paper, and his face melted into a big, fat, shit-eating grin. He grabbed the pen beside the paper and signed it with a flourish. And then he looked up at Stanforth. "Do you want tell them, sir, or shall I?"

"Be my guest," Stanforth replied, grinning widely.

What the hell was going on? She still was too impatient to play political games worth a damn. But at least she now knew how to bite her tongue and wait.

The general turned to face her and her team. "The president and I just signed an executive order creating an adjunct unit to the Delta detachment, to be called the Medusas. Your existence will be known only to the commander of JSOC and the president of the United States. You will work directly for me."

Shock. Disbelief. *Pride*. They all rushed through her in a jumble. And, finally, triumph surged in her heart. *They'd done it*. They'd made it inside the fence for real. "And what will our duties be, sir?" she managed to ask reasonably calmly.

General Wittenauer answered gravely, "To kick ass and take names, Major."

A cheer erupted behind her. She gave her own shout of joy and let her team sweep her into a buoyant group hug. Finally she murmured to her teammates, "We're acting like a bunch of teenagers in front of the president of the United States, you know."

The women disentangled themselves and reformed into a straight, military line. But their smiles stayed.

Stanforth laughed aloud. "Congratulations, Medusas. Welcome aboard."

And then Scott Worthington cleared his throat behind them. Vanessa looked at the new commander of Delta Three in surprise. He looked worlds better after a month of R & R and real food. "Me and the guys wanted to say thanks to you ladies for saving our asses…pardon me, our behinds. We know your existence has to stay secret, and nobody's going to know you're part of the team. But we know. Welcome to the unit."

She frowned as he and the other men stepped forward. Each one of them held out his right hand, palm up, to one of the Medusas. Vanessa looked down at Scott Worthington's callused palm in front of her. And picked up the dollar-size medallion lying there. *A First Special Operations Detachment Delta drinking coin.*

She smiled up at him through a haze of tears. "Thanks," she choked out.

A Secret Service agent showed them out to the elevators, and Jack continued to be silent and withdrawn. She wanted to say something. To break through the wall around him. But he was too far gone. Too far behind the fence to let himself have real feelings for anyone. The tragedy of it stabbed her heart yet again.

They rode the White House elevator down several floors and stepped out into a miniature train station. The guard said, "This tram will take you to the Capitol Building. From there, you may exit normally."

The ride in the open cars only took a couple of minutes. A Capitol guard met them at the other end and showed them to the cavernous rotunda of the Capitol building. She oriented herself and turned to walk out toward the nearest Metro stop, when a hand touched her sleeve. *Jack*. She looked over her shoulder at him.

"Walk with me," he ordered.

She rolled her eyes. He never could get out of the habit of giving orders. The two of them peeled off from the others and headed out the west-facing exit. They strolled down the edifice's enormous marble staircase and walked among the dead leaves littering the Mall, the long grassy strip that stretched past the Washington Monument all the way to the Lincoln Memorial at the far end.

Jack reached into his coat pocket and pulled out a folded piece of paper. "Here are the names and phone numbers of the guys in your father's SEAL team. Nine of them are still alive. And General Wittenauer told me to tell you that he knows nothing about the existence of that list."

She smiled fondly. The old fart had turned out to be a pretty decent guy. She'd have to thank him the next time she saw him. She took the list and tucked it carefully in her pocket.

It was a sunny day and warm for February, hinting at the springtime to come. Families strolled along the Mall. Some kids flew kites, and a guy threw a Frisbee for a bandanna-collared dog. The scene was bucolic. Unreal. "This looks so strange to me now," she said quietly. "Six months ago, I was one of these people. But now I'm not."

Jack looked around. "Innocent, aren't they?"

"Yeah," she breathed. That was it. That was the difference. They lived their lives blissfully unaware of the violence and danger she lived with daily.

"We do our job so they don't have to know our world," Jack commented. "The psychologists are always digging around in my head, trying to find some deep, Freudian explanation for why I go out and kill people. And the answer's right here."

"I figured out somewhere in Bhoukar that it's why my father was a SEAL, too." Yet another realization exploded in her mind. Her father *had* tried to come home. To become part of this saccharine, naive world around her. And he couldn't do it. He couldn't come back from the only place he fit into anymore. He'd gotten lost in the dark world of Special Forces.

Jack shrugged. "I think most of us do the job to protect the innocents. The messed up guys—the ones only in it for the killing—don't last long. They get themselves dead or kicked out pretty quick. If your old man hung around for any period of time, he was probably just one more patriotic bastard who gut suckered into doing a dangerous job and let it eat him up."

"You know, Jack. My father got lost inside the fence. But all he had to do—all *you* have to do—is walk out. The real world is still out there on the other side. It's ultimately a matter of choice. You can hide behind the fence until you die like my father did, or you can take a chance and rejoin the human race."

"Are you calling me a coward?" he asked warningly.

"I don't know. Am I? Are you afraid to walk out?"

"Hell, no."

But he frowned and turned to walk away.

Enough was enough. Jack needed a swift kick in the pants. She put a restraining hand on his arm, forcing him to turn back and face her. "I lost my father. And he lost himself. The cost of his inability to come back from the other side was huge to both of us. If you never even try to come out, to love or be loved, what will it ultimately cost you and the people who care about you?"

He didn't answer that one. Not that she really expected him to. She could very well be speaking so far outside his experience that she wasn't making one bit of sense to him. She might be able to go inside the fence to coax or bully him out, but only he could actually turn around and make the long walk back.

They walked nearly the rest of the way to the Washington Monument in silence. And then her patience failed her yet again. She asked, "Is it enough for you? Do you look back on your career and believe you've made a difference?"

"Christ, you make me sound like an old man. I'm only thirty-seven years old."

She smiled wanly. "Sorry."

They walked for a few more moments in silence. Then Jack said, "I don't *believe* I've made a difference. I *know* I've made a difference. And, yeah, it's damn satisfying."

"But is it enough?" she pressed.

"Is what enough?"

She huffed. Was he willfully being dense, or did he truly not get it? She restated patiently, "Does the satisfaction make up for the sacrifices you've made?"

He frowned. "I haven't sacrificed anything. Other than that I can't tell any of my relatives what I do."

"What about a family of your own?" she asked quietly. "You're thirty-seven years old. Most people have married and are well on their way to having their kids raised by that age."

"I never found a woman who could understand or live with what I do and why I do it."

She walked alongside him silently. Was she willing to make that same sacrifice in the long run? To live a solitary life with only her team as a family?

"Until you."

She looked up in surprise at Jack's words. "Until what?" she asked.

He looked exasperated but explained. "I never found a woman who understood me or my work until you."

She blinked. "Oh."

"Is that all you've got to say?" he demanded.

"What do you want me to say?" she asked cautiously.

When he didn't answer right away, she raised an eyebrow at him, signaling that he got to go first this time when it came to true confessions.

He stopped and turned to face her. His coat collar flapped in a gust of wind against his chiseled cheek. His voice was rough. "I want you to say you still love me and that we're perfect for each other. That we understand each other's commitment to the job and can support each other and be there for each other when the going gets tough. I want you to show me the way out from behind the fence. And I don't want you to get lost in there like your old man."

"Oh." That wasn't bad as true confessions went.

"Well?" he demanded. "Am I right?"

A smile unfolded deep inside her heart. Maybe he wasn't hopeless after all. "Uh, yes, of course. You're always right," she managed to mumble.

He exhaled hard. "I'm being serious, here."

She looked him square in the eye. He was going to have to spell it out this time. She'd accept no less than a complete and unconditional surrender from him. "What exactly are you trying to say, Jack?"

"I'm trying to say I love you, dammit!"

"Oh."

"Will you quit saying that?" he exclaimed.

She grinned up at him. "Maybe you'd better just kiss me, so I can show you how I feel. Apparently I'm not doing too hot at verbal communication."

His arms wrapped around her and his mouth joined with hers in an age-old dance of two becoming one. She'd never get enough of this man. She leaned into him, reveling in finally allowing her true feelings to hang out. Jack met her every step of the way, blowing her away with the passion he barely held in check. It was an embrace to dream about during long night watches. An embrace to come home to safely. An embrace to grow old within. An embrace to last a lifetime.

He lifted his mouth away from hers long enough to mutter, "You're okay with me doing my job?"

"As long as you're okay with me doing mine," she replied.

He looked at her long and hard. "Yeah, I'm okay with it. Just don't get lost inside the fence or I'll have to come after you and kick your butt."

She laughed. "The way I see it, you've already had all the shots at kicking my butt you're ever going to get. And I still owe you a few potshots for everything you put us through in training."

He looked at her innocently. "I was just doing my job."

She laughed at him. "Ha! 'Fess up. You liked ordering us around."

He grinned unrepentantly. "Of course I did."

She disengaged an arm to shake a finger at his nose. "There'll be no more of that, mister. The rules of engagement from here on out are that we're equals. Got it?"

"Got it," he replied crisply.

"And no more stupid risks on missions when there's a more sensible way to get the job done."

"Yes, ma'am."

"No dying in the field, no taking it easy on us because we're women, and you tell me when you're losing touch with the outside."

He mulled that over for a moment. "Okay. I can live with all that. Any more rules?"

She glared at him narrowly. "I'm sure I'll think up some more. I reserve the right to establish further rules of engagement at a later date."

He grinned widely. "That's a pretty broad set of operational parameters you're asking for."

She glared even more fiercely. "Take it or leave it, buster."

He nodded slowly. "I'll take it. But just remember I can still kick your fanny in a fair fight."

She snorted. "Since when do I fight fair?"

Their gazes met in mutual understanding. Between the two of them, they'd be able to bridge both worlds. Together.

A slow smile formed in Jack's eyes.

A matching smile unfolded in her heart. She said softly, "A gap in the fence is right in front of us. Shall we?"

He grinned back at her. "After you. You take point and I'll cover your six."

\* \* \* \* \*

*Don't miss any of the thrilling new books from Cindy Dees!*
*HER SECRET AGENT MAN*
*Silhouette Intimate Moments #1353*
*Available March 2005*
*TARGET*
*Silhouette Bombshell #42*
*Available May 2005*

## Books by Cindy Dees

### Silhouette Bombshell

*Killer Instinct* #16
*The Medusa Project* #31

### Silhouette Intimate Moments

*Behind Enemy Lines* #1176
*Line of Fire* #1253
*A Gentleman and a Soldier* #1307

# Silhouette®
# BOMBSHELL™

## COMING NEXT MONTH

### #33 SILENT WEAPON by Debra Webb
Her entire life changed when an infection rendered her deaf. But Merri Walters used her disability to her advantage—by becoming an expert lip reader and working for the police. Now, her special skill was needed for an extremely dangerous undercover assignment—one that put her at odds with the detective in charge…and in the sights of an enemy.

### #34 PAYBACK by Harper Allen
*Athena Force*
Dawn O'Shaughnessy was playing a dangerous game—pretending to work for the immoral scientist who'd made her a nearly indestructible assassin, while secretly aligning herself with the Athena Force women who had vowed to take him down. But when she discovered that only the man who'd raised her to be a monster could save her from imminent death, she had to choose between the new sisters she'd come to know and trust, and payback….

### #35 THE ORCHID HUNTER by Sandra K. Moore
She was more hunter than botanist, and Dr. Jessie Robards knew she could find the legendary orchid that could cure her uncle's illness—Brazil's pet vipers, jaguars, natives and bioterrorists be damned. But the Amazonian jungle, filled with passion and betrayal, was darker and more dangerous than she'd ever imagined. This time it would change her, heart and soul…*if* she made it out alive.

### #36 CALCULATED RISK by Stephanie Doyle
Genius Sabrina Masters had been the CIA's favorite protégée—until betrayal ended her career. Now she'd been called back into duty—to play traitor and lure a deadly terrorist out of hiding. Only she had the brains to decode the terrorist's encrypted data, which was vital to national security. But when the agent who'd betrayed her became her handler, the mission became more complicated than even Sabrina could calculate….

SBCNM0205